PRAISE FOR THE FORBIDDEN ICELAND SERIES

'Riveting, exciting, entertaining and packed with intrigue, you may be tempted to take a second look at your own family after reading *You Can't See Me*, and wonder if you know them at all … Like *Succession* on ice' Liz Nugent

'A tense, twisty page-turner that you'll have serious trouble putting down' Catherine Ryan Howard

'If you've yet to step into Eva Björg Ægisdottir's Forbidden Iceland – a series of novels as distinctive and atmospheric as the island itself – start with *You Can't See Me*, which reads like *Succession* in the lava fields. As ever, Ægisdottir plots with the fair-play brio of a Golden Age legend – *And Then There Were None* fans, take note – but it's her psychological acuity, her insight into human frailty and flaw, that warrant comparison to Ruth Rendell. In a Forbidden Iceland novel, there's no terrain more treacherous than the mind. Here's a deep-dark thriller to read with the lights on' A. J. Finn

'Your new Nordic Noir obsession' *Vogue*

'Confirms Eva Björg Ægisdottir as a leading light of Icelandic Noir … marshals her huge cast with great skill: none of them – colleagues, relatives, suspects – are mere puppets. She is a master of misdirection and thematic development (babies planned and unplanned play a key role) gradually drawing the many plot strands together in a thrilling climax' *The Times*

'Chilling and addictive, with a completely unexpected twist … I loved it' Shari Lapena

'Fans of Nordic Noir will love this' Ann Cleeves

'Elma is a memorably complex character' *Financial Times*

'An exciting and harrowing tale' Ragnar Jónasson

'Beautifully written, spine-tingling and disturbing ...
a thrilling new voice in Icelandic crime fiction'
Yrsa Sigurðardóttir

'Another beautifully written novel from one of the rising stars
of Nordic Noir' Victoria Selman

'Eerie and chilling. I loved every word!' Lesley Kara

'A creepily compelling Icelandic mystery that had me hooked
from page one. *Night Shadows* will make you want to sleep
with the lights on' Heidi Amsinck

'This is a wonderfully plotted story with so many balls to keep
in the air! ... A brilliant read full of dark secrets. Loved it!'
Lynda's Book Reviews

'Isolated, atmospheric, chilling at times, and with the weather
and electrics being utterly temperamental, allowing for the
sense that literally anything could happen. Another cracking
addition to the series' Jen Med's Book Reviews

'Eva Björg Ægisdóttir is a real rising star in Icelandic Noir, she
just gets better and better, and I look forward to whatever she
pens next – she's definitely an automatic must-read for me'
Leigh-Anne Fox

'As chilling and atmospheric as an Icelandic winter' Lisa Gray

'A born storyteller and she skilfully surprised me with some amazing plot twists' Hilary Mortz

'I loved everything about this book; the characters, the setting, the storyline … had me utterly gripped!' J. M. Hewitt

'Elma is a fantastic heroine' *Sunday Times*

'The twist comes out of the blue … enthralling'
Tap The Line Magazine

'An unsettling and exciting read' *NB Magazine*

'Not just one of the brightest names in Icelandic crime fiction, but in crime fiction full stop' Nordic Watchlist

'Chilling and troubling … reminiscent of Jørn Lier Horst's Norwegian procedurals. This is a book that makes an impact' Crime Fiction Lover

'The setting in Iceland is fascinating, the descriptions creating a vivid picture of the reality of living in a small town … A captivating tale with plenty of tension and a plot to really get your teeth into' LoveReading

'The author writes so beautifully you are immediately immersed into the chilly surrounds … A genuinely excellent novel' Liz Loves Books

'The writing is skilful and the translation impeccable' Fictionophile

'Dark, chilling and tense'
Random Things through My Letterbox

'There is a growing confidence in Ægisdóttir's writing that could easily escalate her to the widespread recognition of her fellow Icelandic crime authors' Raven Crime Reads

'Suspenseful, moving and unsettling. I loved every word' Hair Past a Freckle

'One of my favourite series in crime fiction' Hooked from Page One

'One of the most compelling contemporary writers of crime fiction and psychological suspense' Fiction from Afar

'An intricate tale that burns steadily throughout the pages and positively roars towards the finale … A great addition to a series I can't wait to get back to' From Belgium with Booklove

WINNER of the CWA John Creasey (New Blood) Dagger
WINNER of the Storytel Award for Best Crime Novel
WINNER of the Blackbird Award for Best Icelandic Crime Novel
SHORTLISTED for the Amazon Publishing Readers' Award for Best Debut Novel
SHORTLISTED for the Amazon Publishing Readers' Award for Best Independent Voice
SHORTLISTED for the CWA Crime in Translation Dagger
SHORLISTED for the Petrona Award for Best Scandinavian Crime Novel

The Forbidden Iceland Series
The Creak on the Stairs
Girls Who Lie
Night Shadows
You Can't See Me

ABOUT THE AUTHOR

Born in Akranes, Eva Björg Ægisdóttir studied for an MSc in Globalisation in Norway before returning to Iceland and deciding to write a novel – something she had wanted to do since she won a short-story competition at the age of fifteen. After nine months combining her writing with work as a flight attendant and caring for her children, Eva finished her debut novel, *The Creak on the Stairs*. Published in 2018, it became a bestseller in Iceland and went on to win the Blackbird Award, a prize set up by Yrsa Sigurðardóttir and Ragnar Jónasson to encourage new Icelandic crime writers, and the Storytel Award for Best Crime Novel of the Year. It was published in English by Orenda Books in 2020, and became a number-one bestseller in ebook, shortlisting for Capital Crime's Amazon Publishing Awards in two categories, and winning the CWA John Creasey New Blood Dagger. *Girls Who Lie* and *Night Shadows* soon followed suit, shortlisting for the CWA Crime in Translation Dagger, the Capital Crime Awards, and the Petrona Award for Best Scandinavian Crime Novel. *You Can't See Me* won the Storytel Award for Best Crime Novel of the Year in Iceland in 2023. The Forbidden Iceland series has established Eva as one of Iceland's bestselling and most prestigious crime writers, and her books are published in fourteen languages. She lives in Reykjavík with her husband and three children.

Follow Eva on Instagram @evabjorg88 and on Twitter @evaaegisdottir.

ABOUT THE TRANSLATOR

Victoria Cribb studied and worked in Reykjavík for a number of years and has translated more than forty books by Icelandic authors, including Arnaldur Indriðason and Yrsa Sigurðardóttir. Many of these works have been nominated for prizes. In 2021 her translation of Eva Björg Ægisdóttir's *The Creak on the Stairs* became the first translated book to win the UK Crime Writer's Association John Creasey (New Blood) Dagger. In 2017 she received the Orðstír honorary translation award for services to Icelandic literature.

You Can't See Me

Eva Björg Ægisdóttir

Translated by Victoria Cribb

**ORENDA
BOOKS**

Orenda Books
16 Carson Road
West Dulwich
London SE21 8HU
www.orendabooks.co.uk

First published in the United Kingdom by Orenda Books, 2023
First published in Iceland as *Þú sérð mig ekki* by Veröld Publishing, 2021
Copyright © Eva Björg Ægisdóttir, 2021
English translation copyright © Victoria Cribb, 2023

A catalogue record for this book is available from the British Library.

Paperback ISBN 978-1-914585-72-2
Goldsboro Hardback ISBN 978-1-914585-98-2
eISBN 978-1-914585-73-9

The publication of this translation has been made possible through the financial
support of

 ICELANDIC LITERATURE CENTER

Typeset in Minion by typesetter.org.uk
Printed and bound by CPI Group (UK) Ltd, Croydon CR0 4YY

For sales and distribution, please contact info@orendabooks.co.uk or visit
www.orendabooks.co.uk.

Pronunciation Guide

Icelandic has a couple of letters that don't exist in other European languages and which are not always easy to replicate. The letter ð is generally replaced with a d in English, but we have decided to use the Icelandic letter to remain closer to the original names. Its sound is closest to the voiced *th* in English, as found in *th*en and ba*th*e.

The Icelandic letter þ is reproduced as *th*, as in *Th*ór, and is equivalent to an unvoiced *th* in English, as in *th*ing or *th*ump.

The letter r is generally rolled hard with the tongue against the roof of the mouth.

In pronouncing Icelandic personal and place names, the emphasis is always placed on the first syllable.

Names like Edda, Ester, Mist and Petra, which are pronounced more or less as they would be in English, are not included on the list.

Akrafjall – AAK-ra-fyatl
Akranes – AA-kra-ness
Ari – AA-rree
Arnaldur – AARD-nal-door
Arnarstapi – AARD-nar-STAA-pee
Axlar-Björn – AX-lar-BYURDN
Bergur – BAIR-koor
Birgir – BIRR-kir
Birta – BIRR-ta
Borgarnes – BORG-ar-ness
Breiðafjörður – BRAY-tha-FYUR-thoor

Búðir – BOO-thir
Djúpalón – DYOOP-a-lohn
Elín – EH-leen
Elísa – EH-leessa
Fróðárheiði – FROH-thowr-HAY-thee
Gestur – GHYESS-toor
Gísli – GHYEESS-lee
Hafnarfjall – HAB-nar-FYADL
Hákon – HOW-kon
Hákon Ingimar – HOW-kon INK-i-marr
Haraldur (Halli) – HAA-ral-door (HAL-lee)
Harpa – HAARR-pa
Hellissandur – HEDL-lis-SAN-door
Hellnar – HEDL-narr
Hörður – HUR-thoor
Hvalfjörður – KVAAL-fyur-thoor
Hyrnan – HIRD-nan
Ingólfur Hákonarson – INK-ohl-voor HOW-kon-ar-SSON
Ingvar – ING-varr
Irma – IRR-ma
Ísafjörður – EESS-a-FYUR-thoor
Jenný – YEN-nee
Knarrarklettir – KNARR-ar-KLETT-teer
Líf – LEEV
Maja – MYE-ya
Oddný – ODD-nee
Oddný Píla – ODD-nee PEE-la
Sævar – SYE-vaar
Sigrún Lea – SIK-roon LAY-ya
Smári – SMOW-ree
Snæberg – SNYE-bairg
Snæfellsjökull – SNYE-fells-YUR-kootl
Snæfellsnes – SNYE-fells-ness
Sölvi – SERL-vee

Stapafell – STAA-pa-FEDL
Stefanía (Steffý) – STEH-fan-ee-a (STEFF-fee)
Stykkishólmur – STIK-kis-HOHL-moor
Theódór (Teddi) – TAY-oh-DOHR (TED-dee)
Tryggvi – TRIK-vee
Valgerður – VAAL-gyair-thoor
Viðvík – VITH-veek
Viktor – VIKH-tor

The Snæberg Family

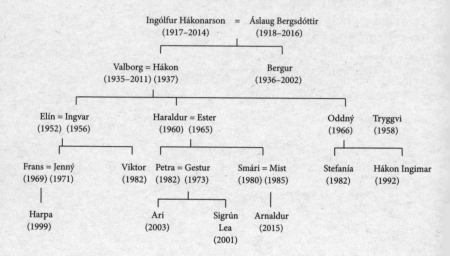

Ingólfur Hákonarson (1917–2014) = Áslaug Bergsdóttir (1918–2016)

Valborg (1935–2011) = Hákon (1937)

Bergur (1936–2002)

Elín (1952) = Ingvar (1956)

Haraldur (1960) = Ester (1965)

Oddný (1966)

Tryggvi (1958)

Frans (1969) = Jenný (1971)

Viktor (1982)

Petra (1982) = Gestur (1973)

Smári (1980) = Mist (1985)

Stefanía (1982)

Hákon Ingimar (1992)

Harpa (1999)

Ari (2003)

Sigrún Lea (2001)

Arnaldur (2015)

Evil creatures here abound
We must speak in voices low
All night long I've heard the sound
Of breath upon the window.

Sixteenth-century verse by
Þórður Magnússon á Strjúgi

Many thanks to my grandfather, Jóhann Ársælsson, for the poem on p. 262.

This book is dedicated to my family.
Here's hoping our next reunion won't be quite as eventful as the one in this book.

Early Hours of the Morning
Sunday, 5 November 2017

She can no longer hear the music from the hotel.

The cold cuts through her flesh to the bone. However tightly she hugs her coat around herself, the wind always seems to find its way in.

Every nerve in her body is screaming at her to turn back. No good can come of running out in the middle of the night like this; she doesn't know the surroundings well enough. She thinks about the family sitting over their drinks back at the hotel. Judging by the state they were in, no one will notice her absence straight away. If anything happens to her, it's unlikely anyone will raise the alarm until the morning.

Lowering her head, she ploughs on, trying to move her fingers and toes, though she can hardly feel them anymore. She becomes aware of movement at the edge of her vision and darts a glance to the side. She sees the outline of a human figure looming through the falling snow, and her pulse starts beating wildly, until she realises that it's only a lava formation in the vague shape of a man. She should be used to this by now.

She toils on, one step after another, trying not to panic. Time must be passing, but she has no idea how long she's been walking. In the darkness and driving snow it's as if time and space have ceased to exist.

Yet, strangely, it's a relief to be outside. The hotel had started to feel like a trap, as if its concrete walls were closing in on her, making it hard to breathe. Now, all she can think about is getting in the car and driving home. Home to their house and her warm bed, and the mundane, everyday life that she's only now realising is so precious to her. But she can't go home yet. First, she has to keep walking, searching in the dark, terrified of what she might find. And even more of what she might not find.

When she turns her head, she can make out the face under its hood, cheeks red with cold. The expression's not unfriendly, but there's something sinister behind the eyes that she's never seen before. Or perhaps she just didn't want to see it.

She starts walking faster, but the feeling of being trapped hits her even more strongly than before. And the thought crosses her mind that maybe it wasn't the hotel that had given rise to the feeling of claustrophobia, but the people staying there. Her family. The person walking only a few steps behind her in the dark.

Two Days Earlier
Friday, 3 November 2017

Irma
Hotel Employee

My eyes flick open the instant I'm awake, like a light bulb being switched on. There's a faint aroma of coffee wafting down from the kitchen above my room, and I inhale deeply, then roll over onto my back and stretch.

Today is Friday. I start work at midday, taking the noon-to-midnight shift, as I do every Friday. As it's still only eight, I could have a bit of a lie-in if I wanted and go back to sleep or read the book on my bedside table, but I'm too excited.

The feeling reminds me of gearing up for a night out when I was younger. That flutter in your stomach at the prospect of having fun.

They're coming today, sings the refrain in my head, and I smile like a small child at Christmas.

I know it's silly to feel so excited. It shouldn't be a big deal; and it isn't – or wouldn't be for most people – but there's going to be a family reunion at the hotel this weekend. Or maybe I should call it a birthday celebration. The woman who rang to make the booking explained that her husband's grandfather would have been a hundred on Sunday, so his descendants are spending the weekend together in his honour. They've booked out the entire hotel, even though they won't be able to fill all the rooms.

It might not sound like a good reason to get in a tizz, but this is no ordinary family. The Snæbergs are only one of the richest and most powerful clans in Iceland. Ingólfur, who would have been a hundred on Sunday, was the founder of Snæberg Ltd, which is pretty much a household name these days – a huge business empire by Icelandic standards, with hundreds of employees and an annual turnover in the billions of krónur.

Not that I know much about the business side of the company or its history. All I know is that the family is super rich.

Rising to my knees, I draw back the curtains. It's almost completely dark outside, as there's still a good hour until sunrise, but it's just possible to glimpse the jumbled, moss-covered rocks of the lava field stretching away on every side. Since starting work here, I've often caught myself wondering if I'll ever be able to move back to the city; to my flat with its view of my neighbour's windows and the dustbins in the alley below.

I fetch my laptop from the desk and climb back into bed, then tap 'Snæberg' into the search engine and study the images that come up. They include a number of well-known faces, people who have made their mark in Icelandic business and political circles, as well as younger family members who are prominent on the party scene. Some of them can barely leave the house or post anything online without the media turning it into a news item.

Hákon Ingimar is one of the younger generation. He was in a relationship with an Icelandic singer until fairly recently, and after that he hooked up with a Brazilian supermodel.

I click on a recent news item about Hákon Ingimar and see that he and the model have broken up, though the report about their split is accompanied by a photo of them in a clinch. With his blond, blue-eyed good looks and the golden tan revealed by the rolled-up sleeves of his shirt, you'd say he should be starring in a film or an aftershave advert. His now ex-girlfriend would cast most girls in the shade, with her luscious lips and those endless legs.

They're both so stunning that it's almost impossible not to feel envious. Not to wonder what it would be like to be them; to be rich and beautiful and free to do almost anything you like. Go on a spontaneous weekend break to Paris, shop for clothes and buy exactly what you want. Whereas I can barely even afford to do a food shop at the supermarket without getting a sinking feeling in my stomach when I present my card.

I bet Hákon Ingimar has never been in that position. You only have to look at social media to realise that he has no cash-flow problems. In his photos he's always dressed in designer clothes (although half the time he's undressed), quaffing expensive wine at five-star hotels, surrounded by friends and admirers. I bet Hákon Ingimar has never been lonely; he's too popular for that.

I've never been popular. I've always struggled to make friends and hold on to them. Had to be the one who knocked on the door or picked up the phone. I've been told I'm too clingy and don't know when to back off. The truth is, you're only seen as too clingy if people don't want you around. Yet another problem I bet Hákon Ingimar doesn't have.

I take a deep breath and remind myself that comparisons like this aren't helpful. And it's not like the Snæberg family were handed everything on a plate, not to begin with, anyway. Ingólfur, Hákon Ingimar's great-grandfather, started his first business at seventeen years old, using the small fishing boat he operated out of a village, here in the west of Iceland. He worked hard all his life for his wealth. His descendants have capitalised on his success, and although that's easier than starting from scratch like him, they must have done something right to have preserved the family fortune.

Scrolling back, I spot Petra, another of Ingólfur's great-grandchildren. As far as I know, Petra Snæberg doesn't work for the family business, though of course she's benefited from its success. Instead, she has her own interior-design and consultancy company. She's got thousands of followers on social media and collaborates with various firms. You can't open a newspaper or online media platform without seeing her face in adverts with the slogan: 'Why not invite Petra round and convert your home into a sanctuary?'

'Sanctuary' is a word she's forever trotting out, like, she'll say: 'Your home is above all a sanctuary, a place that reflects the inner you.'

If people started judging my inner me by the state of my flat in Reykjavík, I'd hate to hear the verdict. It's not like I've put any particular thought into how things are arranged. They're just there because that's where they ended up. The shelves are just shelves; a place to keep things. My flat is just a flat, and I certainly don't regard it in any sense as a sanctuary.

Opening Petra's Facebook page, I scroll through her photos.

She's got a husband called Gestur, and from the pictures it's not immediately obvious how he and Petra got together. All I can say is that he must be a real charmer in person. Gestur works as a programmer at a drugs company, but no doubt he'll end up at the family firm one day, like most people who marry into the Snæberg clan. In fact, I'm surprised he hasn't already made the move.

Gestur and Petra have two children, Ari and Sigrún Lea, always known as Lea. Cute little names, more suitable for small children than adults. And they certainly are cute in the photos from when they were kids: Ari in his sports kit, his hair almost white in the summer sun; Lea, a robust little girl, beaming to reveal oversized front teeth, her dark hair so long it reaches below her waist.

Lea is older than Ari, but not by much – two or three years, maybe. I click on her name, but the page that comes up contains next to no information. She's much more active on Instagram. On her profile there you can see that the little girl with the big front teeth now wears a pout and a crop top. No longer robust but slender, her long hair tied back in a pony-tail apart from two

locks left free to frame her face. She reminds me of a singer –
I've forgotten her name – who's also petite and slim, with long,
dark hair and chocolate-brown eyes.

I examine the background in Lea's pictures, trying to peer into
her room, her life, but I can't see anything of interest. Nothing
that provides any more insight into who she is or what she does.
A lot of the photos on her page have been taken abroad, in big
cities or holiday resorts. In one, Lea's on a beach wearing a bikini;
in another, she's in Times Square, toting a Sephora shopping bag,
and in yet another, at the London Eye with a Gucci one. Only
sixteen but already far more cosmopolitan than me. I wonder
how often she goes abroad each year; what kind of hotels she and
her family stay in.

Pushing away my laptop, I tell myself aloud to stop it. Envying
people is not my style. But no matter how often I remind myself
that the Snæbergs must have their problems, like the rest of us,
I can't help wondering what it would be like to be them.

Later today they'll all be here at the hotel, and I'll get to see
with my own eyes whether they're as perfect as outward
appearances suggest. Perhaps what excites me most is the
thought of looking more closely and spotting all the little cracks
that must lurk under that perfect veneer. Because of course
they're not perfect.

Nothing is perfect.

Sævar
Detective, West Iceland CID

There was a deep gash in the mountainside, as if someone had taken a giant cleaver and split it in two. Sævar raised his eyes to the top of the precipice, many metres above, and felt weak at the knees. A fall from that height would be impossible to survive, as the evidence at their feet made only too clear.

'That was a heck of a drop,' Hörður said, stating the obvious.

'Yes.' Sævar's voice emerged in a croak, and he coughed. Hastily lowering his gaze, he concentrated on his shoes and blinked. He'd suffered from vertigo ever since, as a small boy, he'd witnessed one of his friends falling from the first floor of a block of flats. They'd been climbing on the balcony rail, daring one another to dangle over the edge. When his friend lost his grip and plummeted backwards into the redcurrant bushes below, Sævar had been convinced that he was dead. But, by a stroke of luck, he'd got off with no more than a broken arm and a few scratches, which he boasted about for weeks.

For a long time afterwards, Sævar had suffered from nightmares in which he felt the air rushing past him as he made a headlong descent, as if it was he who had fallen and not his friend. He would wake up frantically clutching the duvet, sometimes on the floor, but usually still in bed, drenched in sweat, his heart pounding. Even now, all these years later, he couldn't stand heights and could hardly even think about them without growing dizzy.

To distract himself, he concentrated on the body lying at their feet. From a distance, it had blended into the surrounding landscape, the grey down jacket resembling a rock jutting out of the snow, but as they drew closer it had resolved itself into a human figure, its limbs sprawling in an unnatural position, dusted with a thin layer of snow.

Sævar watched as Hörður bent down, head on one side, then raised his camera. The clicking as he snapped away seemed incongruous in the profound silence.

Sævar was familiar enough with Hörður's slow, careful working methods to realise that they would be here for a while. They had been colleagues at Akranes Police Station for several years, but Sævar had only been working directly for Hörður for two, when he was promoted to detective. Now they worked closely together every day, as part of a three-man CID team covering the west of Iceland.

Sævar raised his eyes again to survey their surroundings. Beyond the snow-capped peaks of the mountains near at hand, he glimpsed the white flanks of the Snæfellsjökull glacier, rising like a great dome at the end of the peninsula. A few birds floated so high overhead that it was impossible to identify them, though he could hear the distant screeching of gulls from the shore. The nearby road seemed to be little used, apart from the odd car that drove past and almost immediately vanished out of sight down the slope.

There had been a blizzard during the night, but the gale-force wind had scoured the ground clean, leaving only scattered snowdrifts. Now the weather was breathlessly still, beautiful in its tranquillity. The calm after the storm, Sævar thought. Or should that be before? He couldn't remember.

Before he had a chance to study the landscape in any more detail, Hörður called out:

'See that?'

Sævar moved closer. Again, he was hit by a wave of dizziness and had to swallow a mouthful of saliva. The precipice looming over him felt menacing, though common sense told him there was nothing to fear.

'What is it? Can I see what?'

'There.' Hörður pointed to the victim's hand.

It took Sævar a moment to work out what Hörður was referring to, but then he saw it. Saw the dark strands of hair protruding from the clenched fist.

Two Days Earlier
Friday, 3 November 2017

Petra Snæberg

I've been running round the house like a headless chicken all morning, cursing the size of the place – not for the first time. Three hundred and sixty-five square metres, thank you very much: two storeys, a basement and a double garage. Although it seemed like a good idea at the time to put the kids' bedrooms on a different floor from ours, in practice it makes trying to keep the house tidy between the cleaner's visits a total nightmare – not to mention finding anything that's lost. Just now, for example, all the chargers seem to have vanished into thin air, which is unbelievable given how many there are in the house. I suspect they're all lying on the floor in either Ari or Lea's bedroom, but they swear they haven't got them and of course I'm not allowed in there to look for myself. I bet they haven't even bothered to check.

'Lea! Ari!' I call downstairs to the basement, not for the first time this morning. 'We're leaving in ten minutes. Bring up your bags. Dad's packing the car.'

I wait for an answer, but of course it doesn't come.

Well, that's their problem. I run a hand through my hair, glancing distractedly around me. Breakfast still hasn't been cleared away. There are bowls of milk and soggy Cheerios on the kitchen table. No way am I leaving them there all weekend.

While I tidy up, I review my mental list of everything that still needs to be done and everything I'm bound to have forgotten. The house is a tip. After Gestur got home late last night, everything went a bit pear-shaped, and I stormed off to bed without doing any of the chores I had meant to deal with before going to sleep.

It's not like me to leave my packing until the evening before. Usually I'm on top of everything: birthdays, dinner parties, special occasions. I'm the type who makes to-do lists. Few things give me more pleasure than putting a little cross by the tasks I've accomplished. On my computer I have individual pre-prepared checklists specially tailored for beach holidays, city breaks and trips to the Icelandic countryside. Being disorganised is not an option. If it weren't for my organisational skills, I would never have been able to keep the family together while simultaneously setting up my business.

Most people think I got everything handed to me on a plate thanks to my family connections, but nothing could be further from the truth. I built up my firm, InLook, which specialises in interior design and consulting, through my own hard work, and it took several years before it turned any real profit.

Because Gestur studied business and computing, he was able to help me with the practical side of things, like budgeting and project schedules. At first, I took care of all the rest myself: project acquisition, hands-on interior design and social media. But since then I've hired people to take on some of these jobs, and now my role is mainly restricted to conducting the initial meetings with clients, the meetings at which ideas are thrown around and I get a better idea of their requirements. This is harder than it sounds, because people often have no idea what they actually want.

In the beginning, my clients tended to be private individuals, but in recent years I've branched out, designing everything from homes to workplaces. Today, I've got a team of fifteen people working for me, eight of them designers, including me, and I'll soon need to hire more. I can hardly keep up with demand, and in the last year I've paid my parents back every last króna of their original investment in my business.

So it hurts when people say I've been handed things on a plate, because it undervalues all the sheer hard graft I've put in over the last ten years. Sure, my parents provided the initial capital and helped set the company up, but I'm the one who did all the rest. I developed the brand, took care of the marketing, built up a client base and hired the staff. Recently everything's been going so well. Brilliantly, in fact. I should be so bloody happy.

I close the dishwasher and switch it on, though it's nowhere near full. Then I lean against the kitchen counter, listening to the regular sloshing of the machine.

Yesterday's empty wine bottle is still on the table. Becoming aware of the sweetish-sour smell, I chuck it in the bin and shove it down out of sight. I drank most of it alone in front of the TV last night while Gestur was out. I needed something to calm my nerves. For the last few weeks I've had this voice in my head, counting down the days until the family reunion: *three, two, one...*

I smile at Ari, who has finally come upstairs, but my smile fades a little when he fetches a bowl and takes out the packet of cereal I've just put away.

'What are you doing?' I ask.

'Having breakfast,' Ari replies, with that *what's it to you?* tone that comes so naturally to teenagers.

'I've just cleared things away, Ari,' I protest plaintively. 'We're about to leave.'

Ari mumbles something and pours milk into his bowl.

I stand there, watching him in silence. Studying the beautiful blond hair that's far too long but looks so good on him. When he was small, he had white curls, but now it's just attractively wavy. He has the kind of smooth, flawless skin that any beautician would die for, but his sharp, angular jawbone prevents his face from appearing too delicate.

Ari has always been my weak spot, the child I can't say no to and always end up giving everything he wants. The child who makes me smile – just the thought of him is enough. I can't be angry with Ari.

'What happened to your fingers?' he asks.

'Nothing,' I say, clenching my fists to hide my nails. The cuticles and surrounding skin have never looked worse. The fact is, I'm a biter, and would probably gnaw my fingers right off if I didn't restrain myself. But I haven't chewed my nails this badly for years, not since I was a teenager, so I must have done it in my sleep. When I woke up, the pillowcase was spattered with tiny spots of blood and there was an iron taste in my mouth. Two of my fingers are now wrapped in cartoon-animal plasters – the only ones I could find – as if I were a small child.

Ari furrows his brows, which are much darker than his hair. As a child, he was nothing but eyes. His long, dark lashes resembled those of a doll.

Gestur enters the kitchen, accompanied by a cold gust of air. He's left the front door open, and out of the corner of my eye I can see the bushes in front of the house. The wind is whirling the shrivelled leaves around on the pavement. The sound they make as they rustle over the paving stones seems suddenly loud, as if someone has turned up their volume and muted everything else. *Three, two, one…*

'I've filled the tank,' Gestur says.

'Great.' I beam at him and fold my arms across my chest. 'Then we can go.'

Tryggvi

Until three days ago, talk of the weather dominated the Facebook page the family set up to organise the trip. According to the original forecasts, it was supposed to be unusually fine for an Icelandic November: sunny, windless, relatively mild and mostly dry. People posted jokey comments, asking if everyone had invested in sunscreen. Then, on Tuesday, the forecast did a U-turn, and now they're predicting snow and gales; the first depression of the winter is due to make landfall on Saturday, causing temperatures to plummet, or so the weatherman claimed yesterday as he warned people against travelling. I itch to bring up the sunscreen joke again but doubt anyone would appreciate it. Luckily, the bad weather isn't expected to arrive until late in the day, so we should still be able to fit in the cruise of Breiðafjörður, which is scheduled for noon on Saturday.

I find it funny that no one in the family has even mentioned the latest forecast. For the last few days, Oddný has stopped watching the TV the second the weather report comes on. I'm guessing she's refusing to accept the forecast. She's just decided to ignore it.

Perhaps she thinks bad predictions don't apply to the Snæberg clan. Sometimes I think Oddný's family really believe they're not governed by the same rules as the rest of us.

I glance at Oddný, sitting in the passenger seat beside me. She's tarted herself up a bit for the occasion, put on make-up and blow-dried her hair, but she's dressed casually, in a beige, zip-up fleece and black trousers. Smart but not too smart. Oddný has always known exactly how to tread the middle line.

She's in a good mood and turns up the radio as Bon Jovi sings about living on a prayer. Out of the corner of my eye, I can see her fingers tapping in time.

'We should stop at Vegamót,' she says. 'Get something to eat.'

'We can do that.'

'I didn't have any breakfast. And I wouldn't mind trying their seafood soup again.'

We've been up the west coast to the Snæfellsnes peninsula once before, though that was to stay in Oddný's family's summer cabin. The place turned out to be rundown and badly in need of maintenance, so while we were there, eager to do my bit, I oiled the deck and did a spot of DIY. Not that anyone seems to have noticed; at least, no one's said a word.

'It's a fair while since we last saw Haraldur and Ester,' I say. 'When was it again? At the confirmation party last spring?'

'Yes, I suppose it was,' Oddný says. 'Don't be shocked if Ester's changed.'

'How do you mean? Changed in what way?'

Oddný sounds gleeful. 'She's had a facelift. Had all the skin stretched back to smooth out her wrinkles. Ester's always been rather vain. According to Ingvar, she looks as if she's been facing into the wind too long.'

'Has she really had a facelift? You're not pulling my leg?'

'No, I'm not.' Oddný pulls down the sun visor, peers into the small mirror on the back and runs a finger over one of her eyebrows. 'But I bet she won't admit it. Like the time she had her eyelids done and tried to act like nothing had happened. I'm sure Halli made her do it.'

'Halli?' I say. 'You reckon?' Oddný's brother Haraldur is the controlling type all right, but ordering his wife to have plastic surgery is going a bit far, even for him.

'You know what he's like,' Oddný says, pushing the visor up again. Smiling at me, she adds: 'I'm so lucky compared to my sister-in-law.'

'I wouldn't want to change a single thing about the way you look,' I say, and I mean every word.

Really, I'm the lucky one. Oddný's far too good for me. Her family agree. They can't understand what she sees in a weather-beaten, penniless carpenter like me, but then I can hardly understand it myself.

I haven't belonged to this family for long, in fact I find it ridiculous to talk about *belonging* to it. Me and Oddný, we're polar opposites, to be honest. We hardly have anything in common.

When we reach the red-roofed café at Vegamót on the southern side of the Snæfellsnes peninsula, we go inside and order soup and a sandwich, then take one of the tables by the window. The mountainous spine of the peninsula and the glacier at its tip are hidden from view behind the café: all we can see is flat pastureland, then the great sweep of Faxaflói bay. We sit silently watching the passing traffic. I'm halfway through the sandwich when I hear Oddný's name being called in a questioning voice.

Oddný's face lights up when she sees her older brother, Ingvar, and his wife, Elín. Putting down her glass of water, she gets quickly to her feet.

'You here?' Oddný's voice is so loud and piercing that everyone in the café must be able to hear her.

I stand up as well to greet them. There are hugs, kisses and demands for news.

'Shouldn't we toast the occasion?' Elín says, and she and Oddný charge over to the counter.

Ingvar asks about the holiday Oddný and I took in Spain last month. 'Must have been nice to get away to the heat.'

'Yes, very,' I say, because it's the answer people want to hear. But the truth is, I think hot weather is overrated: I get no pleasure from lying beside a pool, knocked out by the heat, with nothing to do. I feel like I can't breathe properly until I'm back in the cold, fresh north wind of home.

The women return with two mini bottles of white wine and two beers.

'It's like that, is it?' Ingvar says, and the sisters-in-law giggle like schoolgirls.

No one mentions the fact we've still got another forty kilometres or so to drive. I don't touch my drink, but then Oddný knew I wouldn't, and once she's finished her wine, when nobody's looking, I nudge my glass towards her.

'Isn't Hákon Ingimar coming?' Ingvar asks.

'Yes, but he'll be a bit late,' Oddný says, as usual smiling indulgently when her son is mentioned. 'Hákon's always so busy.'

'So I gather,' Ingvar says, no doubt referring to all the stories in the news about Hákon Ingimar forever turning up at parties with a new girl on his arm.

'He's appearing in an advertisement,' Oddný says, rather proudly. 'On a glacier.'

'Which glacier?'

'He didn't say,' Oddný replies. 'It's an advert for outdoor clothing.'

'Oh,' Ingvar says. 'I thought you were supposed to advertise swimwear on glaciers.'

We all laugh. I dimly recall seeing a photo of Hákon posing in swimming trunks against a wintry landscape. Then the conversation turns to the upcoming weekend – who'll be there and who won't, and what everyone's children are up to these days.

Oddný has two older brothers, Ingvar and Haraldur, who are both married, with grown-up kids. It took me quite a while to work out which children belonged to who and what their names were, but I've more or less got it straight now – I hope. And I shouldn't forget Oddný's father, Hákon, who'll be arriving on Saturday evening for the party. He's eighty and was diagnosed several years ago with a degenerative disease and has gone downhill a lot recently.

Oddný has two children from before we got together: Hákon Ingimar and Stefanía, known as Steffý. Hákon Ingimar, or Hákon junior as some people call him, is a bit of a special case, to be honest. Oddný always makes out like he's got all sorts going on, but as far as I can tell all he really does is stare into a camera lens day in, day out, though mostly the camera of his own phone, which he's never parted from. Still, it's not my place to judge. After all, I grew up in a different time. I suppose you could say I'm the product of a totally different world.

I've only met Stefanía a couple of times as she lives in Denmark, where she works for some sort of cosmetics company. She has a posh engineering qualification, only I can't remember what kind.

I didn't have children myself until I was thirty, when I met a woman with a five-year-old boy. I raised him as my own kid, and he's been a part of me ever since, though Nanna and I split up donkey's years ago. The boy didn't have a father, at least none worthy of the name, and I saw it as an honour to be allowed to play that role in his life. I was totally unprepared for how tough and at the same time rewarding it was to be responsible for a child – for all life's events, big and small. I took him along for his first day at school, taught him to read, escorted him to swimming lessons and watched, tearful with pride, as he graduated from school. Getting to be his dad is the best thing that's ever happened to me – nothing else has ever come close.

'Well, best hit the road,' Oddný says, finishing my glass.

As she stands up, her bag falls on the floor, and she and Elín burst out laughing. Oddný's cheeks are flushed, as always when she drinks. I feel a twinge of anxiety, but push it down. I'm sure it won't be as bad this time.

During the year and a bit that we've been together, it's been impossible not to notice that Oddný's family is unusual, to say the least. Of course, I was aware of who the Snæbergs were, but I hadn't taken any interest in their affairs, since I rarely read the gossip columns or business pages. Maybe I'd have been better prepared if I had.

The family has its fair share of big egos, and they can be touchy as hell. I've seen how a single innocent comment can trigger a violent quarrel, where one person blurts out something that would have been better left unsaid and another person storms out. To understand what they're like, it's probably best to imagine a herd of hippos wallowing in too small a waterhole, all of them constantly bumping up against the others. When personalities that strong get together, you never know what will happen, but you can bet your life that sooner or later there will be a showdown of some kind.

Petra Snæberg

'Say cheese!' I hold up my phone and take a picture of us all in the car. The kids smile half-heartedly in the back seat, and I'm hit by a sudden memory of how sweet they used to be when they were small, beaming and yelling 'cheese!'. Now they're both sitting with their wireless ear buds in, their faces blank. A lot has changed since the days when long car journeys had to be carefully organised, with hourly breaks and CDs of children's songs or stories playing at full volume, while you crossed your fingers and prayed that the peace would last. Now the silence is absolute, and I almost miss the squabbles. I miss the time when my children's problems mainly revolved around deciding who got to choose the next song.

'Is everything OK?' Gestur asks in an undertone, so the kids won't hear.

'Yes, of course,' I say, my voice artificially cheerful.

Gestur knows me well enough to see through the pretence. 'You had a nightmare last night. I thought you'd stopped getting them.'

'Oh, did I?'

Gestur doesn't answer. He knows I'm lying. I remember perfectly well what I dreamt about last night. It's a recurring nightmare I've been having ever since I was a teenager. In it, I'm standing alone in the middle of the road at the foot of Mount Akrafjall. It's pitch-dark, and after a while it starts to snow. All is quiet and peaceful. Then suddenly there's a blinding white light and I wake up, jolted out of my dream with the gut-wrenching certainty that something terrible has happened.

Mum sent me to see a therapist after the nightmares had been playing havoc with my sleep for several months. My parents always believed a professional should be brought in to solve most problems. When I was having difficulty with maths as a ten-year-old, they hired a tutor, and again, later, when I started making clumsy mistakes on the violin as a secondary-school pupil, a psychologist was drafted in. My parents always assumed they should farm out our problems to experts, rather than simply sitting down and talking to us themselves. I know they meant well, but sometimes I wonder why they didn't just ask us first what was wrong.

Having said that, I'd never have admitted to them that I knew exactly why I was suffering from nightmares.

'And there's that nail business too,' Gestur adds, still in the same level tone.

'Nail business' is what Gestur calls it when I chew my cuticles.

'It's nothing,' I say, instinctively shoving my hands out of sight between my thighs.

Silence envelopes us again. Unlike me, Gestur doesn't have a problem with silences. They don't seem to bother him.

I turn my attention to the passing scenery. It's a beautiful day, and there's an old hit playing on the radio that reminds me uncomfortably of my youth. The feeling is heightened as we pass the turn-off to the little west-coast town of Akranes.

I really want everything to go well this weekend. It's been a long time since the entire family last gathered for a reunion. We used to be so close when I was younger and still lived in Akranes. My grandparents lived next door, and so did Dad's brother and sister, and I used to wander freely in and out of their houses. In fact, my cousins, Viktor and Stefanía, were my best friends. Steffý and I were born the same year and grew up almost like sisters; we were inseparable in those days. 'Joined at the hip,' Dad used to say.

I often think about Steffý. The image of her face comes into my mind when I least expect it: at night before I drift off to sleep; when I'm watching my daughter with her friends, or hear the loud, shrill laughter of children. The emotions it evokes are a mixture of loss, sadness and regret for what might have been.

Strange how our formative years remain such a large part of us, despite being only a small part of our lives as a whole.

We drive on up the coast, past the steep, dark slopes of Mount Hafnarfjall, where the lowland is clothed with birch scrub, the branches winter bare, apart from a few clusters of dead brown leaves. The only buildings are lone farmhouses here and there, flanked by dilapidated barns and cowsheds, until eventually the little town of Borgarnes gleams white on the other side of the fjord.

'Mum,' Ari says, and I turn down the music. 'Can we stop at Hyrnan? I'm thirsty.'

'Me too.' Lea pulls out one of her ear buds. 'And I need the loo.'

'OK, we're stopping at Hyrnan,' Gestur says, and I catch him and Lea exchanging grins in the rear-view mirror.

Lea has a very different relationship with her father to the one she has with me. They go out on runs together and occasionally go swimming in the mornings before work and school. Sometimes I come home to find Lea watching TV with Gestur, but when I'm there she tends to shut herself in her room. Whenever I try to talk to her, she suspects me of having some ulterior motive, as if I'm trying to get her to do something or looking for an excuse to tell her off.

We pull into the car park by Hyrnan, and the kids run inside to the counter. I let Gestur take care of their requirements while I buy some fizzy water and a toothbrush for myself.

When I have paid for these, I find a painkiller in my bag and quickly swallow it. Gestur thinks I use any excuse to take painkillers, so I've started knocking them back furtively, as if I have something to hide. But the truth is that my head is throbbing from that bottle of wine last night.

I'm rooting around in my bag again, this time in search of my sunglasses, when I hear a voice saying my name.

'Petra?' Next minute Viktor is standing in front of me, holding out his arms: 'Fancy meeting you here.'

I smile and step forwards into Viktor's embrace. He was always very touchy-feely as a teenager, and clearly nothing's changed. His hug is tight and intimate, his face so close that I can see every pore and line, not that he has many lines. In fact, he's only got better-looking with age, his features becoming more defined, his smile gentler.

'How are you?' Viktor is studying me, still with his arms round my shoulders. 'It's been such a long time.'

'Yes,' I say. 'Months.'

Viktor and I used to meet up regularly. He'd come round in the evenings, mainly when Gestur was at choir practice, bearing wine and treats like chocolate or mini desserts. But over the years I found it more and more of an effort to keep up our relationship, until in the end it began to feel like a chore. I started inventing excuses to put off seeing him, and in the last few years the intervals between our meetings have grown ever longer.

Eventually, Viktor must have realised that the impulse to keep up our connection was one-sided. It was always him ringing me and me pretending to be busy.

'Is it that long? That's shocking, Petra. Shocking. We'll have to do better in future.' Viktor shakes his head. 'So, what are you up to these days?'

'Oh, same as usual. Running the company and the family. Apart from that, things are pretty quiet.'

'Quiet? That doesn't sound like you,' Viktor says, reminding me how well he knows me. That he knows I can never sit still, that I have to be permanently on the go.

I'm about to add that he's no different himself, when a young woman appears beside him and hands him a hot dog.

'They didn't have any of the hot mustard,' she says.

'Damn,' Viktor replies, then adds: 'This is Maja, my girlfriend. Maja, this is Petra – who I've told you about.'

'Yes, of course. Nice to meet you, Petra.' Maja holds out a thin arm, smiling. I'm struck by how young she is, at least ten years younger than Viktor, closer in age to Lea than to me. She looks foreign, with black hair and olive skin.

'Likewise,' I say, shaking Maja's hand. Then I look back at Viktor: 'I wasn't sure you'd be coming.'

'I wouldn't miss this for the world,' he says, and I can't tell from his tone whether he's being sarcastic. 'But seriously, I've been looking forward to seeing you.'

'Do you know if Steffý's coming?' I ask. When I asked Mum, it was still a bit up in the air whether Stefanía would make it. I don't think even her mother, Aunt Oddný, knew for sure.

'Yes, she is,' Viktor replies. 'I heard from her yesterday.'

'What fun,' I say, and wince at how false it sounds.

'It'll be just like old times.' Viktor laughs.

'Exactly,' I say, gnawing at my cuticles again.

Viktor chucks his hot-dog wrapper in the bin, and they say goodbye. I stand there watching them leave. Viktor puts an arm round Maja's shoulders, and she looks up at him, smiling.

Viktor's changed; he seems so much more relaxed and self-assured than he was in his teens. Now he gives off a laid-back aura that leaves me feeling like an uptight middle-aged woman and makes me oddly nervous around him. It's almost like he's a stranger, although we know each other so well.

I suppose it's always a bit disorientating when you have only casual contact with someone you used to be very close to. Dad's brother, Ingvar, and his wife, Elín, adopted Viktor in 1984 and we pretty much grew up together. Viktor was with me the day I started my periods and the first time I got drunk. When I cried myself to sleep, Viktor held me all night in his arms. Since then, time has created a certain distance between us, despite our sporadic meetings over the years. But the fact that Viktor knows exactly when and with whom I lost my virginity makes all small talk between us feel distinctly weird.

'Who was that?' Gestur asks, finally coming over, loaded down with sweets and drinks.

'Viktor.'

'Oh, he's coming, is he?'

I nod.

'Was he alone?'

'No, actually,' I say. 'He was with his girlfriend.'

'I didn't know he had a girlfriend.'

'Neither did I.'

'Good for him,' Gestur says, though he doesn't sound as if he means it.

He and Viktor have never got on. We tried inviting Viktor over for meals a few times, but the conversation was strained at best. Viktor finds Gestur far too stiff and formal, while Gestur thinks Viktor hasn't moved on since he was twenty.

Sometimes I get the impression Gestur is jealous of Viktor, because Viktor and I are cousins and have known each other forever. It's perfectly natural that we should find it easy to talk to each other and that we know (or used to know) almost everything about each other, as I'm sure Gestur is aware. But perhaps it's just in a man's nature not to want his wife to be close to another man, even if he's a member of her family.

'You're so unlike yourself around him,' Gestur once said, soon after we got together. I can't remember how I answered, but I do recall thinking that it was the other way round: I could be myself with Viktor; it was with Gestur that I felt I had to be somebody else.

'Oh, Petra,' Gestur says suddenly, grimacing at me.

'What?' I say, guiltily jerking my hand from my mouth. When I lick my lips, I taste blood.

*

Once we're back in the car, I find some flesh-coloured plasters in the glove compartment to replace the cartoon ones. It occurs to me that I'm no better than Lea, who went through a phase of gnawing her nails to the quick; or Mum, who, when I was younger, used to spend her evenings pulling out her eyelashes. I still shudder when I remember the crumbs of mascara on her cheeks and the eyelashes littering the coffee table.

Sometime later, we drive past the narrow, white ribbon of the Bjarnarfoss falls, cascading down the sheer rockface of the mountainside, and I attempt to lighten the atmosphere in the car. Twisting round to the back seat, I say:

'Did you know that some people can see a woman in the waterfall?'

'What?' Ari pulls out his ear buds, but Lea's tapping away on her phone and doesn't even look up. Her cheeks are delicately flushed, her lips parted in a smile. I think she must have a boyfriend, or that she's talking to a boy, but she just snorts and rolls her eyes when I ask.

'Some people say there's a woman who sits in the middle of the waterfall, combing her hair,' I continue.

Ari glances out of the window. 'Cool,' he says, then puts his ear buds back in.

I smile at him and surreptitiously study Lea. The daylight illuminates her dark-brown hair, which she's drawn up into a pony-tail on top of her head.

Lea's been unusually quiet lately. I'm sure something's bothering her, but I have no idea what it is. I remember what it was like to be sixteen, though I know Lea would never believe it. She can't believe anyone in the world has ever been through what she's experiencing. Least of all me. In some ways she's right: the world teenagers face today is very different from how it was twenty or thirty years ago. But I still have a vivid memory of what it is like when your self-esteem depends on other people's opinions. The difficulty of finding a balance between fitting in and standing out. Between being ordinary and at the same time special.

Being a teenager doesn't seem to have affected Ari the same way: he's always himself. In contrast to Lea, he seems to find everything so easy. Yesterday morning, for example, he asked me what the hotel was like, and I showed him some pictures.

It's brand new, built in the middle of an old lava field on the south side of the Snæfellsnes peninsula, not far from the village of Arnarstapi and the glacier. Previously there was a farm on the estate, which belonged to the local government official and his family. According to the hotel website, the farm was abandoned after a fire in 1921, but you can still see the ruins. The story goes that the official's wife died in the fire along with their two youngest children. I closed the information window before Ari could read that far.

Apparently, the hotel is designed to be sustainable and environmentally friendly. The concrete walls are intended to merge seamlessly into the surrounding lava field. They're illuminated by exterior lights, set in the ground, which turn slowly, creating the illusion that the building itself is on the move, the walls billowing as if they were alive. The architect says he drew his inspiration from the rich history of the area, with its centuries-old belief in the supernatural – something that persists to this day.

From the outside, the building has a raw, bleak aesthetic, in keeping with the natural setting of glacier, lava field and mountains that inspired it. The interior, by contrast, looks more welcoming, judging from the online gallery, with simple designer furnishings and the highest-quality Jensen beds. In addition, the hotel is equipped with the very latest in smart technology, a detail that attracted Ari's interest. Everything is controlled by app: the lights in the bedrooms, the temperature, the door locks and the pressure in the showers. Literally everything.

The scenery outside the car window is becoming ever more

familiar. I know this route by heart, having driven it so often since I was a child. Every rock, hummock and hill has its name and its story. The mountain crags take on the shapes of creatures of folklore: the bigger rocks and mounds are populated by elves or *huldufólk*, 'hidden people', the mountains by trolls, the sea by mermen.

Of course, I know these stories are make-believe, relics from a past when people didn't know as much as they do today, but part of me still clings to the belief that perhaps they actually knew more then, were more open to the world around them, their senses more acute.

Whenever I visit the Snæfellsnes peninsula and see the dome of the glacier looming at the end, the spine of jagged mountains, and the sheer rock stacks rising out of the sea, I can never quite shake off the feeling that we're not alone.

Lea Snæberg

Mum turns round and points at a waterfall. Ari pretends like he's interested, but I can't be arsed to remind Mum that she's shown us that waterfall a million times before and I know all about the story of the woman who sits there, combing her hair.

Checking my phone, I see that Birgir has written: *Are you there yet?*

No still in car, I reply. *Will let you know when I get there.*

I wait a while, but Birgir doesn't reply, so I start wondering if it was stupid of me to say that. Why should he be interested in when I get there?

I scroll back through the photos I have of him. Birgir isn't on social media much, but he sometimes sends me pictures that I save onto my phone. He's a year older than me and we've known each other for several months. We've never actually met in real life, though, as he moved to Sweden when he was five and hardly ever visits Iceland. But his family are planning to come over at Christmas, so we'll finally get to see each other then.

Although we've never met, I know a lot about Birgir, and he knows a lot about me, more than almost anyone else. I know he plays basketball and that his dog, Captain, always sleeps by his bed. And he wants to work with children when he's older, either as a teacher or a sports coach. But I've never heard his voice and have no idea what he smells like, so I can't imagine what it will feel like to meet him in real life at last, after everything we've shared with each other.

We've talked every day since we met online, and not just about trivial stuff. We've had deep conversations too, about what we want to do in life and about our feelings. Birgir's the only person I've talked to about all the shit that happened at my old school. Like *really* talked. Sure, I went to a therapist (Dad's idea) and we talked a lot in the sessions, but even then I didn't feel I could open up about all the things I've shared with Birgir. Usually I try not to think about that stuff, but when I told Birgir what happened, it was different. We were just chatting, and somehow it came up that I'd changed schools, and he asked: *Wasn't that hard?*

I replied: *No not really.*

Him: *It must have been tough leaving all your friends behind, though I can't believe it would be too difficult for a girl like you to make new ones.*

I remember staring at those words and wondering what *a girl like me* meant. What was Birgir implying?

Sometimes I feel like I've spent my whole life challenging other people's preconceptions about me – the people who assume I'm a stuck-up snob because of who my family are. I wanted to prove that I wasn't the girl Birgir thought I was, so I said: *Actually it's my fault we had to move.*

Him: *Why was it your fault?*

Me: *Because the kids at my old school didn't want me there.*

Then I told him the whole ugly story. How one day when I got to school, my best friend had decided I couldn't sit next to her anymore. How all the kids had whispered and giggled as I looked for somewhere else to sit. How I found wet lumps of paper in my hair after the lesson, and when I was walking home I noticed a strange smell and realised that my coat was wet at the back. I told him how I tried to hide my schoolbag when I got home, taking it to the bathroom and pulling out my books and schoolwork, which were all soaked with milk. Even after I'd washed out my bag in the bath, it still stank of rotten milk, and the smell only got worse with time.

Birgir didn't say anything for a while, then he sent back: *Lea, let's get one thing straight.*

What? I asked, my fingers trembling as I tapped in the letters, my breathing ragged because writing about what happened made me relive all the feelings and it was hard. Just remembering it was so hard.

But Birgir said: *Let's get one thing straight. Your parents didn't move because of you. None of this was your fault.*

Then it was like something burst inside me, and I cried until my stomach hurt and my eyes were stinging. I'm just glad he was a thousand kilometres away in Sweden and that no one was home to see me in that state.

But I don't want to think about that now, so I unlock my phone again and start scrolling through the photos I've posted on my own page, mostly selfies or holiday pics. The beach at Las Cabos, the lake by our summer cabin, and one showing the wing of the plane on the flight to London last spring.

Mum came into my room the other day and asked me to take down one of my selfies because it was too adult. She said I don't really look like I did in the photo. That really hurt me because I was super pleased with that particular shot. I'd spent hours getting ready, doing my hair in a high pony-tail, using gel to slick back all those little stray hairs, and making myself up like in this video I saw on YouTube. Some people say I look a bit like Ariana Grande. We're both petite, with brown eyes and straight dark hair, and the online tutorial I watched showed how to do your make-up to look like her. I used thick eyeliner, drawing flicks at the corners to make my eyes more cat-like, and completed the look with a browny-pink lipstick and big earrings.

The make-up worked really well. I've never received that many reactions to a selfie before, so no way was I going to take it down. And I got a message almost immediately from Birgir, praising the picture – not that I'd tell Mum. She's already freaking out about some bloke who writes comments on all my posts. Though, to be honest, I find it a bit creepy too.

It started a few months ago when a man called Gulli58 started following me. Next day a direct message was waiting: *Hi sweetheart, how are you?*

At first I didn't give it much thought; after all, I get loads of messages like that every day, mostly from foreigners, but sometimes from Icelanders too. I never respond, of course, just ignore them, or block them if they get too much. But if I blocked everyone who sent me a message, I'd lose a big chunk of my followers, and that would mean fewer likes and comments. In spite of everything, these men are the ones I can trust to like every single picture I post and to comment that I'm cute or sexy. Of course, I get some weirdos, but it's not like I'm anything special to them. They behave like that to all the girls. The same guy will often message all my friends. That's just how it works. They're perfectly harmless.

But Gulli58 hasn't messaged any of my friends as far as I know, and I haven't seen him comment on any of their pictures either. It's not like he's rude or anything. Mostly he just writes under my photos that I'm beautiful or reacts to what I've written, which is kind of weird.

Like, the other day I posted a picture of myself holding my friend Agnes's new puppy and wrote: *Can I take him home with me?*

I got a few comments from men saying I could take them home with me, but not from Gulli58. He wrote: *Is that puppy a cavalier king charles spaniel? I used to have a labrador but it died several years ago. Such a lovely dog.*

Not long before that I'd posted a selfie of me sunbathing at our summer cabin and captioned it in English: *Until you've heard my story, you have no idea.*

OK, I know it sounds sad but it's just a sentence I found online when I was searching for something to write, and I thought it sounded quite cool. It's not like I meant it personally or anything. Lots of people write short captions in English under their pictures, and everyone knows they don't really mean anything.

But Gulli58 obviously took it as a cry for help because he DM'd me, saying that if I needed someone to talk to, he was there for me. Of course, I didn't answer and I thought about blocking him, but in the end I decided that he meant well. He was just some lonely guy who hadn't been on Instagram long and didn't know how it works.

But for some reason I can't shake off this uneasy feeling whenever I see that he's commented on my pictures or been the first person to view the videos I put up on Snapchat. Because he's almost always the first, like he's got nothing else to do but wait for me to post.

'Right, we're here,' Dad says, switching off the engine.

I look out of the window at the hotel. It's grey, with big windows and a flat roof, and looks more like a cliff in the lava field than a building.

I undo my seatbelt and get out. After the long car journey it's a relief to breathe in the fresh air, and I raise my face to the sky, which is blue and almost cloudless.

Suddenly I spot this huge bird right over our heads. Its wingspan is enormous and it seems to float there effortlessly, hardly flapping its wings.

'An eagle,' I say, realising. 'Is that an eagle?'

Everyone stops what they're doing to look up.

'Well, I never,' Dad says. 'I do believe you're right.'

For a long moment no one says anything, we're too caught up in watching the majestic bird.

The eagle swoops and, as it comes closer, I see even more clearly its vast wingspan and its power as it rides on the wind. And suddenly I remember a story Mum once told us, about an eagle that snatched up a child in its big talons and carried it off. I can't remember how the story ended, but the memory makes me shiver.

I'm so mesmerised that I almost forget to take out my phone to video it, then realise just in time. But however much I zoom in, I totally fail to capture the moment. On my phone screen, the eagle looks like any other bird; you can't get any idea of the scale.

Suddenly, the eagle wheels round and soars away towards the glacier.

'Incredible,' Dad says, as we watch it go.

Then he opens the boot of the car and everyone takes out their cases. I'm just going to get mine when my phone vibrates. For a moment I think the message is from Birgir, but when I see the name on the screen, my stomach drops.

The message is from Gulli58. *Hey,* he's written. *I see you're on Snæfellsnes. What a nice coincidence. As it happens I'm staying in a summer cabin nearby.*

Irma
Hotel Employee

'Did you hear the noises last night?'

I'm in my room, pulling on my jumper, when Elísa materialises without warning in the doorway.

'You should knock,' I say, a little gruffly.

'The door was open,' Elísa says, but I know she's lying. Her gaze travels downwards, and I realise my bare stomach is showing.

'I thought I'd shut it.' I tug my jumper down.

Elísa smiles. The odd thing is that when Elísa smiles, the corners of her mouth turn down.

'Did you want something?' I ask.

'No.' Elísa goes over to my bed and plumps down on it. 'I just wanted to see you.'

'Oh, right.'

Having the owners' granddaughter, Elísa, here is a bit like having a cat running around the place. She follows you everywhere and has a habit of popping up when you least expect it. I'm guessing she doesn't have many friends at school, so I let her keep me company while I work, chatting to her and trying to show an interest in her life. She's eleven years old, capable of talking nonstop, and eye-wateringly blunt. She's impulsive too, often saying or doing things without stopping to think first. In fact, her company can be so challenging that, up to a point, I do understand her friendlessness.

'What noises did you hear last night?' I ask.

'Like this.' Elísa makes a horrible rasping noise at the back of her throat that sounds like a cross between the growl of a dog and the squawk of a parrot.

'Jesus, no,' I say, laughing in spite of myself. 'I certainly didn't hear that.'

'Granddad says it must have been a ptarmigan, but I don't believe that.'

'What do you think it was, then?' I ask, glancing out of the window. It's nearly twelve and I can't stop my gaze straying to the car park: they'll be arriving any minute.

'I don't know.' Elísa picks up my necklace, which was lying on the bedside table, and starts examining it.

It takes all my self-control not to snatch it away from her. I've told her repeatedly not to mess around with my stuff, but she never listens.

'The guests arriving today are famous, did you know that?' Elísa continues, fiddling with the catch on my necklace.

My self-control crumbles. 'Elísa, can I have my necklace, please?'

She pretends not to hear me.

'Who gave it to you?' she asks, after a moment.

'No one,' I say, reaching out quickly and taking it from her.

'Your boyfriend?'

'I haven't got a boyfriend,' I say, doing up the necklace at the back of my neck.

'Why not?'

'Right, Elísa,' I say, holding the door open, 'I've got work to do.'

Elísa's mouth tightens into a straight line, then she jumps off my bed and flounces out, her thick plait swinging on her back.

Sighing, I watch her go. Elísa is quick to take offence, but I'm not worried. She always comes back and carries on chattering away as if nothing had happened.

Looking in the mirror, I touch the necklace, which has a tiny gold heart pendant with a red stone in the middle, then tuck it inside the neck of my jumper. I run my hands through my hair, trying to fluff it up a little before tying it back in a pony-tail, but it's futile. Whatever I do, my hair is always dead straight. My face is unmade up, my skin a shiny white. I couldn't be more colourless or less memorable.

When I emerge, Edda's in the restaurant, walking from table to table, lighting the tealights. Actually, 'walking' isn't the right word; 'gliding' would be more appropriate. Edda is tall and willowy, and manages to come across as simultaneously delicate yet strong. Her nose is straight, her hair silver grey and her lips a little pursed. If I didn't know better, I'd think she was one of those aristocratic Englishwomen.

'Are all the rooms ready, Irma?' she asks, noticing me.

'Every single one,' I reply with a smile.

A small information pack about the reunion, prepared and sent to us by one of the Snæberg clan, has been placed in each room. It contains a printed booklet with details about the weekend's programme of events, a biography of the family patriarch, who would have been a hundred on Sunday, and a bar of chocolate with nuts. I was responsible for putting the packs in the rooms, arranging each on the bedcover with a small card providing information about the hotel. While I was doing this, I couldn't stop thinking about the fact that they would soon be staying here, sleeping in these beds. I couldn't keep the smile off my face.

Edda nods with satisfaction, then disappears into the kitchen.

I go over to the reception desk and check the computer. Just seeing the names on the screen makes my heart beat faster. I take a deep breath, then release it slowly through my nose. I have to stay calm, I tell myself. No one must notice how excited I am.

To distract myself, I take the stairs to the first floor, which is slightly smaller in area than the ground floor. It consists of one long corridor with rooms opening off it on either side, widening out at the end into a lounge with glass walls and ceiling, like a greenhouse. It gets a bit chilly in here in winter, despite the under-floor heating, but there are woollen blankets for the guests to wrap themselves in.

On dark winter evenings, this is the perfect spot to sit and watch the Northern Lights. Last weekend the sky was clear and black, and the aurora danced across it for a whole hour, undulating streamers of pink and green. The lounge filled with guests, some of them lying on the floor, gazing, entranced, at the natural light show.

The lounge is furnished with upholstered couches, their backs made of the same rough-hewn wood as the tables, which have bowls on them full of smooth black pebbles from the beach at Djúpalón. Sitting down on one of the couches, I pick up a pebble and rub it between my palms, feeling myself growing calmer.

When we don't have many guests, I often sit here, imagining I'm at home. Not so much that I live here, but that I belong in a place like this. Because, the thing is, I suffer from a constant fear of exposure, convinced that it must be obvious to everyone that I don't belong in surroundings like this. Not someone like me, who grew up in a tower block, wearing hand-me-down clothes and eating ready meals.

Yet the hotel has the effect of taking me out of myself. When I'm working, it's as if I step into a role and become another person. Sadly, though, the job is temporary, and I'll be forced to go home soon enough. I'm dreading the moment.

Putting the pebble back in the bowl, I get to my feet and wander over to the window. As I watch the cars speeding along the distant road, I wonder which of them will take the turn-off to the hotel. The road is too far away for me to be able to see the people in the cars, but I sometimes sit here, watching them pass, wondering who they are, what they're doing there, what their lives are like.

A black four-by-four comes into view, and I move closer to

the glass, sure that it's one of the guests. I smile when I'm proved right and the vehicle slows down before taking the turning to the hotel.

It pulls into the car park below, an expensive, glossy black. Both front doors open almost simultaneously, and a man emerges from the driver's side. I know his name: Gestur. He has dark hair and, although tall, he's not particularly broad or muscular. The woman who gets out of the passenger side looks incredibly petite, at least from here.

I recognise Petra immediately and have to bite down on my lower lip to stop my face splitting in a broad grin, all the while taking in her appearance: her clothes, her hair, her shoes. The way she looks around her as soon as she's out of the car, turning in a circle to survey her surroundings. She's wearing pale, slightly distressed jeans, turned up to show tanned ankles. Her trainers are a dazzling white, but I can't see the brand from here. Big, black sunglasses hold her dark hair back from her face, and she's hugging a long cardigan around herself as if she's cold.

A teenage girl climbs out next and looks around. Lea seems younger in the flesh than in her photos, perhaps because she's so small and slight. Her legs are like two matchsticks in their tight leggings, in contrast to her oversized hoodie and clumpy trainers. I spot her brother, Ari, on the other side of the car, his blond hair gleaming in the sun, and even at this distance I can see how good-looking he is.

Lea points in the air, and they all raise their faces and crane their necks. Following their gaze, I see an eagle hovering overhead, a magnificent sight, but I'm much more interested in the humans than the bird.

After a minute or two, Gestur opens the boot and takes out a large suitcase. Ari lifts out a backpack and follows his father towards the hotel, then turns and says something to his mother. Petra laughs, turning too and calling back in the direction of the car.

Lea grimaces and, even at this distance, I'm sure she's rolling her eyes. She shoves her phone in the pocket of her hoodie, only to take it out again almost immediately. For a moment, she stiffens, staring transfixed at the screen, then peers nervously all around her as if she thinks she's being watched. I wonder what's frightened her.

It's a shock when she looks up suddenly and clocks me standing in the window. I back away from the glass so fast that I nearly fall over a table.

Downstairs the front door opens, and I hear Edda greeting them in a welcoming voice. Hastily running my hands over my clothes to smooth them, I run downstairs to help.

Now
Sunday, 5 November 2017

Sævar
Detective, West Iceland CID

The pathologist, a tall, lean, middle-aged man, who had come up from Reykjavík, was standing over the body. Sævar and Hörður kept well back as they watched him work. He took photos and samples, seemingly in a world of his own. His concentration was so intense that Sævar hardly dared breathe for fear of disturbing him. Afterwards, the body was removed on a stretcher and carried to the ambulance that would transport it to Reykjavík for the post-mortem. Only then did the pathologist turn to Sævar and Hörður.

'What can you tell us?' Hörður asked. 'Do you have any idea when it happened?'

'Well, it's a bit difficult to give a precise time of death. We can analyse the stomach contents and see how far digestion had progressed, but I won't be able to do that until tomorrow.'

'Can you give us a rough estimate?'

'Some time last night,' the pathologist said. 'Around twelve hours ago, I'd conjecture.'

'Any injuries?' Hörður asked.

'Only those sustained in the fall. A fractured skull and injuries to the back.' The pathologist hesitated. 'It's quite tricky to establish what caused the fall, because it was such a long drop, but the position of the body is interesting.'

'Oh?'

'Yes. The victim appears to have fallen backwards. The injuries are mainly to the back of the head and back, rather than the legs or front of the body, as you'd expect if someone had jumped from a great height.'

'As you say, though, it is quite a long way down.' Sævar glanced up the sheer rock wall, then hastily averted his eyes. 'Couldn't the body have twisted in the air?'

The pathologist pulled a face. 'When you're talking about a very long drop, it's certainly common for the body to spin round and fall head first, as most of the weight is in the upper half, but I doubt there would have been enough time for that to happen in this case. Besides, the injuries aren't consistent with that scenario. As I said, most of the damage is to the back and the back of the head.'

'As a result of being pushed?' Hörður asked.

'Exactly,' the pathologist said. 'As if someone gave the victim a shove in the chest.'

Sævar pictured the victim clutching at the attacker and pulling a few hairs out of their head before toppling backwards over the edge and plummeting to that sickening impact with the ground below, skull smashing on the rocks.

Before they returned to the car, Hörður stepped aside to take a phone call, leaving Sævar with Valgerður, a female officer from the local Snæfellsnes police force, who had been among the first on the scene.

'Are you going up to the hotel now?' she asked. When Sævar said yes, she went on: 'Be warned, the press are bound to be on their way as soon as they get wind of this.'

'Really?' Sævar wasn't used to the cases he worked on for West Iceland CID receiving much media attention. His job as a detective was nothing like the image presented in films and TV series; and this was Iceland, after all.

'You know who it is, don't you?' Valgerður asked, raising her eyebrows. 'You can be sure the reporters and camera crews will be jumping into their cars and charging up here the minute they hear the Snæberg family's involved.'

'Yes, I suppose you're right.' Sævar felt stupid not to have thought of that earlier, though of course they hadn't initially been aware of the connection to the Snæberg clan. The search-and-rescue team had been called out during the night when it became clear that one of the hotel guests was missing in the blizzard, and towards morning the police had been notified about the discovery of a body.

'Interesting location,' Valgerður said, after a brief silence.

'What's so interesting about it?' Sævar asked, looking over at Hörður, who was still occupied with his phone call and showed no signs of ringing off.

'You haven't heard the stories, then?'

'What stories?' Sævar asked.

'About Fróðárheiði and the Knarrarklettir. About how many people have lost their lives on this very spot, falling over the precipice after getting lost on the moors.' Valgerður pointed towards the famous little black wooden church at Búðir, visible in the distance. 'There used to be a trading post here on the southern side of the peninsula, and people would cross the Fróðárheiði moor to visit the merchant. But the weather could be extreme, and travellers often lost their way, not realising the precipice was there until it was too late.'

'But that can hardly be what happened this time,' Sævar said.

'No, probably not,' Valgerður conceded. 'But the question remains, what did happen? What would someone be doing out here in the middle of the night?'

'Yes, that's the big question,' Sævar agreed.

'Some people say Fróðárheiði is haunted,' Valgerður went on. 'That ghosts lure those lost on the moors towards Knarrarklettir. I don't know if there's any truth in it, but more than a dozen men and women have fallen to their deaths here.'

'You're kidding,' Sævar said.

'I'm not,' Valgerður replied. 'So, as I say, the location is pretty interesting, don't you think?'

Sævar tried to come up with a flippant answer. He was someone who always felt compelled to lighten the mood, though the results could be mixed. Inspiration failed him this time.

His eyes kept being drawn back, against his will, to the mountain. He couldn't stop himself from staring up at the sheer rockface and thinking about what it would be like to stand on the brink, with all that empty space below him.

'Hey, is everything OK?' Valgerður asked.

'Yes, fine.'

'You looked a bit wobbly for a moment there. I thought you were going to fall over.'

'No, there's no danger of that,' Sævar said. 'Just a spot of dizziness.'

Valgerður wrinkled her brow, clearly still concerned, and Sævar forced his mouth into a smile.

In the instant before he'd managed to tear his gaze away from the precipice, he'd thought he caught a flicker of movement at the top; a dark shadow that vanished as quickly as it had appeared. He decided not to mention the fact.

Two Days Earlier
Friday, 3 November 2017

Petra Snæberg

The hotel reception is low-key and minimalist, with a high ceiling and the same grey concrete walls as the exterior. The floors, too, are of smooth grey concrete and there are none of the furnishings you would usually expect in a hotel reception: no rugs on the floor, no paintings or other decoration on the walls. The effect is deliberate, of course. Nothing must distract attention from the real decoration, which can be seen outside the large, floor-to-ceiling windows: black lava, grey-green moss and white glacier. The experience is almost like being part of nature. I immediately start taking pictures to share with my followers.

The only slightly jarring note is struck by the black Gino Sarfatti chandeliers hanging from the ceiling. I've never been particularly taken with the design: there's something insect-like about all those thin, spiky arms. If the chandelier was turned over it would look like a spider with too many legs.

I hate spiders and would have chosen something quite different myself. Something simple and stylish, like the Normann Copenhagen Amp lamp or Alvar Aalto's Artek lights.

In keeping with every other aspect of the hotel, the woman who greets us seems to blend in perfectly with her surroundings, with her light-brown jumper and silver hair.

'I'm Edda,' she says. 'I do hope you'll enjoy your stay with us this weekend.' She smiles as she produces her well-rehearsed spiel. 'Now all I need is your names so I can check you in.'

Gestur supplies them, and Edda enters our names into the computer.

'Has anyone else arrived?' I ask.

'You're the first,' Edda says, without looking at me.

I'm a little surprised by this as I know my parents left before us. But neither of them has tried to ring me. Images flash into my mind: smashed-up cars, smoke, blood. I'm hard-wired to fear the worst.

'I'm going to ring Mum,' I tell Gestur, and step aside. While I'm waiting for an answer, I gaze up at the snow-flecked rock formations of the lava field outside the window. Suddenly a black blur seems to shoot across one of the white patches, so fast that I'm not even sure if it really happened. My pulse shoots up, though I realise it must have been a bird or a mouse. Then again, the shadow had looked too large for that. Could it have been an Arctic fox?

There's a cold draught emanating from the glass, and I draw back.

'Petra?' says a voice in my ear.

'Mum?' I'd almost forgotten I was making a phone call and have to clear my throat. 'Where are you?'

I can hear loud voices and laughter in the background, and to my relief she tells me they've stopped off on the way to get a bite to eat. She reels off the names of various people she's encountered, then gets distracted and starts talking to someone beside her. In the end, I have to shout into the phone to say goodbye.

'Isn't the hotel finished yet?' Lea asks when I rejoin them.

'Yes, of course,' I say, relaying what I read on the website. 'The raw look is a deliberate part of the design. The idea is that nothing should distract from the environment.'

'The environment?'

'Yes,' I say. 'Just look outside, Lea. Look how beautiful it is.'

Lea stares out of the window for a while, but from her expression it's clear that she's unimpressed.

Luckily, Edda doesn't seem to have heard and she's still smiling when she comes over.

'This is a smart hotel,' she says. 'Hopefully you'll have received the email with instructions about how to use the app. Have you downloaded it?'

'Yes, of course,' I say.

'Excellent,' Edda holds out cards and brochures for us. 'You've got two rooms at your disposal, and these are the codes that you'll need to enter when you register with the app. The brochure contains instructions, but in my experience it's all pretty self-explanatory. Once you've opened the app, you'll be able to control the lighting in your rooms, as well as the shower, the thermostat and the TV. There's a selection of films and programmes to watch. If you like, Irma can give you a tour before you go up to your rooms.'

Turning, I see Irma standing there, watching us. She's dressed in black, in a cotton top, skirt and tights, with her name printed on a small badge on her chest. She opens her mouth, as if to speak, but Gestur forestalls her.

'That would be great,' he says.

'Good.' Edda nods. 'I'll have your cases taken up to your rooms.'

As if by arrangement, two men emerge from a door behind the reception desk. One takes our luggage, the other is carrying a tray with four glasses.

'Iced tea,' Edda says. 'Made from wild thyme, flavoured with blueberry syrup. The ingredients are locally sourced, like almost all the refreshments we serve here. Please, help yourselves.'

'Oh, thanks,' I say, taking a glass. The tea is delicious; sweet, fresh, with a perfect balance between the blueberry and thyme.

Even Ari and Lea drink it down and return empty glasses to the reception desk.

As Irma introduces herself, I notice how nervous she seems, as if she's about to burst into giggles any minute or doesn't know where to look.

'Why don't we begin with the restaurant?' she says, then pauses. 'Or … no, maybe the bar.'

'Whatever you think,' Gestur says, smiling.

He's noticed too, I think. I should be used to people recognising us, but I'm not. I've never got over that feeling of discomfort when someone stares at us too long or shows signs of being tongue-tied. Fortunately, few people betray themselves, but I know that most recognise us. Or me, at least. It's me they know, not Gestur. My face appears in the advertisements, and when there's news about us in the media, my name always comes before Gestur's, if he gets a mention at all. After all, he's not actually employed by my company; he only helps out when necessary.

These days it doesn't bother him as much as it used to. Yet wherever we go, I get the feeling he's making an extra effort to let people know that he's in charge. When we meet clients at restaurants or bump into people we know in town, Gestur always tries to take over the conversation as if to ensure that he's the centre of attention.

I don't really mind, though I get the feeling he's trying to compensate for something, as if he needs to show that he's important too.

'So, this is the bar,' Irma says, having led us through a door to the right of the entrance. 'It's open from twelve noon till midnight on weekdays, and until one at weekends. Though it's sometimes open longer, as it will be tonight and tomorrow.'

There are wineglasses suspended from the ceiling on black steel pipes, and the wall behind the bar, lined with countless bottles of spirits, is illuminated with a greenish-yellow glow. Beside it, there is a wine rack built into the concrete wall.

In one corner of the room, upholstered couches and deep armchairs of brandy-coloured leather are arranged in front of an open fire. The furnishings are characterised by pure lines, simplicity, every piece serving a purpose. Everything looks raw but the effect is deliberate. Very Scandinavian. The only decoration is provided by a number of small picture frames containing not paintings but tufts of moss, growing where the picture should be.

'It's real moss,' Irma says, noticing me looking. 'The first time I saw it, I was, like: how on earth are you supposed to water that? But it's easy.'

'Oh?'

'Yes, you just mist it.' Irma smiles again, and I get the impression she's a simple soul. Childlike, even.

'Clever,' Gestur says. 'But then the entire design of the hotel is fascinating.'

We continue into the restaurant, Gestur and Irma talking to each other all the while. I hear him telling her about the hotel I'm designing in Reykjavík and about the philosophy behind this or that decision. You'd think he was the interior-design consultant, not me. Irma can hardly get a word in edgeways, but she doesn't seem to mind. Every time our eyes meet she smiles at me, lips clamped together as if she's afraid of showing her teeth.

'Mum.' Ari comes over to murmur in my ear. 'Can't we just go to our room?'

'We're nearly done,' I whisper.

Despite my job, my kids have absolutely zero interest in architecture or design.

'What do you think?' I ask Ari.

He shrugs. 'Pretty cool, I suppose.'

'Seriously?' Lea asks, overhearing. 'But it's so depressing. So...'

'Cold and unwelcoming?' Ari supplies.

'Exactly.'

'I'm sure it won't seem cold this evening,' I say. 'Not when it's dark outside and they've lit the fire.'

Neither Ari nor Lea says anything to this. We follow Irma upstairs, where she shows us the lounge, explaining that you can sit there when it's dark and watch the Northern Lights.

'It's the most popular spot in the evenings,' Irma tells us. 'Last weekend it was packed out because there was such an amazing display of the aurora. I think the forecast is the same for this evening.'

'Great,' Gestur says. 'We'll have to come up here and enjoy the show.'

'Yes.' Out comes Irma's smile again, then she drops her gaze, and I could swear she's blushing, though I can't imagine why.

We stand there for a while, looking out of the windows. The sun is as high in the sky as it ever gets in November, its rays glittering on the distant sea. If I didn't know how cold it was, I might have been tempted to go outside.

'Well, that's pretty much it.' Irma produces her odd, tight smile, then adds: 'Oh, unless you want something. We can bring anything you like from the bar or kitchen to your rooms. The menu's on the app, and you can order the food there too.'

'We're good for now,' Gestur assures her.

'Thanks so much for the tour,' I say. 'It was very interesting.'

Irma nods but shows no sign of leaving the lounge. I can feel her eyes following us as we go to find our room.

'Nice girl,' Gestur says, once we're out of earshot.

'You think so?' I ask, stealing a glance over my shoulder. She's still standing there, her hands clasped, wearing that smile. 'You didn't find her ... I don't know ... a bit odd?'

'No.' Gestur raises his eyebrows. 'Did you?'

I hesitate, not wanting to sound vain, but something about the young woman's gaze made me uncomfortable. She seemed almost avid, as if she could hardly tear her eyes off us.

❉

'Look, it works,' I say, holding the door open for Gestur when we reach our room.

Our cases are standing just inside the door. As we enter, we're greeted by a smell that's a combination of home fragrance – from a scented candle or diffuser, presumably – and strong soap.

In contrast to the other parts of the hotel we've seen so far, the room has curtains at the window. The bed appears to be an extension of the wall, a concrete base with a mattress on top, white sheets and a charcoal-grey cover spread over half of it. Someone has placed a plastic folder and a bar of chocolate on the bed. I break a bit off and study the photo on the cover.

It shows my great-grandparents outside their house here on Snæfellsnes. They were young at the time it was taken, or at least I think so, though I always find it hard to gauge people's ages in old photos. Neither their clothes nor their hairstyles give anything away. Great-grandfather's face, which became heavily lined in his later years, looks smooth here, which makes it hard to recognise him as the old man I remember so well – the man I feared and avoided as much as I could. In this picture there's no sign of the harshness that later came to dominate his expression.

Opening the file, I read: 'Welcome to the family reunion...' There's information about my grandparents too, about where they lived and when they moved. All their descendants are listed, with their birth dates and professions. Under my name, it says 'architect', and I can feel myself blushing. Architects go to university and study for years. I work with them, of course, but all I did was an interior-design course, which doesn't really give me the right to style myself as anything other than a consultant.

I take out my phone and start posting photos of the hotel on my Instagram and Twitter accounts.

'What do you think?' Gestur reclines on the bed, watching me.

'It's very smart,' I say, shifting away from him, towards the edge of the bed. 'Even smarter than in the pictures.'

'Reminds me a bit of an underground car park,' Gestur says. 'Same concept.'

'An underground car park?' I laugh. 'I suppose I know what you mean, but I still like it.'

I turn to my phone again, pull up the app and select the symbol for the lights. Various tabs appear for ceiling lights, wall lights and table lamps. I try setting the ceiling lights to red and the room becomes slightly brighter. The effect isn't as pronounced as I expected, but I suppose that's because it's still daylight outside.

'We'll have to try it again this evening,' I say.

Gestur's mouth twitches in a half-smile, and he reaches out to me.

'I'm going to the loo,' I say, pretending not to notice his hand, and can feel his eyes on me as I stand up.

When I return, Gestur is sitting up.

'About yesterday...' he begins.

'It's all right,' I say, smiling. 'It was my fault.' I don't know if that's true. Yesterday's row was different from usual. At first it was about Gestur coming home so late, then it moved on to the damage to the roof cladding and ended up being about something completely different. Mainly about me and all the things I do or fail to do.

Gestur smiles and stretches out again.

'Come on,' he says. 'Let's lie down.'

I lie on the bed beside him, though not close enough to touch him.

Gestur closes his eyes and the rising and falling of his ribcage gradually slows. He's always been able to drop off quickly, like a small child. Even when we're having a conversation, he can conk out mid-sentence.

Shafts of sunlight shine in the window, falling on the white bedlinen and on Gestur. On his straight nose, the cleft in his chin and the dark hair that shows no sign of turning grey, although he's almost ten years older than me.

I don't find the age gap as big now as I did when we first got together, when I was eighteen and he was twenty-seven. Looking back now, I find it unbelievable that my parents didn't object. How would I react if Lea suddenly came home with a man who was nearly thirty?

Gestur is from Reykjavík, and for the first few weeks he drove up to Akranes to see me. Our first kiss took place in the car one evening, in the parking area at the foot of Mount Akrafjall. Pitch-darkness all around us, the wind buffeting the car and the windows steamed up from the rain.

Feeling a lump forming in my throat, I close my eyes.

Then open them wide as my breathing becomes rapid and shallow, and stare upwards, counting the cracks in the ceiling, then the arms on the light fitting. Trying to think about something completely different, anything at all.

The room is cold and uninviting, almost like a prison cell. The designers have overstepped the mark in their quest for simplicity, and in spite of the under-floor heating and the sunshine, I feel chilly.

Unable to relax, I get up, put my shoes back on and leave the room, making no attempt to wake Gestur.

Downstairs in the restaurant, the kids already have glasses of some kind of fizzy drink, and no sooner have I sat down than a waiter comes in with a burger and a sandwich that he places on the table in front of them.

'Are you two really that hungry?' I ask.

'Yes,' Lea says. 'It's nearly one o'clock.'

Lea's right, it's long past midday. Some of the others must surely have arrived while we were up in our room.

'Like some chips?' Ari asks, pushing his plate towards me.

'Thanks,' I say. 'Maybe I'll get a drink.'

The young woman who gave us the tour is standing behind the bar. She's so startled when she sees me that she almost drops the glass she's holding, then hurriedly puts it down and comes over.

'Vodka and cranberry, please,' I say quietly. 'No ice.'

I take a big mouthful as soon as she serves me the drink, then go back and join the kids.

'What's that?' Lea asks.

'Cranberry juice,' I say.

The front door opens in reception. At the sound of muffled voices and laughter, I automatically tense up. Mum appears.

'Hi, my darlings. You're sitting in here, are you?'

Her piercing voice fills the room, and her high heels clack across the floor as she rushes over. When she hugs us, I catch a powerful waft of her perfume. Roses and citrus. Dad follows on her heels and envelopes me in an even tighter hug.

'Oh, it's ages since I've seen you. You don't come up to Akranes often enough,' Mum says, with that characteristic faint note of accusation in her voice.

'It hasn't really been that long—'

'Petra,' Mum interrupts in ringing tones. 'What happened to your hands?'

'Nothing,' I say. 'I cut myself.'

Mum gives me a sceptical look. 'Don't tell me you've started biting your nails again?'

'Again?' Lea makes a face. She's never been able to stand it when I gnaw my cuticles. She says even the sound makes her feel sick.

'When your mother was your age,' Mum tells her, 'I thought she'd chew the ends off her fingers.'

Seeing Lea's gaze drop to my plasters, I hide my hands under the table. But I'm saved from having to answer by the arrival of Dad's sister, Oddný, his brother, Ingvar, and their partners. They all make a loud noise about demanding hugs and kisses.

'Where did you stop off?' I ask. 'I thought you'd left home before us.'

'We did,' Dad says wryly, and I immediately notice Oddný and Elín's red eyes and shiny faces.

I shoot a look at Dad that says *Really?* and he nods. Then we both turn to watch Oddný, who's made a beeline for the bar.

The last few times I've seen Mum, her conversation has revolved almost entirely around Oddný's drink problem and her new man, who's apparently no better.

'So it's going to be that sort of weekend,' I whisper to Dad.

He chuckles quietly and shakes his head. 'No, I'm not worried about your mother, but you know how ... how some people carry on.'

I nod. Then a familiar voice says my name, and I turn. My heart starts beating faster when I see Stefanía.

'Steffý?' I say. Her name comes so easily to my mouth, though I've hardly said it aloud for years.

'Long time, no see.' She gives me a quick hug, then takes a step backwards to inspect me. 'You never change.'

I force myself to smile. It sounds like praise, but it isn't really. As a teenager I was shy and self-effacing, and dressed to avoid being noticed. I was chubby too and prone to getting spots. Most people who see pictures of the sixteen-year-old Petra can't believe it's me.

'I wasn't sure if you were coming,' I say.

'No, neither was I.' Steffý grins. 'But I couldn't miss it. How often do we all get together like this?'

'I know.' All of a sudden, I'm conscious of how badly I've missed her, in spite of everything. Missed being around her cheerful presence.

'I mean, compared to how things used to be...' Steffý sighs. 'Then I heard Viktor would be here too and thought I just had to come. The three of us must have a drink together.'

'I...'

Steffý looks away before I can reply and shouts out Mum's name. She laughs and bumps against me as she pushes past.

My face grows hot as it hits home how perfunctorily Steffý has dealt with me. I watch her hugging my parents, smiling and laughing. She's the one who hasn't changed. She's the one who's exactly like she was when we were kids.

'Mum?' Ari's looking at me quizzically.

'I...' I croak, then clear my throat and say: 'I'll be back in a minute.'

I walk quickly to the ladies and close the door behind me.

As I examine myself in the mirror, I see how red and shiny my skin looks under my foundation. 'Don't be silly,' I tell myself. 'Don't let her get to you like this all over again.'

But I can't help it. Stefanía is connected to all my childhood memories. We were together every day. I have a feeling we even slept in the same bed more often than not, though surely that can't be right? We shared a wardrobe, mealtimes, sports lessons and summer holidays. Even our Christmases. The mere thought of her brings back the taste of ice lollies, the smell of chlorine in the Bjarnarlaug swimming pool and the feel of sand under our bare feet as we played on the beach at Langisandur.

When I open my eyes again, everything is black. I blink several times, feeling a rising sense of panic. I grip the sink. It takes me a moment to realise that there's nothing wrong. I haven't gone blind. It's just that the lights in the toilets have automatically switched themselves off and, because there are no windows, the darkness is absolute.

I wave my arm but nothing happens; the sensor must be faulty. I grope my way to the door and open it. The relief when I'm back in daylight is so profound that I let out a long sigh. My heartbeat returns to normal and, after a few breathing exercises, my feeling of faintness recedes.

I've never been able to explain my fear of the dark and of narrow spaces. Luckily, I've managed to keep it under control for the most part. My home is deliberately designed to be open plan. Most of the rooms in the hotel are similarly spacious, so I don't understand why I'm feeling so claustrophobic here. As if something in my surroundings is pressing in on me.

Lea Snæberg

'My bed,' Ari says when we get back to our room, flopping down on the one closest to the window.

'Great,' I say, glad not to have to sleep that side.

I don't care what Mum and Dad say, this hotel's not cool. OK, maybe it looks cool if you're taking photos. Ari took one of me earlier, and the concrete in the background comes out really well. But I'd thought at least the rooms would be a bit cosier – that there'd be colourful rugs or comfy chairs – but the bedrooms are like everything else in the hotel: just concrete, all grey and white and sterile.

When I buy my own flat I picture it having dark-painted walls, mirrors with gold frames and a velvet sofa. A bit like in a palace, but not as kitschy, of course. I don't understand why everything has to be so bright and open and flooded with sunshine nowadays, like you have to spend the whole day in the brutal glare of daylight. How tiring is that?

Take all these big windows in the hotel: it's light outside at the moment and you've got a view of the lava field and mountains, but I still find it creepily exposed. Someone could be standing out there among the rocks, staring in without you knowing. And when it gets dark, there'll be no way of seeing if anyone's outside the window: you'll be on show like an actor on stage or an animal at the zoo.

Maybe I've just got a hyperactive imagination. I mean, when you think about it, who'd want to stand out there and freeze in a lava field in the middle of winter?

Ari's brought his snack up with him and it's stinking out the room. 'Don't you ever stop being hungry?' I ask.

'No, not really.' Ari grins.

The shower suddenly starts up in the bathroom, making me jump.

'What's that?' I sit up and stare in the direction of the en suite. Could there be somebody in there? I haven't even been inside, just took a quick glance through the half-open door.

But then I see Ari's expression and remember that everything's controlled via an app. I pick up a cushion and fling it at him.

'Idiot,' I say.

He laughs, then starts fiddling with the lights, turning them red, violet and green.

'Cool, eh?' he says.

'I suppose.' I get under the duvet and check my phone. Still nothing from Birgir, but there are several messages waiting from Gulli58.

From the few photos I've posted, he's guessed the right hotel. He must know the area well because he's mentioned the names of some cliffs or something on the coast nearby – Svörtuloft and the Lóndrangar. He says we should visit the beach at Djúpalón and go to the café there. He often goes there himself for a cocoa and might be there later, if I want to say hi.

I stare at the messages, feeling my spine prickling. For the first time it occurs to me that he might actually come here to the hotel. Might try to find me.

No, impossible. No one's that crazy, are they?

I try to find out who he is, but his page is locked and the last thing I want to do is get his hopes up by sending him a friend request. The only photo that's visible to everyone is of a small black church with white doors and windows. All I know about him is that he's called Gulli and was probably born in 1958, going by his username. I do some quick mental arithmetic and get a shock when I realise he must be fifty-nine.

Fifty-nine. Almost sixty.

I stare at his name for a moment or two, then go ahead and block him. Now he won't be able to send me any more messages.

I put the phone down on the bedside table and pull the duvet around me.

But despite having blocked Gulli58, I don't feel any better. I close my eyes and try not to think about the fact that he knows where I am. Because even though I've blocked him now, it was probably too late.

Petra Snæberg

Gestur's hair is wet and his white T-shirt clings damply at the back where he hasn't dried himself properly.

'Did you get some sleep?' I ask.

'A little. Then I had a shower.'

'Was it a good shower?'

'It was all right.'

Gestur takes a woollen roll-neck jumper out of the suitcase and pulls it over his head. I've got the same one, but in a different colour. They were presents from my parents last Christmas, and if I'm not mistaken they have the same kind of jumpers themselves. We'll probably end up looking like the Teletubbies, all in matching jumpers in different shades.

'We're leaving in a minute,' Gestur says.

'I know.' The first activity on the Snæberg family reunion programme is a walk to the little fishing village of Hellnar. 'It'll be good to get some fresh air,' I add, smiling at him.

'Aren't we supposed to be downstairs and ready by three?' He doesn't smile back.

'Yes,' I say. 'That's the plan. I'll be along in a minute.'

Gestur nods and leaves the room.

The door closes carefully behind him, and for a moment I stare at the empty space where he had been standing.

For years the future has seemed as predictable as a pre-filled form. None of the details have been worked out, of course, but the big picture has been pretty clear: marriage, work and children. But now it's like someone has taken the form and deleted it or put it through a shredder, and nothing's certain anymore.

Perhaps the future never was predictable. Perhaps that's just part of the illusion of stability and immortality that we create for ourselves. I, of all people, should know how unpredictable life is, how quickly things can change.

Dismissing these thoughts, I put on a jacket that's bright red, like my jumper. Then I pull on my walking trousers and finally a fox-fur headband that was present from Gestur in the days when he still used to surprise me with gifts.

On the way to reception I bump into Viktor and Maja.

'Ready for the walk?' Viktor says, grinning. He's wearing a sporty black windcheater and a headband that has pushed up his black hair.

As we head to reception together, there's a brief, awkward silence.

'It's going to be a beautiful walk.' I clear my throat. 'And the hotel's great, isn't it? So original.'

'Yes, of course, you're involved in this area yourself nowadays,' Viktor says. 'Always designing homes for the smart set ... No, sorry – sanctuaries. You design sanctuaries.'

'Oh, Viktor.' I shake my head. 'Sanctuary' was Gestur's idea. He said I had to come up with key words that people would associate with the company, that would define our mission statement.

Viktor winks at me. 'Seriously, though,' he says, 'I think it's amazing what you've achieved. I always knew you'd go far.'

'Thanks.' I've missed the way he makes me feel. When we were younger, he had a unique ability to cheer me up.

Judging by the hum of talk and laughter coming from reception, a large contingent of the family are already there waiting. There's Mum with my uncle and aunt, and their kids and partners. Lots of people I don't really know that well, though they're still a part of me. I let out a scream when someone grabs me round the waist and squeezes.

Spinning round, I encounter Smári's grinning face.

'Really? Aren't we too old for that?'

Smári laughs, puts his arms round my shoulders and crushes me in a hug.

'Never, Petra,' he says. 'Never too old.'

Although Smári's two years older than me, for some reason he always feels like my younger brother. He's the one who did everything right in our parents' eyes: completed a degree abroad, married the girl he'd been with since sixth form, got a good job with the family firm, and only after all that had a child. All by the book, not once stepping out of line. The most annoying part is that Smári's great. I can understand exactly why they dote on him so much. He reminds me of Ari; always happy and infecting others with his good mood.

I greet my little nephew, who's in a baby carrier on his father's back. Arnaldur's only two, his parents' first child. Yet another reason why I always feel so much older. Smári has a toddler; I have teenagers.

'Where are Ari and Lea?' Smári asks.

I glance around and notice that Gestur's talking to Stefanía. She's got her back to me, and I can tell that she's in full flow, regaling him with a story, no doubt. She was always good at telling stories.

She's wearing her hair in a pony-tail, which sways gently as she moves her head. When we were younger, she grew her hair down to the small of her back and always wore it loose. Now it's shorter but the same beautiful colour, like dark cherry wood or mahogany.

Gestur and Stefanía have met before, of course, a long time ago now. I try to remember the last time they saw each other, but can't. On the other hand, I can clearly recall Gestur's first encounter with her. We'd just started seeing each other, and Stefanía insisted on having a look at him. Gestur drove up to Akranes in his old Chevrolet and picked us up outside the shop where we were standing with glass bottles of orange and liquorice straws. Steffý had got us into the habit of drinking the orange through the tubes of liquorice. I remember how nervous I was, because Steffý had never been impressed with the boys I liked, and this time I longed for her approval.

I got in the front and Steffý in the back seat, where she leant forwards until her head was almost between us. When Gestur dropped us home later that evening, she said: 'He's all right, Petra; better than the last one, anyway.' She gave me a wicked grin. It was then that I knew I had to get away from her.

'The kids are probably still in their room,' I say in answer to Smári. 'I'd better check what they're up to.'

Lea and Ari's room is at the end of the corridor on the ground floor. I knock twice, then put my ear to the door. It's very quiet here; I can't even hear the chatter of the group in reception, as it's separated from the bedroom wing by a heavy fire door.

'Lea,' I call, knocking again. 'Ari.'

At the sound of footsteps, I turn, startled. The man coming along the corridor must be my father's age. His clothes are dirty, as if he's been working outside.

He's not a member of the family, so he must belong to the hotel, though he seems totally out of place here. All the other staff are neatly dressed and friendly. This man is the opposite. In fact, he looks at me with such disgust that for an instant I shrink away, afraid he's going to swear at me.

Abruptly, the door of Lea and Ari's room is flung open, and Lea is standing in front of me. 'What?'

For a moment or two I can't utter a word, inhibited by the menacing presence of the man behind me.

'Mum?' Lea is waiting for an answer.

'I ... I just wanted to check if you two were coming,' I say, hearing the footsteps moving away. 'Everyone's ready downstairs.'

'Yeah, we're just getting changed,' Lea says, though evidently she hasn't put on her outdoor clothes yet.

I tell her to hurry, and she mutters something inaudible.

Alone once more in the corridor, I look for the man, wondering where he's gone and who he is. I've always been perceptive about people, and this man makes me uneasy. I feel as if he's recognised me.

But now that I think about it, I realise that this sense of disquiet has been lurking at the edges of my consciousness ever since we arrived at the hotel, or maybe even before, so it may not be entirely the man's fault.

I don't know what exactly is causing it, whether it's the setting or the hotel, which looked so tasteful in the photos but in reality is cold and impersonal. Lea was right: all these high concrete walls are oppressive. But I expect it's probably the experience of being surrounded by my family, the feeling that memories I've tried to bury are threatening to break through to the surface again.

Irma
Hotel Employee

The weather is deteriorating and the wind has started whining through the gaps of the coffee-room window. Although the sea isn't visible from down here, I imagine it's dark and choppy. Outside the window, the gulls are circling. They must have spotted something in the lava field – a mouse or some small birds, perhaps. Once I came across a whole flock of them tearing into the carcass of a mink.

I peer at the jagged, moss-covered rocks but can't see what's attracting the gulls' attention. On my first day here, I spotted an Arctic fox poised with its forelegs on a stone, looking straight back at me. Its pelt was grey with white patches where it was moulting, losing its winter coat.

I fill a cup with boiling water and warm my fingers on it. A short respite before the group returns from their walk and I have to get the restaurant ready for supper.

'What are you drinking?'

I don't need to turn my head to know that it's Elísa.

'Tea,' I say. 'Peppermint tea.'

Elísa sits down across the table and watches me. I've got used to the way her searching eyes scrutinise my face and no longer let it bother me.

'When are you going home?' Elísa asks.

'Home?'

'Yes, you know – back to where you used to live.' Elísa sweeps the crumbs on the table into a little pile. 'No one stays here long. Everyone goes home again in the end.'

Elísa's question is more personal than she realises. The word 'home' means so many things to me, perhaps because I've been lost and adrift for many years, like a stray cat.

I've lived in six different flats in Reykjavík, always renting, never able to save any money. Living from pay cheque to pay cheque, only just making ends meet.

When I think about home, I think about the flat I lived in longest with my mother, a two-bedroom place in a block. I was a happy child, which is a strange thing to say because I now realise we weren't well off, at least not in today's terms. We were chronically short of money, but I can't remember that causing me any distress until later, when I was old enough to understand.

Sometimes I think it wasn't my mother who was the problem but all the teachers and kids at school. I didn't even think about my clothes until the other kids started making fun of them. Just as I never had any doubts about my mother until I was older and got to visit flats where everything was tidy and well ordered, with supper on the table at seven o'clock and clean sheets on the beds.

I was happy until I started to compare my life to those of other people. Slowly but surely it was impressed upon me that I was disadvantaged.

'I may never go home,' I say to Elísa.

She seems pleased with this answer and asks if she can taste my tea. She takes a sip and looks thoughtful.

'It's quite good,' she says. 'A bit like toothpaste.'

I laugh.

'Bring up the bottles from the cellar.'

I start, because I hadn't noticed Gísli come in. You certainly couldn't accuse Edda's husband of having a winning personality. His eyes are permanently overshadowed by thick, louring brows, so I still haven't worked out what colour they are. Perhaps his surly appearance is why he has little contact with the guests and sticks to maintenance work and keeping the grounds tidy. I don't think I've ever seen him in clean clothes.

The first time I met him I could hardly believe this was Edda's husband, but I know he didn't always look this way. Elísa has shown me old photos of him and Edda: thirty years ago he was young and handsome.

Most of what I know about the family I've learnt from Elísa. She told me that her mother, Edda and Gísli's daughter, died when she herself was a baby.

She whispered the story to me one evening, over a glass of milk and biscuits here in the coffee room. 'I was only one,' she said, licking the milky moustache from her upper lip. 'Mummy used to live with Granny and Granddad in those days because I was only a baby and Mummy needed to work. One day she woke up early and went out while I was still asleep. She was crossing the road right outside the house where we lived when *bang*!' Elísa clapped her hands together, making me jump.

'Bang?'

'Mm.' Elísa nodded. 'A bus.'

'Was she knocked down?'

'Yes. She died instantly,' Elísa said. 'And that's why I've always lived with Granny and Granddad. Granny says Granddad changed when Mummy died. Have you noticed how he's always in a bad temper? He never smiles, and Granny says his smile died with Mummy. Do you think that's true? I don't, because smiles don't die like people.'

I was disconcerted by the lack of emotion in Elísa's voice as she spoke of her mother's tragic death. She ate another biscuit, then started talking about something completely different. But of course she was very young when it happened, so I suppose you wouldn't expect her to be sad.

'The bottles,' Gísli says again, pouring himself a cup of coffee.

'Yes,' I say, getting up as he sits down, and opening the door to the cellar.

The flight of stone steps leading down there is narrow and

made even more cramped by the work jackets reeking of oil and mildew that hang from a row of pegs on one side.

I press the light switch at the top of the stairs. The fluorescent bulb flickers a few times before coming on properly, its yellowish glow illuminating the cellar. There's a large chest freezer in one corner. The walls are lined with wine racks and open shelves stacked with miscellaneous items. On the floor there are suitcases left behind by guests and sacks of forgotten clothes. It's amazing what guests leave behind. On one shelf there are at least two tablets and several sets of headphones, as well as a basket of jewellery. Some people hardly seem to notice that they've forgotten something and don't bother trying to recover it, even when it's valuable.

I'm met by a smell of damp earth as I descend the steps. Picking up a laundry basket, I begin laying bottles of wine in it, when I'm startled by a noise behind me.

'God, you made me jump,' I say, seeing Gísli on the stairs.

He merely grunts, then starts moving things around on one of the shelves. I turn back to the wine rack and add two more bottles to the basket.

I don't know why but the atmosphere in the cellar feels vaguely menacing with the two of us alone down here. I wasn't at ease before, but now I feel an urgent need to get back upstairs as soon as possible.

I don't like Gísli, though I can't say that without a pang of guilt. He hasn't done anything to me. I should pity him for the loss of his daughter. Should be filled with admiration at the way he and Edda have taken in their granddaughter and brought her up. But there's something about his eyes and his presence that makes me jumpy.

I pick up the laundry basket with a clinking of bottles. Gísli seems to have found what he was looking for – a pair of rather ancient-looking binoculars, which he holds up and examines. But as I try to pass him, he grabs my shoulder, stopping me in my tracks.

His hand is heavy and his fingers dig into me. He's so close that I can smell his breath when he says: 'Take some of the strong stuff too.'

'Strong stuff?'

'Hendrick's. Or Bombay.'

Realising he means gin, I nod. But he doesn't release his hold on my shoulder until I back away. I quickly scan the shelves, trying to find the right bottles.

'They're in the freezer,' Gísli says.

Putting down the binoculars, he opens the chest, reaches inside for the bottles, then holds them up, brushing off the frost.

'They're bound to want spirits,' he says, without looking at me. 'There should be plenty of whisky upstairs but make sure there are enough mixers.'

I nod, and Gísli goes back up the steps. Relieved by his departure, I hurriedly track down what I need. I can't stay in this cellar a minute longer.

Suddenly the light goes out and I'm left standing in pitch-blackness. In the same instant, I hear the loud slam of the cellar door.

I can't bear being shut in. The blood starts throbbing in my ears and I stand there as if paralysed, not daring to shout for help. After a moment, I recover the power of movement and reach out my arms, groping until I feel the wooden shelves in front of me, then I start edging sideways, only to stop dead when I hear a noise. A quiet scratching somewhere nearby. Mice.

They're everywhere in the lava field. Gísli always lays traps around the cars so the mice don't crawl into the engines. Each morning without fail there's a mouse in every single trap, its tiny body crushed by the metal. I always avert my eyes.

I clench my jaw and continue fumbling my way along the shelves until my foot encounters the bottom step.

When I get back up to the coffee room, Elísa is still sitting there, drinking a glass of milk. She smiles when she sees me and licks her lips.

'Did you shut the door, Elísa?' I ask, more sharply than I'd intended. My heartbeat is booming in my ears, and I can still hear the scratching noise, though I've closed the cellar door behind me.

Elísa smiles and shakes her head, but I can tell she's lying. I can always tell when people are lying.

Tryggvi

The plan is to walk the two kilometres from Arnarstapi to Hellnar. We start by the sculpture of Bárður Snæfellsás, a great pile of stones with a roughly hewn head, built to commemorate the guardian spirit of Snæfellsnes, who was supposedly a descendant of giants and trolls. From here, we're to walk along the coast and through the lava field to the beach at Hellnar. It's a scenic route, short and not too demanding, though it has its share of hazards, as the path runs along a sheer line of cliffs with nothing below but the icy waves. This is no place for small children or drunks, as it's easy to slip and fall.

Luckily, Oddný has sobered up a bit after her rest, though she still smells of booze and her eyes are a bit bleary. We used to drink together in the early days of our relationship, but I've been sober for almost a year now, not that it's anything to boast about. A year is a short time, and I can't say it's made much of a difference to me, not in the way that some people would like to believe.

Maybe my drinking wasn't serious enough for the difference to be that obvious. I've never missed work on account of it, never let anyone but Oddný see me the worse for wear. My benders happened at weekends, alone in front of the TV – never inconvenienced anyone else. Mind you, I suspect the blokes I worked with must have smelt the booze on my breath on Monday mornings, though they never commented on it.

Oddný still drinks. I want her to quit on her own terms, not mine.

'It's all right,' Oddný says, when I try to hold her hand as we set off.

I know why I used to do it, but I can't really work out what's behind Oddný's drinking. Though we've been together for more than a year, our relationship still feels quite new, as if we're still getting to know each other. Our paths first crossed when Oddný rang the workshop about getting an old armchair restored. I take on jobs like that from time to time, giving old furniture a new lease of life. I have an upholsterer who can perform miracles on a shoestring. The chair Oddný brought in was a classic Icelandic design, a quality piece of work that I enjoyed doing up. I took extra care, lovingly polishing and oiling it until it looked like new.

Oddný and I got to know each other while I was working on the chair. She took an interest in my job and asked if she could watch me oiling the wood, then spent ages dithering over what material to cover it with. In the end she chose a patterned fabric in a nice shade of blue.

To my surprise, when she came to pick up the chair she suggested going for a drink. 'To celebrate,' she said.

And we celebrated. Oh yes, we celebrated, all right.

'I'm just going over to talk to the others,' Oddný says, moving away. She's got a hipflask in her bag that she keeps taking nips from.

The group comes to a halt, and I gaze at the pillars of rock rising out of the sea, carved by the waves into strange, troll-like shapes. The sun is still up, though it's going down quickly now. The surface of the sea is bathed in its rays, the lapping of the waves mingling with the cries of the gulls. I inhale the salty smell, filling my lungs and holding the breath for a moment before releasing it.

'Tryggvi?'

I've fallen a bit behind, when Oddný's sister-in-law, Ester, comes over.

'It's beautiful here,' I say.

'Yes.' Ester coughs. 'How, er ... how's Oddný been doing recently?'

'How's she been?'

'Yes, I get the impression...' Ester sighs '...that she's drinking more. Is that true?'

I don't know how to answer this. Is she drinking more?

'I couldn't really say,' I reply.

'No, of course, you haven't been together that long,' Ester says. 'Sorry, I didn't mean ... I just mean that maybe it's hard for you to judge.'

'I suppose so. A year isn't a very long time.'

'No, quite,' Ester says. 'It's just ... I'm afraid Oddný's taken it rather badly.'

'What?'

'The business with the company.' Ester rubs her temple. 'Halli and Ingvar weren't trying to oust her. They just thought it might suit her better not to have it hanging over her. Oddný's never been ... How shall I put it? She's never been interested in business or the management of the company. Halli and Ingvar both did stints working for the family firm, but no one can even remember the last time Oddný bothered to turn up to a board meeting.'

'No, I see.'

'So they just thought ... they thought maybe she'd rather take the money and ... and travel, or something,' Ester says. 'Was that such a bad idea?'

'No,' I say. 'Not at all.'

'Would you let Halli and me know if the situation gets any worse?'

I nod and turn to watch Oddný, who's some way ahead of me. I can tell from the way she's walking that she's been taking a few too many swigs from the hipflask.

Sometimes I wonder if Oddný had a falling-out with her

brothers when they were young; it would explain why Haraldur and Ingvar are so close, why they've got their shit together, while Oddný's like she is. Because under the surface she's like a rebellious teenager.

I just can't work her brothers out. They're polite enough, that's not the problem, but I always get the feeling there's something rankling underneath. Something unsaid hovering in the air.

If you ask me, they take after their father: strong, determined and sure of their own worth. From the little Oddný's told me about her childhood, I've learnt that their father was a harsh, cold man. Not that Oddný's really aware of that herself. She's never directly said anything bad about him, just mentioned, as if by chance, that she was often beaten, which used to be common practice here in the old days, and sometimes locked in her room as a punishment.

But one thing stayed with me. An incident Oddný told me about when she was drunk. Once, when she was a teenager, she'd sneaked out to meet a boy. Late that night she came home to find her father waiting up for her. While her brothers slept upstairs, he took out his belt and thrashed her.

It didn't seem to be the beating itself that hurt Oddný most, but the fact that she was the only one to be punished; her brothers always got off lightly. She'd muttered: 'I could never understand why Dad only wanted to punish me and not them when they did bad things. Was it just because I was a girl and they were boys? Or was it more personal? Was there something wrong with me?'

Petra Snæberg

I find myself walking beside Maja. Viktor's up near the front; I can see his dark head towering over the rest of the group. He's tall – taller than the other men in the family, but then, technically speaking, he's not related to any of us; he's got different genes.

'So, how did you two meet?' I ask, after a couple of minutes of awkward silence.

Maja seems grateful for the choice of subject.

'At the gym,' she says. 'We were both training at the same club.'

'Club? What sort of club?'

'Mixed martial arts.'

'Really?' I say. I hadn't a clue that Viktor was into martial arts, let alone that he trained in them. The Viktor I used to know couldn't stand any form of exercise. During games lessons we used to sneak down to the gym and lie on the piles of mats. But then he was completely different in those days, so tall and thin – a bit gangly. Now he's much more muscular, so I should have guessed that he did some kind of physical training.

'Yes,' Maja says. 'After one session he offered to hold the punch bag for me. I wanted to practise my striking techniques. You know, my arm movements.'

'Mm,' I say, though I can't for a minute picture it. Maja's so tiny and delicate. I can't imagine her hitting anything, not even a punch bag.

'Anyway, after that we started meeting up.' She smiles in embarrassment, and I guess that something more must have happened after she had finished practising those striking techniques.

The group pauses, and we take in the view. The rocks rising out of the sea form a spectacular natural arch, like a bridge. Although there's only a light breeze, the sea is foaming and splashing against the cliffs, filling our noses with salt. Gulls are perched on ledges, and the rocks below are streaked white with their droppings.

'You two grew up together, didn't you?' Maja asks. 'At least, that's what Viktor said.'

I nod. 'Yes, Viktor was like a brother to me.' The word 'was' bothers me a bit. Because I don't see him like that anymore, do I?

Maja doesn't seem to notice anything.

'What was he like?' she asks. 'When he was younger, I mean?'

What a strange question, I think. Childish, even. Like a teenager in love who wants to know all about the boy she fancies.

'Viktor was...' I pause to think. 'He was very quiet and easygoing, maybe a bit shy. There when you needed him. He always hung around with us girls. He never really seemed to fit in with the gangs of boys, but then you know what they're like.'

'Didn't he have any male friends?' Maja asks.

'Yes, of—' I break off in mid-sentence to reflect. Did Viktor ever have any male friends? I don't remember any in particular. He sometimes sat with some boys during break, and once he went to a party at one of their houses, but were they his friends? 'He just wasn't that type, if you know what I mean? The boys all used to be so competitive, always showing off, but not Viktor; he was just laid-back.'

'OK.'

Maja doesn't seem to understand, and I feel an urge to defend Viktor, as if it's necessary to apologise for the fact that he preferred our company to that of boys. It was like that when we were younger too. Lots of people assumed he was gay because he chose to hang out with us. Not that it would have mattered if he was, but we knew he wasn't, and, besides, this stereotypical view of men gets on my nerves.

Before I can say anything else, Uncle Ingvar, our self-appointed guide, starts talking. He suggests that we walk down to the jetty, then take the path along the stony beach before returning to the hotel through the Arctic tern colony.

'The nesting area's empty at the moment,' he adds, grinning, 'which is probably just as well since none of us came equipped with helmets or sticks.'

The terns come here to nest every summer. They can be pretty aggressive in the breeding season, swooping at you with ear-splitting screeches if you get too close to their nests. Unlike most people, I love terns. I've always admired their fiercely protective nature, the way they work so hard to defend their chicks. They're beautiful too, with their streamlined white bodies, black caps and narrow, pointed wings.

We often used to visit the nesting area to collect eggs when I was young, armed with sticks that we held up over our heads. Not to hit the birds but so that they would attack the sticks rather than us. Entering the screeching colony was a nerve-racking business, like being in the middle of an air raid. Your heart pounding, your nerves stretched and the noise so deafening that you could scarcely hear yourself think.

But now – now the colony looks a bit sad. All the little tern chicks have grown up and flown away with their mothers on their great migration to Antarctica.

Ingvar is pointing to the dramatic rock stacks rising out of the sea. While he's talking, I seize the opportunity to move away from Maja.

Oddný tugs at my sleeve before I've gone far. 'Would you like a drop to combat the cold?' She holds out a flask and I eye it for a moment before accepting it and taking a generous slug.

I choke when the liquid is halfway down my throat but manage to smother the cough until I can breathe normally again. The whisky burns my stomach, and I feel its heat spreading through my body.

'Good, eh?' Oddný smiles wryly and takes a mouthful herself before putting the flask back inside her coat. She's always drunk a lot. I remember her years ago, staggering around at birthdays and during camping trips. Once she was so wasted that she fell over backwards while taking an al-fresco pee and fell asleep with her trousers round her ankles. I've rarely seen a sorrier sight. Luckily, she doesn't remember, but every time we meet, the image of her lying there pops into my head.

'It didn't occur to me that it would be this cold,' I say.

'I stopped feeling the cold long ago,' Oddný says, and laughs. She passes me the flask again. We're at the back of the column now, and I'm glad no one can see us.

'Oof,' I groan, wiping away a tear that trickles from the corner of my eye. I don't know whether it's because of the wind, the cold or the strong spirits.

'How's it going with all that...' Oddný waves a hand '...design and so on?'

'Well,' I say. 'It's going well. How about you? What are you up to these days?'

'Oh, you know.' Oddný sighs. 'This and that. I can always find something to keep myself occupied.'

I bite my tongue. I'd completely forgotten that Dad and Uncle Ingvar relieved Oddný of almost all her responsibilities a while ago, because they didn't trust her to look after any aspect of the family business. I'd assumed that Oddný didn't mind, but perhaps I was wrong. Perhaps she's bored by having nothing to do.

'Is it a long time since you were last here?' I ask, to change the subject.

'Yes, quite a long time. The three of us – Ingvar, Halli and I – used to visit in the summers and stay in the cabin on Dad's land.' Oddný thinks for a moment. 'I suppose we must have been teenagers the last time we came here together.'

'What was it like growing up with Dad and Ingvar as brothers?'

'I'm the youngest, as you know.' Oddný rubs her nose on her

sleeve. 'Your dad's in the middle, and Ingvar's the oldest, of course.'

'I bet it was quite challenging at times?' I laugh.

Oddný smiles, but I sense a hint of sadness there.

'Oh yes.' She takes another nip from her flask. 'It was challenging all right.'

Oddný comes to a halt, and I stop with her. Suddenly she doesn't seem herself. I look around for Tryggvi, thinking that he should probably be by her side to support her. But the others have continued walking and drawn some way ahead of us. If I call out, either no one will hear me through the wind and their headgear, or I'll attract everyone's attention to us, which would be embarrassing.

'Oddný?'

'You know,' Oddný says, without taking her eyes off the sea. 'One summer a child fell over the cliff here. We'd been playing with the boy that morning. He was only four.'

My stomach takes a dive, though I've heard the story before.

'He vanished from outside the summer cabin he was staying in,' Oddný continues. 'His parents looked all over for him, and ... and then Ingvar said he'd seen him playing by the edge of the cliff, and they found his toy car in the grass here.'

'That's ... awful,' I say.

Oddný takes a step forwards and cranes her neck to see down to where the waves are crashing on the rocks below. Suddenly, I feel alarmed.

'Oddný,' I say. 'Don't stand so near the edge...'

Lost in her own world, she doesn't seem to hear me. She's so close to the brink now that I tense up with fear. She reaches a hand inside her coat to fish out her flask, then takes a sideways step or, rather, staggers.

'Oddný, be careful, I...' I don't get any further because at that moment she slips. One of her feet starts sliding down towards the edge of the drop and she loses her balance.

I reach out, trying and failing to grasp her coat. I can feel the material slipping through my fingers as Oddný falls.

Sævar
Detective, West Iceland CID

Although the scene of the fall wasn't that far from the hotel as the crow flies, getting to the hotel by car proved to be a much more roundabout business. As Sævar and Hörður drove slowly along a rough gravel track, the car juddering and lurching into potholes, Sævar contemplated their next steps. The Snæbergs were still at the hotel, and it would be best if the police could talk to as many of them as possible before they all returned home.

He wasn't entirely clear about how many people were staying there. According to what he'd been told, the clan had gathered at the hotel to celebrate the hundredth birthday of their patriarch, who had died some years previously. If the police were lucky, it might only be one branch of the family. In the phone call CID had received that morning to notify them about the body, the background to the events had been hazy, so he and Hörður were on their way to the hotel to collect more information.

'What do you know about the family?' Sævar asked. 'Any internal feuds or tensions you're aware of?'

'I know the Snæbergs originally came from Snæfellsnes.' Hörður paused for a moment, thinking. 'I don't actually remember hearing about any tensions, except of course between the brothers, a long time ago. Ingólfur had two sons, Bergur and

Hákon. Bergur was a bit of a recluse and didn't have any kids, but Hákon had three, and it's that side of the family who've got together for the reunion.'

'Ingólfur's grandchildren, in other words.'

'Exactly,' Hörður said. 'That is, Ingvar, Haraldur and Oddný. They're the ones at the hotel, with their partners and kids, and their father Hákon as well, though I hear he's in pretty poor health these days.'

'What about Hákon's brother, is he still alive?'

'No,' Hörður said. 'Bergur's dead. Hákon and Bergur stopped talking to each other after their father died. They quarrelled over some land out east, and it ended in a court case that Hákon eventually won.'

'Not much of a victory,' Sævar remarked.

Hörður slowed down to avoid a particularly deep pothole. 'How do you mean?'

'I just mean what's the point of winning a court case over a piece of land if you forfeit your relationship with your brother as a result?'

'I suppose it depends which you value more, your family or the money.' Hörður smiled drily. 'And we're talking about pretty substantial sums. After all, they own Snæberg, the fishing business that Ingólfur Hákonarson founded way back when. These days most of the workforce are foreign, apart from the office staff and managers. In recent years the family have invested heavily in the latest fishing technology, as well as in a number of other areas. Ingólfur's grandchildren all sit on the board, along with their partners.'

'Is the business doing well?' Sævar knew the answer but asked anyway.

'Well?' Hörður snorted. 'Better than well. The dividends they pay themselves seem to get more generous by the year. They're among the top taxpayers in Iceland. And they're behind the construction of all those blocks of flats on the new estate in

Akranes, as well as being involved in all kinds of other investments and wheeling and dealing on the property market. Judging from a news story I read recently, one of their subsidiaries turned a profit of several billion krónur last year. The money, the businesses, the holding companies and the management positions are then doled out among the family members. They all get their share of the profits from the family firm and the business directly associated with it.'

Sævar sighed. He found it hard to get his head round this sort of stuff: billionaires, investments and property deals were part of a world he neither understood nor had any interest in understanding. Though he couldn't help wondering for a moment what it would be like to have all that money. Whether it would change anything, maybe even change him?

Sævar regarded himself as pretty comfortably off, although the police salary wasn't anything to boast about. He owned his flat outright, and had a small lump sum in a savings account, inherited from his parents, who had died in a car crash when he was twenty. This put him in a better position financially than many of his contemporaries, not that his situation was exactly desirable. If he'd had a choice, he'd rather be up to his neck in debt and have his parents still alive. But of course that's not how the world worked. And there was nothing Sævar could do about it.

'Anyway,' Hörður went on. 'I haven't heard about any friction in recent years, though that doesn't mean it doesn't exist. Now that the siblings' father, Hákon, is in poor health, new disputes could have arisen about the inheritance. It would hardly be unusual.'

Sævar had never understood how inheritance disputes could destroy relationships between siblings and between cousins, though of course such quarrels were commonplace. No doubt it was all much more complicated than he realised.

As they drove up to the hotel, he wondered whether a conflict of this kind could have led to murder.

Lea Snæberg

A piercing scream cuts through the wind, the screeching of the gulls and the crashing of the waves.

Everyone spins round, and I'm shocked to see Mum hanging onto Aunt Oddný, who's lying right on the edge of the cliff. If she rolled sideways now, she'd go straight over.

For a second, nobody moves, then Tryggvi and Granddad start running. They grab hold of Oddný and drag her back from the edge, while she swears and tuts at them as if they're overreacting.

'Oh, my God,' I hear Mum saying. She sounds like she's in a real state. 'God, I thought she was going to fall.'

Oddný is muttering and trying to push the men away.

'Stop it,' I hear her slur, then I see Tryggvi bending over her and whispering in her ear.

After a minute or two we start walking again, with Tryggvi and Oddný at the back.

The path through the lava field is narrow and uneven underfoot. I have to pick my way and keep my eyes on the ground to avoid tripping. My trouser legs are wet and my fingers are numb. But every now and then I pause to look back at Stapafell, the little mountain above Arnarstapi. I love it because it's a perfect triangle, like a mountain in a child's drawing. There's a rock poking out of the top that looks like a man wearing a hat, and another on the side that from some angles reminds me of a cat or some other creature crawling up the slope. Maybe it's all these rocks shaped like men or trolls or animals, but I always feel as if the landscape is more alive here than anywhere else, as if it's awake and watching us.

My thoughts are interrupted by Granddad's brother, Ingvar.

'This here,' he's saying, 'is Oddný Píla's Fissure. The story goes that back in the eighteenth century, some boys from Hellnar raised the ghost of a teenage girl called Oddný Píla. When they found they couldn't control her, Latin-Bjarni, the vicar of Breiðavík, had to be summoned to lay her ghost to rest. But, after he'd done so, the boys refused to pay the agreed fee, so Bjarni raised her ghost again. Oddný started killing livestock and maiming people, until in the end the inhabitants of Hellnar had to hire Latin-Bjarni to exorcise her again. Ever since then, the place is said to have been haunted.'

The fissure in the lava isn't that big, just a small hollow, really, but I peer down it, hearing the sea crashing on the rocks behind me. The wind whips cold spray onto the back of my neck, making my skin break out in goose pimples.

'Who was she?' I ask, surprising myself. I'm not usually the type to speak up in class or ask any questions.

'Who?' Ingvar asks.

'Oddný Píla. The teenage girl.'

'Oh, I don't remember.' He scratches his head. 'The story doesn't tell.'

He carries on talking about the vicar and various spooky events that have happened here since, like animals being killed or sightings of Oddný's ghost, but I can't stop thinking about Oddný herself – the living girl, not her ghost. I wonder who she was and why she died in her teens. Had the boys known her when she was alive? Had they been cruel to her – was that why she was so angry? Could they even have murdered her?

The group moves off again, but I'm suddenly finding it hard to swallow.

Stupid, I think to myself. That's a stupid idea. There's probably no truth in the story, any more than there is in any of the other tales they tell about this area.

I hurry after the others, ignoring the shiver at the back of my neck, which feels as if a cold breath has found its way inside my jumper and all the way down my spine to the small of my back.

The lava field finally comes to an end, and the path leads down to a rocky beach. A concrete jetty stretches out into the sea, and on the other side of it is an even smaller, sandy beach.

Next minute the sun comes out from behind the clouds. It's low in the sky now and its rays gleam red on the surface of the sea and on the white tops of the mountains across the bay. The wind drops, and everyone stops to admire the view.

I close my eyes and let the sun warm my face.

'As if on command,' Dad says beside me. 'Come on, I'll buy you a hot chocolate.'

I follow Dad up to the building that stands just above the beach. A concrete house with a red roof and a sun deck. Fjöruhúsið – the café that Gulli58 was talking about.

'What are you waiting for?' Dad turns back and smiles.

'I'm not terribly hungry,' I say.

'We're only talking about a mug of hot chocolate,' Dad says. 'Just to warm up. Get a bit of energy for the walk back.'

In the end I let him persuade me. As we go inside, I nervously scan the little room and breathe easier when I see that there are no other customers.

Dad and I are followed by Granny and Granddad, and my aunts, uncles and cousins. People I've known all my life, who've watched me grow up since I was a baby but don't really know me at all.

Dad and I take a seat outside with our drinks, and I warm my hands on the hot china mug. The chocolate is delicious, sweet and warming.

'You still do it,' Dad says, smiling.

'What?'

'Close your eyes when you're enjoying something.'

I laugh. I hadn't realised my eyes were closed.

'You always used to do that as a child,' Dad continues. 'You'd close your eyes and moan with pleasure whenever you got something nice to eat.'

'Oh, stop it, Dad.' I pretend to be annoyed but I'm not really. I like it when Dad remembers things like this; the way he looks at me as if I'm special.

When Uncle Smári comes over and joins us, I take out my phone. Birgir's sent me a message, a song by Kodaline called 'All I Want'. I've heard it before but I put in my ear buds and listen anyway. The music is sad and beautiful, and as I gaze out across the cliff-ringed bay, I feel like I'm floating above it, like this moment isn't real, just a dream.

I tell Dad that I'm going to walk down to the beach. I pick my way over the flat rocks on the shore, being careful not to step on the slippery seaweed, then watch the waves licking the sand in front of me.

I still feel a bit detached from reality. I don't know why, but I've been feeling like that ever since I got here. Like I've gone back in time and am twelve years old again; it was then that this feeling started coming over me. I remember standing in front of the mirror and feeling I wasn't myself but somebody else. Like I was watching myself from a distance. I was both familiar and unfamiliar at the same time, like my body no longer had anything to do with me. At that moment the feeling was good, as if everything that had happened at school and in other places didn't matter anymore.

But now I'm finding it hard to get into that state of mind. The story of Oddný Píla has raked up memories. Though I don't know what really happened to her or how she died, I imagine her undergoing some horrible experience. I imagine that she came back as a ghost to get her revenge.

The more I think about it, the more I realise that's exactly what I'd like to do. Something was taken away from me when I was twelve and I'll never get it back; those last few years when I should have been allowed to stay an innocent, trusting child, believing the world was a good place and that people were either good or bad. But now I know that's not true, and, like Oddný Píla, I'm burning for revenge.

Petra Snæberg

'Petra.' Stefanía is coming over, and there's no way I can pretend not to have heard her. 'I didn't get to talk to you earlier,' she says, a little out of breath.

She's well kitted out, in a hat and gloves and a down jacket with a fur-edged hood.

'No.' My first instinct is to be petulant but then, realising how childish it is to act hurt, I smile. 'How are you, anyway?'

'Oh, I'm fine,' Steffý says. 'But how are you? I mean, I know InLook's going well, but what about you personally? How are you doing?'

Typical Steffý, I think. Always straight in there with the personal questions. Behaving as though we were still close friends and I'd want to tell her my most intimate thoughts.

'I'm fine,' I say, determined not to give anything away.

Most of the others have gone into the café for a hot drink, but I don't feel like anything. I'm still a bit jittery after Oddný's close shave on the cliff top. The adrenaline that rushed through my body when I grabbed her has mostly ebbed away now, leaving me feeling utterly drained.

'Great,' Steffý says, and I can feel her eyes boring into me. 'I'm thinking of moving back home.'

'Are you?'

'Yes, I always meant to come back sooner.' She smiles. 'Always wanted my kids to grow up in Iceland.'

'Are you ... Are you and...?'

'Oh God, no, I'm not pregnant.' Stefanía laughs. 'I just meant if I ever have children.'

'Oh, right.' I pretend not to notice the undertone in Steffý's voice. The fact is she's never liked children and never shown the least interest in my kids. When I told her I was pregnant, she asked if I'd made an appointment for an abortion. To her, anything else was unthinkable. In her defence, I was only nineteen at the time and it wasn't the done thing in our family to have kids young, at least not in our generation.

I hug myself against the cold and gaze out to sea. The sun that broke forth so strongly earlier is now hidden by cloud again.

'I'm quite excited at the thought of moving home,' Steffý says. 'I was just saying to Gestur that we should meet up more often.'

'When did you talk to him?' I say, far too snappishly.

'Earlier,' Steffý replies. 'In the hotel reception.'

'Oh, right.' I force myself to smile. 'That might be fun.'

We notice that the others have congregated outside the café and are putting their hats on again, ready to head back to the hotel. The sun will soon be setting, and the light will fail very quickly after that. With all the cloud about, the evening will be pitch-black, making it dangerous to return along the cliffs.

We head back to join the others outside the café, making small talk.

I feel stupid to have overreacted like that when she mentioned talking to Gestur, but I've always been wary when it comes to Steffý and the men in my life. Not that she's ever done anything, but she could never leave them alone. She used to claim she was helping me, putting in a good word for me, but I saw the way she was always finding an excuse to touch them, stand close and whisper to them, so close that her lips would brush their ear. Inevitably most of them ended up falling for her and losing interest in me.

We may not be at school anymore, but I've never quite lost my insecurity around Steffý.

She's always been prettier than me. Cleverer too, with more self-confidence. Once, a girl in my class asked what it was like to be Steffy's lapdog. It was meant as a joke, but it rankled, perhaps because there was a grain of truth in there.

My thoughts often return to the evening when we all got drunk together, me, Steffy and Gestur. For some reason I got completely wasted and can't remember much about the evening, apart from knocking back glass after glass and at some point having to be carried to my room. When I woke up, music was still playing in the sitting room, it was getting on for four a.m. and Gestur wasn't in bed beside me, so I got up and went out into the hall. It sounded as if something was happening in the sitting room, but I couldn't hear any voices, just rustling on the sofa and heavy breathing. On my way to find out what was going on I accidently kicked an empty bottle that had been left on the floor and it fell over with a loud clonk.

When I entered the room, Gestur and Steffy were both sitting on the sofa. Steffy's hair was ruffled, and Gestur was red in the face.

I asked what they were doing, and they both hastened to assure me that they were only listening to music. Gestur said he'd been about to come and join me.

After we got into bed, I couldn't stop thinking about what I might have seen if the bottle hadn't fallen over. I was sure I'd heard familiar noises over the music, like small, smacking sounds.

Now, as we approach the café, I see Gestur standing there, watching us. Or no: as far as I can tell, his gaze is resting solely on Steffy.

Irma
Hotel Employee

The restaurant is looking great. The tables have all been laid with white cloths and tall black candlesticks. Gothic chandeliers hang from the ceiling, casting a subdued, yellow glow, which has transformed the ambience. The hotel is at its best in the evenings, when the austere, grey concrete walls take on a warmer, though still sombre appearance. It's as if the cool Scandinavian chic has melted away and the hotel now resembles a cosy cave. The glasses hanging above the bar reflect the candlelight, looking more like an artwork than anything of practical use.

There's a delicious smell coming from the kitchen. Apparently, the Snæbergs are quite traditional when it comes to food. This evening it's fish and tomorrow leg of lamb. This might sound plain, but it's not going to be served with your bog-standard boiled potatoes. On the contrary, the cod comes with a soy butter sauce, grilled tomatoes, olives and capers. The starters are beef carpaccio and tiger prawns. Then there are the desserts, of course. The chocolate lava cake they make here is something I could happily live on for the rest of my life.

Only the best for our guests. Everything has to be perfect.

I wish I wasn't working but could be enjoying the dinner myself with my nearest and dearest. But my family on my mother's side is small, and none of us have any money. My grandmother's dead, and my grandfather's even more confused than my mum. My uncle, Mum's brother, is much older than her, and they were never that close. I'm in touch with his daughter,

Svana, but she has a husband and four children, so most of our interaction is about whether I can babysit for them.

My phone rings, and I recognise the number. For a moment or two I consider not picking up, but the thought makes me feel so guilty that I answer cheerfully: 'Hi, Mum.'

'Hello, dear.' I can hear immediately that Mum's in a good mood.

'How are you doing?'

'So, so – you know how it is.' Mum starts complaining about the bad food and her dirty room. She lives alone but gets support from the council on the grounds of chronic mental illness. 'They never clean properly,' she goes on. 'They always leave a grimy line in the corners when they mop, and the toilet – don't get me started. Do you remember how clean we used to keep things, Imma dear?'

Imma's the name Mum's always used for me. No one else has ever called me that. 'I remember, Mum,' I say placatingly. 'I remember.'

'They just don't care,' Mum grumbles. 'They don't have to live here themselves, so they don't care.'

I long to tell Mum who's staying at the hotel, but I stop myself. I'm not sure how she would react.

When I hang up after talking to her, I have a knot in my stomach. Guilt, probably. I haven't visited her in such a long time and I always find talking to her a bit disorientating, especially when I'm at work. Here I can forget myself among the beautiful surroundings, playing a role I've become pretty good at. But when Mum rings, it brings me back down to earth; I'm just myself again.

Mum and I never belonged to this posh world. That's not necessarily a bad thing, but sometimes it's nice to be able to forget the fact.

'Excuse me, but I'd like to check in and there's no one on reception.'

When I look round, there's a young man standing in the doorway, leaning on the handle of a small wheelie case. I recognise him instantly. Hákon Ingimar's wearing a short-sleeved shirt, open at the neck in spite of the cold weather, and ripped jeans.

'Yes, of course,' I say, hearing how odd my voice sounds.

As we go to the reception desk together, I keep wanting to pinch myself to be sure this is real; that I'm standing here beside this man. I feel like I know him, which is stupid because I've never met him before. But I've been following him for years, though of course following someone in the news and on social media isn't really the same as knowing them. I am aware of that.

My hands tremble a little as I type his name into the computer, but by taking deep breaths I manage to steady them.

'Hákon Ingimar,' he says, leaning on the desk.

Oh God, he smells so good. Like a freshly polished oak table … vanilla and citrus – lemon … no, orange.

'Right, here you are.' I find his name and check him in. 'Have you downloaded the app?'

'The app?' He's not looking at me but taking in the surroundings. Furtively, I study his straight nose, the finely shaped eyebrows and the thick stubble completely covering the lower half of his face, with not a single hair out of place.

'Yes, we have an app here that you'll need to download,' I say, holding out an information booklet. 'You control everything from there: the lighting, the room temperature, the curtains and—'

'Yeah, OK,' Hákon interrupts. Smiling, he adds: 'I've stayed in hotels like this before.'

That smile … Even as I think it, a noise escapes me. A gurgle of laughter. Such a girly sound that I feel myself blushing scarlet. He must be used to staying in the most exclusive hotels on his endless travels. Yesterday evening I scrolled through the photos on his Instagram page one more time before going to sleep. They featured either magnificent Icelandic scenery, like waterfalls and glaciers, or tropical beaches. And selfies, of course.

'Are you alone?' I try to adopt a professional smile, not too wide, just right, because I'd hate him to think I'm some crazy fan.

'Yup,' Hákon says. 'Where is everyone?'

'They've gone for a walk. They set out for Hellnar about an hour ago, so they should be back anytime now.'

'Oh, OK. Best make myself scarce, then.' Hákon grins.

I suppress another giggle. 'Shall I show you to your room? I mean, show you the hotel? Where everything is and so on?'

Why can't I talk normally?

'No, there's no need,' Hákon says. 'I should be able to find my own way.'

He walks off, and a frisson of excitement zings through my body. What would my friends say if they knew I was here with these people? What would Mum say?

Tryggvi

I haven't let Oddný out of my sight since she nearly fell over the cliff. Though I don't believe it was really that narrow an escape: it was just Petra being dramatic. Or at least that's what it felt like to me. There was absolutely no need for her to let out such a blood-curdling scream.

Still, to be on the safe side, I've kept a tight hold on Oddný's arm on the return journey, though she just laughs it off. She flatly refused to go back early, complaining that everyone was overreacting.

'It wouldn't be such a bad thing if I had fallen,' she whispers to me. 'At least then I'd be free.'

I suspect that Oddný has been dreading this family weekend for a long time, though she hasn't said anything to me. Her anxiety has been obvious from the way she's been so distracted lately, unable to concentrate, and there have been times when I've come home from work and noticed a smell on her breath that she's tried and failed to disguise with perfume. It's new for her to feel she has to hide her drinking from me, and I couldn't understand why she was doing it. Couldn't understand what made her think she needed to put on this pantomime for me.

'Oddný, don't you think you've had enough?' Ester asks in a low voice, gesturing at the flask in Oddný's hand.

Oddný laughs. 'Don't you start, Ester. You used to be much more fun in the old days.'

Ester's lips tighten.

From what Oddný's told me, Ester certainly knew how to let

her hair down when they were younger. The sisters-in-law used to be closer at one time and would go out partying while Haraldur stayed at home studying.

Back in the hotel room, I take a shower, then put on a clean shirt and some aftershave. I've never felt at ease in a suit, being more of a jeans man, so I pull them on now.

I ask Oddný if she wants me to wait for her, but she tells me to go on down.

I take a seat at the bar and order a Coke, and I'm still sitting there when Haraldur, comes in.

'Started already, eh?' he says, beckoning to the barman. He takes the stool beside me and orders a whisky. 'What's that you're drinking?'

'Coca-Cola,' I say and grin.

Haraldur raises his eyebrows. 'What, aren't you going to have a proper drink?' he asks.

'Nah, not today.'

He continues to look at me, as if waiting for an explanation, so in the end I give in and add: 'Sober for a year now.'

'Well, well,' he says, taking his drink from the barman. I can tell that he's not impressed by my answer: he's already glancing around for someone else to talk to. Perhaps he thinks denying yourself alcohol is a sign of weakness.

But I'm not denying myself out of necessity; it was my own choice.

'What brought that about?' Haraldur asks, slurping his whisky.

'I didn't like who I became when I drank,' I say. 'I wasn't myself.'

'Is that such a bad thing?' Haraldur laughs.

'In my case, yes.'

'Well, not in mine, I can tell you.' He gives another bark of laughter. I'm about to answer when Ingvar comes into the bar and the brothers start talking about something else.

I drink my Coke, not even trying to listen in on their

conversation. I could have told Haraldur that when I'm drunk it's not just that I'm unlike myself; I don't even recognise myself. I become angry and aggressive, I take things further than I would dream of doing when the booze isn't in charge. When I drink, it's like all my demons rise to the surface. That's why I haven't touched a drop for nearly a year. Because I'm afraid of what I might do.

Sævar
Detective, West Iceland CID

The name of the hotel is carved on a wooden signpost by the road.

The place opened back in the spring. Sævar had read a news report about it while it was still under construction: a luxury hotel on Snæfellsnes, designed to be environmentally friendly. Some big-name foreign architect had been involved, but Sævar couldn't remember who, as he wasn't well informed about that sort of thing.

Though he did remember the architect saying that special emphasis had been placed on the lighting design. Now, in daylight, the lighting was barely noticeable, but presumably it must come into its own at night. From outside, the hotel looked like nothing so much as a block of concrete dropped into the lava field.

The upstairs level jutted out slightly from the main building to form a glass-enclosed room, supported by concrete pillars flanking the entrance on the ground floor. That must be the lounge. Sævar had seen a photo of it and remembered that the architects had called it a viewing lounge, an area of seating where guests could watch the Northern Lights in warmth and comfort on dark winter evenings.

It all sounded terribly romantic, but Sævar couldn't see how it would work in practice, unless all the lights were switched off and the glass was regularly cleaned. What's more, the room was bound to be freezing in winter and like a greenhouse when the sun was shining in summer.

'The family has hired the hotel for the weekend,' Hörður said, as they parked beside a black Range Rover.

'The entire hotel?' Sævar counted the floor-to-ceiling windows on the upper floor, which must belong to the bedrooms. On the side facing them, he counted fifteen.

'Yes. The entire place,' Hörður said.

'How many people are there again?'

'Between twenty and thirty, I believe.'

The family evidently weren't short of money. The fleet of vehicles outside the hotel was proof, if you needed it, that none of them were bothered about playing down their wealth. Although Sævar had no interest in cars, even he could work out that there were vehicles worth tens of millions in the car park.

'Which one would you most like to own?' he asked.

Hörður was far more of a car enthusiast than he was.

Hörður looked around, clicking his tongue. 'Hard to say,' he replied. 'But probably the Benz. Or the Range Rover.'

'Really?' Sævar had always regarded people who drove around in Range Rovers as show-offs. He had no hesitation in dismissing them as attention-seekers, though this judgemental attitude probably said more about him than it did about them.

Hörður didn't reciprocate by asking which car Sævar would have chosen, but then he wasn't the type to play what-if. Especially not in the current circumstances. Sævar, on the other hand, felt a need to lighten the atmosphere and distract himself briefly from the case. He surveyed the fleet, thinking that if Hörður asked, he'd say he'd like the most expensive car, but only so he could sell it and invest the money in something more worthwhile.

He looked up at the hotel again and spotted a figure standing at the glass wall upstairs, a woman with long hair, wearing loose clothes. When their eyes met, she retreated from the window and vanished from sight, but not before Sævar had sensed something in her movements. Fear, perhaps. He wondered at this.

'Well, shall we go in?' Hörður asked.

Sævar nodded, and they walked up to the hotel entrance together. Although Sævar could no longer see the woman, he had the skin-prickling sensation of being watched.

Lea Snæberg

What should we do if we meet up?

Er I don't know ... see a film maybe? I curse myself for not being able to think of anything more original. Going to the cinema is the last thing I'd want to do with Birgir.

Mmm, maybe. But a film wouldn't give us much chance to talk. What about going swimming?

Maybe. If it was in the dark.

Why in the dark?

Oh you know.

I'm sure you'd look great in a swimming costume.

I start to write a reply, then delete the message. I don't want Birgir to think I'm shy or insecure, but the thought of him seeing me in a swimsuit stresses me out.

I hesitate, then write: *OK swimming. Deal. Will you turn up in Speedos?*

Maybe. Unless I'm wearing my thong.

Ha ha.

What about you? Bikini?

God, could I wear a bikini in front of Birgir? The last time I went swimming in Iceland was about two years ago. Actually, I do have a newish bikini that I bought in Mexico, but it's not exactly very Icelandic. I mean, it's got these rhinestones sewn onto it, so I'd never wear it in a chlorinated Icelandic pool. It's more like beachwear. But it doesn't matter, because before I can answer, Birgir adds:

I think you'd look great in a bikini.

Thanks. But maybe I wouldn't bother with one.

My heart beats fast as I send the message. We don't usually talk like this, but I want Birgir to understand that I'm serious. I want us to meet. I don't want him to see me as some whiny little girl, and I've whined enough to him in the past. Now I need to show him that there's another side to me.

You'd wear a swimsuit instead? he asks.

Nope.

Oh...

Birgir starts typing, then stops.

I think we'd need to find a natural hot spring or deserted swimming pool, I add.

Why?

Because I wouldn't want anyone else there.

I get butterflies in my stomach just thinking about it. I've talked openly about various things before, but not like this.

Don't you want to meet up somewhere first so we can talk?

Staring at Birgir's message, I feel a rush of shame, as if I've said something I shouldn't have.

Maybe, I write eventually. *Is that what you want?*

Of course.

Birgir doesn't write anything for a while, then sends: *You never know, we might have some fun afterwards...*

I can't help smiling as I wonder what those dots mean.

'Who are you talking to?' asks Ari, who's still sitting on his bed, though he's supposed to be hurrying up and getting in the shower.

'No one,' I say. 'Just Villa.'

'OK.' He doesn't sound convinced.

Anyway, I've got to go out, Birgir writes. *Shall we chat this evening? Send me a photo.*

What kind of photo?

A selfie, of course...

When I put down my phone, I'm both excited and nervous. What does dot, dot, dot mean? Does he want a normal selfie or one that's a bit more … unusual?

Not that I'd ever send a photo showing anything. But what if that's what he wants?

We've often sent each other pictures, but nothing daring. Once I sent a photo of myself with a huge *bragðarefur* – that's like an Icelandic McFlurry or ice-cream mix-up – and Birgir sent me a photo of his dog licking his cheek. But we know each other really well now, as well as you can know anyone online. As soon as he comes to Iceland we're going to meet up, and then who knows what will happen?

In a way I'm sure it was good for Birgir and me to meet online. I feel like I know him better than the boys I've talked to before. Perhaps because over the last few months there's been nothing to get in the way of our chats. I don't need to worry about looking good when we talk, or whether I smell OK, or whether something I say is going to sound stupid. Sometimes I think this is the only proper way to meet someone, to really get to know another person.

I've had two boyfriends in the past, but neither relationship lasted long. The first was for two months, the second for four. The first was when I was fourteen, and all we did was kiss at my friend's birthday party. The second was last autumn, and I still feel sick every time I think about Sölvi and how it ended.

My feelings for them both were only like a childish crush that quickly wore off, though my friends don't believe me. They think I'm still hung up on Sölvi because he dumped me. They don't believe that I couldn't care less, that it's exactly what I wanted to happen. To be honest, I think they were pleased when Sölvi broke up with me. At least, some of them didn't hesitate to continue liking his pictures and posting comments on them.

My relationships with those boys were totally different from this thing with Birgir. He's my friend, and that's something I've never had before: friendship with a boy. I feel like I can trust him. Like, totally.

'I'm going to get a drink,' I say to Ari, bored of sitting there.

In the bar, I order a Coke, and I'm about to take it back up to our room when I notice this girl. She's sitting on the windowsill at the end of the corridor, looking at something on her phone.

Of course I know who Harpa is. Her dad's married to Jenný, Uncle Ingvar's stepdaughter. That's why we're not proper cousins, more like sort of step-cousins, if such a thing exists. We used to play during Christmas get-togethers when we were kids, at the age when you can still play with someone though you don't know each other. Back then, Harpa had light-brown hair, which was always elaborately styled, in tight braids, a French plait or a bun. Now her hair is dark with pink highlights, and she has a thick fringe. She's wearing heavy, black army boots and a hoodie that comes down below her bum, over tight leggings; clothes that say she doesn't give a shit what anyone thinks, that she's cool. Or at least I'm guessing that's how she thinks.

Impulsively, I go over to her.

'Hi, I'm Lea,' I say. 'You might not remember me but, er...'

Harpa smiles. 'I remember you.'

'Cool,' I reply, then don't know what else to say.

Harpa's dark-ringed eyes look me up and down, but not in a way that makes me uncomfortable. More like she's interested.

'Er...' I cough, when Harpa doesn't say anything. 'Don't you live in Sweden?'

'Yes,' Harpa says. 'And I don't speak Icelandic.'

'Oh. I, er...' I can feel my face growing hot.

'Joke.' Harpa grins.

I laugh, feeling she must be able to hear my relief. I'm a bit stressed, though I don't quite know why. Perhaps it's because Harpa seems so self-assured and sophisticated, not like me.

'How old are you again?' Harpa asks.

'Sixteen, and you?'

'Nearly eighteen.' She stands up. 'Come on, let's go to my room.'

'Oh.' I hesitate. I hadn't expected her to invite me along.

'Are you coming?' Harpa asks.

'Sure,' I say. 'I'm coming.'

We climb the stairs, and Harpa opens the first door on the landing.

'Have you got a room to yourself?' I ask.

'Of course,' Harpa says. 'Haven't you?'

I say no and explain that I'm sharing with my brother.

'He's cute.'

'I know,' I say, looking round her room. There's a large make-up case open on the desk, a set of hair straighteners and a leather jacket. Harpa picks up a pair of trousers that are lying on the floor and chucks them over the back of a chair. The bed has been made and there are two bottles of Coke on the bedside table, one empty, the other half full, and a bag of chocolate-coated liquorice balls.

'He's going to be mega hot in a few years,' Harpa says. She flings herself down on the bed, then turns to me with her hand under her chin. 'Not that I've got any designs on him myself, but all the girls are going to go crazy about him.'

'I suppose,' I say, though I expect she's right. Ari's popular at school. He's good at sport and at his studies. Good at most things, in fact. And he almost never gets on my nerves, which is pretty incredible, considering that he's my younger brother.

'Are you seeing anyone?' Harpa asks, when I don't add anything.

'No, no one.' I sit down on the end of the bed.

'Then who are you always chatting to on your phone?' Harpa asks. 'Isn't that your boyfriend?'

'No, nothing like that,' I say, wondering when Harpa's been

watching me. I pick at the varnish on my thumbnail. 'It's just …
I don't know. I'm just talking to this one guy.'

'Let me have a look at him.'

I hesitate for a moment, then take out my phone and find a
photo. I might as well show Harpa a picture of him. It's not like
she and I are going to meet again anytime soon.

'He's cute,' Harpa says, after studying the picture. She asks how
old he is and where we met.

I lie and tell her we first met several months ago. It suddenly
feels embarrassing to admit that we only know each other online.

'He lives in Sweden, but we're going to get together again soon
– the next time he's in Iceland.'

'Cool,' Harpa says, apparently losing interest. She sits up,
opens the suitcase on the floor and takes out a bottle. 'What do
you say to making this evening a bit more interesting?'

'What's that?'

'Vodka,' Harpa says, finding some glasses. 'Don't worry, I've
got juice too. There's no way I'm going to drink it neat.'

'But … but won't they notice?'

'No chance. Did you see them earlier? They're so pissed
themselves that they won't notice a thing,' Harpa says. She looks
at me. 'You have drunk alcohol before, haven't you?'

'Yes.' The second lie I've told this evening, and I don't know
why. Don't know why I feel I have to lie to impress Harpa. It's
not simply that she's older; there's something exciting about her
that's having this effect on me.

I've never drunk before, though most of my friends have tried
alcohol. I went to a junior prom with my class, where lots of the
kids were trying it for the first time. At the warm-up party I
watched as they seemed to get really lit up at first, but as the
evening went on, some of them were in a terrible state. One of
the boys never even made it to the prom because he started
puking up at the party; others could hardly stand up and kept
falling into people's arms, and one girl, who's usually terribly shy,

told the boy she fancied that she loved him. When I got home I lay awake in bed for a long time, thinking I'd rather die than behave like that. Besides, I had fun at the prom despite not being pissed. I danced without worrying about whether anyone was watching. There was a kind of freedom in being almost the only person there who wasn't wasted.

But now I'm here, with Harpa, who I barely know, and somehow it doesn't seem to matter if I get a bit drunk. I'm quite curious to know what it feels like. If I'm ever going to try alcohol, this is probably my best chance.

So I accept the glass Harpa hands me, take a big gulp and try not to let it show that the drink is burning my throat. I manage OK and it gets easier after a few more sips. Harpa starts fiddling with her phone and for a while neither of us says anything. I check if Birgir's sent me any more messages, but he hasn't.

Suddenly, Harpa screams, making me jump. After that she has a massive laughing fit, then sits up and pats the bed beside her.

'You've got to see this video,' she says.

I move up and sit beside her with my glass. We watch the video and drink until the world turns all soft and fuzzy and warm.

Petra Snæberg

There's still an hour till dinner when we get back to the hotel. I curse my outdoor clothes. They're supposed to be wind- and waterproof, but my back is soaked and I'm freezing. By the last ten minutes of the walk it was so dark that we could only see a few metres in front of us. The landscape, which had seemed so beautiful by daylight, was transformed by nightfall. The crashing of the waves no longer seemed soothing but menacing, the noise they made as they broke on the cliffs was like a reminder of the sea's true cruelty. I couldn't stop thinking about the little boy who fell off the cliff all those years ago, imagining his small body being tossed to and fro by the waves, vanishing under the water, only to reappear briefly before disappearing for good. What thoughts must have gone through the poor kid's head during the last few seconds of his life?

It's a long time since I've been so powerfully aware of the darkness closing in on me. A long time since I've let it get to me like this.

At least the hotel, in contrast, seems cosier now that it's evening, the yellow glow of the lights softening the rawness of the concrete and a fire burning in the bar. The crackling of the flames, the scent of wood smoke and the delicious cooking smells go a long way towards dispelling my feeling of disquiet, and I begin to relax.

'Do you want first shower?' Gestur asks.

'No, you go ahead,' I say. 'I'm just going to sit down for a bit and have a coffee. Get the chill out of my bones.'

I don't want to go upstairs yet. Don't want to be alone with Gestur in case I come out with something I'll regret. He and Steffý were talking to each other all the way back. They were too far away for me to hear what they were saying but I couldn't miss Steffý's laughter, and now I can't shake off the image of the two of them in a clinch on the sofa while I was crashed out drunk in the bedroom. I never questioned them or told them my suspicions. At the time it seemed too absurd ... or at least that's what I told myself. Now I wonder if the reason I didn't ask was because I was afraid to hear the answer.

I order myself an Irish coffee at the bar and sit down by the fire. The heat of the flames is welcome, and after a while I take off my coat and hat. My hair's probably sticking up in all directions, my curls frizzy from the damp outside.

The young woman from the bar materialises at my side with astonishing speed.

'Here you are,' she says in a sing-song voice, handing me my drink.

I thank her, but she doesn't immediately leave.

'I...' she begins, then laughs awkwardly.

I raise my eyebrows. 'Yes?'

'I'll be behind the bar if you need anything else.'

'Thanks.'

I watch her trot away, trying to remember her name. Irma, wasn't it? She can't be much younger than me, in her early thirties probably, yet she comes across as oddly childlike. Which is strange, because her face doesn't actually look that young. Perhaps the childlike effect has more to do with her manner. She seems shy and gauche, as though she doesn't quite know how to behave. There's something vaguely familiar about her too. I feel as if I've seen her face before.

Irma, seeing me watching her, smiles and cranes her head forward, as if to ask if I need something. I look away.

Ever since I can remember, I've had a bad habit of staring at people. I get caught up in studying them, watching how they move, how their expressions change. Most people have unconscious habits, like touching their faces, fiddling with their hair or pursing their lips.

I take out my phone and start updating my social-media accounts with the photos I snapped before it got too dark.

'Hi, coz.' Hákon Ingimar takes a seat facing me and signs to Irma. 'Tough walk?'

'No,' I say with a sigh. 'Not physically, anyway.'

Hákon orders a beer with a charming smile. I notice how Irma's cheeks turn pink.

When she's gone, Hákon says: 'I hear you. I seriously considered making up some excuse to avoid coming here this weekend.'

'Did you?'

Hákon doesn't answer for a moment, then smiles at me.

He's so much younger than me and Steffý that when we were eleven or twelve, we used to babysit him. We looked after him one whole summer, forcing him into the buggy he was determined not to sit in and taking him to the playground. Hákon was a difficult child. He used to run away whenever he got a chance and was always hurting himself; falling off the castle at the playground or tripping over his own feet. He's still difficult now, though he's stopped falling flat on his face. He insists on going his own way and won't listen to anyone who tries to tell him what to do.

'How's Mum been?' he asks, licking the beer froth off his upper lip.

'Oddný's been...' I don't want to mention the drunken incident on the walk when she almost fell over the cliff. I smile. 'You know.'

'Mmm.'

For a moment a shadow crosses Hákon's face and the careless expression is replaced by something darker.

'She hasn't been that bad,' I say and change the subject. 'What's new, anyway? I saw the other day that you and Ivana have broken up.'

'Oh, yeah,' Hákon says. 'It was never going to work. She wanted me to move to Brazil.'

'Doesn't that sound tempting? Sunshine and white beaches?'

'What am I supposed to do with myself there?'

'I don't know. Sunbathe and enjoy yourself?' I say. 'What do you do here?'

Hákon's mouth twitches up at one corner. 'Whatever I like.'

I shake my head. People think Hákon Ingimar takes himself too seriously. They see the clothes, the hair and the selfies he shares and have him down as a certain type. But really he's the first person to laugh at himself. No one finds the photos sillier than he does. The thing is, though, he's indifferent to what other people think. Hákon Ingimar has always done what's necessary to get his own way, to get the column inches, attention, and, most importantly, the girls.

'So you're not about to get hitched anytime soon?' I ask.

'Darling coz, you ought to know me better than that.'

'Do you think it'll ever happen?'

'What?' Hákon gives his twisted grin again. 'That I'll find a nice girl? Become a dad? Have little brats that keep me awake all night and shit themselves during the day?'

'Something like that.'

'Maybe.' Hákon leans back and props one foot on the armchair opposite him as he takes out his phone, adding: 'Who knows?'

I feel a stab of envy for Hákon and his carefree lifestyle. What must it be like, not having to take responsibility for anything?

'What about you, coz?' he asks. 'What are you up to?'

'You know, same old, same old.'

'Playing at being mummy?'

'You've got it,' I say. 'Playing at being mummy.' Because isn't that what I've been doing for the last few years? Playing at being a mother and wife? Trying to be good on all fronts at once: at work, at home and in the media? I can feel how tired I am from trying to juggle all these roles. I try to imagine what it would be like to drop them all and be fancy free, like Hákon.

'Anyway, I'd better go and jump in the shower.' Taking my coat, I stand up.

'You do that,' Hákon says, without raising his eyes from his phone. But as I'm moving away he adds, 'Hey, Petra?'

I look round. 'What?'

'I reckon you could do with a pick-me-up.'

'What do you mean?'

Hákon beckons me to come closer, then takes my hand and presses something into the palm.

'What's this?' I ask, though I have my suspicions.

Hákon winks. 'Give it back to me later, once you've had your shower.'

On the stairs I finally open my fist to discover a small plastic bag of white powder.

Sævar
Detective, West Iceland CID

There was absolute silence in the hotel when they entered, and the noise of the door slamming behind them was like a bomb going off in the lobby.

Sævar looked around the reception area. Stepping inside was more like entering a cave hewn out of rock than a building. For a moment, he and Hörður both stood there, wordlessly taking in their surroundings, then they heard the sound of approaching footsteps, and a tall, thin woman came round the corner. Sævar noticed that she was wearing flat-soled shoes, yet oddly they emitted the same clicking noise as high heels.

She extended a hand in greeting.

'I'm guessing you're Edda, the manager,' Hörður said, as he took her hand.

'Yes, manager and owner. My husband, Gísli, and I had the hotel built a few years ago.' She corrected herself. 'That's to say, we started the process five years ago, but the construction wasn't finished until spring this year.'

'Yes, right,' Hörður said. 'And I gather you've been quite busy?'

The corners of Edda's mouth twitched, as if she found the question ridiculous, but she didn't say as much, merely smiled. 'We've been booked out all summer and had to turn people away. Most of the guests have been foreigners, though we've had

Icelanders staying with us too. Their numbers increased during the autumn, and they probably made up a third of our bookings in September and October.'

'It's beautiful,' Hörður said, looking around again. 'Very tasteful.'

Again, Edda smiled, but Sævar thought he detected a hint of condescension in her expression. Part of him could understand why. The hotel had been designed to precise specifications by architects who were leaders in their field. 'Tasteful' wasn't the word Sævar would choose to describe the place. He used tasteful about things that had been neatly arranged and went well together. The word seemed hopelessly inadequate in this case, since the hotel was more like a work of art than a building.

'Thank you,' Edda said.

'The guests are all still here, aren't they?' Hörður asked.

'Yes, no one's left today, as you requested.'

'Good,' Hörður said. 'We'll need to interview both guests and staff.'

'Of course.' Edda clutched the necklace she was wearing, rubbing it against her chest.

Sævar wondered if she'd already got wind of the fact that the missing guest had been found dead, since she didn't ask any questions. Unless she was simply the type of person who found it easy to contain her curiosity, who avoided prying. It must be a desirable trait in her profession.

Before they could say anything further, they heard hurried footsteps in the corridor, as if someone was running towards reception. When Sævar saw the man's face, he felt the slight sinking of his heart that always accompanied having to inform the next-of-kin of a death.

The instant the man saw Hörður and Sævar, his footsteps slowed and shortened, as if he was finding it difficult to force himself to keep going. Sævar watched his face slacken, his chin drop and his eyes grow distant; his hope disappear. Before the man could reach them he sank down, as if his legs had buckled beneath him.

Irma
Hotel Employee

I don't know why I'm so stressed. My hands are shaking as I serve the drinks. My cheeks burn as I carry them over. I can't stop staring at them while I'm lining up the clean glasses on the shelves. I keep having to remind myself that they're no more interesting than anyone else, but it's hard not to feel inferior. I might as well have a different kind of blood flowing through my veins, which isn't true, of course, but I feel as though it is.

When Petra walks past the bar she smiles at me, but her smile is gone as quickly as it appeared. Even now, with bedraggled hair, in wet clothes, she looks amazing.

'Thank you,' I call after her, then bite my tongue. *Thank you.* I sound like a desperate fan, like a little girl who can't contain her excitement.

Hákon Ingimar is still sitting in the bar, absorbed by his phone. He's got his shoes up on one of the chairs, but I'm not going to say anything. Besides, they look spotless, the soles a brilliant white. I doubt he's ever walked on anything but tarmac in them.

'Another.' Hákon raises his empty beer glass and points at it. I nod to show I understand.

His eyes linger on me as I bring him a fresh glass, several drops spilling over the rim onto my fingers.

'Thanks,' Hákon says, as I hand him the beer. I smile and am about to go when Hákon stops me. 'Look...' He runs his tongue over his teeth, his eyes narrowing slightly. 'I feel like I know you.'

'Really? I don't think we've met before but ... but you never know, do you?'

'Where are you from?'

I've always found it hard to answer this question, like when Elísa asks me when I'm going home.

Where am I from? There are so many possible answers. Most people would probably mention their birthplace, but I only lived there a few months and of course I don't remember it, so I've never felt it's right to say I'm from there.

Mum and I were always moving when I was younger, first between towns, then between suburbs of Reykjavík. I used to love settling into new places. Arranging my things in a new room, putting my cover on the bed and hanging up the picture of the child with the plump cheeks, which Mum always said was just like me when I was small. I was always the new girl in the class and told the other kids proudly that I'd lived in five towns and been to eight schools. I used to enjoy the way they gaped in wonder.

I suppose some people might pity me, but there's no need. I enjoyed moving regularly; I expect I'm one of nature's nomads, like my mother. And it was quite fun always being new. New people are exciting, aren't they? And if anything went wrong, I got a chance to disappear and make a fresh start somewhere else. To mend my ways without anyone knowing about my earlier mistakes or sins.

A psychologist I once saw told me that this constant moving was responsible for my inability to settle down. I get bored of most things sooner or later, whether it's places or people. But my own take is that I just like novelty. When it comes down to it, the world is an exciting place, full of variety, and I simply want to experience everything.

'Here and there,' I finally answer Hákon, hoping that it sounds intriguing rather than off-putting. To avoid being too curt, I add: 'I've always moved a lot. Never put down roots anywhere.'

'I see,' Hákon says.

'I'd like to move abroad. Try living overseas.'

'Really? Like where?'

'Japan, maybe. Or Cuba.' I fiddle with the end of my plait. 'Somewhere sunny.'

Hákon's laugh is so loud it startles me. 'Awesome,' he says. 'Excellent.'

Hákon Ingimar thinks I'm awesome, a little voice cries inside me. *He thinks I'm excellent.*

'Well, anyway. Better get on...' I gesture awkwardly at the bar.

'Yeah, right.' Hákon leans back, digging around in the pockets of his ripped jeans. Not that they're worn; they were obviously distressed like that when he bought them. Every tear is deliberate.

Hákon sniffs, then rubs the tip of his nose with a finger. His jaws are working oddly and one of his legs is jiggling as if he can't control it.

As I walk away, I wonder if he's on something. Cocaine or some other stimulant. I'm familiar with the movements, the little tell-tale tics, as I've seen them all before. It shouldn't come as a surprise to me: lots of the comments under the news stories about Hákon Ingimar have hinted at it. Cocaine is the rich people's drug, isn't it? But I'm disappointed that the cliché is true in his case. I expected more of him. Hoped for more, to be honest.

Anyway, so what. It probably doesn't mean anything. I expect he's only a recreational user, taking a hit when he's out partying at weekends, like so many other people.

Inside, I'm jumping for joy because I've had a conversation with Hákon Ingimar. He was interested in getting to know me. I smile to myself and am almost overwhelmed by anticipation at the thought of this weekend.

I can't wait to get to know them all better.

Lea Snæberg

'Is that the bag?' Harpa points at my bag, grinning.

'What?'

'You know, *the bag*.' Harpa rolls her eyes at how slow I'm being. 'The one the online comment system went crazy over.'

'Oh, you mean that? Yes, this is the one and only bag.' I start to giggle, though I didn't feel like laughing when the news about the bag broke in the media.

Mum brought it home with her as a late birthday present. A present that was supposed to make up for the fact that she'd forgotten all about my birthday and booked herself onto a course in Paris that weekend. She pretended she'd made a terrible mistake, and for a while I let her believe I was genuinely hurt. It made a nice change to have her all humble and anxious to please. Then she came home with this bag from YSL that cost more than two hundred thousand krónur.

'The bag reminded me so much of you that I just had to get it,' Mum said, eagerly watching my face as I opened the box.

For once, she got it right. The bag was exactly my style, black with a gold logo on the front and more gold woven into the leather strap.

That evening I took a selfie of myself with the bag and next day the media headlines screamed: 'Petra Snæberg Gives Daughter YSL Bag for Her Birthday', beside a photo of me.

For two days the story was on the list of most-read items. I felt like everyone at school was talking about it. Like I couldn't go anywhere without feeling all eyes were on me.

I've hardly used the bag since. After the media frenzy, I didn't get any pleasure from looking at it anymore. The news ruined everything that was good about this gift from Mum.

'We'll need to go down to dinner soon,' I say to Harpa, and she hands the bag back to me.

'Yes, I suppose so.' She yawns. 'See you shortly.'

❀

As I walk along the corridor to my room everything seems to be moving up and down. The floor and walls are dancing around me, and the door handle won't stay still. For a moment I forget how to open the door and just stand there in front of it, my body swaying slightly. I giggle. The situation seems funny until I hear voices and try to focus. I don't want to meet anyone, not yet, not like this.

Then I remember the app and manage to open the door.

'Half an hour till dinner,' I whisper to myself as I close it. 'Half an hour.'

To my relief, Ari's nowhere to be seen. Not that I'm afraid of meeting him, as he'd never say anything to Mum and Dad.

I check the time, then go into the bathroom and take off my clothes. For a minute I linger in front of the mirror, studying myself. Then I go and sit on the bed, running my fingers over the gold letters on the bag Mum gave me.

One evening, I made the mistake of reading the comments on the news story. Most were about how horribly spoilt I was, and one said that I must be totally out of touch with reality. Others asked if this was really news and pretended not to have a clue who me or Mum were. I think they must have been lying, though, because everyone knows who Mum is since her company became so successful. There are regular adverts on TV, in the papers and on advertising hoardings all over town, featuring a big photo of Mum wearing bright-red lipstick, her hair styled in attractive waves.

In one of the comments a man asked just who I thought I was and whether there was something wrong with me. A few people came to my defence, saying I was only sixteen and couldn't help who my parents were.

The comments made me wonder if this was what people really thought about me and my family. People who didn't even know us. I feel as if they think we're somehow different from them. Like we have no feelings or can't read the stuff they write.

I longed to answer back and went as far as writing a reply to one of the comments. Once I'd started writing, I couldn't stop. My fingers flew over the keyboard, and when I came to myself sometime later, my hands were damp and my breathing was fast and shallow, like I'd been running. Reading back over what I'd written, I imagined what the reaction would be if I actually posted it online.

My heart was crashing against my ribs as I rested my finger on the enter key.

Just one small movement, I thought. *One tiny movement and everyone will know what happened to me.*

In the end, though, I jerked back my hand, then deleted the whole thing. Now I wonder if it would have been a relief to unburden like that. If anyone would have believed me, or if my words would have been torn to pieces by the comments system, like the news story itself.

Petra Snæberg

Gestur's just finished in the shower when I get back to our room.

He's standing in front of the mirror, buttoning up his shirt, his hair still wet and the room full of steam. I open the window and a cold gust whips up the thin curtains.

'The temperature's dropped,' I say, looking out. I can't see far, as the blackness outside is impenetrable and all the lights are on in our room.

'Where were you?' Gestur asks.

'I got chatting downstairs,' I say. 'To Hákon Ingimar.'

'Ah.' Gestur puts his tie round his neck. He's never been a fan of Hákon, regarding him as behaving like a teenage slacker with no ambition or direction. Which, if I'm honest, is a pretty fair assessment. 'What's he up to?'

'Not much. He's split up from his girlfriend.'

'That singer?'

'No, the Brazilian model,' I say. 'He and the singer broke up ages ago.'

Gestur stares into the mirror with a look of concentration as he knots his tie.

I tell him I'm going to have a shower and head into the bathroom, locking the door behind me. I put the plastic bag Hákon gave me on the vanity unit beside the basin and contemplate it. The bag looks so small and innocent, sitting there, but I feel oddly light-headed, not only because of the drink I had in the bar.

The sensible thing would be to empty the bag down the loo,

but Hákon wouldn't exactly be pleased by that. What was he thinking, giving it to me? Surely he doesn't imagine I'm going to start taking drugs this weekend?

I have a sudden memory of bumping into Hákon in town two or three years ago. I'd invited the staff of InLook out for a meal. We'd gone to a restaurant in the city centre and got horribly drunk, or perhaps it was only me who got horribly drunk. I remember finding a karaoke bar with some of the others and singing 'All By Myself', clutching a red cocktail that slopped onto my white shirt – like a scene from *Bridget Jones's Diary*, now that I come to think of it. No doubt looking as wrecked and tragic as she did.

Hákon Ingimar came up while I was smoking a cigarette outside the karaoke bar, and I went with him to another bar, where everyone was unbelievably young, the music was ridiculously loud, and it was so packed I could hardly move. Worst of all (I can't help grimacing when it comes back to me), I went into the toilets with Hákon and he took out a little bag, just like the one in front of me now, and, without even stopping to think, I snorted the contents up my nose. Without pausing for one second to consider whether it was a good idea.

'Pathetic' is the word that comes to mind. I'm pathetic.

I take the bag and shove it to the bottom of my handbag, then strip off my clothes and get in the shower. It's an overhead shower, and I close my eyes, raising my face and letting the powerful jet of hot water pound my skin.

Over the drumming of the water I become aware of someone knocking and turn off the tap.

'What?'

'I'm going downstairs,' Gestur calls.

'OK.'

The door to the corridor slams, and I step out of the shower, wrap the towel around me and emerge into our room.

The curtains are still open, but nothing can be seen outside because of the reflection on the glass. I grab my phone and work out how to turn down the lights with the app, then go over to the window and touch the cold glass with my fingertips. In the distance I can make out a tiny pinprick of light, like a moving, orange-yellow flame. A cigarette?

As I move closer, the light disappears. There's no way of guessing how far away it was. The darkness outside is so thick that I can't see a thing, even with the lights dimmed in the room.

But anyone could see me.

I draw the curtains and back away from the window, clutching the towel around me, then decide to get dressed in the bathroom. I opt for a pair of high-waisted, skinny black trousers, heels and a top that is fitted where it counts and loose everywhere else. It cost almost as much as the shoes, which most people would probably regard as a ludicrous amount to spend on a shirt.

I bought it in Paris several years ago, back when Gestur and I regularly went on trips abroad together. When Lea and Ari were small, Gestur and I lived for our foreign breaks. Our most precious time used to be the evenings when we fled the responsibility of home, the mess and the whining, and relished being together, just the two of us. We went to nightclubs, wrapped up in our own little world, with eyes only for each other. Then we'd head back to the hotel and have sex that lasted for hours. I miss those times. Nowadays we never do anything together. I drink at home, and Gestur goes out with his friends. It dawns on me now that it's ages since I even thought about our good years.

The phone rings and Mum's name flashes up.

'Aren't you coming down, Petra? Everyone's taken their seats. What on earth are you doing?'

I assure her that I'm on my way, put the finishing touches to my make-up, spray perfume on my wrists and rub them behind my ears. My bag's beside the sink and my eyes keep being drawn to it. The thought of spending a whole weekend in the same place as Steffý is overwhelming.

But I can hardly blame her for the fact I find her presence so difficult – not without a sense of guilt and fear. My bad conscience never goes away, but around Steffý it becomes almost unendurable.

Being burdened by secrets is such a strain. For many years this burden has tainted everything around me, damaging my relationship with my family and friends. I can never be completely myself because I feel as if I don't deserve to be happy after what I did.

Irma
Hotel Employee

'Will the starters all be arriving together or one at a time?' Haraldur makes it sound as if this is a matter of supreme importance. Beside him, his wife, Ester, is chatting to her sister-in-law.

'The starters will be served together,' I say, adding that there are only two of them, beef carpaccio and tiger prawns.

'Great. I think it's best to make the speech during the starters.'

I assume he's talking to himself but I answer anyway: 'Good idea. I'll make sure there's enough of a gap between the starters and the main course.'

'Good,' he says, and walks away without paying me any further attention.

Haraldur never once looked me in the eye during this short exchange. He rarely does, I've noticed. Even when he looks, he's not really looking, not actually seeing you. Haraldur's a man who sees only my clothes and my position, not who I really am. That's of no interest to him.

I survey the restaurant, which has now filled up. I'm fairly confident that few of the people present would be able to remember my name unless they checked the badge on my chest.

'Irma.' Edda beckons me over. 'You can put the bread baskets on the tables now.'

'Will do.'

I go into the kitchen, where the bread baskets are standing ready along with little lava platters of whipped butter.

'Don't forget to smile,' Arne, one of the waiters, whispers.

'Shut up.' I stick my tongue out at him.

Arne has often seen me massaging my cheeks after a busy evening when I'm afraid the professional smile will become permanently fixed to my face. There's no doubt that this evening will be one of those times. The dinner will go on until late, everyone will drink a bit more than they should and say stuff they'll probably regret later.

After putting the bread and butter on all the tables and taking countless orders for the bar, in spite of the bottles of wine on every table, I retreat briefly into the shadows to study them unobserved.

They're a noisy family. They're all talking at once, laughing a lot and speaking in loud voices. I always longed for a big family, though I never told Mum that. Particularly at special occasions, like Christmas and Easter, and during the summer holidays. When I was young, I used to ask Mum if I could have a brother or a sister, but she said she needed a man before she would consider having any more children.

I couldn't understand why. After all, she had me without a man, though I was perfectly aware that she'd needed someone's help in the first place.

This family is lucky because they're part of something bigger, though I wonder if they have any appreciation of how fortunate they are. Whether it ever crosses their minds that some people are more or less alone in the world. That they belong to a minority – a small, privileged elite for whom all doors are open.

Somehow I doubt it ever occurs to them.

After Mum's illness became more serious, there was a long period when I felt desperately lonely. I got pretty low at one point, to the extent that I felt life wasn't worth living. But then I saw the light, so to speak, and now I have something to live for again.

Now, for the first time, I feel as if I have a purpose.

Petra Snæberg

The tables have been arranged to form four long rows. There's an empty seat next to Gestur, which is presumably intended for me. Scanning the room, I spot Steffý at the table furthest away from us. Next to her is Viktor.

'Have you got it?'

I flinch as Hákon whispers in my ear.

'Not here,' I mutter, and beckon him to leave the room with me. Outside in the corridor, I dig what he wants out of my handbag and slip it to him as unobtrusively as I can.

Hákon laughs at my embarrassment. 'Are you scared the cops will turn up or something?'

'The police are the least of my worries,' I hiss.

'Did you take some?' Hákon asks.

'No, I didn't.'

He grins disbelievingly.

'Seriously, Hákon, I—'

'Relax.' Hákon puts his hands on my shoulders. 'Chill. It's not a problem.'

I look straight into Hákon's eyes, and gradually his mouth curls in a smile. When an answering smile appears on my lips, quite against my will, he starts laughing.

'You're a menace, Hákon. An absolute menace.'

'If you only knew...' He winks at me, then waves towards the toilets. I needn't ask what he's intending to do there.

I go back into the restaurant and take my seat between Gestur and Mum. I'm starving, so I'm glad to see that there are bread baskets on the table and whipped butter. But just as I'm reaching for my second roll, I meet my mother's stern gaze and change my mind.

My entire youth was dominated by Mum's constant attempts to control my eating and prevent me from having too much food. I expect she finds it hard to stop. In her defence, I was quite a chubby kid and ate enough for an adult. Whenever Mum had sweets in the house she'd hide them, but I always tracked them down. But it's not like weight is an issue for me these days. I started to lose weight when I was seventeen, and for a while I became so thin that Mum sent me to a doctor. He couldn't find any signs of anorexia but did think there were various indications that I was suffering from post-traumatic stress. Mum had never heard such nonsense.

Brought back to the present by a sudden crash, I twist round sharply to be confronted by the sight of Oddný lying on the floor, having fallen off her chair. She's swearing and tutting and laughing. Tryggvi jumps to his feet and helps her up.

I can tell from Mum's strained smile that she's not amused.

'What are we going to do about Halli's sister?' she whispers to me as she butters herself a roll. 'Things can't go on like this.'

'Can't she just go into rehab?'

'Rehab?' Mum snorts. In her opinion, rehab is for a different class of people. Not that I have any direct evidence that this is the way she thinks, but I've always had the feeling that Mum's view of the world is rather black and white. Us and them. People like us never show any weakness or too much emotion, we're always strong and behave with dignity. Then there are *them*, the other type, who are weak and don't know how to exercise self-control.

Not that she's ever unpleasant or rude to anyone. Her manner has never been arrogant, quite the opposite. Yet there's something there, something I've never quite been able to put my finger on; an impression I've always had that Mum makes a distinction between us and them.

'There's nothing wrong with going into rehab, Mum,' I say. 'It might be good for her.'

'Oh, it's not like that.'

'Like what?'

Mum sips her white wine. 'She's just going through a stubborn phase. She's not been happy since Halli and Ingvar raised ... raised the subject with her.'

'What subject?'

'You know.' Mum repositions her glass on the table.

'They didn't seriously go ahead?' I remember Dad musing a while ago over whether to suggest they should buy Oddný out, but I never thought he'd actually do it.

Mum exhales heavily. 'They just thought it would be easier for her. She's got enough on her plate as it is with Hákon and her own problems.'

'But Mum...'

My mother tightens her lips. 'And that man she's with...'

'Tryggvi?'

'Exactly.' Mum sighs, as if the name alone is painful to her. Then, leaning a little closer, she adds in a low voice: 'Oddný was talking recently about getting married. Can you believe it?'

'So?'

'So my sister-in-law has never been known for her common sense,' Mum says. 'I'm just afraid she'll do something impulsive. Something she'll come to regret, that will have ... well, consequences.'

I want to snap at Mum that it's not Oddný she's worried about but the Snæberg money, but I bite back the comment. Turning to look over my shoulder, I see that Tryggvi is holding Oddný's hand under the table. She seems to have calmed down but is still knocking back the booze, undeterred. I notice that there's nothing but a bottle of Coke on the table in front of Tryggvi – no alcohol at all.

I don't suppose Tryggvi has done anything to earn my

mother's hostility. I expect she took one look at him and decided that he was one of *them*, not *us*. In a way I can see why. He dresses as if he came from Texas, favouring checked shirts and cowboy boots, and his hair is long and straggly. But I know nothing but good about him, and I can see with my own eyes how much care he takes of Oddný. He seems totally harmless.

As if Mum can read my mind, she leans over to me again and whispers: 'Oddný's not in a good place. She hasn't been for a long time. And there are men who are prepared to take advantage of the fact.' Up close like this, I can see how Mum's lipstick has bled into the fine lines around her mouth. She leans back, putting on a smile that's completely out of keeping with our conversation, and picks up her glass. 'We need to take care of what is ours, Petra. Only have people around us who we can trust. You understand?'

I understand, though I don't want to.

We're interrupted by the clinking of metal against glass.

Uncle Ingvar has taken the stage and is waiting for silence. 'Dear family, dear in-laws. Dear friends.'

I'm going to need something stronger than wine. It's going to take something much stronger than mere alcohol to help me get through this evening.

Tryggvi

The more the drink flows, the louder everyone talks. I feel sorry for the waiters, who can hardly keep up with running back and forth to take the orders. People have started mingling now that we've finished eating, and Oddný's brothers and their wives have moved over to our table.

'Plenty to do at the workshop?' Ingvar asks, faking an interest.

'Can't complain,' I say. 'There's generally enough to do in winter.' I notice his gaze wandering as I speak. No one in the family has the slightest interest in what I do, though they always ask out of politeness. It's like they can't think of any other subject of conversation apart from how things are going at work.

'Right.' Ester smiles politely and sips her champagne, leaving a smear of wine-red lipstick on the glass. We don't have much to talk about. It's a safe bet that she's never set foot in a carpentry workshop. I don't want to start pigeonholing people, but the fact is we belong to completely different social groups. With no experiences or views in common.

'We pranged our car the other day,' Haraldur says, after a silence lasting several long seconds. 'I was stopping at a red light when it just sort of slid forwards into the back of the car in front. The bumper took most of the impact, but the other car came off pretty badly. A Yaris. They're such junk.'

I'm fairly sure Haraldur has forgotten that I'm a carpenter and has me pegged as a mechanic instead. Maybe there's not much difference between them in his mind. After all, they're both people who work with their hands. I don't correct him, just make some remark about small cars. Haraldur laughs, and that's that dealt with. Now the conversation can get back to people they know, friends of the family and business associates.

There are no tradesmen in the Snæberg clan. They go to work in suits and ties, not in dungarees and vests. And they come home as well-scrubbed and smart as when they went to work in the morning, not covered in sawdust and splashes of paint, with the smell of oil in their nostrils.

'How's business going?' I ask Ingvar.

'Excellently. Times are...' Ingvar hesitates. 'Times are good. There's enough fish in the sea, and that makes everybody happy, doesn't it?'

'Yes, sure,' I agree.

Ingvar turns and says something to Haraldur.

Ever since my first dinner party with Oddný I've been struck by how formal her family are. Conversations with them are too polite to be sincere. At first I thought it was because I was new, but since then I've discovered it's just that some things are never discussed except in private.

I often get the feeling they think I'm trying to work out how to ride on the family's success, that this is the only reason I got involved with Oddný. Nothing could be further from the truth. I have no interest in money, to be honest – never did. The fact is I enjoy seeing the fruits of my own labour and would hate to be a small link in a big chain at some company. That's why I've mainly been self-employed over the years, supporting myself with carpentry work. I've not done badly from it either, though I'm unlikely ever to get rich.

The way I see it, money causes more problems than it solves. That's why I've tried to think of it as no more than a means to buy the basic necessities. That said, a reasonable sum has built up in my account in recent years. The carpentry workshop has been doing well, there's no shortage of work, and I don't spend much beyond what I have to.

Unfortunately, Oddný has been careless with her money over the years. That's why I don't like the idea of her selling her share in the company, as her brothers are obviously pushing her to do. I wonder when Oddný's planning to tell me or whether she ever will. Talking about money bores Oddný; I suppose because she's always been able to take it for granted.

'Let's dance,' she says, as the music starts.

And we dance. I twirl her round, then put my arms round her waist, holding her close. Breathing in her sweet scent.

We're good together, Oddný and me, whatever her family think.

Lea Snæberg

Harpa is sitting at the table in front of me, and I can see her sneaking frequent sips of her father's drink. He's either pretending not to notice or isn't bothered, but then Harpa told me her dad is well aware that she drinks. He even buys her alcohol sometimes.

I suppose there's nothing odd about that. Harpa's nearly eighteen and most people her age have started drinking.

The vodka I drank with Harpa seems to be wearing off, at least I can hardly feel it now. On the way to my room earlier I thought I could feel something, but now I wonder if I imagined it. Perhaps the dizziness was just caused by excitement.

Now they're playing some Icelandic golden oldie, and lots of people are dancing. Dad's disappeared, I can't see him anywhere, and Mum's standing at the bar with Hákon.

'Who are you thinking about?'

Harpa has come over. She's holding a glass and orders me to try it, so I know it must have alcohol in it. I take a tiny sip to please her, because I'm always trying to please people. The moment this occurs to me, I realise it's true. For the past few years I've been constantly trying to please everybody. I want to do well at school to make the teachers happy and I always try to do everything my friends want me to; say whatever they want to hear: that they're hot, that their clothes are great or that some guy is definitely into them.

How long is it since I did something purely for me? Seriously, when was the last time I did something just to please myself?

'No one,' I reply.

'Birgir?'

'Yeah,' I say.

'You know,' Harpa pushes the glass back towards me, 'I reckon you should look at it like this: if he's interested, he'll send you a message. If not, so what? There are a trillion other guys out there, you know? So why get hung up on one?'

'Yeah, maybe.' I want to say that perhaps she's right, but that none of them are like Birgir. Most of the boys I know are selfish and immature.

Sölvi, the last boy I was seeing, invited me round to his place, and while we were sitting watching a film, he put his sweaty hand on my thigh. Every time he moved, his hand crept a little higher. It felt like a slimy snake crawling on me, and in the end I got up before the film ended and went home.

'Let's dance,' Harpa says, seizing hold of my arm.

I try to resist but she's determined.

It's different from the parties I've been to before. They're playing nothing but old Icelandic hits, and I feel like I'm in some alternative reality where I'm watching my family and distant relatives dancing around me. It's so weird seeing Granny and Granddad dancing together.

Harpa and I jump around like idiots, making faces at each other and singing along to songs we hardly know. She passes me a glass containing alcohol and some kind of mixer, and I wonder where she got it.

Then suddenly someone grabs me from behind, one hand gripping my waist, the other my arm, and spins me round. I laugh, expecting to come face to face with Dad, but shrink away when I see that it's Hákon Ingimar standing in front of me.

He doesn't say anything, just smiles and twirls me away from him, then back again. I smell his strong, heavy smell, and close my eyes, thinking I'm going to faint. My knees are trembling.

'What, aren't you pleased to see me?' he whispers in my ear.

I swallow and open my mouth, but I can feel my throat tightening and no words will come out. Then I realise it's not words that are about to gush out of me.

My stomach churns and, tearing myself free, I start running and don't stop until I'm in the toilets.

Petra Snæberg

'I think it's time to call it a day, Petra,' Gestur murmurs in my ear. I've got two shot glasses on the table in front of me.

He grips my upper arm, but I jerk it away.

'Are you taking the piss, Gestur?' He's behaving like I'm wasted when I'm not. Or no more than he is.

'You need go to bed now,' Gestur says levelly.

'Fine,' I say. 'Great.' I flounce off. Something falls over behind me but I don't look round. I don't want to see the disapproving expressions on Gestur's and Mum's faces.

But I don't go upstairs. Instead, I go into the bar and take one of the seats by the fire, which is still burning merrily, and sit there, gazing into the flames. I feel suddenly tired; the world is spinning, the ground is moving up and down underneath me, and all I want is for it to stop. On reflection, perhaps I am a bit drunker than I thought.

'Can I bring you something?' asks the waitress with the funny name, who always seems to be hovering within reach. The perfect member of staff, I think to myself; invisible but ever present.

'Whisky,' I say. 'No ice.'

It's not until she returns with the drink that I notice Maja is sitting there too, towards the back of the room. She's staring into space, lost in her own thoughts, but then she seems to sense that I'm looking at her.

'Oh, hi,' she says, when our eyes met. 'I didn't see you.'

'No,' I say, with a short laugh.

Maja hesitates, then gets up and comes over to join me. I take the drink from the waitress, who starts wiping the tables around us. They must be wanting to close the bar soon, but the party's still going strong in the restaurant, with Icelandic music blasting out at full volume.

'I was feeling a bit tired in there,' Maja says.

'Me too.' I yawn. 'I was thinking of going up to bed soon.'

'Mm.' Maja lowers her eyes and picks at her cuticles.

As we sit there, I realise that she's probably younger than I originally thought.

'How old are you, Maja?' I ask.

'Twenty-two,' she says, almost shyly.

I have to stop my jaw from dropping. Twenty-two! She's no more than a child. What must her parents think about her being involved with a man thirteen years older?

But then I remember that at twenty-two I was in a relationship with Gestur, who was nearly ten years older than me, and I'd already had Lea.

'And where are you from?' I'm aware of my maturity all of a sudden. Maja's closer in age to my daughter than to me.

'Innri-Njarðvík,' Maja says, referring to a town down south on the Reykjanes peninsula, close to Keflavík Airport. 'I've always lived there. Well, until I moved in with Viktor a few months ago. But you know, my parents are still there and my room and everything, so I've sort of got one foot there and one foot in Reykjavík.'

'I didn't know you two were living together.'

'No.' Maja gazes into the fire and takes a deep breath. 'No, I ... it just happened.'

'What do you do?' I sound as if I'm interrogating the poor kid.

'At the moment I'm at uni, studying to be a social worker,' Maja says. 'I want to apply to work for children's services or something like that. Or maybe at a juvenile treatment centre.'

'Wow,' I say. 'I've always admired people who do jobs like that. It must be incredibly tough.'

Maja's face brightens. 'Yes. Tough but rewarding. I ... I've got a little sister who Mum and Dad fostered, then later adopted. Since then I've always wanted to help children in her situation.'

I nod, sensing that Maja's got something else on her chest but doesn't know how to say it.

'Lóa, my little sister, she ... she was five when she came to us and ... she had all these marks on her arms. Bruises and...' Maja closes her eyes briefly. 'Anyway, you should see her now. She's ten and she's a completely different kid from when she first came to live with us.'

'It's so great that you could give her a better home.' Ridiculously, I feel myself choking up.

'Yes.' Maja smiles. 'Anyway, that's what I want to do in the future.'

'Do you have much time left at university?'

'No, but...' Maja sighs. 'But I'm probably going to have to take a bit of a break.'

'Oh?'

Maja glances round, then leans forwards and whispers: 'I'm pregnant.'

'Seriously?' My heart turns over. 'Does Viktor know?'

'No, not yet,' Maja says. 'I don't know how to break it to him. It wasn't planned or anything, and so far I've only told Líf, my other sister.'

'He's sure to be pleased,' I say, thinking about Elín, Viktor's mother, who's always complaining about her lack of grandchildren. After all, Harpa's only her step-granddaughter and she doesn't get to see her that often. So Elín will be happy. But what about Viktor? Will he welcome the news?

'Yes. Yes, sure.' Maja looks doubtful. As if by instinct, she runs a hand over her stomach, then gets to her feet. 'Well, best get to bed.'

'Good night,' I say.

'Um...' Maja hovers in front of me. 'I wanted to ask you something about Viktor.'

'Yes?'

'Do you think ... Has he ever...?' Maja looks down, looping her wrist with the fingers of her other hand. 'No, it doesn't matter.'

'Are you sure?' I ask.

Maja wavers. 'Could I maybe talk to you tomorrow?'

'Of course,' I say.

'OK.' Maja smiles. 'Good night, then.'

I watch until she's disappeared round the corner before I open my bag. In it, I find a sleeping pill, which I swallow, washing it down with what's left of my drink.

Now
Sunday, 5 November 2017

Sævar
Detective, West Iceland CID

Sævar was looking out of the window of the coffee room, trying to concentrate on the rugged black lava, the grey-green moss and the raven that was turning circle after circle in the air. Anything to avoid having to think about the face of the grieving man. It had been hard enough looking at the body earlier, but that was nothing compared to watching someone's world collapsing. Sævar knew that the moment the man's expression had changed as he took in what had happened would be etched on his memory for a long time to come.

'How was the weekend going?' Hörður asked.

'Extremely well,' Edda said. 'They all partied into the early hours both nights and I don't believe the last ones went to bed until four. Of course, the bar had been closed for hours by then, but we allowed them to go on sitting in there, as there were no other guests staying at the hotel for them to disturb. Since they've got the place completely to themselves, I didn't feel I could interfere.'

'I see,' Hörður said.

'What was the atmosphere like yesterday evening?' Sævar asked. When he was a kid, family reunions had involved camping and barbecuing in the great outdoors. He remembered people clad in traditional *lopapeysur* jumpers passing round a hipflask. He'd been allowed to stay up late and had watched, fascinated, as all the happy grown-ups sang and played the guitar by the bonfire into the early hours. The entertainments here had no doubt been rather more sophisticated, he reflected. At an exclusive hotel like this, they'd hardly be passing round hipflasks and necking straight from the bottle. No doubt they'd toasted with champagne, dressed in evening gowns and suits.

'The atmosphere was good,' Edda said.

'Much drinking?' Sævar asked.

'Yes, certainly. As you'd expect at a gathering like this.' Edda shifted in her seat, which made Sævar wonder if there was a bond of confidentiality between hotel staff and guests, perhaps similar to that between doctors and patients. But while he doubted that the same laws applied to hotels, it was clear that Edda found it uncomfortable to discuss her guests.

'Actually...' she said. 'Actually there was heavy drinking all weekend.'

'Is that so?' Hörður said.

Edda clutched her necklace again and rubbed it between her fingers. 'Yes, I suppose it shouldn't have come as a surprise, but I hadn't anticipated that it would be quite on that scale. They've almost drunk our cellar dry, and that's never happened before.'

'Were there any incidents during the weekend?'

'What sort of incidents do you mean?'

'Rows,' Hörður said. 'Tensions or confrontations.'

'No, I don't remember anything like that, or not as such. At least, not until ... until what happened last night.' Edda let go of her necklace and clasped her hands on the table in front of her. 'Well ... come to think of it, there was a bit of a situation yesterday. A girl turned up here searching for her sister. She seemed sick with worry about her; she'd rung earlier in the day. Her name was Maja – the girl she was searching for, I mean.'

'María Sif?'

'That's right,' Edda said.

Sævar and Hörður exchanged glances. They were both familiar with the name.

Two Days Earlier
Friday, 3 November 2017

Tryggvi

Haraldur places two drinks on the table and slaps me on the back.

'Men like you,' he says, 'are undervalued in our society. I've always admired people who can work with their hands. Create things.'

I nod and mumble something. When blokes start talking like this, it's best to make an excuse and go to bed.

'You were married, weren't you?' Haraldur continues.

'Yes. For fifteen years.'

'Well, well. No children, though?'

'She already had a child.'

'But you didn't have any together?'

'No.' Nanna and I did try, but it never worked. We went for all kinds of tests, but the doctors couldn't find anything wrong. Everything was in perfect working order, they said. But despite that nothing happened.

'That's OK,' Haraldur says. 'It's OK not to get involved in all that if you don't want to. Being childless has its advantages, I expect.'

I could tell him that it wasn't like that at all. That I've never regarded myself as childless. Because Nanna and I did have a child. But for some reason I don't feel like explaining this to him.

'Ester always wanted more kids,' Haraldur says. People are still chatting around us, but someone's turned the music down. Probably the hotel staff trying to bring the evening to a close. 'I said no. Two are more than enough.'

'We have to be thankful for what we've got.'

'Yeah, yeah.' Haraldur shrugs. 'Ester didn't agree. She was pissed off when I had the snip – you know, told the doctor to get the scissors out.'

'Oh, I see.'

'Yes.' Haraldur leans closer. 'I didn't think the marriage would last, the old lady was so spitting mad.'

'But it worked out in the end.'

'Eh?' Haraldur sits back again. He seems lost in his own world, staring at the wall behind me. 'Yes, I made some bloody stupid decisions back in the day. But that's life: you can't always do the intelligent thing.'

'No,' I say, conscious that I have nothing to add. But then I don't think Haraldur has the slightest interest in hearing my opinion anyway.

'Yes,' he goes on. Then he chuckles quietly and takes another slurp of his drink. 'I slipped up.'

'Oh, in what way?'

'Well, just between ourselves, maybe I didn't always have my eye on the consequences. There was a hell of a lot of pressure on me at the time, and Ester was permanently pissed off and...' Haraldur strokes his chin and grimaces slightly.

I watch him, wondering what he's trying to say.

'Still, nothing that money couldn't smooth over,' Haraldur adds, taking another generous slurp from his glass.

Before I can respond, Oddný suddenly appears beside me. 'So, Tryggvi,' she says, 'time for bed.'

I don't wait to be told twice, and we say goodnight to the people who are still lingering downstairs.

Oddný goes out like a light the moment her head touches the

pillow, and starts snoring gently. Whereas I sit there for a while, staring into the blackness outside. The conversation with Haraldur has raked up old memories. Of Nanna and our life together. I rarely think about what things could have been like, but now I let my mind wander.

A scream shocks me out of my thoughts.

Jumping to my feet, I glance around. Where did it come from?

The world outside the window is pitch-black, but I'm pretty sure the noise didn't come from out there. It was someone inside the hotel who screamed. I strain my ears, then move slowly over to the door, hardly daring to breathe, but I can't hear anything. I'm starting to wonder if I imagined it, if it was the old scream that sometimes wakes me with a jolt in the middle of the night, but then I hear it again, fainter this time but still unmistakable.

A scream that seems to stem not from terror but from rage.

Petra Snæberg

After swallowing the pill, I take my bag and get to my feet. The floor seems to be moving in waves, and I collide with a chair, almost losing my balance, but luckily I manage to save myself. I don't look round to check if anyone saw.

'Ari,' I say, spotting my son sitting on the sofa in reception, absorbed in his phone. 'Shouldn't you be going to bed soon? It's so late.'

'Yeah, I'll go in a minute.'

'Good boy.' Leaning down unsteadily, I kiss him on the top of his head.

Upstairs I pull out my phone and let myself into our room with the app.

I'm met by such an icy blast of air that I gasp. I grope frantically along the wall, searching for a light switch, then remember that the lights are controlled via the app as well. Clever as the idea seemed at first, I'm now starting to curse it.

When I finally succeed in turning on the lights, I see that the window is wide open and the curtains are flapping wildly. A small puddle has formed on the floor. Hastily, I close the window and fetch a towel to throw over the water.

The weather has grown worse. The wind is howling and rain is lashing against the glass as if it's trying to break in.

I undress, throw my clothes on the chair and brush my teeth with record speed. Then, deciding I feel dirty, I turn on the shower, mentally counting, as I do so, the minutes since I took the sleeping pill. If I'm quick in the shower I should be in bed by the time it starts to take effect.

The jet of water is powerful and hot, but I turn it up even hotter, feeling my skin warming up as the evening is flushed down the drain: the look in Mum's eyes, Steffy's smile, the disappointment on Gestur's face. I immediately feel a little better.

Then I hear a noise over the drumming of the water, like the door of the room banging. Gestur must have come up.

I turn off the tap and wring out my hair. As I step out of the shower, I'm hit by a wave of dizziness, and I have to crouch down for a few moments to recover. No doubt it's the combination of the hot water, all that booze and the sleeping pill on top. I listen, still crouching there, but can't hear what Gestur's up to. I picture him sitting on the bed, waiting. Perhaps he wants to talk to me about my behaviour. About the state I'm in.

It's normally Gestur who wants to talk about our relationship; he always wants to discuss everything in depth, to know how I'm feeling and why. He's convinced that talking helps, but he doesn't understand that it only makes everything worse. Our conversations put me in a position where I'm forced to lie, widening the gap between us with every word.

I turn on the cold tap and have a drink. When I wipe the condensation from the mirror, I get a shock at the sight of myself. The mascara has run down my cheeks in the shower, making me look like a character in a horror film. Once I've washed my face, I look a bit better, but not much. I'm still glassy eyed and can feel the effects of the sleeping pill growing stronger by the minute. I have to get to bed, quickly.

The room is dark, and when I say Gestur's name, there's no answer.

He's not here. The lights seem to have gone out of their own accord and I fumble my way to the bed, where I know my phone's lying.

'Gestur,' I say again, almost in a whisper. Although I know I'm alone in the room, it feels as if there's another presence in here. Suddenly, I'm convinced someone is watching me in the darkness.

I definitely heard the door banging a few minutes ago, didn't I? Or did I imagine the sound?

I grope on the bed until I find my phone, then open the app and switch on the lights. When I look around, everything's just as it was before I got in the shower. Nothing's been moved, the window is still closed and the curtains hang perfectly still.

I crawl under the duvet before turning the lights off again. Immediately, drowsiness begins to steal over me and my mind sinks towards sleep.

Just before the welcome oblivion takes hold, the lights come on again. The ceiling light illuminates the whole room with such a blinding whiteness that I can barely open my eyes. There must be a bug in the system.

Sitting up quickly, I grab my phone and switch off the lights again. The darkness seems even blacker than before. There are no streetlights outside the window here to cast their glow into the room. I close my eyes, but my drowsiness has receded. My body is on the alert, my heart beating faster than normal.

Next moment, the room is bathed in light again. I grimace, shielding my eyes with one hand.

'You must be joking,' I say aloud.

Yet again, I turn off the lights via the app but this time they come on again immediately. They flash on, then off, three times in succession as I watch helplessly, not knowing whether to scream or cry. What the hell is going on? Tomorrow morning I'm going straight down to reception to complain. What's the point of having such a hi-tech hotel if nothing works properly?

Next minute there's a loud bang from the bedside lamp, following by a fizzling sound, then everything goes black. For a few seconds I watch as the glow in the light bulb fades into invisibility. Although I want the room to be dark while I'm sleeping, I pick up my phone and try to turn the lights on again. Nothing works.

The prospect of being trapped in blind darkness fills me with unease, yet in spite of that my thoughts are ebbing away, I can't keep hold of them, and my eyelids are growing increasingly heavy. I struggle against my drowsiness for a little while longer, trying to pin down my thoughts, but they seem to dissolve into nothing. Finally, I sink into a deep, dreamless sleep.

❁

When I wake up again, it's still night but the room is brightly lit. Blindingly bright, the ceiling light shining in my eyes. I have no idea how much time has passed or how long I've been asleep. Gestur's not beside me; I'm alone in bed.

Outside, the rain has stopped, and the wind seems to have died down as well. There's silence in the room, but suddenly I hear a rustle, followed by a quiet metallic click.

The door.

'Gestur?' I whisper.

I try to sit up, squinting against the glare, but my body won't obey. So I lie there deathly still and hear the noise again, as if it's right by my ear. My heart pounding, I force myself to move my fingers. After another moment or two I manage to slide my legs out from under the duvet and get to my feet. I start walking towards the door, intending to open it and let Gestur in. Or perhaps I want to get out.

Then I see the door and stop dead. Every nerve in my body is taut and I can hear my breath coming fast and shallow.

The door to the corridor is standing slightly ajar.

Lea Snæberg

I feel awful, my head is splitting and I can hardly stand up.

Harpa calls after me as I leave, but I pretend not to hear her. In the loo, I grip the sides of the basin, noticing, as I do, that I look like a car crash. Terrible. My eyes are huge and swimming, my face chalk white.

But in spite of everything, none of the adults have said a word. Not one of them has noticed how drunk I am.

Suddenly, I can't hold back any longer. I only just manage to bend over the basin before the contents of my stomach come gushing out with such force that they splash the surrounding tiles. I can hear noises too, horrible, rattling noises, then I realise it's me. They're coming from me.

Afterwards I stand there for a long time, hunched over, retching.

Eventually, I move to the other basin and wash my face, splashing it with cold water, then dry it with a paper towel. When I've finished, I peer out of the door and, seeing no one nearby, hurry as fast as I can to my room. As I'm using the phone app to open the door, I hear my grandmother's voice approaching and my heart goes into overdrive.

I tiptoe inside and close the door softly behind me, only to discover that I'm alone. Ari's still downstairs.

I take my time in the bathroom, brushing my teeth and washing my face again. Noticing some vomit in my hair, I rinse it off, but the smell won't go away. Still, I'm too tired to worry about it.

When I lie down in bed, the world starts spinning.

I take out my phone and have to blink several times before I can focus on the message from Birgir.

How's the hotel? As cool as in the pictures?

He sent the message more than an hour ago, but I answer anyway, taking care over my spelling. I tell him the hotel's awesome, that everything's great.

I wait a little while for an answer but nothing happens. He's probably gone to sleep. Sweden's an hour ahead of Iceland, so it's very late over there.

I scroll through the photos of him. He hasn't sent me many and they don't show much, just his face as he sits in front of the computer screen.

Birgir isn't really into social media apart from Instagram, and he hardly ever posts any pictures on his page. There are a few from his home town in Sweden, though. The house he lives in is yellow, with a reddish-brown roof and white window frames. Very Swedish. One of the photos is of his dog, Captain. He's a Labrador Border Collie cross, with a black-and-white coat. Birgir loves his dog more than almost anything else in the world.

Perhaps it's because I'm an only child, he told me once. *Captain's the closest thing I have to a brother or sister.*

I often get the feeling Birgir's lonely, which is strange because he's so good-looking and has loads of friends. But I should know better than most how you can be alone even when you're surrounded by people.

Birgir says he sometimes sits in a café and watches the passers-by, making up stories about them, trying to guess what they do for a living and where they're going.

I stare at his name on the screen, wishing he was here with me. The connection I feel between us is unlike anything else. It's real and deep, and I long to show him how serious I am about him.

I scroll up and read our conversation from earlier today, and my eye catches on something he said: *Send me a photo*. Then, when I asked what kind of photo, he'd said a selfie, followed by that dot, dot, dot.

Smiling to myself, I hold up my phone. My selfie is a bit out of focus and the flash is so bright that I look totally washed out, like a ghost.

I switch on the bedside light and try again. Take several pictures of myself smiling, then some other ones; ones that show rather more. Pictures I'm hoping will make him want to jump on the next plane to Iceland.

Irma
Hotel Employee

My back is aching with tiredness, the pains shooting right down to my toes. I can't wait to crawl into bed once my shift is over.

Most of the guests have gone back to their rooms, and silence has fallen over the hotel. I always enjoy walking around the place late at night or early in the morning, when all is quiet.

The evening turned out to be livelier than I'd expected. I'd thought a family like this would be better at handling their drink, a bit more sedate. But of course they've got the hotel to themselves, there's no one here to spy on them and leak the story to the press, so I suppose they've allowed themselves to let their hair down and be less careful about what they say and do.

'Someone's been sick in the ladies. Could you by any chance...?' Edda looks apologetic as she knows cleaning isn't, strictly speaking, one of my duties, but since arriving here I've had various things dumped on me that weren't in my original job description. What can I say? I'm an incurable people-pleaser.

'Of course,' I reply. 'I'll sort it out before I go to bed.'

'It was quite an evening,' Edda says, massaging the back of her neck.

'They certainly had a good time,' I agree.

'Yes, didn't they?' Edda smiles. 'I reckon they were all pretty satisfied.'

'I think so too.'

Edda inclines her head slightly, then says goodnight. I hear the front door open, the noise of the wind outside, then the sound of Edda carefully closing it again. She's such a nice woman and this hotel is her passion. She pulls out all the stops for her guests and radiates pleasure when they're satisfied. I've never understood how she ended up with a man like Gísli, whose anger and disappointment seem permanently etched on his features. I suppose he's never got over how his daughter, Elísa's mother, died.

When I check the ladies, I see that most of the vomit is in the basin. Who can have been drunk enough to throw up in there? Could it have been Lea? It was obvious to me that she'd been drinking, though I doubt her parents noticed anything amiss.

Lea is a sensitive soul, but I don't think her parents realise how fragile she is. I can see it, though. I can see it from a mile off.

Ever since I was a child, I've been one of life's observers, rather than a participator. Because we were always moving house, I got used to never having a chance to get close to people. In the end, I gave up trying to make friends, as there was no point clinging on to friendships that were forever being cut short. Every time I joined a new class at school, I would watch the other kids, trying to guess what kind of lives they led. I used to keep a diary where I wrote down their names and my first impressions of them.

Anna – rarely smiles, reads books and loves animals. An only child.

Thór – hates losing, good at sport but bad at lessons. Has older brothers and parents who fight a lot.

Then I would observe them and, when it was time to leave the school, I would compare my first impressions with what I'd subsequently learnt to be true. By my final years at school I'd got so good at this game that there would be very few details that turned out not to match the reality.

'Hey.' Hákon Ingimar is standing in the doorway of the ladies. His voice is husky, and he's squinting as if he's having trouble keeping his eyes open.

'Hi,' I say, pulling off my rubber gloves.

I wait for Hákon to say something else, but he doesn't, he just stands there, leaning against the door frame and squinting at me with a slight smile on his face. An unsettling smile.

Suddenly I'm aware of how confined the space is. None of the other guests are still up, as far as I know, and the rest of the staff have gone home. We're alone here, Hákon and me.

The blood is pumping through my veins, my pulse is racing, but I try not to show it.

'Right, best get to bed,' I say in a deliberately normal voice, picking up the bucket of cleaning fluids.

But Hákon doesn't budge, he's still blocking the doorway.

'Is there something I can help you with?' I ask, forcing my lips into a smile.

Hákon laughs and bites at his lower lip. His eyes are black, the pupils so dilated that you can't tell what colour his irises are. He reminds me of a wild animal.

Outside, the wind wallops the windows in the corridor, making me jump, and the roaring of the storm redoubles its volume, until the rain sounds like someone hurling gravel at the glass.

Hákon seizes his chance to make a move. It happens so fast; one minute he's standing in the doorway, the next he's right in front of me. I drop the bucket and it crashes onto its side, but the rain is so loud that it even manages to drown out the sound of it hitting the concrete floor.

Then his hands are tearing at my body.

'What are you doing?' I cry, but my voice is muffled, as if it's coming from a great distance.

I don't try to scream because I know it won't do any good. And in the end I stop struggling.

The Day Before
Saturday, 4 November 2017

Petra Snæberg

I wake up to find one of Gestur's legs draped over mine, cutting off the circulation. For a moment I study his face, which is half buried in the pillow, his cheek squashed, his lips slightly parted. Adults are not beautiful when they sleep; only children enjoy that privilege.

I ease my leg from under Gestur's, warily, so as not to wake him, then wriggle my toes, feeling the painful tingling as the blood flows back into them. My head is in a surprisingly good state, considering how much I drank last night, but I have a raging thirst.

As I drain a bottle of water from the minibar, I look out of the window. The sun is rising, the wind has dropped and there's a thin layer of snow on the ground.

In the daylight, the events of last night seem remote, yet I shudder when the image of the open door comes back to me. I try to recall what happened yesterday evening, struggling to put my memories into some kind of order, but they're so hazy that it's difficult. The sleeping pill has left me feeling groggy, unable to think straight. But I do remember hearing the door banging while I was in the shower. Had I checked that it was locked when I came in?

Impossible to remember. Then there was the hassle with the

lights, but I think I dropped off shortly after that. I'm pretty sure I did.

But can it be right that I woke up in the middle of the night, unable to move? That rattling of the door handle, as if someone was fiddling with it, had seemed so close to my ear that it can't possibly have been real. Yet my recollection of that is clearer than the rest. And I remember too that when I eventually managed to get up, drugged with sleep, the door to the corridor was open.

Had it been open the whole time? While I was in the shower, while I was sleeping? Unsettling though this idea is, it's the only logical explanation. It can't have closed properly when I came up to our room. That would explain the sound I heard while I was in the shower – the wind banging the door.

As I pull on my running gear and shoes, I tell myself that there's no reason to feel spooked. The only people here are my family; there's nothing to be afraid of. I doubt I need to worry about the hotel staff, though the memory of the man I encountered in the corridor yesterday gives me pause. But I've subsequently learnt that he's Edda's husband, so presumably he's quite harmless, in spite of his appearance.

There's a delicious smell of bacon and waffles wafting up from the kitchen downstairs, but I walk straight past the restaurant and out of the front door. The instant I fill my lungs with fresh, crisp air, the fog in my head clears and the last remnants of sleep are blown away. I survey my surroundings, wondering which way to go, but all I can see is the lava field, so that doesn't leave me with much choice. I decide to run along the drive towards the main road.

There's not a single car in sight, and I run fast, feeling the wind in my ears and hearing the slapping of my footsteps on the wet tarmac. The further I get from the hotel, the better I feel, and I experience an urge to keep going forever.

A car comes up behind me and slows down. I slow down too and move to the edge of the road, but the moment I step on the loose gravel, my foot skids and over I go, just managing to break my fall with my hands. The sharp stones bite into my palms and my knee scrapes along the ground.

Shit. I grimace with pain. The car slows down even more, and for a second I see the face of the driver watching me in the rear-view mirror. Then he accelerates and is gone.

I'm left sitting there, picking grit out of my wounds. My knee is stinging and I can feel something wet collecting in the hollow behind it, but there's no point pulling up my trouser leg here. Instead, I start to limp back in the direction of the hotel, all the energy from my run dissipated.

When I enter reception, there's a hum of conversation and clinking of cutlery coming from the restaurant. My stomach rumbles, but I decide to take a shower first. On my way to the stairs, the manager, Edda, calls out to me.

'I'm sorry, could you help me a moment?' she asks, quickly coming over. She's holding a sheet of paper, and I notice that she has unusually long, thin fingers.

'Sure,' I say, trying to straighten up and hide my grazed palms.

'I've just had a young woman called Líf on the phone. She was asking to speak to Maja.' Edda smiles apologetically. 'I'm afraid I can't remember who Maja is, and I can't find her name on the guest list, so I was hoping you could tell me.'

'Of course, she's in the room that'll be under Viktor's name,' I say. 'Viktor Ingvarsson.'

'Viktor Ingvarsson. Right, thank you.' Edda opens her mouth again, as if to say something else, then changes her mind.

'If you like, I can pass on the message,' I say, and immediately realise that this was what she had been hoping.

'That would be great,' Edda says. 'It sounds urgent, but apparently Maja's not answering her phone.'

'I'll let her know.'

'Thank you,' Edda says, and gives me Viktor's room number.

I try to brush the dirt off my tracksuit bottoms and tidy my pony-tail. Perhaps this would be a good moment to have that chat with Maja. There was something she wanted to discuss yesterday, and I'm curious to know what it is. And I want to find out if she's told Viktor she's pregnant and how he reacted.

Viktor and Maja are in a ground-floor room, like Lea and Ari. I listen at the kids' door, wondering if I should wake them, but decide to leave it. They're sure to think I've no right to disturb them this early on a Saturday morning.

Viktor's room is number twelve. I stand outside the door for a moment, dithering about what to do. They might still be asleep. But the message is urgent, according to Edda, so I ought to let Maja know. Bracing myself, I tap cautiously on the door. Too cautiously, probably, because no one opens up and there's no sound inside. I knock again, louder this time, and the door opens.

Viktor is standing before me, dressed and recently emerged from the shower, judging by the smell of soap.

'Good morning,' he says, studying me. 'Some people are up bright and early.'

'Yes, I prefer running in the morning. Sorry to knock so early,' I say.

'Is there a gym at the hotel?'

'No, I went out,' I say. 'Actually, it was Maja I wanted to speak to. Is she here?'

'Maja?' Viktor asks, his brow furrowing.

'There was a phone call,' I say hurriedly. 'Someone was trying to get hold of her.'

'I see.' Viktor's expression turns grave. 'Er, Maja had to go home.'

'Did she?'

'Yes, some family issue. Nothing serious, but she wanted to go home anyway. She left last night.'

'Oh. I see.'

'Was there anything else?' Viktor asks.

'No, I just wanted to let Maja know that ... that Líf was trying to get hold of her.'

'Ah, right. Líf's her sister.'

'But...' I hesitate. 'Doesn't she have a phone? Do you think something could have happened to her on her way home?'

'No, I'm sure it hasn't,' Viktor says. 'The signal can be a bit dodgy on the way. She'll turn up.'

'Right.' As far as I can remember, my phone had a signal all the way here. If the connection had dropped out, I'd have heard complaints from the kids. But I don't say anything, just smile. 'Maybe you could pass on the message when you talk to her.'

'Will do.'

'Anyway, I'd better jump in the shower.'

'You do that.' Viktor smiles. 'See you shortly. The cruise should be great in this weather.'

Hearing Viktor close the door behind me, I turn and look back at it.

If Maja set off last night, she should be back by now, with her family, so I'm a bit puzzled by Viktor's lack of concern. Is it possible that they've had a row? Could he have taken Maja's news so badly that he couldn't care less whether she got home all right?

I climb the stairs, Maja's face vivid in my mind's eye. Her expression when she told me she was pregnant, the way she stroked her belly and the corner of her mouth twitched in a smile, the picture of happiness.

Sævar
Detective, West Iceland CID

'Remind me, what details were we given about the girl's disappearance?' Hörður asked, once they were alone. Edda had gone to fetch them some coffee.

Sævar cast his mind back to the phone call he'd received the previous day. Maja's sister had initially rung the local police in southwest Iceland, where she lived, explaining that María had gone with her boyfriend to a hotel on Snæfellsnes for the weekend. As the hotel was in the region covered by the West Iceland CID, the sister's call had been forwarded to Sævar.

She had introduced herself as Líf and told him she'd last spoken to Maja on Friday evening. At the time, Maja had been a little nervous because she was intending to break it to her boyfriend that she was pregnant.

'I haven't heard from her since,' Líf had told him.

'Is that unusual?' Sævar had asked. He'd been scrolling through the online menu for a nearby restaurant at the time, wondering whether to buy a burger or go for something a bit healthier.

Líf had said yes it was, adding that Maja always kept her phone switched on.

'Could she have forgotten her charger?'

'No, it's nothing like that,' Líf had replied, her exasperation breaking through. 'I rang the hotel and her boyfriend said Maja had left during the night due to a family issue.'

'Oh?'

'Except none of us had been in touch with Maja. It's obvious that something's happened.' Líf had sniffed at this point, and Sævar could hear from the wobble in her voice that she was close to bursting into tears.

He had closed the online menu and got to his feet. 'What makes you think that?'

'Maja's pregnant. She was planning to tell her boyfriend yesterday evening and she was very stressed about it,' Líf had repeated. 'And now she's vanished. Apparently, she left the hotel in the middle of the night, though she doesn't have a car, and her phone's switched off. Something must have happened to her. She didn't go home because of some family problem, like her boyfriend claimed. None of us have heard from her.'

That had caught Sævar's attention. Could the young woman have had a fight with her boyfriend after telling him her news? Had he thrown her out in the middle of the night?

Having promised to look into it, Sævar had rung off. Then he'd got straight on to Snæfellsnes police and asked them to take a drive around the hotel and see if they could spot Maja anywhere. But none of the officers had come across any signs of her.

The Day Before
Saturday, 4 November 2017

Tryggvi

Oddný's getting ready when I wake up.

'Hi, love,' she says. 'How did you sleep?'

'Fine,' I say, though I hardly got a wink until late. Just lay there, not moving a muscle, straining my ears to hear if there were any more strange noises.

After I'd heard the scream, I went out into the corridor and stood there for a while, as if there was something I should do, though I didn't know what. The scream hadn't been a normal cry, the kind someone would make if they bashed their toe, for example. No, it was a very different kind of sound: a scream of rage.

Oddný tilts her head on one side as she puts on her earrings. She's always so smart when we go out, wearing a blouse, jewellery and lipstick. My ex was quite different. I can't remember Nanna ever bothering with make-up or high heels. She wasn't that kind of woman. Not that I'm comparing them, I've tried to avoid doing that, but it's hard to stop the odd detail coming to mind. Small things that you'd think I'd have forgotten.

Although it's many years since Nanna and I parted ways, Oddný's my first relationship since her. By the time I met Oddný, I'd got used to being alone. In fact, I thought that's how it would be for the rest of my life.

'Did you hear anything in the night?' I ask.

'When?' Oddný picks up a jumper, considers it, then chooses another.

'I heard something just before I fell asleep, like a scream.'

When I see Oddný's face, I wish I hadn't mentioned it.

'A scream?' She comes over and sits on the edge of the bed. 'Weren't you just dreaming?'

'No, I don't think I was. But it was probably nothing.'

I pull on my jeans and dig out a T-shirt. Something in Oddný's tone sets my teeth on edge. Because the fact is I do suffer from nightmares, as she's well aware; I start awake, drenched in sweat. Oddný always tries to pry out of me what I've been dreaming about, but I don't want to tell her.

'You know dreams can be premonitions,' Oddný says. 'Sometimes it's the dead, trying to get messages to us. Apparently we're particularly receptive in the moment between sleep and waking. That's when they visit us.'

'Don't...' I close my eyes and turn my head away.

'I'm just saying...'

'Yes, but don't. Not now.' I get up and go into the bathroom, where I sit down on the toilet seat, trying to calm my breathing.

I know the scream I heard was no dream and I know too that the dead don't visit us any more often between sleep and waking than they do at other times. If there is an afterlife, I just hope for all our sakes that it's nothing like the world we live in now.

As for the nightmares, they've become less severe since I stopped drinking. I no longer hear the cries as I'm drifting off. No longer feel someone pulling at me, begging me for help.

Lea Snæberg

When I wake up, the first thing I see is my phone. There are several notifications on the screen, but none are from Birgir. He hasn't replied, hasn't said anything about the pictures I sent him last night. I'm mortified when I see them in our chat.

What was I thinking?

I put down my phone with a knot in my stomach. My mouth is so parched, I feel like I could gulp down a gallon of water. Little by little, the events of last night come back to me. Harpa and me on the dance floor, leaping around like idiots. Sneaking into the ladies to take swigs from the bottle she was hiding in her bag. Throwing up in the basin of the ladies at the end of the evening. I try to remember if anyone noticed. It would be unbelievable if they hadn't. If no one noticed the state me and Harpa were in, it must mean that my whole family was as drunk or even drunker than us.

Beside me, Ari's getting dressed.

'I'm going to go and get something to eat,' he says.

'OK,' I say. 'I'll be along in a minute.'

'I'd take a shower first if I was you.' Ari wrinkles his nose. 'And chew some gum.'

I make a face and sigh. 'Ari?'

'Yes.'

'Don't say anything to Mum.'

Ari laughs. 'No, I won't. Don't worry. But you know, if you don't take a shower, I won't have to say anything.'

When I get up, my stomach's so empty that it constricts. I open the little fridge, take out a bottle of water, drain half of it in one go and immediately feel better. The water trickles down into my stomach, so cold that I can feel its icy progress.

Then my phone vibrates and I jump, almost dropping the bottle as I grab it to answer.

The relief that surges through my body is so great that I can't help smiling. Of course, I think, of course Birgir's got in touch. I'm both excited and stressed about what he's going to say about the photos. My hands are trembling as I unlock the phone. But the message isn't from Birgir; it's from a name I don't recognise. The disappointment's so acute that it's like a punch to the stomach.

Where is Birgir and why hasn't he replied?

I peer at the name, which is a meaningless jumble of letters and numbers, as if a small child had got at the keyboard. But when I open the message, it's as if the ice-cold water from the bottle has found its way into my veins and is spreading through my whole body.

Hi, Lea. Something must have gone wrong because I couldn't send you any messages from my old account. But it's all right, I set up a new one and now I've found you again. Beautiful new selfie. Best, Gulli.

Petra Snæberg

I'm still so preoccupied with thinking about Maja when Gestur and I go down to breakfast that I'm momentarily thrown when he holds out a hand to me. He smiles, and I wonder if he's apologising, asking my forgiveness for something. I still haven't asked him where he was or what he was doing until so late last night.

Our marriage has reached the stage where we've stopped asking questions. We don't make any demands on each other's time, not like we used to when the children were small. Then we would ask if it was OK to go out for a drink with colleagues or visit the gym after work. But since the children have got older, that's changed. Now I don't ask where Gestur's going when he heads out in the evenings. Perhaps because I don't want to be asked the same questions in return. The truth is, when I go out in the evenings, all I do is drive around in a daze.

So I don't ask any questions now either, but I'm surprised at how good it feels to hold Gestur's hand, like revisiting an old memory.

The magic wears off as soon as I see my parents sitting in the restaurant with my brother Smári and his family. At the table behind them are Stefanía and Hákon Ingimar.

'This all looks very tempting,' Gestur says, surveying the breakfast buffet. He starts piling bacon, pancakes and cocktail sausages onto his plate.

I help myself to scrambled eggs, bread, jam and fruit. But the moment we sit down and I take the first mouthful, I start to feel sick. Nevertheless, I force myself to eat some bread with a thick layer of jam, hoping the sugar will get my circulation going.

'How did you two sleep?' Dad asks.

'Well. Very well,' I lie.

'Did you hear the racket in the night?' Dad asks.

'When?' I prod at the scrambled eggs, which look as if they've already been digested once, then returned to the plate.

'When was it, Ester?' Dad looks at Mum. 'One, two o'clock?'

'Yes, a quarter past one,' Mum says with her usual conviction. Even when she's wrong, she's right, a characteristic she's cultivated for as long as I can remember.

'What kind of racket?' Gestur asks, his mouth full of sausage.

'Well, it sounded like screaming,' Mum says. 'Didn't it, Halli? Didn't it sound like screaming?'

Dad says 'Mm' in agreement.

'And a noise like something smashing,' Smári adds.

Gestur and I lock gazes.

'I was asleep. What about you?'

'I didn't hear a thing,' Gestur says, apparently failing to pick up on the note of accusation in my voice.

'Anyway,' I say, deciding to leave it for now, 'the lights in my room were a bloody nuisance. They kept switching on and off, whatever I did with the app. Did you have the same problem?'

They all shake their heads.

'You should talk to reception,' Dad says.

'The place must be haunted,' Smári adds with a grin.

'I'm going to wake the kids,' Gestur says, wiping his mouth with the napkin, then laying it on his empty plate.

My brother and his family leave too. They say they're going to fetch some warm clothes for the cruise. Dad says something along the same lines, though I'm well aware that really this is an excuse for him to sneak out and take some snuff. That just leaves me and Mum.

'Coffee?' Mum asks, after a short silence.

'Yes, please.'

'So, what's going on?' Mum asks, once she's filled my cup.

'Going on?'

'Last night,' Mum says. 'I expected Smári to overdo the drinking, but not you, Petra. You usually know better than that.'

I can feel my cheeks growing hot. I wasn't that pissed yesterday. Besides, why's it always OK for Smári to overdo it and not me? I know I wasn't myself yesterday evening, though, and that I wasn't drinking for fun. I drank because I was in a bad way, and that's always fatal.

'I didn't have that much,' I protest.

Mum sips her coffee, watching me over the rim of her cup.

'Your father and I went through a difficult patch years ago,' she says, apropos of nothing.

'Things are fine between Gestur and me,' I reply. Naturally Mum assumes the problem must lie in our marriage. I take a mouthful of coffee, trying not to let Mum's searching look get to me.

'You probably won't remember,' Mum continues, as if she hasn't heard me. 'You were only about six.'

'What happened?' I ask.

'Your father was unfaithful,' Mum says, in the matter-of-fact tone of someone discussing the weather.

'What?' My jaw drops. 'Dad cheated on you? But...'

Mum hushes me, then straightens her shoulders. 'Like I've said before, you have to make some sacrifices in a marriage. It's not always plain sailing.'

'But...' I don't know what to ask first. When? Who with? Why? But no sooner have the questions formed in my head than I wonder if I really want to know the answers.

'It doesn't matter now,' Mum says, her lips tightening. 'What matters is that we got over it.'

'Why are you telling me this? Gestur's not having an affair,' I say. 'We're fine. Last night was just ... just because I was tired.'

'All right, dear,' Mum says, in the tone she uses to small children.

Her expression changes as Ingvar and Elín enter the room, immediately becoming warmer and more cheerful. She waves at them to come and sit with us. They pour themselves coffee, and Elín asks me how work's going. Then Viktor comes along with a heaped plate and joins us.

'You've got an appetite,' Elín remarks.

'I'm still growing, Mum.' Viktor grins.

'How's your back today, Ingvar?' Mum asks.

Ingvar goes into a long account of the back pain he's been suffering from since being involved in a minor collision two weeks ago.

'There was hardly a mark on the car,' Elín chips in. 'Not like that time you almost wrote our car off, Viktor.'

'Hm?' Viktor wipes his mouth with a napkin.

'That time you hit a sheep when you were in your teens,' Elín says. 'The dent in the car looked more like you'd hit an elephant than a ewe.'

'Oh, that.' Viktor shakes his head ruefully.

'You always were a terrible driver,' I tease him.

Viktor gives me a nudge in return. But I don't feel up to taking part in any more small talk, so I excuse myself and leave the restaurant.

As far as I knew, my parents had always had a good marriage. Now I feel as if something has been stolen from me, from my childhood memories.

My dad cheated. Betraying not only Mum but me and Smári too.

The hotel lobby gradually fills up. Everyone's wearing raincoats and waterproof trousers, ready for the cruise. I go up to our room to fetch my outdoor clothes. My trousers are still wet from yesterday's outing, but I pull them on anyway with a shiver.

When I come downstairs, Lea and Ari are standing in the lobby. Ari's saying something to his sister, who's smiling vaguely. Lea's face is very pale and her eyes are glazed.

'Are you all right, sweetheart?' I brush a hand over her forehead. She flinches as if I've burnt her. As if my touch makes her uncomfortable.

'Don't, Mum,' she protests.

'I thought you might have a temperature,' I say.

'Can I stay behind, then?' Lea's face brightens.

'Not if you're not ill,' I say.

'But I've got an upset stomach.'

'That's probably because you didn't have any breakfast,' Gestur says, tugging at her pony-tail. I hadn't noticed him there and jump when he suddenly appears beside me.

'I'm not hungry,' Lea mutters.

'You're coming too,' I say, more sternly than intended.

'Anyway, you'll need to leave some room for the sushi later,' Gestur says.

'Is there going to be sushi?' Ari asks.

'Yes.' Gestur laughs. 'Viking Sushi. Food fit for a king.'

The look of anticipation is wiped off Ari's face. 'Why does that sound so grim?'

I can't help smiling at Ari's look of horror.

As we walk out to the car, my spirits rise slightly, in spite of everything. We're greeted by sunshine, brilliant but cold. It's a beautiful day, the sky's cloudless, there's not a breath of wind. What's done is done, and if Mum could forgive Dad, so can I. Gestur smiles at me before getting in the car, and I think about how different he is from Dad. Gestur's generally good-humoured and always friendly, whereas Dad's domineering and stubborn. He lets his temper get the better of him, which means Mum often has to tiptoe around him. Gestur would never behave like that, nor would he do anything to hurt me.

Just as I'm about to open the car door, I notice a scrap of paper stuck through the handle. I take it and smooth it out. It's a small yellow Post-it note on which someone has written just two words. Or three. I stare at what it says in disbelief, thinking I must be imagining it.

Be careful. M.

Irma
Hotel Employee

I'm not going to kick up a fuss. Of course not. I've worked in enough bars and clubs to know that men aren't always themselves. They become the drugs they're taking or the alcohol they're drinking. It sounds as if I'm inventing excuses, and maybe I am. I suppose I've grown too used to pushy men, the type who want their own way, whatever the consequences. I've become inured to their behaviour. It doesn't bother me any longer.

I step out of the shower, wrap a towel round my hair and inspect my right arm. The bruise is turning blue, and I can make out the shape of a hand. It's like a brand, the imprint of the four fingers clearly visible and, on the inside of my arm, the thumb.

As I contemplate the marks on my body I wonder what would have happened if we hadn't been disturbed by a noise in the corridor. Hákon stopped and looked round, loosening his grip on my arm as he did so, and I seized the opportunity to tear myself free and get the hell out of there.

Naturally, he didn't follow me. Dark deeds belong in small, enclosed spaces, don't they? But I could hear his laughter as I fled down the corridor. Laughter that implied we'd only been messing about; that it had been nothing but a joke.

It seems there are black sheep in every family, even those who appear perfect on the surface.

✳

I report for duty before the clock has struck twelve, and Edda smiles, pleased. She likes me, I can tell. But then what's not to like? I'm punctual, conscientious, good-tempered and I go out of my way to do more than is required of me. An exemplary member of staff in every way.

'Ah, Irma,' Edda says. 'Would you mind checking if they need more soap and so on in the rooms? The beds have been made, but you know how it is.' She leans closer, lowering her voice. 'One just can't trust that things are done well enough.'

Edda gives me a conspiratorial smile. She knows we're alike in this at least: we have the same exacting standards. We care about the guests and want the hotel to be more than just a place to stay. People's time here should be an experience. Everything has to be perfect, and we go out of our way to achieve that. There are almost no lengths we wouldn't be prepared to go to in search of perfection.

'Of course,' I say, and hurry off.

One of the most interesting aspects of my job is going into the rooms when there are guests staying in them. It's unbelievable how many people leave personal items lying around, though they know the staff will be coming in. So far I've come across quite a few sex aids, in addition to dirty underwear, condoms, drugs and even a wig. I always feel as if I'm looking through someone's window or reading their diary. It's so personal.

I have to admit that I can hardly wait to see what these particular guests have left lying around in plain sight.

Disappointingly, I find very little juicy stuff in the first few rooms. Most of them are actually quite tidy compared to what I'm used to. I make sure there are fresh sheets on all the beds and clean towels in the bathrooms. I top up the bottles of body wash and shampoo, and replace the wild thyme and birch fragranced soaps that Edda has custom made for the hotel.

When I enter Hákon Ingimar's room, I stand very still and look around, making sure he's not there. The room smells of him, a heavy male odour with a tang of sweetness. I take in the leather jacket hanging in the wardrobe and the wash bag on the desk. It is open and I see that it contains aftershave, hair gel and packets of condoms. I open his suitcase warily, then hear a noise outside. Footsteps. I recoil in a panic, my pulse shooting up, and glance around frantically for an escape route, then tell myself there's nothing unnatural about my presence in his room. The footsteps recede into the distance, and everything is quiet again, apart from the blood throbbing in my head and my rapid breathing.

When I resume my task, I realise my hands are shaking, and I need a moment or two to recover. I stroke the bruises on my arm and close my eyes, concentrating on steadying my breathing. I tell myself it was no big deal, just a bit of harmless fun.

I go through the next rooms without taking much notice of them, too distracted and preoccupied by my thoughts.

It's not until I enter a room on the floor below that I see something unexpected. It's tidy enough; there are no clothes or rubbish lying around. What attracts my attention is the absence of the large vase that should have been on the desk. Glancing around, puzzled, I wonder what's become of it. Surely a well-off family like this wouldn't go around stealing vases?

I peer under the bed, but instead of a vase, I see shards of glass.

I fetch a broom and sweep the broken pieces of the vase into a dustpan. Then I notice that there's an item of clothing under there too, perhaps something left behind by a previous guest. With the help of the broom, I fish the garment out and see that it's a strappy vest with a large stain on the front. I don't need an expert to tell me what kind of stain it is. Blood has trickled down the front of the vest, as if someone's had a violent nose bleed.

I put the vest top in a bag, check that there's no glass left under the bed, then go straight to the room where the hotel supplies are kept: duvet covers, sheets and hopefully a replacement vase. As I walk by reception, the phone starts ringing on the desk.

The young woman on the other end is in a real state. 'I'm

looking for my sister – she's called Maja. I mean, María Síf Pálsdóttir, known as Maja.'

'One moment,' I say, and I'm about to check on the computer when Edda comes over.

'Is she asking about Maja?' she whispers, and adds that Maja has gone. She left last night.

When I tell the young woman on the phone this, she sounds surprised.

'Are you quite sure? I just ... No one's heard from her since yesterday evening.' The woman hesitates, then adds: 'Could you check, just in case?'

'I don't know quite—'

'But how?' the young woman suddenly interrupts.

'I'm sorry?'

'How's Maja supposed to have left the hotel?' she asks, her voice cracking. 'Maja doesn't have a driving licence. She hasn't got a car. So could you please explain to me how she's supposed to have left the hotel in the middle of the night?'

Lea Snæberg

'Hold on to the rail, dear, the steps could be slippery.'

When I look round, Tryggvi, my great-aunt Oddný's partner, is standing behind me at the bottom of the gangplank that leads up to the deck.

'OK,' I say, grasping the rail.

I can sense him behind me as I walk up. I can't stand it when men call me 'dear' or 'love'. Especially men I don't even know, like Tryggvi.

The other day, when Granny came round, I heard her bitching about Oddný to Mum. About what she was doing with a man who was not only uneducated but unwashed too.

Before I met him, I thought this was a bit harsh, but now I understand what she means. His grey hair is too long and straggly. It looks greasy, and I doubt he ever uses shampoo, let alone conditioner. His clothes are terrible too. He always wears threadbare, flared jeans, a T-shirt with some band name on it and an anorak from a brand I've never heard of. Not only that but he walks around in these ridiculous cowboy boots. But the worst part is the way he smells – of unwashed hair, sweat and something else I can't identify. Maybe some kind of chemical, like oil or paint, which would make sense as, according to Mum, he's a carpenter.

Now, though, the stench of the sea drowns out almost everything else. I screw up my face when I arrive on board. The boat stinks of fish guts and salt.

'Don't look like that,' Granny says, putting her arm round me. 'It's not that bad. You know your ancestors grew up on boats like this. Out at sea in all weathers...' Granny takes my hand and leads me across the deck, telling me about how once, when she was young, she went out fishing with her father.

'Weren't you seasick?' I ask, because I'm already nauseous, although we haven't even started moving yet.

'Goodness, yes,' Granny answers with a laugh. 'I had my head stuck over the rail pretty much the whole time. That's why I only ever went on that one fishing trip and decided it wasn't for me.'

It's hard to imagine Granny Ester at sea. She's always so dressed up, in high heels and jewellery, that the thought of her in fisherman's overalls and a *lopapeysa* is ridiculous. As weird as the idea of Granddad in a ballerina's tutu. I try to picture Granny as a child but I can't do it. I imagine her face as it is now on the body of a child, and the result is just creepy.

The boat seems steadier once we're moving, and my seasickness fades as soon as the cold breeze begins to play over my face. Granny has started talking to someone else, so I hold on to the rail and turn my face up to the sun.

The sea air doesn't smell so bad now, and there's an amazing view across the bay. The water foams around the boat and the sky is pale blue. In the distance I can see the islands of Breiðafjörður, some just rocks poking out of the sea, others larger, covered with grass. There are all kinds of birds swarming in the sky or perching on the rocks.

I close my eyes and breathe.

'Did you know there are too many to count?'

'What?' When I open my eyes, Oddný's boyfriend, Tryggvi, is standing beside me at the rail.

'They say there are too many islands in Breiðafjörður to count,' he says. 'But actually there are around two thousand seven or eight hundred, so that's not quite true.'

'Oh, OK.'

I already knew that about the islands, though I don't say so. Again, I have an uncomfortable feeling that I can't explain.

'Yes,' Tryggvi continues, as if talking to himself. 'There are a lot of them, all right.'

He leans against the rail, resting his elbows on it, gazing into the distance, and I suddenly remember the man with the handle Gulli58, who's been sending me messages. An old man sending messages to a sixteen-year-old girl. It's strange and creepy.

I wonder how he'll react when he sees that I've blocked him again.

Gulli58 knows where I am this weekend and he says he's somewhere in the area. I've always pictured him as a lonely, old bloke, but what if he isn't? What if he has a family, even kids? What if he doesn't look like someone who'd be messaging a sixteen-year-old girl online?

What if that man is Tryggvi?

The thought occurs to me so suddenly that I almost jump. Could the man calling himself Gulli be Tryggvi? If '58' means he was born in 1958, could that age fit Tryggvi? After working it out in my head, I realise it could, though Tryggvi's probably a little older. A man born in 1958 would be fifty-nine years old. I find it hard to guess Tryggvi's age. He's just an older man, older than Dad – he could be the same age as Granddad, maybe. But Granddad and Tryggvi are so different that it's hard to compare their ages.

My phone starts ringing, giving me a good excuse to move away.

'Lea?' It's my friend Solla, and I can tell from her voice that she's worked up about something. Relief floods through me.

'What?' I glance behind me and see that Tryggvi's still gazing out to sea.

'Lea, are you there?'

'Yes.'

'I've been selected,' Solla says.

'What?'

'For the national team. Or, you know, the under-sixteens.'

'Oh.' I'm still so distracted that it takes me a moment to remember to be excited for her. Then I add belatedly: 'Wow, congratulations, Solla. That's awesome.'

Solla carries on talking for a while, going on about who has and hasn't been selected. I find a sheltered spot, against a white wall, and try to concentrate, but her words go in one ear and out the other.

I watch Tryggvi talking to Smári and Dad. He doesn't once glance in my direction, so I start to calm down. I've probably just gone a bit mental. I'm a nervous wreck after everything that's happened over the last few years. In a state because I can't stop thinking about Birgir. I check my phone every few minutes, twitching every time I think I hear a notification or feel a vibration in my pocket.

'Lea?' Solla sounds annoyed. 'Are you there?'

'Yes.'

'I asked you a question,' Solla says. 'Do you think you'll definitely be home tomorrow? Because I'm not going on my own with Tara, you know. She can be so bossy.'

'I don't know when I'll be home,' I say, suddenly aware how much I long to be back in Reykjavík. The scenery that seemed so beautiful before, now feels menacing. Instead of refreshing, the wind is freezing, and since the boat slowed down the stink has become unbearable. I'm stuck here, I think to myself. I couldn't get away even if I wanted to.

By the time I say goodbye to Solla, the cold has found its way inside my down jacket, and before long I'm chilled to the bone. I lean over the rail, trying not to think about the cold and the horrible smell.

We're sailing past a small island, just a rock really, poking out of the waves. There are birds on it, gulls mostly, perching very upright and looking out to sea with their staring eyes. Then, among all the gulls, I see a bird that looks very different: black, with a long neck, the feathers on the back of its neck ruffled up.

The bird turns its head towards me, and I feel as if it's watching me, though I know it can't be. Then, without warning, it spreads its wings and flaps them, but doesn't take off. The movement is threatening, as if it's warning me off, and instinctively I back away, retreating a few steps until I'm up against the wall again, hidden in the shadows.

In the end the bird takes to the air, and I see it flying away, far above all the other birds.

I shake off my spooked feeling, zip my jacket right up to my chin, then check my phone again. Although Birgir hasn't replied, I want the reassurance of seeing his face and knowing that he's out there somewhere. I often scroll through the photos of him when I'm feeling down or lonely. The sight of his face makes me smile and fills me with feelings of happy anticipation.

I type Birgir's name into Instagram search, but instead of his picture coming up, a completely different Birgir appears. I try again but can't find his account. I check if I've typed his name wrong, though I know I haven't.

My heart is pounding and there's a bad taste in my mouth, as though something's rising up my throat. My breathing is so fast and shallow that I think I'm going to faint. I can't get enough air in my lungs.

I tap in his name again and again, staring at the screen. Run my finger down the list in search of Birgir, but nothing comes up. His page no longer exists.

He's vanished.

Petra Snæberg

The boat slows and I gaze down at the sea, gently rising and falling beneath us. The surface looks like a soft mattress, like something you could lie down and sleep on.

Be careful, M.

The words echo in my head as I wonder what Maja meant by them. Because 'M' must stand for Maja, surely? Who else could have written the message?

I suspect it's connected to the thing she wanted to discuss with me last night. Since she didn't get a chance to talk to me, she's resorted to leaving me a warning. But why make it so enigmatic?

The only answer I can think of is that she was afraid someone else might find the message. She wanted to be sure only I would understand it; but I don't – I don't know why I'm supposed to be careful.

I try to put myself in Maja's shoes. Imagine her rushing out of the hotel in the early hours, hastily writing me the note and sticking it on my car in the hope I'd find it.

Be careful.

She must have thought I'd understand immediately who I'm supposed to be careful of, but the only person I can think of is Gestur. Because he's the person closest to me, the one I trust most.

'Is everything OK?' Gestur asks. He stands behind me, leaning against my back, gripping the rail either side of me and resting his chin on my shoulder.

'Everything's fine,' I say. I wonder if I should tell him about the note but decide not to.

He puts his hand over mine, and I feel the warmth radiating from him.

'We need to make some use of that hotel room when we get back,' he whispers in my ear.

When I don't answer, I feel him pressing closer, breathing in the scent of my hair. And in spite of everything, I feel the longing stir inside me.

Maja can't have been referring to Gestur in her message. I've no reason to beware of him; I never have. Perhaps Maja didn't mean I should be careful of anyone specific, just that I should be careful in general. Like worried parents telling their children to be careful when they go out.

We're so close to one of the islands now that I can see the birds on the rocks: gulls, fulmars and puffins. I always forget how small puffins are close up. With their stubby red-and-blue beaks and the red marks encircling their round eyes. I stare at them, mesmerised, and they return my gaze from their rocky ledges.

Someone calls out that they've spotted an eagle, and Gestur immediately lets go of me and reaches for the binoculars. He has a strange passion for birds that I can't even pretend to share. Yet I look up like everyone else and see the eagle soaring with outstretched wings high overhead. Its flight seems completely effortless, its wingspan is so great that the updraft can hold it aloft for ages. It comes closer and closer, eventually landing on a nearby islet, where it perches on the highest rock, haughtily surveying the bay.

I shiver and release my hold on the icy metal rail. I have a sudden sensation of being watched, and when I glance round, I see Viktor standing there.

'They're beautiful creatures,' he says, smiling.

'Yes,' I say. 'They are.'

But instead of turning my attention back to the bird, I study Viktor's face, noting how carefree he looks.

I find it unlikely that Maja can have left the hotel by car. I remember meeting the two of them at the Hyrnan service station and seeing them both getting into Viktor's vehicle. She can hardly have borrowed his to drive home in. I expect she got someone to come and fetch her or walked to the next village, which, come to think of it, would take an hour or more. Bearing in mind what the weather was like last night, I hope she got a lift, though it seems unlikely. After all, if someone had come to pick her up, surely her family wouldn't be wondering where she is today? She would have let them know. Unless she accepted a ride with a stranger. Perhaps she meant to walk to the next village, but someone stopped to give her a lift, offering to drive her there. A shudder runs through me when I think about the implications, because nothing has been heard from her since she left.

I know it's probably stupid of me but I can't help being chilled by the sinister history of the area. Axlar-Björn, one of Iceland's most notorious serial killers, once lived at Búðir, not far from our hotel. He used to rob and murder travellers who passed his farm and bury his victims in the lava field near Knarrarklettir. Although this all happened hundreds of years ago, I sometimes find myself wondering about the bones that may still be lying out there, never finding rest in a proper grave. For all my fondness for this part of Snæfellsnes, I feel as if the horrific events that happened here have seeped into the place itself. After Axlar-Björn was executed, his body was chopped into three pieces and buried not far from Hellnar, where we were yesterday – three pieces, to prevent him from coming back to haunt the district. It's not that I'm afraid of his ghost, more that I'm afraid the evil might still cling to the landscape somehow.

It's impossible to think about Maja alone in the lava field at night without being affected by this story.

Tryggvi

I've had enough of standing on deck for the moment and go below to the saloon, where I buy two mugs of coffee and a chocolate-covered flapjack. Then I take a seat beside Oddný, who can't have spent more than a few minutes outside before taking refuge in here.

'How are you doing?' I ask, handing her one of the mugs.

'Oh, fine,' she says, smiling gratefully. 'It's bitter out there.'

'Yes, it is a little nippy.'

Oddný doesn't ask how I'm doing and, though I don't want to complain, the truth is I've felt better. But then it was to be expected that it would be a difficult day. The fact is, I haven't been sober on this day for seventeen years, but there's a first time for everything. Apparently you're never too old to mend your ways.

I've been thinking recently about how I can become a better man. When you make a start and it goes well, this acts as an incentive to continue down the same path. But, despite having given up drinking for a while, I still can't kick various other bad habits: I sleep too little, work too hard and seldom say what's on my mind. The way my life has panned out has meant I haven't been able to do many of the things I once dreamt of, like travelling in the Scottish Highlands or the American Deep South.

'I'm feeling a bit out of sorts,' Oddný sighs. 'I can't wait to get back to the hotel and have a lie-down.'

'Oh, yes. That'll be nice.' I break off a piece of flapjack and put it in my mouth, and as I do so it occurs to me that I can't picture myself travelling to those places with Oddný.

I push the plate over to her. 'Don't you want something to eat?'

She stares at the flapjack, as if weighing it up, before breaking off a tiny corner and nibbling at it. When she looks away, I notice a wound on her forehead, just above the temple. A small cut and a bruise that's turning blue. Her make-up can't quite hide it.

I feel a gnawing guilt and decide not to have any more flapjack. As if denying myself a treat will change anything.

'Had enough sea air?' Haraldur asks, thumping down beside us. He's clutching some mini bottles of wine he bought at the counter and starts sharing them out, as if he's allocating jobs. Strange how one minute Oddný's family are so worried about her drinking, the next they insist on offering her booze. Oddný accepts, but I don't.

'What, are you always this boring?' Haraldur asks with a bark of laughter, then drains his bottle in one go.

They talk for a while about the formation of a new government, about the media's attacks on the right, and the nonsense on the left.

'I just can't understand what right a slip of a girl like that has to be prime minister,' Haraldur says. He takes out a tin of tobacco and shakes it. 'Do people really think it'll improve anything? That breaking up the coalition over some silly scandal will solve any problems? What do you think?' Haraldur rounds on me. There's an edge to his voice, as if he's expecting the worst and gearing up for a fight.

'Well...' I could tell him I've always voted for the left, that I regard myself as a social democrat, not a capitalist, but that would only lead to a row. 'I haven't made up my mind yet,' I say diplomatically, 'but she's perfectly up to the job, isn't she?'

'Oh, come off it, Tryggvi.' Haraldur scowls, then addresses Oddný. 'What do you say, Oddný, which side is your boyfriend on?'

Oddný smiles faintly. 'We rarely discuss politics.'

'Thank God,' Ester says, as she comes over to join us,

accompanied by Ingvar and Elín. 'Please, Halli, let's change the subject.'

Haraldur puts some snuff on the back of his hand and snorts it noisily up his nose.

'Oh, dear, what on earth happened to you, Oddný?' Ester exclaims, noticing her sister-in-law's face.

'It's nothing,' Oddný says. 'I just bumped into something.'

Ester raises her eyebrows, and I can guess what she's thinking. She saw for herself the state her sister was in yesterday. But she quickly changes the subject, saying with fake cheerfulness: 'I've heard that the food at the place we're going to afterwards is fantastic.'

'What's it called again?' Elín asks.

'Viðvík,' Ester says. 'Apparently they do an awfully good shellfish soup.'

After a moment, she turns back to me. 'Have you been to this area before, Tryggvi?' I suspect she's trying to make up for Haraldur's behaviour. Seeing how red he is in the face, I realise he must have put away a fair amount of booze already.

'Hey!' Haraldur calls, giving a sign to the waitress.

I don't think they have table service here, but the girl comes over anyway to take his order and returns with more mini bottles of wine.

'What do you think of the hotel, by the way?' Elín asks. 'I slept so well last night. Like a log.'

'It's all very smart,' Ester says. 'And talk about powerful showers ... I've never felt so clean in my life. I was just going to congratulate you on making such a good choice.'

'Me?' Elín shakes her head. 'I'd never heard about the hotel before.'

'But wasn't it you who posted a link to the hotel on Facebook?' Ester asks. 'On the page we set up to organise the reunion?'

'No, that was somebody else. I'm not on Facebook; Ingvar takes care of that side of things.'

'Oh, I see,' Ester says. 'Well, it was a good choice, anyway. I'm very impressed with everything.'

'Mind you, the soap smells a bit iffy,' Ingvar says. 'A bit like ... like...'

'Birch,' Ester says. 'They're fragranced with birch and wild thyme.'

'Is there thyme in everything?' Elín asks. 'It was in the tea they gave us when we arrived too. That was really good, by the way.'

'I agree with Ingvar. Odd smell, odd taste. Whose is that?' Haraldur points to the flapjack on the table.

'Help yourself,' I say.

He breaks off half and shoves it in his mouth. Crumbs rain down on his royal-blue waterproof jacket.

'Can't complain about the service, though,' Ingvar says. 'That girl's pretty obliging.'

'Obliging, yes,' Haraldur says. 'I hope she'll be taking care of my massage later.'

'None of that, Halli,' Ester says, elbowing him. Haraldur lets out a loud guffaw, and, seeming not to mind when no one else joins in, drains another bottle in one go.

I want to point out to him that we still have a fair way to drive after the boat trip. We left our cars in Stykkishólmur, on the northern side of the Snæfellsnes peninsula, where we boarded the boat. Once we get back there, the plan is to drive round the western tip of the peninsula, stopping for lunch at the Viðvík restaurant in Hellissandur at two p.m., then continue to the beach at Djúpalón before returning to the hotel. That must be more than a hundred kilometres in total. But I know that men like Haraldur think they're above the law. They believe they're different from us plebs and can do what they like. Maybe there's some truth in that, because, after all, money is power. Haraldur wouldn't even notice a big fine. Come to think of it, he'd probably offer a bribe if necessary. And although I find it hard to believe that anyone would accept a bribe in Iceland, the sad fact is it happens.

This selfish arrogance, this total lack of consideration makes me so angry that I'm almost shaking. These bastards who drink-drive and show no respect for everyone else's right to travel safely on the country's roads. I'm disgusted by their lack of consideration for other people's lives.

I watch Oddný accept another bottle from Haraldur and suddenly I'm gripped by a desperate urge to get out of here, off the boat, somewhere far away. I don't belong here and I can't sit still for a minute longer.

'They're about to lower the net,' I say, getting to my feet.

Although I'm seething with righteous anger, I know I'm the most shameful sort of hypocrite. Because in my worst moments I've done exactly what I'm judging them so harshly for – and other things that are far, far worse.

Now
Sunday, 5 November 2017

Sævar
Detective, West Iceland CID

Edda came back bearing coffee and chocolates.

'Right, let's go over what happened last night,' Hörður said.

'Yes, of course.' Edda rubbed her hands together. 'Though actually I'd gone home by that time. Several members of staff stayed on to attend to the guests who wanted to order drinks at the bar and ... and, well, there are always staff on night duty.'

'When did you first learn that one of the guests was missing?'

'I got a phone call at four in the morning to say that one of the guests had gone outside and hadn't come back. Understandably, people were worried. The weather was terrible, it was freezing and there was a blizzard raging, so it didn't make sense to go out. Besides, the nights are so dark here that it's hard to find your way if you don't know the area. It's easy to get lost...'

'Who rang you?' Hörður asked.

'One of our staff,' Edda said. 'Arne, the young man who works behind the bar, told me that three people had gone out into the snowstorm for some reason, and only two had come back.'

'What happened next?'

'I told Arne to get on to the search-and-rescue team straight away, which he did. They arrived quickly and immediately started the search.' Edda stared down into her cup. 'I don't suppose I need to tell you that in weather like that every minute counts.'

She fell silent and took a sip of coffee, but Sævar already knew what had happened next. He knew that the search party hadn't found the body until dawn. That it wasn't a question of a person succumbing to the elements, as sometimes happened on cold, stormy nights in Iceland, particularly in the olden days. This time nature had only played a supporting role, if any, in the victim's fate.

Petra Snæberg

'I've got a niece,' Mist, my brother Smári's wife, tells me, 'who's mad about interior design. She's living in a student flat at the moment, but you should see how beautifully she's decorated it. I'm telling you, she has a really good eye for detail.'

Mist opens her eyes wide and uses her hands a lot when she talks. 'Anyway, I said I'd ask if you were hiring people for summer jobs. Honestly, you'd hardly have to pay her – she'd work for free.'

'That's nice,' I say. 'As a matter of fact, we haven't been in the habit of taking on summer temps, but I'll see what I can do.'

'That would be fantastic. She'd be so thrilled.'

I smile and fake an interest, though in reality I'm searching for an excuse to extract myself. Mist and I have never really hit it off. She and Smári got together when I was still living at home with my parents. The first time I met her, I'd come home early from school and thought the house was empty. I was just going to my room when I heard a noise, so I stopped in the hall and called Smári's name but there was no answer. Then Mist emerged from my bedroom, scarlet in the face with embarrassment.

'Sorry,' she said. 'I ... I was looking for a hairbrush.'

'A hairbrush?'

'Yes. I, erm ... I'm Mist.'

Smári had mentioned her. Mist was the girl who was

constantly ringing our house, the girl Smári's friends teased him about. I don't know what I'd been expecting but certainly not this. Mist was wearing a T-shirt with a picture of Minnie Mouse on it and a small hole over the navel, and she had mousy hair, a jutting chin and round glasses. There she stood, blushing at being caught snooping in my room, and we both knew she was lying about the hairbrush. I instantly took against her.

I've never really forgiven her for snooping like that, though nothing in my room appeared to have been touched. If I'm honest, perhaps I've never forgiven her for hooking Smári, who could have done so much better for himself.

It's a relief when a crew member shouts to us from the stern of the boat.

'Time to haul in the net,' he calls, beckoning everyone to gather.

I leave Mist and find Ari standing towards the front of the onlookers.

'Are you going to try it?' I whisper to him.

He screws up his face, then shrugs. 'Yeah, sure.'

The net attached to the dredge comes up so full it's overflowing. The sailor heaves it onto the long table in front of him. The passengers line up on the other side, watching as he opens the net from the bottom and the catch pours out.

'Here you have your Viking Sushi, as fresh as it comes, straight from the bottom of the sea.' The man spreads the contents on the table. 'We've got some delicious scallops and urchins for you to taste. And I see we've scooped up some nice big crabs too, though we'd better remove those before they do any damage, as their claws can be pretty lethal. Then here we have some starfish and a sea cucumber.'

Several crew members clad in oilskins take out knives and begin prising open the shells.

'We'll have to try them, won't we?' Viktor says. He's standing right next to me, so close that I can feel the heat emanating from his body.

'Yes,' I say, picking up one of the open shells and inspecting the white muscle inside. It looks horribly slimy, but I drop it into my mouth and swallow fast.

Viktor watches me closely to see how I'll react.

'Mmm,' I say, nodding. 'It's good. Have a taste.'

The briny ocean tang isn't that good actually, but I manage to convince Viktor.

He picks up a shell, raises it to his face and examines the contents dubiously.

'Was it really good?' he asks.

'Yes. Honestly.' I adopt an innocent expression and give him a nudge. 'Try for yourself.'

'For you,' Viktor says, then closes his eyes and slides the contents of the shell into his mouth. For a moment he looks as if he's going to spit it out. He jerks convulsively, then swallows with an effort.

'You traitor,' he says in mock outrage. 'I'd forgotten how mean you could be.'

I can't say a word; I'm laughing so much that tears come to my eyes.

'Would you like to try this?' the man with the dredge says, holding out some roe. 'It's a real gourmet delicacy.'

'No, thanks,' Viktor says. 'I couldn't.'

'No, thanks,' I say.

'Listen, why don't you come down to my room for a drink before supper this evening?' Viktor suggests, once the man has given up trying to persuade us to feast on more raw seafood. 'I can't leave tomorrow without having had a chance for a proper chat with you.'

'Yes, sure,' I say. Perhaps Viktor wants to discuss what really happened between him and Maja.

'Great. I've got some of that champagne you like so much.'

Viktor gives a wicked grin and I feel my cheeks growing hot. A few years ago he came round with a bottle of champagne when Gestur was away on a business trip in Poland. We drank the whole bottle together, followed by a bottle of red wine. I fell asleep on the sofa while Viktor was still there and woke up in the morning to find Lea shaking me. 'Mummy, why are you sleeping on the sofa? Are you ill?'

Luckily, Viktor had removed the incriminating bottles and glasses from the table. He had also spread a throw over me and brought a pillow from the bedroom to tuck under my head.

'Oof,' I say. 'I don't know if I should touch that stuff again...'

Viktor doesn't answer but smiles, and there's a glint in his eyes that I haven't seen before. Someone bumps into us, pushing us even closer together until I can feel his body pressed against mine.

I laugh in embarrassment and try to move away, but I'm pinned against the table with all the slippery sea creatures on it. Brown-and-purple urchins, upturned crabs helplessly wriggling their legs, gaping scallops, their slimy insides ready for eating.

Then I'm hit by the stench, a pungent sea smell that makes me feel as if I've got a head full of fish guts. All around me I can hear people laughing and smacking their lips. Our family aren't the only ones on board; there are tourists too, mostly foreigners. Someone's pouring white wine into glasses, adding a sickly-sweet smell of alcohol to the mix. The nausea curdles in my stomach and rises up my throat, making me gag. I can't get away. Behind me Viktor seems immovable, as if he has no intention of letting me by. In fact, it feels as if he's leaning closer, pressing against me so hard that I can scarcely breathe.

Lea Snæberg

By the time we pull into the car park by Djúpalón Beach, the sun is setting and the air is full of fine spray. I've been here loads of times. When I was little, I used to pester my parents to stop here every time we visited Snæfellsnes. Because of the pebbles. All the pebbles on the beach are smooth black ovals, polished by the sea until they look like beads. I used to spend ages searching for the best ones to take home with me, then arrange them in rows in my room or give them to friends as gifts.

'Are you coming?' Dad calls back. He's walking on ahead of me, holding Mum's hand.

I pick my way down the path until I'm standing between the strange black lava formations that rise like walls on either side of me. A little further on, the sea comes into view. I take off my beanie because I want to hear it, the crashing of the waves and the hissing of the water as it trickles over the pebbles on its way out again.

Down here on the beach it's like being in another world, and for a while I feel better. Like I can breathe again. As I stand there, gazing at the pebbles and the sea, it strikes me how long it's been since I was happy. Genuinely happy.

Thoughts like that always make me feel guilty. I'm the girl who has everything, so why can't I be happy? I should be happy.

I'm much better off than so many other people. Whenever I think that, I always remember this one girl I made friends with when I was nine. Her name was Dagbjört, and she had only joined our class that autumn. One day I suggested going round to her house instead of mine. She agreed, but only after I insisted.

I was shocked when we entered her flat. I paused in the doorway and just stared. It was like a junk room. Worse than a junk room. The floor was covered in stuff, or that's what I thought at first, but when I looked closer, I saw that it was rubbish: pizza boxes, drink cans and fast-food packaging. Inside, the TV was on but the place was really dark. The curtains were drawn, even though it was sunny outside. But the worst part was the smell – a horrible stink, like something rotten. Then Dagbjört's father came out, wearing strange clothes, with a strange look on his face. He snapped at us to keep the noise down, then disappeared back into one of the rooms.

When I had friends round to my house, my parents would always talk to them and offer us snacks to eat.

Dagbjört asked if I was going to take my shoes off, and I invented an excuse on the spot and ran home. After that, we never spoke again unless we had to. Every time I saw Dagbjört I turned my back on her or walked away.

I often think about Dagbjört and that flat, the horrible smell and the expression on her father's face. I don't know why, but Dagbjört has stayed at the back of my mind, like a thought that won't go away, though I haven't seen her for years. It's probably my conscience nagging at me and reminding me how ungrateful I am, how wicked and prejudiced, to have gone home, abandoning Dagbjört in that miserable flat. I sometimes saw her walking home alone after that, lingering on the path to watch the rest of us, but I always pretended not to notice her.

I was only a child then and perfectly happy, avoiding anything uncomfortable. It wasn't until several years later that I finally learnt what it meant to be an outsider like Dagbjört.

Everyone started saying that I'd become so quiet all of a sudden. I withdrew into my shell at school and stopped sticking my hand up in lessons or asking the teachers for help. I stopped wanting to play with the other kids after school. My friends thought I was snubbing them, and somehow the whole thing became my fault. Sometimes I think they saw a weak spot in me and took advantage of it. They understood that this was a golden opportunity to bring me down.

Mum always believed I'd changed because of what happened at school – that the other girls had that effect on me. I never told her the real reason. She never found out about the Christmas party the year I was twelve, when I fell asleep in Granny's bed and woke up to find someone's hand groping under my jumper, inside my vest. I shrank inside when I realised what was happening, but I couldn't move.

Hákon Ingimar laughed when he noticed that I was awake. 'You're beginning to develop,' he said.

I felt as if he'd destroyed something fragile that I couldn't explain. With a single touch, in a single moment, he had stripped me of the innocence I hadn't even known I had until it was gone.

Now I wonder what will happen if Birgir, or whatever his name is – the boy I've been writing to – starts sharing the selfies I sent him or our chats. What would Mum and Dad say? And the kids at school?

My stomach feels as if it's full of stones, as if all the pebbles I collected as a child are weighing me down.

Then I start thinking about something quite different: Dad making me hot chocolate when I came home from school as a little kid and was so cold that my teeth wouldn't stop chattering. Or the evenings when we used to go swimming as a family, when I was younger, and Ari and I were allowed to stay up long past bedtime. Dad tucking me in at night, so tightly that I couldn't move my arms. I don't know what has made me think about that now, but the memories flood into my mind and I get a lump in my throat.

I take a deep breath and slowly release it. Close my eyes. Forget the people around me. What if it all simply disappeared? What if...?

I walk right down to the water's edge. A wave slides up to my shoes, licking the pebbles, before being sucked out again.

I pick my way further out. The next wave comes up to my ankles and the water pours into my trainers, wetting my socks. At first it's freezing, but after a while my feet get used to it.

I keep walking.

Petra Snæberg

OK, so I had a glass of wine with lunch and I'm feeling a bit better. The heaviness in my head isn't as bad now. I'm fairly sure I must have imagined what happened with Viktor on the boat. He wasn't deliberately pressing himself against me; it's just Maja's note confusing me and making me paranoid. The note might not even have been from her, or intended for me. Maja doesn't know what kind of car Gestur and I have, and, besides, how could she know that Gestur would be driving, not me?

By the time Gestur pulls into the car park at Djúpalón Beach, I'm feeling pleasantly numb from the alcohol. Not that I've drunk much, only a couple of glasses, but it's enough to make everything seem a little easier. The world is pleasantly fuzzy.

'Whoops.' I slip on the wet moss as I pick my way down to the beach.

Gestur grabs hold of me. 'Careful,' he says, and I start laughing. But my laughter's too loud, and Ari turns to look at me, raising a quizzical eyebrow.

Gestur smiles wryly. He finds me amusing when I drink – most of the time – as it gives him a chance to try his luck, knowing that I'm less likely to reject him at those moments.

I don't care. Gestur used to turn me on, but I haven't felt like that for a long time – until now.

When you've been married for years, you learn how to treasure the rare occasions when the spark is ignited. We walk down to the beach together, hand in hand, and I can hardly wait for us to be alone together.

'You look good,' Gestur says.

'Liar,' I retort, laughing. 'But thanks for lying.'

'I'm not lying.' Gestur bites his lower lip. His eyes rove over my face and neck, and I can feel the heat spreading inside me. Then he asks: 'Where's the necklace I gave you?'

'The necklace?'

'Yes, the necklace.' He doesn't need to explain. He gave it to me when we first got together, and I've worn it constantly for the best part of sixteen years. But a few months ago I took it off before getting in the shower and it must have slipped down behind the furniture or something because I couldn't find it anywhere. I turned the bathroom upside down, searching for it in vain. It seemed to have vanished into thin air.

'Oh, I forgot it at home,' I lie, stroking my throat. After wearing the necklace all these years, I feel as if something's missing. Every time I unconsciously raise my hand to stroke the little gold heart, I'm disconcerted by its absence.

'Just as well.' Gestur smiles at me. 'Anyway, it's about time we found something new to put there.'

I give a sigh of relief and we carry on walking.

Although I've visited the beach at Djúpalón many times, it never ceases to take my breath away. It's one of my favourite places. When I was young, Steffý and I used to come here with our grandparents, filling our pockets with beautifully polished pebbles that we would line up on the windowsills in our summer cabin. We would hide in the caves formed by the lava formations and pretend to be elves. Later, I brought Ari and Lea here and watched them collect stones in their turn and run away, shrieking, from the waves.

It's a peaceful place in spite of the crashing of the surf and the screeching of the birds. As you stand here, everyday life recedes into the distance and your perspective gradually alters. Suddenly your priorities seem clear.

I pause by the information board about a shipwreck that took place here in 1948. Only five of the nineteen crew members survived. You can still see bits of wreckage scattered here and there on the shingle, reddish-brown with rust, like a memorial to the tragedy.

I gaze out over the sea, watching the waves rising and falling, as if the world is breathing. The sun is still up but there's a line of dark sky on the horizon, as if night is waiting in the wings, ready to settle over the land.

I catch sight of Steffý standing nearby, staring out to sea too, as if hypnotised. She's wearing a bottle-green raincoat and a pair of walking shoes that look too smart to be practical. Her hair is held back by a furry headband, and her pony-tail stirs gently in the breeze.

Perhaps I've been too hard on her, projecting all the bad stuff onto her, as if the whole thing was her fault. It's easy to forget how young we were. When you're sixteen or seventeen, you feel as if you have the whole world in your grasp. I thought I knew what I wanted and who I was. That I had everything sorted. But I only have to look at Lea to realise we were just children who thought we were grown up. Yet I've been punishing Steffý for eighteen years.

Eighteen years. How is that possible? Most of the time I feel I'm still in the same place as I was then. That I haven't changed; I'm still the same girl who came home that evening all those years ago.

Steffý doesn't notice me at first, but then, as if sensing my presence, she looks round.

'This place hasn't changed a bit,' she says.

'No,' I agree. 'Do you remember coming here with Granny and Granddad?'

'Of course.' She smiles. 'We could happily spend hours here, collecting stones.'

'Hiding in the caves.'

'Imagining the elves,' Steffý adds.

I smile and turn my face up to the sun, but the cold breeze blowing off the sea strips its rays of any warmth.

'You know, I nearly rang you the other day,' Steffý says. 'I was sorting through some old junk and came across the scrapbook we made. The one we asked all our friends to contribute something amusing to.'

'Like "Be happy but not in a nappy"?'

'Yes, or "Remember me, I'll remember you..."'

'"...you all. And if you ever need me, here's my number to call",' we chime in chorus, and burst out laughing.

'I'd completely forgotten that,' I say.

'I brought the book with me,' Steffý tells me.

'Really?'

Steffý seems a little embarrassed, which is a strange sight. I don't think I've ever seen Steffý embarrassed before. 'Yes, in case you wanted it back.'

'That would be great.' I hesitate. 'Er ... if you like, Viktor and I were planning to meet up in his room before dinner.'

'Oh, I'd love to...' Steffý breaks off, making a face. 'That *was* meant to be an invitation, wasn't it?'

'Yes, it was.'

'Thanks.' Steffý smiles, and a small silence develops.

'Did you find anything else?' I ask after a moment or two. 'Among the old junk?'

Steffý immediately perks up, and we start reminiscing about the glossy pictures of angels and elves we used to collect, about cut-out dolls and stamps.

'Did we really always have to have a craze for something?' I ask. 'Couldn't we just have played with our Barbies?'

'We did play with our Barbies,' Steffý points out. 'But you always wanted to do such ... inappropriate things with them.'

'No way,' I protest. 'It was you who always insisted on taking all their clothes off.' I've just started to remind her of the time she left them naked together in the Barbie bed and her mother,

Oddný, made us sit down and explain what was going on, when I hear someone shouting Lea's name.

I look around and it takes me a moment or two to work out what's happening, then I catch sight of my daughter.

My heart lurches. Lea has waded out, fully clothed, until she's knee deep in the freezing seawater, seemingly deaf to Gestur's shouts. She keeps going, slowly and steadily, one step at a time.

When my eyes meet Gestur's, I see the despair in his face. He doesn't understand what's happening any more than I do. What the hell does Lea think she's doing?

In the end, Gestur gives up trying to call Lea, as she's not responding, and plunges into the sea after her. Lea doesn't look round until her father grasps hold of her shoulder. Then she turns her head to stare up at him, and it strikes me what a bizarre scene it is, the two of them standing in the icy water, which is up to Lea's waist now, just staring at each other. They don't exchange a word, as far as I can see, but some sort of communication has obviously taken place, because Lea eventually starts wading back to shore with him.

'What were you doing, Lea?' I ask when I reach them, my voice shaking.

Lea pauses and looks at me. Her eyes are huge and staring, as though she's looking not at me but through me.

'I only wanted to touch the water,' she says, after a short delay. 'I just wanted to know what it would feel like.'

Irma
Hotel Employee

Everything's ready for their last evening at the hotel. I can hardly conceal my excitement, because the odds are that this evening is going to be pretty eventful.

Earlier I heard the staff in the kitchen saying that interest in the hotel's social-media accounts has exploded. We've got countless new followers and the bookings are flooding in. We're already booked out for the whole of December. Imagine one family having that much influence.

Mind you, I reckon the biggest influencers are Hákon Ingimar and Petra. Their social-media accounts are among the most popular in Iceland, and I know they've posted loads of photos of the hotel and its surroundings. I follow them both online – have done for ages – though I doubt they've ever noticed. For them, I'm no more than one name among thousands.

'Talk about crazy,' Edda says, coming in and dropping heavily into a chair. She rubs her knees, grimacing.

'Are they giving you trouble?' I ask.

'Argh, yes, they're hurting like hell for some reason.'

I sit down opposite her and pour us two mugs of coffee.

'Thank you,' she says. 'But I shouldn't have too much caffeine this late in the day or I won't get to sleep tonight. And if I do, it won't last long, or at least that's how it's been for years.'

'Really?' I say. 'Why's that?'

Edda thinks about it. 'I suppose I haven't slept properly since Elísa's mother died. I know that was years ago, but her death seems to have robbed me not only of her but of the ability to sleep as well.'

Edda's smile takes some of the sombreness out of her words, making them sound almost casual.

'Wasn't Elísa only one when ... when...?'

'When her mother died?' Edda finishes.

I'm ashamed of my inability to come out and say it, but Edda doesn't seem offended.

'Yes, Elísa was one when Marta killed herself,' she says.

'Oh.'

Edda gives me a questioning look.

'It's just...' I hesitate. 'Elísa said she'd died in an accident.'

Edda's smile doesn't reach her eyes. 'You know what Elísa's like. She has a vivid imagination.'

I laugh, then realise how inappropriate it must sound and try to explain: 'I was exactly the same. Always making up stories. Like about the father I never knew.'

'Yes, children are good at that.' Edda gets to her feet. 'It's a pity our imagination seems to lose some of its power with age. There are times when it would be good to be able to forget oneself like that.'

I nod and put my mug in the sink, suddenly finding the thought sad, because when I was younger and had a better imagination, life was easier. It was so easy to deceive myself and pretend that everything was better than it was.

Out in the corridor, I come across Elísa, standing staring out of the window. I creep up behind her.

'See anything interesting?' I whisper in her ear.

She doesn't jump, doesn't even look round.

'Yes,' she says.

'What?'

'It doesn't matter – you won't be able to see it.'

I peer outside but can't see anything unusual, so I give Elísa's plait a gentle tug and go into the restaurant, leaving her at the window.

It looks lovely in here now, with all the chairs in straight rows and tealights decorating the tables. In the gathering gloom, the hotel takes on a mysterious, faintly sinister atmosphere. It makes you instinctively lower your voice, in case someone overhears what you're saying. If there's anything I love about this hotel, it's the evenings. The darkness. Sometimes I roam the corridors, sitting in the armchairs in the bar or lounge and pretending it's another world, a place where anything could happen.

I go into the kitchen and survey the trays of starters. This evening is the main event, and the menu is even more elaborate than yesterday.

'Can I pinch one?' I ask, pointing at the chocolate-coated strawberries.

'Help yourself,' Arne says. 'Have you tasted the prawns too?'

'No, what's in those?' I ask with my mouth full.

'They're tempura prawns,' he says, handing me a small plastic bowl. 'With chilli mayo.'

'Oh, wow, that's good.' I close my eyes and emit a loud moan.

Arne laughs. 'Now I know what you sound like when—'

'Shut up.' I give him a nudge, then leave the kitchen.

Hákon Ingimar is in the bar, having a drink. The look he shoots me suggests he thinks last night's incident will have turned me on. I feel sick but smile at him blandly, watching until he looks away. But when I go behind the bar, my knees feel shaky. I tell myself to get a grip and start lining up the clean glasses.

My thoughts stray back to Elísa and her imagined alternative world in which her mother died in an accident rather than deliberately abandoning her when she was only one. I feel sorry for Elísa, and it occurs to me that perhaps we're more alike than I realised.

Mum always said I had an overactive imagination. As a child I lived in a world that no one else could see. One that was much brighter and better than the real one, like a fairy tale or story, because as I turned the pages of books I *became* the characters.

I used to immerse myself so fully in the world the author had created that I was able to continue the story after the last page.

But the older I got, the more difficult it became. I started comparing myself to other people. I realised that the flat Mum and I lived in probably wasn't that tasteful, and the life we lived wasn't actually that exciting. Perhaps it wasn't so desirable after all to be constantly moving from place to place, constantly changing schools and spending most of my evenings alone at home.

A small voice inside me suddenly became louder. The voice said it wanted what I deserved. Wanted all that I'd been denied but had every right to.

Tryggvi

Since the incident on the beach, Oddný has seemed a bit shaken. All she can talk about on the drive back is Lea. She seems to have forgotten about the flask in her coat pocket.

'Petra's just like her mother,' she announces, once we're back in our room.

'How so?' I ask.

'Ester was always so self-obsessed, too selfish to notice how the people around her were feeling. She couldn't see further than the end of her nose.'

I wondered if this means that Oddný's own nose had been put out of joint by Ester's arrival in the family. Apparently, when Haraldur brought his new girlfriend home, his father, Hákon, was very taken with Ester and treated her like a favourite daughter, and that must have been tough on Oddný.

'And you think Petra's the same?' I ask.

'Obviously. Petra's just like her mother. She's oblivious to the fact something's upsetting her daughter. Lea seems so lost. Remember what a cute little thing she used to be?'

'No...' Lea was fifteen when I arrived on the scene. For me, she's never been a cute little thing. I've always thought her beautiful rather than cute, and quite grown up for her age.

'She used to be adorable,' Oddný continues. 'Always so cheerful whenever you met her. Now she seems so ... miserable. Don't you think?'

I make a noncommittal noise that could be taken for agreement, though to tell the truth I don't really have an opinion on this. To me it seems natural that teenagers aren't the same simple, happy souls they were as children.

'Such a shame,' Oddný mutters as she pulls off her socks. 'Petra was the same.'

'In what way?'

'Petra and Stefanía used to be inseparable when they were younger. All the way through school, in fact. They were joined at the hip, always up to something together, either at our house or at Halli and Ester's. I was almost like a second mother to Petra.'

As Oddný continues, a disapproving note enters her voice: 'Then she met Gestur and it was like Stefanía no longer existed. Petra just vanished, casting her cousin aside. Steffý was so hurt – I think it's part of the reason why she decided to study abroad.'

'Oh, right.' I nod, wondering if the disapproval in Oddný's voice is really directed at Petra. Oddný's always had a hard time accepting that Stefanía lives in Denmark, but I didn't know she blamed Petra for the fact.

'Yes,' Oddný sighs. 'So it's not exactly a surprise.'

'What isn't?' I ask, not quite following.

'This business of Lea being so unhappy. I often get the impression that Petra's too wrapped up in herself and her own success to take any interest in her daughter. Poor kid.'

Oddný goes into the bathroom, and I hear the sound of the shower starting up.

I wonder if there could be anything in what Oddný says. Whether both Ester and Petra lack a level of maternal affection and care towards their kids. I picture Lea's frozen expression when she came ashore and remember how she looked at her mother. Had there been hatred in her eyes? Accusation? Not that I could see. From all I've observed, Petra seems a perfectly good mother.

The problem with Oddný is that she finds it so easy to judge other people but maybe doesn't always see herself that clearly. I sometimes wonder what kind of upbringing Stefanía and Hákon

Ingimar had if her drinking was the way it is now. I get the feeling that Hákon Ingimar didn't get much support or discipline when he was growing up, and I suspect that Stefanía may have been escaping more than just a cousin who dropped her for a new boyfriend.

But it's probably not worth thinking about. Nowadays everyone's always going on about their feelings and everyone has a sob story to tell. The attitude used to be that bad things happen but there's no point wallowing in the fact. Now, though, people seem to be diagnosed with PTSD or anxiety, or whatever they call it, over the slightest thing. Sometimes I wonder if what does the most harm isn't the incident itself but all the talking about it – all the reactions afterwards.

Of course you can argue about that just as you can about anything else. People who are wiser than me would probably say that traumas need to be processed. In my experience, though, you can live with life's knocks. I've never felt any desire to blab about my problems. I've learnt to live with the grief that's part of me, just like everything else I've been through.

I open my bag, take out the photo and study it. I've kept it encased in a plastic sleeve, so it's still smooth and uncreased, although I've carried it about with me for years to look at whenever my thoughts turn that way.

From the sounds in the bathroom, I can tell that Oddný has finished her shower. She emerges after a minute or two, wrapped in a towel. It's dark in the room as we didn't turn on the lights when we got back.

Oddný perches on the edge of the bed next to me and raises a hand to my cheek, turning my face to meet her gaze.

'I'm so glad you're here, Tryggvi,' she says. 'I don't know what I'd do without you.'

I close my eyes and we kiss. It's nice of her to say it and I should feel warmed by her words, but instead a shiver runs through me.

Lea Snæberg

I'm not cold, which is weird, because the sea was freezing. I knew that, and I could feel that it was cold, but somehow it didn't affect me at the time.

When I get in the shower, my feet feel oddly numb in the heat. It's painful at first, but then I get used to the temperature and feel the blood streaming back into my toes until they're warm. Burning hot, in fact.

The strange thing is that I don't remember the moment when I decided to walk into the sea. I remember doing it and what it felt like as the water seeped into my shoes, soaking my socks, then my trousers. But I don't remember actually making a decision; it was more like someone else was making it for me, taking over my body.

For a moment I felt like I was floating above myself, watching my body walking into the waves. As if it didn't really have anything to do with me, as if I was no longer connected to myself but part of something bigger.

It sounds mental, I know, but I can't describe it any more clearly than that.

On the way home, Mum said I didn't have to be such a drama queen all the time, but I didn't mean to, it just somehow felt so beautiful to be standing there. Faced with the sea and sky, I felt like nothing else mattered. I was just this insignificant dot in the universe, and nothing I did or said was of any importance at all, and that felt good. More than good: it felt amazing.

Because then none of the bad stuff would matter anymore.

I close my eyes, letting the hot water stream onto my face. Open my mouth to taste the droplets.

I feel so stupid to have let Hákon Ingimar get to me like that. And to have believed that Birgir was genuinely into me and that I could trust him. A boy I've never met. I don't even know if he's real. More than anything, I feel so incredibly stupid for sending him those selfies.

They're in the hands of a stranger now. I picture him as a dirty old man, like in a TV documentary I saw about people who create fake online profiles. It would be so humiliating to have fallen for a scam like that.

I get out of the shower and dry myself. I just hope the photos won't be shared online, because if they are ... if they are, I don't know what I'll do.

'Why did you do that?' Ari asks when I come out of the bathroom. He's sitting on his bed, as if he's been waiting for me. His expression is genuine, a little shocked, and it strikes me that his question is quite different from Mum's, though the words are the same. Ari's tone is caring and affectionate; Mum's was accusing.

'I don't know,' I say and it's the simple truth.

Ari looks at me without speaking. Then he holds out a bag of sweets. 'Want some?' he asks.

'Thanks,' I say, selecting a few.

'Er, I'm going to see what's happening downstairs.' He hesitates. 'Or would you rather I stayed here?'

'Ari,' I say, laughing. 'You don't need to babysit me, honestly.'

'No, I know. I just...'

'Seriously, Ari. I wasn't going to ... I was never going to walk out very far.'

'You went quite a long way,' Ari points out.

'Yeah, but...' I search for a way of explaining it to Ari without sounding overdramatic. 'I just suddenly wanted to know what it would feel like. Haven't you ever wanted to do something crazy, just to know what it would be like?'

'No.' Ari laughs and stands up. 'You're mental, Lea.'

'I know.' I smile. 'Completely mental.'

'Crazy.'

'Batshit crazy,' I agree.

Ari smiles at me, and for a moment I think he's going to hug me. Then he goes out, leaving me alone in the room.

I pull on jeans and a jumper and comb my hair. Wearing no make-up, and dressed down like this, I look like a child. It's almost like seeing myself at twelve or thirteen, when I was always wondering what I could change about myself. What I'd look like with bigger lips or higher cheekbones.

Now that I stop to think about it, I realise how stupid that is. I'm suddenly angry with myself and with society, because young girls shouldn't be thinking about things like that. They shouldn't be so obsessed with their appearance. But before I can follow this thought through, there's a knock at the door. At first I think it's Mum, but she always calls out when she knocks. Her knock is firm, but this one is light and tentative, as if the person standing outside barely wants it to be heard.

'Hello?' I say through the door. 'Who is it?'

There's no answer.

I stand there, staring at the door. The wind is picking up outside and it's whining in the window frame. I wait with my breath caught in my throat, not really sure why my heart is beating at a million miles an hour. It's not like I'm afraid of anyone here at the hotel. The only people staying here are my family.

My phone lights up; I've received a new message. Again, it's from someone whose name is an incomprehensible jumble of letters and numbers. I open it, but there's no message inside, just a video.

The video is dark, taken outside at night. Instinctively I bring the phone closer to my face, to see better. I turn up the volume. The sound crackles with the wind, then I hear a crunching of gravel. Footsteps. Someone is walking outside, along a gravel path. The video ends with the sound of a throat being cleared and a cough. I turn to the window, feeling the sweat break out all over my body. Isn't there a gravel path leading to the hotel?

Again I hear a rustling sound outside the door, then more knocking. Two taps, like before.

Tap, tap.

Sævar
Detective, West Iceland CID

'This is the room,' Edda said.

Sævar was rather disconcerted when, instead of opening the door, Edda took out her phone and started fiddling with it. Was she going to keep them standing there while she answered a message or checked her notifications on Facebook?

He nearly jumped when there was a click and Edda opened the door.

Noticing his expression, she said: 'The doors are controlled by an app. It's possible to use keys too, but the app's more convenient.'

'Ah, right.' Sævar glanced round the room.

'As you can see, it hasn't been cleaned.'

On the desk were several bottles of champagne, confirming Sævar's suspicion that there had been no swigging vodka straight from the bottle here, but fizz, drunk from elegant glasses. The one on the table was half full, and perhaps that accounted for the stale smell of alcohol in the room. The window was closed and the air was stuffy, though they knew no one had slept in there that night.

'Will it be necessary to ... to examine the room?' Edda asked.

Hörður nodded. 'We'd better close it off. I'll get forensics to carry out an examination later.'

Sævar peered into the bathroom but couldn't see anything of interest at first glance. It was neat and tidy. A used towel hung from a hook, and the bin was almost empty.

But there was something in there. A small blister pack. He took it out of the bin and read the name: Sertraline. He knew it was a drug used for depression and anxiety: not that interesting in itself, but it might turn out to be significant.

He opened the bathroom cabinet and saw that the shelves contained cosmetics for both men and women. His gaze was caught by something on the back of the cupboard door, and he called over his shoulder.

'Hörður, you need to see this.'

The Day Before
Saturday, 4 November 2017

Petra Snæberg

'Something's been up with her for a long time,' Gestur says. 'You'd notice if you...'

'If I what?' I ask. Gestur looks away but he doesn't need to finish the sentence. I know full well what he's insinuating.

The spark that had been ignited between us earlier has gone out. Although we're in the same room, we could hardly be further apart than we are now. Instead of the alcohol high, the pleasant numbness I experienced earlier, I have a relentless whistling or whining in my ears.

'If you showed any interest in her.' Gestur shakes his head. 'Can't you see, Petra?'

'Can't I see what?'

'That she's constantly trying.' The anger has left Gestur's voice now and he's looking at me as though with pity. Or disappointment. 'Lea's constantly trying to please you.'

'And I'm constantly trying to please her.' Even as I say it, I know that I sound like a petulant teenager.

Gestur rubs his temple and closes his eyes. 'I think it would be best for her to see a therapist.'

A therapist, I think to myself. Then I'd be in the same position as my parents, choosing to let professionals take care of my children's problems rather than tackling them myself.

'Perhaps we should just talk to her,' I say. 'See if she's willing to open up to us. It might not be that serious. It might...'

'Are you saying you think it's normal to walk into the sea in the middle of winter, Petra?' Gestur asks. 'What if we hadn't been there? How far out would she have gone?'

'She said she never intended to go any further,' I say quietly. Before Gestur has a chance to have another go at me, I add: 'But I know she needs help. Of course. And we'll help her. I'll talk to someone on Monday.'

Gestur hesitates, then his shoulders sag a little. 'Good. We have to do it, Petra. I'm afraid for her.'

'Me too,' I say, letting Gestur hug me. I stand very still while he wraps me in his big arms. He moves his head back slightly to kiss me, but I turn my head away, pretending I hadn't realised what he wanted, hadn't noticed his attempt to kiss and make up.

I regret it immediately. Gestur releases me and moves away, roughly enough that I can tell he's hurt.

'I'm going to have a shower,' I say.

Gestur doesn't look at me, and as I'm closing the bathroom door, I see him opening the minibar.

Once I'm alone, I start feeling sick with fear for Lea. What if there's something seriously wrong with her? Up to now, I've assumed that her bad moods and temper tantrums are the result of the usual teenage hormonal fluctuations, but what if it's something worse? I thought she'd got over the problems at her old school with that spiteful gang of girls she hung out with there, but what if she still hasn't recovered from the experience? Maybe Gestur's right and I am too uncaring as a mother. Too self-centred.

Gestur thinks I'm both distant and self-obsessed, though he's never come right out and said it. I can tell by the way he looks at me. He's never entirely trusted me as a mother. I remember one incident when Lea was three. I was cooking and turned away for a moment to search for something in the fridge. Next minute I heard Lea let out a terrible scream. She had reached her little hand up to the kitchen worktop and grabbed the blade of a sharp knife I'd been using to slice onions.

I don't think she hurt herself as badly as her scream suggested – she was just frightened when she saw the blood pouring from the cut and dripping onto the floor. She was still holding the knife, and I seized her hand and carefully prised her fingers off the sharp blade.

At that moment Gestur came into the kitchen, and the first thing he said was: 'What have you done, Petra?'

Not what happened, but what had I done.

Gestur scooped Lea up in his arms, wrapped a tea towel round her hand and carried her out to the car. He drove off without even waiting for me, leaving me staring after them, my hands covered in blood, the dinner still in the oven.

I've never felt as useless as I did in that moment.

In reality, my remoteness isn't caused by indifference but by my fear of making a mistake. My fear of saying or doing something stupid and losing Lea.

I open my bag and dig out the miniature bottle of vodka that's been there since I went on a business trip to London last year. I down it in one, feeling the burning in my throat, followed by the warm glow in my stomach. And I resolve not to worry anymore tonight about Lea; there'll be plenty of time to deal with her problems later.

Normally I'd use this time to update my social media, but it occurs to me that I've hardly taken any photos all day. I've been so preoccupied that I haven't even thought about documenting my every move, and the last thing I feel like doing now is sharing the events of the day with my followers.

When I emerge from my shower, Gestur has gone. A smell of aftershave lingers in the air and his clothes are neatly folded on the chair by the desk. His smart shirt and shoes are missing from the wardrobe. He must have got ready and gone downstairs without bothering to take a shower or let me know.

Lea Snæberg

'Hello,' says Harpa, walking in. 'Sorry, I didn't know if you were alone or not.'

'I'm alone,' I say, faking nonchalance, as if I haven't just nearly wet myself with terror, wondering who could be knocking.

Who did I think it might be? The man who calls himself Gulli? Or Birgir?

I put down my phone and wonder if the video could have been sent by Gulli. In spite of everything, his messages have always been polite and he's never sent me anything directly inappropriate. Well, apart from the fact that it's pretty inappropriate for an older man to be sending messages to a teenage girl he doesn't even know.

I go over to the window and pull the curtains back a little, peering out into the blackness, but I can't see anything because of the light in the room.

'What's up?' Harpa asks. 'Something exciting going on outside?'

'No.' I turn away from the window. 'The weather's getting worse.'

'So?' Harpa laughs. 'We're not going anywhere, are we?'

'No, I suppose not.'

Harpa gives me a searching look. 'Are you ill or something?'

'No,' I say, running my hands through my hair. 'I've just got out of the shower.'

'OK.' Harpa smiles wryly and sits down on Ari's bed. She's wearing a black dress and nylon tights with black spots on them, and holding a black backpack with a red tassel dangling from the zip.

'What?' I ask, when she continues to stare at me.

'Nothing.'

Something's changed since yesterday. Harpa's looking at me differently and it takes me a moment or two to realise that it must be connected to what happened at Djúpalón. Harpa's bound to be wondering what's wrong with me. Whether I'm a bit weird in the head.

It hasn't occurred to me until now that the other members of my family must be talking about me. I suppose everyone must think there's something wrong with me.

But Harpa's expression radiates not concern but interest.

'Are you going home tomorrow?' I ask.

'No. We've got to stay until next week.'

'Don't you want to be here?'

'No. I mean, sure. But...' Harpa strokes the red tassel on her backpack. 'But it's kind of tiring not sleeping at home, you know? Always being in a strange bed and having to live out of a suitcase. And then there are all the endless visits where I don't really know anyone. Not properly.'

'I hear you.'

'Yes.' Harpa sighs heavily. 'But it's always like that with Dad.'

'Do you find it boring being with him?'

'Oh, no,' Harpa says. 'Not now, anyway.'

We smile at each other.

'We should go down,' I say.

'Yes. Yes, we should.' Harpa looks serious for a moment, then laughs, and her expression turns mischievous. 'Actually I've already been downstairs. You know, with that bartender.'

'The woman?'

'What woman?' Harpa raises her eyebrows. 'No, with the guy. The hot one.'

'What? What were you doing with him?'

'Nothing special. Just talking.'

'What about?'

'What about?' Harpa fiddles with the zip of her bag. 'About getting him to spike our glasses every time we ask for a drink. Without anyone seeing.'

'What?' I stare at her in astonishment. 'Seriously? But ... but...'

'I've paid him in advance,' Harpa says. 'All we need to do is go down and ask for a Sprite or, you know, some other non-alcoholic drink.'

I feel my heart beating a little faster with excitement. I can hardly believe how brazen Harpa is. Or that the guy has actually agreed to do it. He must know what would happen if our parents found out.

'He said it was his last weekend here, anyway,' Harpa adds, as if reading my mind. 'So it doesn't matter if he gets caught.'

'But what about us?'

'What about us?' Harpa asks.

'What if someone guesses?'

'Lea.' Harpa opens her backpack to reveal a bottle of vodka. 'You remember what it was like last night? They wouldn't have noticed if we'd come in puking our guts up. They were too wrecked themselves. Anyway, in the UK you can buy booze at my age.'

'I suppose so,' I say.

'So, I think we should just do what we like. Agreed?'

I nod. 'Agreed.'

Petra Snæberg

When I go downstairs to Viktor's room he's already holding a glass of foaming, golden liquid. The good champagne, I assume.

'Wow, you look smart,' I say, taking in the tailored blue suit and waistcoat with a handkerchief in the breast pocket. He looks as if he's been cut out of an advertisement, with his dark beard perfectly groomed, his neatly brushed-back hair, and his gleaming, cognac-brown shoes.

Viktor has always been good at putting an outfit together. He always dressed well when we were younger. If I wanted an honest answer about what to wear, I would ask Viktor rather than Steffy.

'You're not so bad yourself,' Viktor says, handing me some champagne.

'Where did you get the glasses from?' I ask, taking a seat at the desk, while Viktor perches on the bed.

'I fetched them from the bar.'

'How posh,' I say, sipping the sweet drink as I survey his room.

It's pretty much the same as ours, same kind of furniture and bedspread, just a little smaller and much tidier. Everything in its place, a coat on a hanger and nothing on the desk or bedside table that doesn't belong there. No vase, like in our room.

'What a shame Maja had to leave,' I say. 'Do you know what the family problem was?'

Viktor shrugs. 'Something to do with her sister.'

'Have they found her yet?'

Viktor doesn't answer, just smiles and says: 'To be completely honest, I'm not sure it's working between us.'

'Oh?'

'We're just too different.'

'Oh, OK.' I finish my glass, and Viktor gives me a refill. 'I get the impression you're different from quite a lot of women...' I add.

'Let's just say...' Viktor looks down at his champagne, a small smile playing over his lips '...I'm not exactly in a hurry.'

'No, you men have all the time in the world.' I sound bitter without meaning to, and explain: 'To have children, I mean.'

'Would you have done anything differently?' Viktor asks. 'If you could choose?'

'Yes.' I feel guilty the moment the word slips out. 'Well, you know, I wouldn't exchange Ari or Lea for the world, but I wouldn't have minded having them a bit later...'

'What about Gestur?'

'Gestur?' I look at Viktor, puzzled. 'You mean, would I have chosen to be with him?'

Viktor nods.

'I ... I...' The words stick in my throat. I want to say yes, of course I'd have chosen him if I had my time again, but is it true? I've often thought that Gestur was a safe choice of husband. He's a reliable man and most people like him. But there was never any real spark between us, never any passion, at least not on my side. That's never bothered me, though; I'm not particularly romantic and regard that kind of love as a naive dream. I've always thought that anything that blazes that hot is sure to burn out fast.

Gestur ticked all the boxes, for me and for my family: a good job, a fun personality, reliable. But recently he hasn't been particularly reliable, has he? He's been behaving differently from usual. His fuse has been shorter and suddenly it's like there's something missing when he looks at me. A sort of tolerance that used to be there. All of a sudden I'm no longer sure of him, and I ask myself if he's finally given up on me. Had enough.

'You don't need to answer that,' Viktor says. He studies me over the rim of his glass as he drinks. No doubt he can see how much trouble the answer is giving me. The smile on his lips is a little teasing, as though he's amused by something.

'What?' I ask nervously. Strange, because I always used to feel safe with Viktor when we were younger. But now I feel as though the balance of power between us has shifted.

'Nothing,' Viktor says. He's silent for a while. 'It just reminds me of the old days, the way we used to spend our evenings sitting on the bed at my house and gossiping.'

I smile. 'I used to enjoy that.'

'It didn't take much for us to have fun.'

I think back, aware that he's right. All we needed was each other. We usually went round to Viktor's house because his parents would let him get away with almost anything.

Viktor was the child his parents had dreamt of, but who kept them waiting for his arrival for many years. Elín had Jenný with a previous partner when she was just nineteen, but when she met Ingvar, their attempts to have children together failed. When Viktor finally arrived thirteen years later, admittedly via the adoption agency, Elín and Ingvar were so relieved that they couldn't bear to deny their child a thing.

I raise the glass to my lips to take a sip, only to discover that there's no champagne left. Viktor fetches the bottle and gives me another top-up. I'm drinking far too fast – it's already going to my head. I don't just feel tipsy – the whole room is moving around.

I remember the days when I didn't have to bear my secrets alone. Everything I was, all the feelings I had, I shared with Viktor and Steffý.

'I've invited Steffý to join us,' I say.

'Oh?' Viktor seems surprised. 'I thought you two were ... Well, I don't really know what to say.'

'Neither do I.'

'You've never told me why you fell out.' Viktor is studying me. 'I thought you'd just gone in different directions, but now, after watching you together here, I get the impression something happened between you.'

I look down at my glass, tipping it until the liquid touches the rim.

'What did happen?' Viktor asks.

'Nothing,' I say, but my voice has no power to persuade.

'Come on,' Viktor persists. 'Out with it. What the hell happened?'

'Nothing happened.' I drink, then look up at Viktor. He's staring at me as if he can compel me to speak by the force of his gaze. I laugh, unable to stop myself, and feel briefly as if things are back to how they used to be.

'Petra,' Viktor says.

'OK, OK.' I give up, but as I begin talking I can feel the effect of the alcohol changing, turning my mood sombre. I don't feel like laughing anymore. I swallow and say: 'Do you remember Teddi?'

'Yes.'

Of course Viktor remembers him. It was Viktor who held me in his arms when I wept every time I got drunk for months afterwards. Comforted me, stroked my hair and whispered that everything would be all right. I smile at the thought, though the memory is painful. Viktor made everything more bearable, but I doubt he would have comforted me like that if he'd known the truth.

'OK.' I empty my glass down my throat and ask for more. 'You remember what happened.'

'Of course,' Viktor says, more seriously now. 'We don't need to—'

'No, I want to.' I close my eyes, hoping that this will make it easier to talk. Then I put down my glass, because my hands are shaking. 'Anyway, you know … the evening it … it happened…'

I take another deep breath and prepare to say out loud the thing I've never spoken about before, though it preys on my mind constantly. The thing I just can't forget, however hard I try.

Tryggvi

I tell Oddný to go down ahead of me, then I sit and stare at my phone as if it is somehow more than just plastic and metal.

My decision to have a drink has been taken unconsciously and I don't even try to fight it. The first mouthful of beer is icy cold and so good that I close my eyes. Another mouthful immediately after the first, then a third. After a little while I sit there staring at the empty beer can, wondering if it was worth it. Was all the time I've been sober really worth the effort? Perhaps it would have been – before. In fact, I'm sure it would have been worth giving up the booze before it happened, but not now. Now it's too late.

When I finally pick up my phone, there are two empty beer cans on the desk and I'm halfway down the third. There's only one can left in the fridge, and that's all the booze there is, so I'll have to go downstairs if I want more to drink.

Glancing at the clock, I see that I'll have to act fast. Oddný's bound to come up soon to tell me to come down for dinner.

The phone call has been on my mind ever since I woke up, as it's an annual tradition on this day and I know Nanna will be waiting. She answers straight away too, as though she's been sitting with the phone in her hand.

'How are you?' I ask.

'Fine. I'm fine.' As always when I call, Nanna sounds indifferent. But then she was like that when we first got to know each other. I was sure she wasn't interested in me the first few times I rang her. She was so curt and seemed in a hurry to hang up. Later, I realised she was testing me, checking if I was really interested. She didn't have time to waste talking to men who were just playing around. She had a son and wanted a man who was prepared to be a father. A man who wouldn't do a runner the first chance he got.

'Did you do anything to mark the occasion?' I ask.

'Not much,' Nanna replies. 'Though I did bake a cake. An almond cake. You remember? The one with the pink icing.'

'I remember,' I say, smiling at the memory. 'It never disappoints.'

Neither of us says anything for a while, then Nanna comments: 'You're on Snæfellsnes.'

It's not exactly a question, but I answer it anyway. 'Yes, we're here at a posh hotel.'

'Of course.'

I laugh inside, though of course Nanna can't hear me. She's always been a bit strange about Oddný. When she first found out we were seeing each other, she was very nosy, asking all sorts of stuff about the family. Funny questions, like what did we eat and how did they treat me.

Nanna's never been keen on people with money. She feels they must have cheated somehow, as if no one deserves to be rich.

Money used to be an endless topic of conversation in our relationship. Or rather the lack of money. We had to watch every penny, spending as little as we could get away with or we wouldn't be able to make ends meet. Nanna was seldom happier than when she bought something on sale, and she was good at producing cheap, hearty meals. In fact, she was a genius at making a little go a long way. Her resourcefulness was one of the things I liked best about her.

'Yes, it's a very posh hotel,' I say, imagining Nanna here with me; how she'd shake her head over all the extravagance. 'We're here until tomorrow.'

'I visited him earlier,' Nanna says, ignoring my last comment.

'Oh, did you? I must drop by myself when I get a chance.'

'You won't regret it.'

'Yes, I know. I still talk to him,' I say, cracking open another beer. 'In the evenings, mostly.'

'I know,' Nanna says. 'Me too.'

Silence.

'I got, er, my brother Tóti to scan in some pictures,' Nanna says then, in a lighter tone. 'Photos of photos, so to speak. Do you want me to send them to you?'

'Please,' I say. 'You've got my email address, haven't you?'

'Yes, I should have it somewhere,' Nanna says. Then: 'Are you drinking?'

'It's been a long time.'

'I'm not judging you.'

I hear a click like a glass being put down on a table and realise that Nanna's drinking too. I suddenly picture her sitting on the sun deck outside our old house. Remember how she used to drink white wine, closing her eyes and turning her face up to the sun as she savoured every drop. Remember how she used to laugh at those moments. Nanna used to laugh a lot. It was fun being around her. She was a bit of a butterfly in those days, chattering away, often without thinking.

But in the end alcohol became another topic of discussion between me and Nanna – my drinking, that's to say. I didn't seem to be able to control it, once I got started. The trouble is that I become a different man when I drink and do things I'd never normally do.

We sit there on the phone for a while, barely talking, but it's a comfortable sort of silence. I know that, like me, Nanna's not really present in the moment but lost in her memories. Of our shared past. In spite of everything, most of the memories are good. Or perhaps that's because I only remember the good times. The quarrels and our divorce have left little trace. It's the laughter and affection that stay with me. The evenings when I used to stealthily breathe in the scent of her hair as we lay watching TV or when Nanna woke me after I had dropped off while putting our son to bed.

We could have had a good life together, Nanna and me. I often think our break-up would only have been temporary if it hadn't been for what happened afterwards. In fact, I'm sure of it.

When I ring off, I feel empty inside. I stand up and trip over the suitcase on the floor but recover my balance before I fall over. I open the minibar again, but all the booze is finished, as I already knew.

I stand there in the middle of the room for a minute or two, wondering what I should do. Perhaps I should just leave. The thought isn't so bad.

Outside a storm is raging, making the huge windows vibrate, yet, even so, I'd rather be out there than in here.

'You haven't a clue what became of us, have you?' I say aloud to someone who no longer exists. Yet I could swear that he answers, telling me not to be such a fool.

Petra Snæberg

To my relief, Steffý knocks before I can tell Viktor what happened that evening. Generally I'm a pretty good talker; I can communicate well when I'm giving my sales pitches or presenting my ideas to clients. But now I'm sure that it would have come out all wrong, if I'd been able to say anything at all.

Steffý is wearing a long-sleeved gold top that seems to shift colour according to how the light falls on it. Her lipstick is scarlet and there are several gold bracelets on her slim wrists.

'Right, raise your glasses,' she orders once Viktor has supplied her with a drink.

We obey, toast, then drink. I've been downing mine too fast and have to blink several times to get the world around me to stop spinning.

'Have you got any water?' I ask Viktor.

He fetches a bottle from the minibar and hands it to me. I gulp down half of it but don't feel any better. While Steffý and Viktor are talking, I wonder hazily what I'd have told him if Steffý hadn't knocked just then. Whether it would have been better to begin the story on the fateful evening – or on the day I first met Teddi.

Teddi started at our school in the autumn of our second year, when we were sixteen going on seventeen. I'd been trying to find out which room our maths class was in and arrived late for the lesson, red-faced and out of breath. I slipped into the first free seat I could see and had barely sat down before the teacher came over to me.

'What's your name?' she asked, her thin lips turning up at the corners, though there was no corresponding warmth in her eyes. Her voice was deep and resonant, as if it belonged on the radio.

'Petra,' I managed to stammer.

'Stand up, Petra, and face the class.'

At first I thought she was joking, but when her eyes continued to bore into me, I got hesitantly to my feet. My hands were shaking, and my heart was thudding so fast I was sure all the other kids could hear it.

'Now apologise to your fellow pupils for arriving late and interrupting the lesson,' she said, in the same tone, the smile still fixed on her face.

I turned, if possible, even redder. My face was burning like a light bulb, and there was cold sweat running down my spine and under my arms. I knew, rather than sensed, that my deodorant would fail to disguise the smell.

'So ... sorry I was late.' I scarcely recognised the weak, trembling voice as my own.

For a moment there was complete silence, then I heard the teacher speak behind me.

'Thank you, Petra,' she said.

Humiliated, I sat down again, trying to hold back the tears. I could hardly concentrate or follow the lesson, which is why I didn't immediately notice when the boy next to me pushed over a piece of paper.

He'd drawn a caricature like the kind I'd often seen in the papers. It didn't take me long to work out that it was the teacher, though Teddi had exaggerated her features, giving her a huge nose and reducing her lips to a thin line. He'd captured her so well that I had to clamp my hand over my mouth to stop a laugh from escaping.

Teddi was unbelievably good at drawing, and I learnt later that his caricatures were just something he did for fun. At home he drew closely observed portraits of people, which showed them in a different light from photographs. He seemed to capture their essence in his sketches, depicting them with expressions illustrative of their character. Expressions that few people would notice but were nevertheless instantly recognisable when Teddi caught them with his pencil.

I couldn't take my eyes off him the first time I watched him drawing, his face so focused, his movements so deft. His pencil danced over the white paper, and the drawings took shape as if by magic. I didn't understand how it happened, not really, but I did know that Teddi had an unusual gift – and that I liked him. He made me laugh so much I couldn't breathe. His smile had the same effect on me.

'Petra, hello?' Viktor's voice jerks me back to the present.

'Yes?' I say, pretending nothing's up. 'What?'

'Is everything OK?' Viktor frowns. 'Bring your glass over here, I reckon it needs a refill.'

I try to refuse but can hear how feeble my protests sound. Because the truth is I don't want to be sober. Being confined in a small room with Steffý and Viktor fills me with a mixture of nostalgia and suffocation. I feel as if I've been transported back in time. We could easily be in Viktor's bedroom, shortly after the millennium.

Viktor hands back my glass and asks what I was thinking about.

'Nothing special,' I say, and raise the glass to my lips. I can see that Viktor doesn't believe me though he pretends he does. He turns to Steffý.

'So, what happened with you and ... and...?'

'Per,' Steffý finishes. 'It's all right, I can hardly remember his name myself.'

'What happened? The last time we talked you two were planning to buy a house, weren't you?'

'Yes, we'd reached that stage.' Steffý laughs, then sighs. 'Not a house actually, a flat. We were going to buy a flat and even got as far as looking round a few. There was one absolute beauty in the centre of Copenhagen with high ceilings and arched doorways and windows. It was so romantic, with decorative mouldings, ceiling roses, French windows, the works. Honestly, Petra, you'd have loved it.'

'So what happened?' Viktor asks.

'Well, one day I happened to see a message on Per's computer and...' Steffy raises her glass and laughs again. 'I mean, if you're going to cheat on someone, the least you can do is remember to log out of your email and lock your computer.'

I gaze at Steffy in astonishment. Someone cheated on her? On the girl who used to wind boys round her little finger? When she was younger, she would never have let anyone treat her like that – she was always one step ahead.

'You're joking?' Viktor says. 'What an idiot.'

'Yep.' Steffy holds out her empty glass, and Viktor fills it. 'Here's to fucking Per.'

'I'm not drinking to him,' Viktor says.

'OK, who should we drink to, then?' Steffy asks. 'Any suggestions, Petra?'

'To...' I cast around for something neutral. 'To being together again.'

'To being together again,' Steffy repeats. 'Not very snappy, but, OK, I can drink to that. May it be the first reunion of many.'

We raise our classes, and there's a ring of crystal as they clink.

'Right, I know what we should do,' Steffy says. She adopts a pose, as if she's about to deliver a speech. 'Never have I ever—'

She gets no further because Viktor bursts out laughing.

'Are you for real, Steffy?' he asks. 'Never have I ever? Aren't we a bit old for that game?'

'Hush,' Steffy replies. 'Don't say that. Can't we pretend we're sixteen again, just for this evening?'

Viktor and I exchange glances.

'Please,' Steffy says, her mouth turning down in a pout. 'I really need a distraction from thinking about Per and that slut.'

We give in. 'All right,' I say. 'You start.'

'Yesss!' Steffý beams, then puts a finger to her lips, pretending to think. 'Never have I ever peed in my pants as a teenager.'

I take a gulp of my drink and shoot Steffý a dirty look. 'So we're going to play it like that, are we?'

'OK, what am I missing?' Viktor asks.

I sigh. 'It was when we were twelve.'

'Thirteen,' Steffý corrects.

'All right, thirteen,' I say. 'We went to the cinema to see some film.'

'*Clueless*,' Steffý supplies. 'We both wanted to be Alicia Silverstone.'

'Quite right,' I say, hit by a vivid memory of the group that had formed outside the cinema, all the boys and girls jostling to get to the ticket office. The window outside the foyer where everyone held out their money in return for a ticket. The smell that hit you as you entered, of carpet impregnated with old popcorn and of the overheating projector, and the anticipation once we had settled into the soft red seats and the film started. In the background the quiet hissing of the projector and the rustling of popcorn bags.

'We noticed straight away that the fittest boys in the school were sitting in the row behind us. Boys from year ten. Boys we'd never have dared to talk to. Then, during the interval, Steffý had to go to the loo and ... and the boys were standing there and one of them asked...'

Steffý takes over because I can't hold back my laughter any longer. 'One of them asked: "Have you got a light, girls?" As if a couple of thirteen-year-olds like us would have a lighter in our pockets.'

'Then what?' Viktor asks, squinting at us from under his brows. 'Did you wet yourself?'

'Petra got in such a tizz that she turned scarlet and got the giggles,' Steffý says. 'You remember how she always used to giggle uncontrollably when she was embarrassed?'

'I remember.' Viktor is amused.

'Well, she couldn't stop laughing and she'd just drunk a bucket of Coke...'

'Anyway,' I say loudly, though I can't help laughing now myself.

We carry on with the game, doing several rounds. The shots are innocent enough. I've never cheated in an exam or I've never cried during a film at school. As we laugh, I forget about all the negative stuff. Don't even spare a thought for Teddi. I just think about all the good times – because there were far more of them than the bad times. I'm starting to believe that perhaps everything will change now: Steffý will move back to Iceland and the three of us will start meeting up regularly, picking up the thread as if nothing had ever come between us. It's a happy thought, as if I've finally found my feet again after dangling in thin air for years.

I'm just thinking how much I've missed them, when Steffý darts me a wicked look and says: 'Never have I ever kissed my cousin.'

Oh, God. I feel my face growing hot as I remember me and Viktor kissing.

At some point Steffý had said she was worried I wouldn't be good enough at kissing when the time came and suggested I practise on Viktor. I thought it was a bad idea, but one evening, when we were all drinking round at my house, she persuaded us that it would be no big deal. That Viktor would be the perfect person to practise on, as he could tell me where I needed to improve my technique.

She had watched us critically, even directed us. At the time I found a way of justifying it to myself, and Viktor didn't put up any objections either. I remember seeing the swelling bulge in his trousers while we were kissing but didn't draw attention to it as I didn't want to embarrass him.

I put it down to his inexperience in matters of sex. He'd never been with a girl. Never shown any interest in them. The only girls he showed the slightest interest in were me and Steffý, but we never thought of Viktor as a boy. He was just one of us. We didn't hesitate to get changed in front of him, or talk about sex, periods and all the things girls discuss with each other. He never seemed bothered by any of it, just sat and listened without contributing much.

I glance at him now. He doesn't seem to find the memory as excruciatingly embarrassing as I do. He raises his glass, waving it around as he talks: 'Technically speaking I'm not actually your cousin,' he says, heedless of the drops spilling from his glass.

'Technically speaking, you bloody well are our cousin,' Steffý insists.

'Not a blood relation.'

'No, but according to the law.'

'OK, OK.' Viktor throws up his hands. 'Then I had my first kiss with my cousin. How tragic is that?'

'Oh, Viktor, sweetie,' Steffý says. 'Was that your first kiss? Of course, how could I have forgotten? But, hang on. Petra, wasn't that your first kiss too?'

'Sure,' I say. 'And now let's change the subject, please.'

Steffý roars with laughter, but Viktor seems a little thrown. Clearly, the realisation has made him uncomfortable, and again I catch a glimpse of the Viktor I used to know. The shy Viktor. The Viktor who didn't dare talk to other girls or go swimming on his own.

I sigh, and Steffý notices. 'Are you thinking about Lea?' she asks.

'Lea?' It takes me a moment to work out why Steffý should bring her up. Then I remember my daughter walking into the sea and am shot through with guilt. 'Yes, actually. I don't understand what happened.'

'It's a difficult age,' Steffý says. 'Is she seeing a boy?'

'No, I don't think so,' I say, though of course I have my suspicions that she is. I've noticed the way she smiles at her phone and writes messages with more anxious eagerness than when she's just chatting to her friends.

'Bound to be a boy,' Steffý says. 'Has she just broken up with someone? I remember what you were like after...' She breaks off and smiles apologetically when she sees my face. 'Sorry.'

I feel myself growing cold and get abruptly to my feet. Steffý grabs my arm. 'Petra, don't go.'

'I'm not going,' I say, forcing a smile. 'I just need a pee.'

In the bathroom I lean against the basin. A broken heart. Is that the reason why I can't stop thinking about Teddi? We were so young, only kids, and at that age attraction is so heightened and overwhelming. It's all so thrilling, beautiful and fragile.

No, I wasn't broken-hearted. I didn't know what love was.

Opening my bag, I hunt around for a pill to calm my nerves. Then I chuck the empty blister pack in the bin. I want to splash my face with cold water, but that would smudge my make-up. Instead, I run icy water on my hands, hoping that will stop them from being so clammy. I can smell a whiff of sweat from my armpits and open Viktor's cabinet in search of something to disguise it. Finding a woman's deodorant, presumably left behind by Maja, I use it under my arms.

Maja. Since entering Viktor's room, I'd forgotten all about her. I'd been meaning to ask him about her, to find out what happened between them and why he isn't more worried about her, but the only thing I can think about is me, me and me again.

Self-centred. Gestur is right.

Having carefully replaced the deodorant in the cabinet, I'm about to close the door when I notice a dirty mark inside. A brown smear or streak.

When I rub the mark with my finger, it spreads and the colour grows lighter and changes, appearing redder.

Irma
Hotel Employee

The wind is whistling through the gap in the coffee-room window. It has been picking up strength fast in the last hour or so. To me, the weather seems like the perfect background for the upcoming evening, but then I've always loved this time of year. Winter is my favourite season. There's nothing cosier than being safe inside a warm house while a storm is howling outside. All the unexplained noises and shadows make everything that little bit more dramatic. It creates a certain atmosphere, doesn't it? But then I suppose I've always been drawn to the dark side.

I move closer and breathe in the damp odour. It's familiar, reminding me of the smell of my bedroom window in the flat Mum and I lived in longest. The wood was rotten, the frame swollen, the paint flaking. When I had nothing to do, I used to amuse myself by picking it off. In bad weather, the wind would whistle through the cracks, as it's doing now, and there was always the same smell of wet wood. Of damp. It's odd that the hotel window should smell like this, because it's new and shouldn't be suffering from any problems of that sort.

'Irma, shut the window, would you?' Edda says, as she enters the coffee room. She wraps a shawl around her shoulders and switches on the kettle.

I obey, closing the window then mopping up the water on the sill with a cloth.

'It's freezing in here,' Edda remarks.

'Sorry,' I say. 'I just needed a bit of fresh air.'

Edda rubs her upper arms, shrugging her shoulders almost up to her ears. 'The weather's getting worse. I just hope the wind will drop by tomorrow lunchtime, when they're due to leave.'

'I'm sure it will.' At the thought of tomorrow lunchtime my breathing quickens, because by then they'll be gone. By this time tomorrow their rooms will be empty or occupied by new guests.

Having to say goodbye always makes me feel a little sad. Every time Mum and I moved, I would look round our flat or my classroom at school and think: I'll never come back here. The thought always left me feeling hollowed out – the same sensation of emptiness every time, as if someone had died.

I can't stand goodbyes.

Mind you, I have seen lots of the kids again over the years, though they don't realise who I am. I'm unusually good at faces and never forget them, which is ironic, since I'm apparently so unmemorable myself.

Recently, I bumped into a girl who used to be in the same class as me. She always found it hilarious to say my name with a bleating noise like a sheep every time I walked by – *Irmaa-a-a*. So original.

I spotted her at the supermarket with two little boys who were constantly whining and pestering her. She looked tired, in spite of her smart clothes and heavy make-up. I noticed the tiny details: the mascara smudged on her eyelids, the belt on her coat all dirty at the end as if it had trailed in the mud. She literally bumped into me by the dairy section, gave me a tight-lipped smile and apologised without once looking at me.

I've seen other former acquaintances around town. Or looked them up and followed them online. I'm interested to see what's become of people, what path they've chosen in life and what sort of trail they leave in their wake. Which of them get the good jobs, have children and are active on social media. Who goes off the rails or gets left behind, only to crop up in the back pages of the papers, their name accompanied by a small photo and the caption: 'Our beloved son and brother.'

Edda pats me on the shoulder. 'We should probably get cracking.'

'Yes, I suppose so.' I get to my feet.

Edda smiles, then turns serious. 'By the way, I noticed something strange earlier.'

'What?'

'There was a man prowling round the hotel. I didn't see him clearly enough to be sure he wasn't one of the guests, but he was behaving oddly...' Edda hesitates before continuing: 'I was wondering if it might be someone connected to the family or just some oddball who wants to get a closer look at them. After all, they haven't made any secret of the fact they're staying here.'

'I'll keep my eyes open,' I say, darting a sideways glance at the window.

'Thanks, dear,' Edda says. 'And there was something else I wanted to talk to you about too: I know your contract only runs up to Christmas, but is there any chance you could stay on longer? The bookings are pouring in, and it looks as if we'll be needing another pair of hands.'

'Yes,' I say. 'Yes, of course. You can rely on me.'

'Thanks, dear,' Edda says, then leaves the kitchen.

I watch her go, thinking how nice it would be to carry on working here. But the truth is, everything depends on what happens this evening. I can't make any promises.

I go to the reception desk to check that the lights are correctly adjusted. The illumination is all-important on evenings like this. Without the twilight, I'm not sure the guests would enjoy themselves as much. Because some things work better in the shadows. The moment they emerge into the daylight they change shape and appear more unsettling.

I've just managed to achieve the perfect night setting for the bedroom corridors when the front door opens with a bang and a figure comes in. My first thought is that it's the man Edda noticed skulking around outside the hotel, but it turns out I'm wrong. It's a girl, who can't be quite twenty, wearing a woollen hat and a bulky down jacket.

'Sorry,' she says. Walking quickly over to reception, she places her hands on the desk. 'My name's Lif. I talked to someone here on the phone earlier.'

'Yes?'

'I'm looking for my sister.'

'She isn't here,' I say, realising straight away that this must be the sister of Maja, the girl whose family can't get hold of her.

'She must be here,' Lif says sharply. Then her voice breaks, and she has to cough and straighten up. 'Her phone's still here. I used that ... that app to locate it. The phone is here in the hotel, so Maja has to be here too.'

Lea Snæberg

Harpa laughs so loud I'm afraid the whole hotel will hear. I tried to tell her that it was a bad idea to leave the room, but she insisted, saying no one would notice; we were as good as invisible. Warily, I open the door to the corridor and check in both directions before we set off.

'Just a weeny bit more,' Harpa says, almost tripping on a rug.

I grab her arm. 'Harpa, people will hear us.'

'Hear what?' Harpa says. 'Hear that I'm totally—'

At that moment the door of one of the rooms opens and she clamps her lips shut, shaking with suppressed giggles. I'm not so amused when I hear Mum's voice.

But Harpa straightens up and starts walking more or less normally, so that when we meet Mum with Uncle Viktor and Auntie Stefanía, they don't seem to notice anything odd. They all look pretty far gone themselves, in fact. Stefanía lurches sideways and clutches at Viktor, who shakes his head. Mum's in the same state, except she's wearing a more serious expression. When she looks at me, it's like it takes her a moment to recognise me.

'Lea,' she says in a singsong voice.

'Mum,' I reply.

Mum grins, then looks me up and down and says: 'Didn't you bring any other clothes?'

'I think she looks cool,' Viktor says, giving me a wink. 'Very *I don't give a shit.*'

I bestow a grateful smile on Uncle Viktor. I've always liked him, though it's quite a long time since he last visited us. When he did, he came into my room and we chatted for ages about various singers. He examined the pictures on the board above my desk too and pointed to a photo of me at the Tivoli in Copenhagen, saying I was the spitting image of my mother. I suppose I can agree, up to a point. I've inherited her hair, her eyes and her lips. When I study old photos of Mum, I can see the resemblance, but Mum was chubbier and taller, while I'm not even 165 centimetres.

'That's exactly the look she was going for,' Harpa says, her expression mock serious as she catches my eye.

I shake my head.

The sound of voices from reception make us all glance round to see two women, the one who works at the hotel and another, much younger; no more than a girl, in fact.

'You can't just—' the woman who works here is saying, but breaks off when she sees us standing in the corridor.

The girl is probably only a few years older than me. She's wearing a down jacket, a red beanie and walking boots that have left dirty wet marks on the floor. Her nostrils flare as she breathes, and her eyes are wide and show the whites, like a frightened puppy.

When she sees Viktor she stops dead.

'Maja,' she says. 'Where's Maja?'

'Líf,' Viktor replies. 'I don't know...'

He breaks off when Líf starts coming quickly towards him. Viktor takes a step backwards, raising his hands as if in self-defence, and for a second I think the girl's going to attack him. But she stops in front of him, leans forwards and says in a low voice: 'What have you done to Maja, you disgusting creep?'

Petra Snæberg

Viktor stays with Maja's sister, who broke down into agonised sobbing after calling him a creep. I'm trying to get my head round what's happened as I make my way towards the restaurant. Maja's family must be frantic if she still hasn't turned up. But why isn't Viktor showing the least concern? And why was Maja's sister so angry with him?

When Steffý and I left, Viktor was talking soothingly to Líf. I didn't hear what he said, but she seemed to have calmed down. At least her sobbing had been reduced to sniffing by the time we walked away.

But I heard her say that she'd traced Maja's phone here to the hotel and, if that's true, I'm not sure what to think. It's impossible that Maja's still here. Could she have forgotten her phone? Did she rush out in the middle of the night without a car or her phone? Again, I picture her standing on the side of the road in last night's storm and shudder at the thought.

I remember the marks inside the cabinet door in Viktor's bathroom. Could they have been blood?

'Where do you think she is?' I ask Steffý when we reach the bar.

'Hang on.' Steffý signals to the barman and orders two cocktails before replying: 'Haven't the foggiest.'

'Don't you find it strange that Viktor's not worried about Maja?' I ask.

'I have to admit that I haven't been following what's happened.'

Clearly Steffý doesn't share my concern. She doesn't even seem to think that anything serious has happened.

'Viktor said some family problem had come up and that's why Maja went home last night. But it's not true,' I say. 'If it was, her sister wouldn't be here looking for her, would she?'

'What do you mean?'

'I just mean: if Maja didn't go home, where did she go?' I take my drink from the barman.

Steffý smiles. 'She'll turn up. Don't worry about it.'

'But Viktor—'

'Petra, don't read too much into it,' Steffý says. 'Maja and Viktor hadn't been together very long. Maybe that's why Viktor doesn't seem too bothered.'

'But what if something's happened to her?'

'Like what?'

I hesitate, wondering if I should tell Steffý that Maja's pregnant and that I saw something odd in the bathroom. If it was Maja who left that note on my car, warning me to be careful, she may have had reason to be afraid herself. Had she been running away?

Steffý watches me, waiting for me to reply.

'I don't know,' I say eventually. 'I just thought her relationship with Viktor was becoming more serious.'

Steffý raises her eyebrows. 'I don't think that's about to happen anytime soon.'

'What do you mean?'

Steffý doesn't explain, only smiles and sips her drink.

With my straw I stir what's left of the orange cocktail Steffý ordered for me. It's almost finished, though I hadn't been intending to drink any more this evening. My head's buzzing, and I'm finding it hard to focus.

My thoughts return to Maja and the look of happy anticipation on her face as she stroked her stomach and told me she was pregnant. What else did she want to tell me?

Out of the corner of my eye, I see Viktor enter the room. When he spots me and Steffý, he smiles broadly and starts walking in our direction but, to my relief, his father intercepts him. I go to put my drink down on a table, but my glass collides with a candlestick and I drop it. The loud crash as it falls on the floor makes the people around me look up.

I apologise and move away from the table, feeling my cheeks turning red. A friendly waitress fetches a cloth and starts wiping up the spilt drink and sweeping together the broken shards of glass. But my eye is drawn to the sight of the rapidly spreading liquid. On the table it appears viscous and bright red.

Lea Snæberg

Everyone's so busy chatting, laughing and drinking that none of them pay much attention to me and Harpa. As I pass the kitchen I can hear the staff talking and I get a whiff of delicious cooking smells. I'm suddenly terribly hungry and realise I've hardly eaten a thing today.

Harpa orders drinks from Arne, a cute boy in a black shirt, who's working behind the bar. When he smiles at me, I drop my eyes. I take the glass Harpa hands me, and we go and sit down at a table in the corner, well away from the noisy grown-ups.

The drink's so strong that I inadvertently grimace.

'Don't make that face,' Harpa whispers. 'People will realise it's not just Coke.'

'Sorry.' I put down the glass, trying to fake an interest in what Harpa's telling me about some boy at school.

I peer around for Frans, her father, who clearly doesn't keep much of an eye on her. Harpa lives with her mother but visits her father and Jenný from time to time. Earlier she told me that her stepmum, Jenný, had asked if she wasn't too old now to be coming round so often. And whether maybe next time she could sleep on the sofabed as the new baby needed her room.

'...although we've slept together—' I'm only half listening but I do hear when Harpa says that.

I interrupt her. 'You've slept together?'

'Yes.' Harpa sips her drink, apparently amused by my expression. 'Haven't you ever done it?'

'No,' I say. 'I ... I've done other stuff, but...'

'Like what?'

'Just...' I don't know why I'm finding it so hard to admit to Harpa that I've only kissed a boy, nothing more. 'You know.'

'What?'

I give up. 'I've snogged someone.'

Harpa bursts out laughing, but I don't join in.

'Sorry,' she says, looking serious again. 'Why not?'

Why not? Perhaps because every time things start to go further, I'm overwhelmed by panic. It's like going back in time, being twelve again and waking up to find those disgusting hands on me.

The sound of smashing glass lets me off the hook. We look up. I can see Mum standing at the bar, staring at the staff who are cleaning up after her. A few tables away, I meet a gaze that I know only too well. Hákon Ingimar raises his glass in my direction. I look away, pretending not to see him.

Then the image of Birgir comes into my mind and I miss him so badly, which is stupid because Birgir almost certainly doesn't exist. But there was someone behind the computer profile, and I miss talking to him. The more I think about it, the sicker I feel. Up to now I've been angry and a bit hurt. Ashamed. It hasn't really occurred to me that although Birgir may not exist, someone has been replying to me and talking to me all this time. And I think: someone out there, who I don't know at all, knows everything about me.

'Are you OK?' Harpa asks, breaking into my thoughts. 'You look so pale.'

'Yes,' I say. 'I'm just going to the loo.'

'Do you want me to come with you?'

'No,' I reply, too quickly. Then add with a smile: 'I'll manage.'

But instead of going to the ladies, I head into reception and open the front door. It's almost torn out of my hand by a freezing gust, but the cold is refreshing. I fill my lungs, closing my eyes and letting the snowflakes whirl around my face.

Nothing matters, I think, trying to recapture the sensation I had when I was standing in the sea; trying to leave myself behind.

'Why, hello there!'

I open my eyes at the voice and quickly glance around but can't see anything except the paving stones outside, lit up by the dim outdoor lights. Could the voice have come from inside?

I turn round but can't see anyone there either.

When I turn back, I almost jump out of my skin, because now there's this man standing right in front of me. He's smiling through his thick beard, he's got his hands in his pockets and his face is red like he's been outside for a long time.

'Lea,' the man says. 'So we meet at last, Sigrún Lea.'

I open my mouth but no sound comes out.

'Didn't you get my messages? The video?'

He moves closer, and I take a step backwards. The fact I'm alone hits me so hard that I can feel my whole body stiffening with fear. I'm alone here with this man.

And I can't move.

Sævar
Detective, West Iceland CID

After they had carried out a quick examination of the room, Sævar and Hörður took a seat in the coffee room again to discuss their next steps. They pondered whether to start with the guests who had gone out into the storm the night before, in search of their companion who had gone missing, but Sævar wasn't sure that was the best approach. Perhaps it would be better to talk to the guests who'd stayed inside first – get their version of events. The ones who'd gone outside were the people who must have seen the victim last, so it made them the most likely suspects. It would be better to have an idea what happened in the hotel before questioning them. The police still couldn't be absolutely certain that they had a murder case on their hands, although the hairs in the victim's fist and the position of the body pointed strongly to this conclusion.

'So it all began with Lea's disappearance?' Sævar asked Edda.

She nodded. 'Yes. I understand she'd been having a few problems since she got here, though I don't know why.'

Edda seemed suddenly embarrassed, and Sævar noticed a hint of colour in her pale cheeks. He wondered if she had said too much, if she'd been eavesdropping on the guests' conversations.

'What gave you that impression?'

'Well...' Edda rubbed her hands together. 'She came in sopping wet after their trip yesterday and I gather – not that I was actively trying to listen but you hear all kinds of stuff without meaning to – I gather from what her family were saying that she'd been in the sea at Djúpalón. I don't know what happened but ... but it was rather peculiar. The poor kid was soaked to the skin.'

Sævar glanced at Hörður. In the sea at Djúpalón? In this weather? That did sound odd. Sævar had visited the beach a long time ago and couldn't remember any obvious spots where someone could have fallen in. At least, not down on the beach itself. Nor had he heard anything about dangerous currents there, unlike some places in the country where the waves were unpredictable and could snatch people off the shore if they were standing too close to the water's edge.

Hörður seemed equally baffled.

'So Lea disappeared and they went out in the middle of the night to look for her,' Hörður said. 'Was she with them when they came back?'

'No.' Edda shook her head. 'No, Lea wasn't with them.'

Sævar sighed. He didn't know what to think.

After a brief silence, Edda asked if she could lend them a room to use for their interviews. They accepted the offer gratefully.

'Shall we just get on with it, then?' Hörður asked, once Edda had gone.

'Yes, there's no reason to hang around,' Sævar replied.

But just as they were standing up, the phone rang in Hörður's pocket. He stepped outside while he was taking the call, and Sævar waited. When Hörður came back, his expression was unreadable.

'Who was it?' Sævar asked.

'That...' Hörður sighed. 'That was Maja's parents.'

Tryggvi

The food's …OK, which is a bit of a disappointment really, as it smelt so promising while it was cooking. The starters were the best part, though even they were nothing to write home about. The lamb for the main course is overcooked, and the sauce was rationed out a bit stingily. But no one else seems to be complaining, so I'm not going to say anything. Sometimes food is just food, serving no other purpose than to fill an empty stomach.

Opposite me, Haraldur is attacking his roast with gusto. His jaws work fast as he chews, and in the dim light the shadows fall oddly on his face, sharpening and coarsening his features.

'Tryggvi,' Ester says, and I start, realising I've been staring.

'Yes?'

'Have you always lived in Reykjavík?'

'No, I grew up in the West Fjords,' I say. 'In Ísafjörður. I lived there until I was thirty.'

'That must have been a nice place to live,' Ester says. 'Such a pretty town. Do you remember when we were there three years ago, Halli? We stayed at that … that hotel. Hotel Horn, wasn't it?'

'Yes,' Haraldur says, washing down his mouthful with a gulp of beer. 'Hotel Horn. Decent hotel but uncomfortable beds.'

'There was nothing wrong with the beds.' Ester smiles.

Sometimes I think she couldn't stop herself even if she tried. Her smile seems to break out at the slightest excuse.

Ester starts praising the hotel again, and everyone except Haraldur agrees. The conversation over dinner is polite but they're drinking hard. One bottle of wine after another is emptied, and the waiting staff watch closely, whipping away the empty bottles and replacing them with full ones, which makes it impossible to tell how many the company have got through.

We're in the middle of dessert when I feel the phone vibrating in my pocket. I take it out, though I know this will earn me a dirty look from Oddný. Neither she nor the other members of her family will put up with people taking their phones out at the dinner table. But this weekend they seem to have relaxed the rule, since lots of them are using their phones to take pictures of the food and each other.

So I'm not expecting anyone to make a fuss if I get mine out. After all, it's not like I'm always checking it. I regard my phone as no more than a tool for communicating with people. But I know that a phone isn't just a phone anymore. I've only recently learnt how to open my email and Facebook on it, so now I'm always getting notifications. I need to find out how to turn off this constant vibrating.

The notification is to say that Nanna has emailed me the photos. As I scroll through them, my surroundings fade and I forget where I am.

Petra Snæberg

Gestur barely says a word to me during dinner. It's not until we've both finished our lamb that he leans over and asks: 'Where were you earlier?'

'You know I was with Viktor,' I say. 'Where did you go?'

'I needed to get out.' Gestur sighs. 'Sorry about earlier – I shouldn't have blamed you.'

You always do, though, I want to say, but I clamp my lips together. Gestur leans even closer and puts a hand on my thigh.

'Petra, should we maybe go and see someone when we get home?'

'Like who?'

'Get help.' Gestur looks deep into my eyes. 'I think it ... it would be good for us.'

I laugh and can hear how fake it sounds. 'Why?'

Gestur doesn't smile. 'Because you ... *we* haven't been ourselves lately. I feel as if you want nothing to do with me.'

The fact we're discussing this at the dinner table tells me that Gestur has put away his fair share of booze, though you wouldn't know it from looking at him. I take his hand and watch as our fingers entwine in my lap, feeling myself relax.

'We can think about it,' I say. 'About seeing someone, I mean.'

Gestur looks at me without speaking. After a long marriage he knows when I mean it and when I don't. He knows that something's been weighing on me for a very long time. In the first years of our marriage he believed that I'd eventually open up to him, but now he knows that's unlikely to happen. He knows

I'll never be entirely present, I'll always be just out of reach. The question is whether he's prepared to put up with that.

When he withdraws his hand, it leaves my thigh feeling cold. The moment his attention is distracted and he starts chatting to someone at the neighbouring table, I slip my hand into my bag, find the foil sheet of Sertraline, press out another pill and swallow it with a mouthful of red wine.

During dessert, my brother Smári takes the vacated seat next to me. I assume Gestur's gone to the bar.

'Had a drop too much, have we?' Smári asks.

'Is it that obvious?'

'Yes.' Smári reaches for the water jug, fills a glass and hands it to me.

'Thanks,' I say.

Smári mutters in an undertone: 'What's going on with you, Petra?'

'Nothing.'

Smári's expression is sceptical.

'It's just...' I finish the water. 'It's just this. Everything.'

'What do you mean "everything"?'

'Everything,' I say, my voice coming out so shrill that Mum looks up on the other side of the table. Oh God, I'm so drunk. I lean over to Smári and whisper: 'I'm screwing everything up.'

'Screwing what up?'

'Everything.'

'Don't be silly, Petra. Not now.'

I have a sudden memory of the last time Smári told me off. The memory is more vivid than the people around me: I'm climbing in through the window of my bedroom when my shirt gets snagged on the catch and rips. I fall onto the floor inside and lie there laughing helplessly, though my head hurts. Fumbling at my forehead, I feel something wet. Then I see Smári's face dancing above me. He says: *Don't be silly, Petra. Not now.* Suddenly I hear Dad knocking on the door: *What's going on in there?*

Someone taps a glass with their spoon and the ringing of crystal cuts through the roar of conversation in the room. Smári doesn't take his eyes off me immediately, as though he wants to reassure himself that I'll obey. The moment he does look away, I scan the table for booze, spot some, nab it and take a swig.

All eyes are turned to Granddad Hákon, who's arrived at the hotel without my noticing. He's so frail that he needs help standing up. Mum waves away his carer and assists him to his feet herself. Granddad takes up position in front of the tables and extracts a piece of paper from the pocket of his jacket. His hands are trembling so badly that the paper shakes, and for a moment I think he's going to drop it, but then he seems to get a grip and straightens his shoulders. His veins are bulging and he works his jaw several times, clearing his throat.

Dead silence falls on the restaurant as everyone's attention is fixed on the stage. Even the gale outside seems to fall into a brief lull. Then Granddad starts intoning in a hoarse, threadbare voice:

'The wild wave beats against the icy ness;
None can tame its elemental force
Or strike a bargain with the lord,
Controller of the ocean tide.
A lone raven flew from Enni head.
He who has travelled far and wide
Will have no fear of the walking dead.

Deserted are the huts by the fjord,
Forgotten the bodies cut down by the sword,
Worm-eaten flesh is the bog-hole's hoard.
Yet when your forebears couldn't afford
A rag for their back, a beggarly horde,
They found safe haven there on board.'

Granddad's voice seems to get under my skin, piercing my flesh to the bone. I can't take my eyes off him; I haven't any room for my own thoughts. Something about the words and the tone they're uttered in sends a cold shudder down my spine. Only when he's finished reading do I realise that I've been holding my breath.

I glance around and see that I'm not the only one to have been affected by Granddad's recital. Smári shakes his head, then starts clapping. The others join in, and somebody whistles.

Granddad barely reacts. He folds up his paper and returns it, shaky handed, to his pocket, then Mum helps him back to his seat.

'That was awesome,' Smári whispers to me, once the applause has petered out and the hum of conversation resumed.

I nod in agreement. Granddad has achieved so much in his life, and the family owes him almost everything. I'm aware of a deep sense of inferiority. What have *I* ever done? I ask myself. What have I achieved?

I turn my gaze to the window and peer out into the blackness. Ice has formed on the outside of the glass and drops are trickling down it, like tiny rivulets.

Without warning, the sounds around me fade into the distance and the lights seem to be going out, one by one. All I am aware of is the glass, as if I'm sitting alone in the dark restaurant, right next to the window. Then I see it. The hand. A palm pressed against the outside of the glass.

I gasp, only just managing to stifle the scream that rises in my throat.

'What? What's wrong?' I hear someone ask.

I can't say a word, just sit there, staring rigidly at the window. When I finally blink, the hand has vanished, and the drops are still sliding down the glass.

Irma
Hotel Employee

The first thing I notice is the cold. It's obvious as soon as you approach reception that an icy draught is blowing inside. Next minute I see that the front door is open and Lea's standing in the gap, gaping at something outside. I don't see the man until I'm right behind her.

'Is everything OK?' I ask.

The man standing at the door is short but stocky. He's obviously been outside for some time as his face looks weather-beaten, the tips of his hair and beard are freezing and his cheeks are a blotchy red.

'Everything's fine here,' he says hoarsely, and I can smell the alcohol fumes rolling over to where I'm standing, despite the wind gusting outside. 'I'm just saying hello to my friend.'

I work out at once that this must be the suspicious character Edda saw skulking around outside the hotel.

'Do you know this man, Lea?' I ask.

Lea shakes her head. 'No,' she says, her voice so low I can scarcely hear it.

'I see.' I smile pleasantly at the man and take up position in the doorway, in front of Lea. 'I'm afraid I can't invite you in. The hotel's closed for a private party.'

'I just wanted to—' the man begins, but I flip the catch and shut the door in his face before he has a chance to say another word.

'That's the way to do it,' I say, giving Lea a wink.

She smiles, hesitantly at first, but I can see how relieved she is.

'Are you all right?' I ask. 'Did you get a shock? Do you know who that man is?'

'No ... I mean, yes. He's been sending me messages.'

'What kind of messages?'

She lowers her gaze to the floor. 'Just on social media. But I don't know him. He's ... old.'

'I see.' I put my hand on her shoulder. 'There are a lot of strange people on the internet. Take it from me, it makes sense to be careful what you share.'

Lea nods.

'But hey,' I add. 'It's not your fault, I wasn't suggesting that. All I meant is that the world is full of weirdos. You can't really trust anyone.'

Lea laughs, though her hands are still trembling a little. 'I know exactly what you mean.'

'Anyway, shall we just forget it and go back to the party? I promise to make sure no one gets in, so you can relax.'

'Thanks,' Lea says, smiling, then braces herself to go back and join her family.

'Maybe you should get a dog,' I say.

'What?' Lea turns round.

'You should get a dog. Whenever I felt scared when I was younger, I used to get my dog to sleep by my bed. That always made me feel better.'

'Oh. Yes, maybe.' Lea gives me a strange look, then blinks and smiles. 'Thanks again.'

I watch her until she has turned the corner into the restaurant and disappeared from sight.

Tryggvi

I'm in the habit of looking through the photos at least once a year. At first I found it a strain but it's become easier. I suppose the pain has dulled with the passing of time.

In the early years after the accident I found it so hard to open the photo album that I would put it off for days, always telling myself there was something else I needed to do first. Now I have no problem scrolling through the pictures and find myself doing it increasingly often. It fills my heart with warmth and, yes, a touch of sadness too, but mainly gratitude. Not everyone is lucky enough to have children, let alone bonus ones. I always found the 'step' word so ugly that the last thing I wanted to be was a stepdad. I've heard that in Scandinavia they talk about 'bonus dads', which sounds much better. But in fact I was always just plain 'Dad'.

The first pictures in the folder were taken before my time, so they don't awaken the same feelings of familiarity as the rest. There's Nanna in the maternity ward, cradling a handsome baby boy with striking features and scarcely a hair on his head. Snapshots of his first steps, of camping trips and Christmas celebrations follow. I pause at the picture of him aged five. That's how I remember him when I first got to know him, in his cowboy costume with the Stetson and revolver.

By the last photos he's a teenager. He stayed on at school and was planning to read medicine at university, but then studying had always come easily to him. He would have made a good doctor, not only because he was clever but because he was kind and considerate; he really cared about people. He was good at getting on with them. He could have been an artist too – an actor, for example. That was obvious when his school put on *The Little Shop of Horrors*. And he had a real talent for drawing. Perhaps that's where his true passion lay – in art. But then everything seemed to come easily to him.

I pause my scrolling at a photo of him on stage at school. The picture was taken from the audience, by me or Nanna, I assume. We enjoyed watching him act so much that we went to see the show four times. I smile at the picture of him standing up there, flanked by several girls in lacy tops with back-combed hair.

'Tryggvi, dear, what are you looking at?' Oddný asks, leaning over to me. Her breath catches when she sees the photo, and she puts a hand over her mouth. 'I didn't realise what the date was, Tryggvi. I'm so sorry.'

'It doesn't matter,' I answer slowly. But the truth is I'd be lying if I denied that I was a bit hurt by her forgetfulness.

Oddný presses closer to get a look at the pictures, and I can feel myself tensing up. I had no problem scrolling through them against the background noise, as I've always been able to shut myself off from my surroundings without any trouble, but I can't do it with Oddný's head on my shoulder.

I decide to wait until I'm alone later to go through the rest, but just as I'm about to lock my phone, Oddný stops me.

'But...' she says. 'What's that?'

'Pictures,' I reply. 'Drawings.'

'I know, but that portrait,' she says. 'She looks so familiar.'

I examine the picture Oddný's pointing to. It's one of the portraits from his sketch pad. Nanna and I found drawings of various people in it, including faces of individuals we didn't necessarily know, though we'd seen them around. This particular sketch is of a girl in a roll-neck jumper, with curly hair and a shy smile. She appears to be biting her lower lip slightly, like she's trying to suppress a broad grin.

'That's Petra,' Oddný exclaims after a moment. 'Can't you see? When she was much younger and still a bit plump, with that thick, curly hair. I'm positive it's her.'

As I stare at the picture I can certainly see a likeness to Petra, Ester and Haraldur's daughter, though not enough to convince me. But before I realise what's happening, Oddný has taken the phone from me and is calling out to her sister-in-law.

'Look, Ester,' she says, holding up the phone. 'Isn't that like Petra?'

Ester bends forwards to peer at it, then nods. 'What is that?'

'A picture drawn by Tryggvi's son,' Oddný tells her.

Ester regards me with an unreadable expression, then asks who my son is, what he's called.

'Teddi.' Even just saying his name fills me with pride. 'My son's name was Theódór.'

Irma
Hotel Employee

When I check the toilets after supper, I find them in a pretty good state, but I fetch some new scented candles anyway and, having made sure no one's in the gents, I pop in to place them by the sink. While I'm there, I notice some traces of white powder on the dark wood of the vanity unit and run a finger over it.

The powder feels fine between my fingertips, and I know only too well what it is.

It's not like I'm surprised. I've observed a certain person blowing his nose. Seen the dilated eyes and frenetically working jaw. What surprises me is how little effort he – or any of the others for that matter – makes to hide it.

I'd never have guessed that this family would indulge in behaviour like that. I assumed they would be as careful here as they are anywhere else. But, on second thoughts, perhaps it's precisely here, in the bosom of their family, that they can afford to let their hair down without having to be afraid of what other people might think or say. And of course they don't have to worry about us – the members of staff – because they know we'd never say a word. As far as they're concerned, we're just part of the hotel furniture.

I'm about to leave the gents when I come face to face with a large figure. Haraldur, I think to myself. He has sweat stains under his arms, and his face breaks into a grin when he sees me.

'You're a bit lost, aren't you?'

'Just making sure everything's clean and tidy,' I say with composure.

'Trashing the place, are we? Keeping you on your toes?'

'No, not at all, I was just—'

'Dad, stop teasing the maid,' says his son, entering behind him.

Smári has taken off his tie and undone the top two buttons of his shirt. He doesn't look a bit like his father – he's much slimmer, with kindly eyes. Smári's the sort of guy you'd want as your doctor, while Haraldur looks like the kind of man who enjoys bossing other people about.

As I'm squeezing past them towards the door, Haraldur pats my bare arm with a sweaty hand. He gives off an odour of perspiration and bad breath, which his expensive aftershave fails to mask this late in the evening.

The door has no sooner closed behind me than I hear the sound made by a stream of liquid hitting the porcelain. I hurry away to avoid having to listen to father and son use the urinals.

Back at the bar, Arne hands me a shot, and we drink with our backs to the party. When I turn round to take the order of a man who's being unnecessarily loud and obnoxious, despite the smile on his face, I notice that Haraldur has come back and now has his arm round his daughter, Petra.

While I'm taking someone a beer in the restaurant, I see them dancing together, Petra looking so delicate in her father's embrace. I see how he smiles at her, his eyes shining, and feel a stab of pain in my stomach. Because although I lived in some kind of alternative reality as a child, convincing myself that everything was perfect, I never entirely succeeded in picturing a father for myself.

Sometimes I pretended my father got in late every evening and was gone before I woke up in the morning. In one place where Mum and I lived, I told everyone he worked abroad, doing an important job in the army. That was before I knew that Iceland didn't have an army.

But I could never form a clear picture of my father. Couldn't decide whether he was dark or fair, whether he had a friendly smile or a stern face. I couldn't imagine what his voice sounded like.

I used to beg Mum to tell me about him, asking if we were alike and whether he knew I existed. She always replied that I was like myself and that my father was no more interesting than any other man you'd meet about town. Just someone whose only contribution to my existence had been on that one night.

OK, maybe she didn't come out and say the last part that bluntly when I was a child, but as a teenager I put two and two together. It wasn't until my late teens that I learnt that the 'sperm donor', my father, was aware of my existence. He knew where I lived and could have come round to visit me anytime.

The truth was that he'd never got in touch for the simple reason that he couldn't give a shit about me.

Tryggvi

Things turn a bit awkward after I say Theódór's name. Ester's first question is what he does for a living. Sometimes I think that's how this family judges everyone, how they calculate their worth. When I explain that Teddi is dead, Ester makes flustered noises and shoots Oddný a dirty look for not warning her. She's even more taken aback when I say that Theódór was living in Akranes when he died.

Ester remembers the accident, or at least she says she does. But I'm not sure she's telling the truth.

Some people might think it strange that this is the first time Theódór's name has come up in conversation with Oddný's family, but during the year we've been together we've only met Haraldur and Ester on a handful of occasions, and the talk has never been that personal. They haven't asked many questions and have made it very clear that they have no interest in hearing about my family. And for some reason I've never felt the need to talk about Theódór to people who didn't know him. It's like I can never do him justice, and no one will ever understand what losing him meant to me or the shattering grief that followed his death.

Nanna and I had only recently moved to Akranes when we split up. I lived there for less than a month, and later, after the accident, Nanna moved back to Ísafjörður. Neither of us had any particular connection to Akranes. We moved there simply because Nanna got a job there and we thought the fact it was near Reykjavík would be convenient for Teddi's university studies further down the line. House prices were much lower there than in the city, and the opening of the Hvalfjörður tunnel a year earlier had cut the commute to forty-five minutes.

After dinner, I go to the bar, order a beer and sit there on my own for a while.

Out of the corner of my eye I can see Oddný watching me, tortured by guilt for having forgotten that it's eighteen years today since Theódór died. Which is why I've been out of sorts and can't stop myself from drinking this evening.

When my glass is empty, I go back into the restaurant, where the tables and chairs have been pushed aside to make room for a temporary dance floor.

I spot Petra immediately: she's dancing with her father. Haraldur's too pissed himself to notice how unsteady she is on her feet or the blank look in her eye.

Nanna and I wasted a lot of time wondering who Teddi had gone to meet that evening. When he said goodbye, Nanna had suspected it was a girl he was going to see.

Of course, I didn't even know he was going out that evening. I've blamed myself often enough for not being there. I knew he'd fallen for a girl because Teddi had told me so himself the last time we met and promised to introduce her to me soon. I was pleased that Teddi had confided in me. He was glowing, and I could see from a mile off that he was in love.

Not that seventeen-year-old kids know what love is. Few people do, however old they are. But Teddi wasn't like most. He didn't waste time on stuff that didn't matter; he was determined, focused and true to himself.

So all Nanna and I knew was that someone had picked him up that evening. We never knew how he came to lose his life on the Ring Road near Mount Akrafjall. It's a mystery we've had to live with all these years, and sometimes I believe it's the uncertainty that's the real killer – the not knowing what happened or why.

As I watch Petra, I wonder if she could have been the girl Teddi was going to meet that evening. Whether she's kept quiet all these years about something that could have given us answers.

When I meet Petra's gaze she seems to stare right through me. She's obviously very drunk. Suddenly it occurs to me that maybe she, too, is in mourning today.

Petra

Dad lets go of me and pulls Steffý to him instead. She's always been a favourite of his and he's always made a fuss of her. When he and Mum went on their trips abroad he used to buy two of everything, so Steffý and I would receive identical gifts of clothes and toys. I always felt bad for being jealous. I couldn't understand why I found it so unfair that Steffý should get the same gifts as me. I used to sulk, though I didn't dare show it and it only made me feel guilty.

I back away from the dance floor until I'm pressed against the wall, then glance over at the window again but can't see a thing. The world still feels as if it's moving up and down, and I realise I need to go to bed. Some voice of reason at the back of my mind tells me that the hand I saw was probably nothing more than a hallucination, brought on by mixing anti-anxiety pills with booze.

I've had hallucinations before, though they've never been as vivid as the one earlier. Once I was so sure there was a man in our garden that I woke Gestur up. I'd woken in the middle of the night and been unable to get back to sleep, so I'd gone to the TV room and sat on the sofa, which has a good view of the garden. I can still remember what a peaceful night it was. The trees were wearing their autumn colours, the brown, red and yellow leaves hanging unmoving in the still air. You get so used to the constant sound of the wind in Iceland that you don't even notice the rustling of the leaves. It's only when they fall silent that you become aware of them.

But all of a sudden the tree by the window started moving, in fits and starts, as if someone was pushing past it. I went over to the window and scanned the garden but couldn't see anyone. Not at first.

We'd been burgled a few months previously, and since then I'd been waking up frequently in the night, convinced that there was somebody in our house. I even heard the front door opening downstairs, the creaking of the parquet and the sound of the cupboard doors. None of this had any basis in reality. The burglar alarm we'd had installed never went off, so there can't have been anyone in our house, but that didn't stop me becoming rigid with terror every time. I'd lie there, unable to move, straining my ears and waiting.

But as I stood there, peering out of the upstairs window, trying to work out if the rustling of the leaves had been real or imaginary, I spotted a human figure in the garden. It was wearing a hood and dark clothes, and vanished as suddenly as it had appeared. I was sure the person had seen me standing there, watching them. Gestur didn't believe me. He was convinced it was the pills. He'd read the patient information sheets accompanying the Sertraline and sleeping pills, and drew my attention to the possible side effects, which included hallucinations.

I leave the restaurant and head to the bar, though I don't want any more alcohol.

'We're just talking about Steffý's job abroad,' Smári says, beckoning me over to sit with them. 'Did you know she's working for Chanel now?'

'Yes, I did,' I reply.

'I haven't been making a big deal out of it,' Steffý says, twisting a lock of hair round her finger. 'I only started this autumn, after an application process lasting months. But if you want any cosmetics, feel free to give me a bell.'

'Thanks.'

Smári gets to his feet. 'Anyway, better let you two catch up.'

He leaves me and Steffý sitting there. The barman asks if we want to order anything, but I shake my head, aware that I can't cope with any more alcohol tonight.

For a while neither of us says anything, then I remark: 'We should have told someone.'

'Petra,' Steffý says, waving her hand. 'You can be so melodramatic.'

I feel sick. Melodramatic, I think. Steffý thought I was being melodramatic when I stopped sleeping and lost my appetite. She found me melodramatic when I couldn't go into school anymore and stopped going out to meet people. For her, keeping quiet wasn't a problem. But then she hadn't given a shit about Teddi. He'd meant nothing to her.

I get up, leaving Steffý in the bar. I hear her calling me, then coming after me.

But I keep walking, my eyes shut. Maybe the drugs help. All of a sudden the image of Teddi is crystal clear in my mind. I remember exactly how he was dressed the evening Steffý and I picked him up: in an Adidas top, a dark-blue windcheater and a new pair of Converse trainers that he'd been given for his birthday a few weeks earlier. I was sitting in the car and when our eyes met, we both broke out into spontaneous smiles and couldn't have suppressed them if we'd been paid to. A memory of two teenagers who believed they were in love. A memory that should stir up warm feelings but instead rouses nothing but horror.

'Sorry, Petra,' Steffý says, catching up with me in the corridor. 'I didn't mean to offend you.'

She reaches out to take my arm, but I back away from her. The expression on her face is long-suffering, as though she's dealing with a child.

'What's going on with you?' she asks. 'Why are you behaving like this?' She leans closer, her gaze fixed on me. 'Are you ... are you on something?'

She's staring right into my eyes, and I realise that out here in the bright corridor it must be glaringly obvious that my pupils aren't reacting normally to the light. The drugs have this effect, making my pupils larger than usual. Making me look like a ghost.

'What's the matter with me?' I ask slowly. 'You make it sound like it's some kind of joke. Like ... Like it's funny.'

'I don't find it funny,' Steffý says, glancing around. 'I never said that.'

'Teddi died because of us.' I raise my voice, not caring who might hear us. 'He died because of us, Steffý. Because of you.'

'Will you shut up,' Steffý snaps. She comes a step closer, adding: 'I was helping you. You know that.'

'Helping me?' I give a mocking laugh. 'Helping me?'

Teddi and I had been sitting in the back seat, kissing, when I found my breath coming too fast and my heart beginning to race. But I didn't want to stop, I just hoped I could get through the anxiety attack without too much trouble. Soon, though, I found I couldn't catch my breath and the world started going black. I begged Teddi to stop but he just went on kissing me, holding me tight. The music in the car was so loud that either he didn't hear me or he didn't realise I was serious. He didn't stop until I shoved him away with all my strength.

Everything happened very fast after that. Steffý braked violently and ordered Teddi to get out of the car. I tried to argue with her, though I was still fighting for breath.

Teddi didn't mean to hurt me. He'd never have done that. The last time I saw him was through the rear windscreen as he stood, bewildered, in the middle of the road. His arms were hugging his body and his open jacket was flapping in the wind.

It's this vision that haunts me at night.

'We left him behind, Steffý,' I say.

'Oh, come on.' Steffý snorts. 'You know, you've always behaved like it was my fault and I've had enough. It was an accident, Petra.

When are you going to accept the fact and stop wallowing in self-pity? We didn't kill Teddi. We didn't knock him down. It was an accident.'

'Don't you think we bear any responsibility?'

'No.'

'How can you say that?'

'We would have gone back for him,' Steffý says.

I was still begging Steffý to turn round as we drove into town, but she wouldn't listen, so I grabbed her arm, causing the car to swerve into the opposite lane, straight into the path of the oncoming traffic.

We weren't badly hurt, but the police came and an ambulance took us to hospital for a check-up. Then our parents arrived, Dad reeking of booze and tobacco, Mum in a knitted jumper over the T-shirt she always slept in.

When I woke up next morning, the kitchen was full of the smell of the porridge Mum was cooking.

'I heard some terrible news from Sigrún this morning,' Mum said as she ladled porridge into the bowl in front of me. As I stared at the grey muck, Mum talked about a boy who had been found dead by the Ring Road. 'They think it was a hit-and-run,' she said. 'But I can't imagine what he was doing out there on the main road in the middle of the night. Running away from home, perhaps? What do you think, Petra? Was the boy having problems at home?'

Instead of answering, I threw up into my porridge bowl.

Steffý came to see me later that morning.

'We can't tell anyone what happened – Dad would kill me,' she said, pulling my duvet over her toes. 'Promise me, Petra?'

And I promised. I promised not to say anything. Promised to keep quiet about the fact we'd left him behind, just because Steffý was afraid her parents would be angry.

'We should have gone back for him,' I say now, rubbing my temples. I can feel the headache beginning between my eyes.

In the restaurant I hear the volume being cranked up and people starting to dance again. Dad's guffaws of laughter carry from the bar, and I know he'll soon be slurring his words and spilling drink down his shirt. I can't take any more, I think. I'm going upstairs.

I turn to Steffý, determined to have the last word. 'We should at least have let his family know.'

'I asked Viktor to go and pick him up,' Steffý says. 'What more could I do? Don't forget that Dad wouldn't have let me out again after what happened. The car was a write-off and everything.'

I'm suddenly wide awake. 'What?'

'The car was a write-off. I—'

'No,' I cut across her. 'I mean the thing about Viktor. Did you ask Viktor to pick him up?'

'Yes, I called him right after our accident, Petra,' Steffý says. 'Why do you think I went and asked if I could use the phone in the shop?'

'I thought you were ringing your dad.'

'Yes, of course I rang him, but I called Viktor too. I asked him to go and pick Teddi up because I didn't want to leave him out there in the middle of the night. Then Dad called the police.'

'But...'

'Viktor couldn't find Teddi,' Steffý says. 'He looked for him but couldn't find him and, OK, maybe it is all our fault, but I never meant ... It wasn't supposed to end like that. It wasn't deliberate.'

'But...'

Steffý comes a step nearer, and this time I don't move away. She leans close, looks deep into my eyes and says firmly: 'Teddi was hit by a car and died, but it wasn't my fault. It was an accident.'

'If your conscience is clear,' I say, 'why don't we tell people what happened?'

Irma
Hotel Employee

We've been kept on our toes all evening, the staff, and we're beginning to fray at the edges. I just saw Edda go into the kitchen, close her eyes and count to ten before going back out there again.

'If anyone snaps their fingers to get my attention one more time...' says Vala, one of the waitresses hired for this evening. She lets out an exasperated sigh.

'Oh, don't let them get to you,' I say. 'They're not that bad.'

'Not that bad?' Vala exclaims. 'While I was serving that bloke over there, he ran his hand over my hip and called me *darling*. *Darling*! Honestly.'

I shake my head and pretend to be shocked. Some of the girls are simply more sensitive than others.

Vala shudders, then goes back out there.

Admittedly, the guests are demanding. I've hardly been able to take two steps without someone prodding me or tugging at me to order a drink or telling me they've knocked over their glass. Sweat is trickling down my back, making my shirt cling to my skin.

But I enjoy watching them. Families hold a powerful fascination for me; this collection of people forced to spend time together solely because the same blood flows through their veins. It's intriguing to think about what binds individuals together and how far some people are prepared to go, just because of this link.

It was like that with Dad. I was prepared to forgive him his indifference. I would have forgiven him all these years, if only he'd accepted me with open arms.

After Mum finally told me who my father was, I started watching him. Once I had his name, I found out everything I could about him, and finally got hold of his address. And when I knew where he lived, I discovered that he was a loud man and noticed that he often stayed up late, going to bed long after his wife.

This makes it sound as if I spied on him every evening, but it wasn't like that at all. I just drove past the house sometimes when I was at a loose end. On my weekends off or when I was bored in the evenings. People-watching has always been a hobby of mine, and doing it systematically, deliberately, like that was exciting. It's unbelievable what you find out; what people do when they think no one's looking.

My father picked his nose and always flicked the snot away with his thumb afterwards. I never saw him lift a finger at home. The only exception was the barbecue, and I'm pretty sure he only took responsibility for that as an excuse to show off to his neighbours and down a few beers while he was at it. The evenings he stayed up late, he sat in the living room, in front of the large, picture window, emptying one glass after another as he surfed the net.

I watched him without his having the faintest idea I was there, without his having the least suspicion that he was being observed.

The longer I watched him, the more it came home to me that I hadn't missed out on much by not knowing him. I had little interest now in meeting him or involving him in my life. There were other possibilities that were far more appealing.

Lea Snæberg

Harpa keeps forcing me to drink with her, and I don't dare refuse. The drunker she gets, the pushier she is. To please her, I take tiny sips, pretending to drink more than I actually do. I chose a seat as far away from my parents and grandparents as possible, but no one's watching us anyway. The adults are all too drunk themselves. The room's so dark and the music's so loud that it's almost like being in a nightclub.

'Another?' Harpa asks, and charges off towards the bar without waiting for an answer. She has a bit of a wait as Arne, the barman, is serving some other people. He's getting tired of us and looks around nervously before handing us our drinks, saying loudly, 'Soft drinks for the ladies,' so no one will suspect anything.

'I think I'm going to fuck him,' Harpa says, picking up one of the glasses.

'What? Who?'

'The bartender. I know he wants it. You should see him staring at my tits.'

Really, it's not surprising if he stares at Harpa's breasts: they're almost bursting out of her dress.

'Isn't he much older than you?'

'Nah. He can't be more than twenty.' Harpa wipes her mouth and leans towards me confidingly. 'But if I had a choice, I'd take Hákon Ingimar over him anytime.'

She glances over at the neighbouring table, where Hákon Ingimar is sitting. He notices us and smiles. I feel my stomach lurch and immediately drop my eyes, my face burning. Then I take a great slug of my drink and see that Harpa's smiling with satisfaction.

'How old is he, anyway?' she asks.

'Twenty-something,' I say, though I know perfectly well that he's twenty-five.

'That's OK,' Harpa says.

I make a face.

'Don't be like that.' She elbows me. 'Even though he's your cousin, you must be able to see how hot he is. He really reminds me of that actor ... What's his name again?'

'I don't know.'

Harpa swears as she racks her brains for the name. I seize the chance to take out my phone, then realise that for a split second I'd forgotten that Birgir doesn't exist and was hoping for a message from him. No chance of that now. But when the screen lights up, I see that there is a message waiting for me after all, or rather an email, and I feel a shiver run through me when I spot the name of the sender.

Before I can read it, someone grabs me round the shoulders.

'Hi, coz.' Hákon Ingimar leans forwards and whispers the words in my ear. Feeling his breath on my cheek, I jerk away and the phone flies out of my hands.

I mutter, 'Hi,' so quietly it's almost inaudible, but Harpa's face lights up as she greets him in a shrill voice.

My phone has slid right under the table, and I have to get down on my hands and knees to retrieve it. My hand encounters something sticky on the floor as soon as I bend down. I become aware of something touching my back, so light that at first I'm not sure if it's real. Then I realise that it's Hákon's fingers brushing my skin like little insects crawling on me, and I go rigid with disgust.

'Need any help?' he asks.

Harpa laughs.

'No,' I reply, and shift so that Hákon's hand slides off my back.

When I get up again, Harpa and Hákon are in the middle of a noisy conversation. He's dragged his chair over to hers and neither of them so much as glances at me.

I tidy my hair and brush the crumbs from my trousers.

'I follow you on Instagram,' I hear Harpa saying flirtatiously.

Hákon Ingimar passes her his phone and asks her to type in her name so he can follow her back. I sneak away.

In the bar, Dad grabs my arm. His eyes are unfocused, his voice too loud.

'Lea, love, are you going to bed?' he asks.

'No, I...' I say. 'Er, yes, I am a bit tired.'

'All right, sweetheart, just shout if we're making too much noise.' Dad winks at me. 'And I'll pull the speakers out of the wall for you.'

I smile, give Dad a hug and say good night.

He doesn't notice that, instead of heading to my room, I go out to reception. Sitting down in a chair, I take out my phone again. I'm short of breath, and there's a throbbing in my head as I open the email from someone calling himself Birgir.

Petra Snæberg

Once Steffy's gone, I stand quite still, listening to the distant hubbub of voices and sound of music from the restaurant. Outside the window, the wind is slamming against the glass. A shiver runs through me.

Not our fault.

Steffy's convinced that Teddi's death wasn't our fault, but that's not true. We left him behind on the Ring Road in the middle of winter. It was getting on for one in the morning and there were no street lights, no shelter anywhere. It would have taken Teddi about two hours to walk the ten or twelve kilometres back to town, but he was found not far from where we left him. On the news they said he was lying on the side of the road and that, from his injuries, it appeared that he'd been knocked down by a car. The driver was never found; either they fled the scene deliberately or didn't realise what they'd done. Since it happened in the early hours of Saturday morning, there was a good chance that the driver was drunk.

Suddenly I make a move, walking rapidly towards the ladies, keeping my head down so no one will see my red eyes. I don't want anyone to stop me and ask what's wrong. Outside the loos I bump into someone and mutter an apology without looking up, though I can tell from the cowboy boots that it's Tryggvi, Oddný's boyfriend. To my relief, he doesn't try to talk to me.

Luckily, there's no one in the loos. I stand there, wondering what to do, wondering if I can go on like this.

I've got teenage children, a husband I don't know if I want to be with anymore and a secret that has been weighing on me for years and destroyed so much. Changed who I am and who I could have been. Because deep down I never stopped being that frightened teenage girl. I feel as if I can never get away from her, however hard I try.

I wipe my face and drink straight from the tap. When I come out, Viktor is standing in the corridor, waiting for me.

'How are you feeling?' he asks. 'Steffý said you were a bit under the weather.'

'Under the weather?' I shake my head and clear my throat. 'No, I'm fine.'

I make to walk past Viktor, but he blocks my way.

'Petra, what's wrong?'

I don't answer immediately. I feel that I'm seeing Viktor in a new light. How could he have known what happened, yet never said a word?

After Teddi died, Steffý and I never talked about that evening. Steffý banned the subject, and I thought it was our secret. I hadn't a clue that Viktor knew we'd left Teddi behind. In fact, I didn't see either of them for a while. I went to school, or pretended to, came home and stayed in my room, listening to music. I slept badly. Whenever I dropped off, I would jolt awake with a gasp, or hover in an uneasy state between sleeping and waking.

Later, when the three of us started meeting up again, nothing was the same. At least not for me. Then I met Gestur, Steffý went to study abroad and I got pregnant.

Viktor and I carried on seeing each other, though our meetings became less frequent over time, but he never once said a word about that night.

'Why did you never say anything?' I ask now.

'About what?'

'About Teddi,' I say. 'You never told me you'd gone to look for him.'

'We agreed not to discuss it,' Viktor replies. 'And I didn't find Teddi. So what was I supposed to say?'

I think back over the conversations we've had, all those intimate, heartfelt conversations. Viktor knows I've been on anti-anxiety drugs for many years and that I see a therapist regularly, but, now that I stop to think about it, he's never asked why.

For years I've longed to be able to talk to someone about what happened, and all the time Viktor has known but never said a word. I feel as if everything is spinning inside my head, my vision is blurred and I'm nauseous.

'Viktor, I ... I can't take any more,' I gasp.

Viktor laughs at first, then he sees that I'm serious. 'What do you mean?'

'I just can't take any more.'

Again, Viktor blocks my way when I try to walk past him. 'Are you ... are you planning to tell someone?'

'Maybe,' I say, thinking that it might be for the best. Maybe what I need is to close this chapter of my life.

'But Petra,' Viktor protests, 'you can't do that now.'

'Why not?' I ask. He is standing so close to me that I can feel his breath on my face when he talks. 'Why should you care?'

'I don't,' Viktor says, scratching his neck. An old habit that shows he's nervous.

I stare at him for a long moment, then ask: 'If you went to look for Teddi straight away, how come you didn't find him? How could you have missed him?'

Teddi must have been dead by the time Viktor went to search for him or they'd have met. Viktor would have seen him. Had Teddi really only been standing there for a few minutes before he was knocked down by a car?

'Petra,' Viktor says. 'Teddi was found by the side of the road, remember. I wouldn't have been able to see him in the dark.'

Viktor was right, yet I can't shake off the feeling that something doesn't add up.

'OK, so it doesn't matter if I confess,' I say. 'Actually, I think it would be for the best.'

'Yes.' Viktor nods. 'Yes, maybe.'

'Yes.' I flash him a quick smile. 'Anyway, I'm going up to bed.'

Viktor doesn't answer. He seems distracted.

Then, as I'm walking away, I remember something Viktor's mother said at the breakfast table.

When I turn round, Viktor's still standing in the same place, looking after me. He's frowning, and for an instant I barely recognise him. But then he seems to realise and turns back into the Viktor I know.

'Hey...' I say. 'Your mother said something this morning.'

'What was that?' he asks.

'About the car,' I remember. 'She said you'd hit a ... what was it again?'

'A sheep.' Viktor laughs. 'What are you implying, Petra?'

'When?'

'What?' Viktor rubs his nose, his gaze fixed on me.

'When did it happen?' I ask. 'Your mum didn't say, just that you'd been a teenager at the time. When exactly did you hit a sheep?'

When we were kids, we knew everything about each other, but I don't ever remember hearing about any car accident of that kind. It didn't occur to me this morning, but now that I think about it, it's odd. If Viktor had hit a sheep, I'd definitely have heard about it.

'I can't remember, Petra,' he says. 'For Christ's sake, don't start making stuff up.'

'Maybe I should ask your mother.'

'Wow.' Viktor rubs his forehead. 'Steffy was right.'

'About what?'

'You're losing it, Petra. And what's wrong with your eyes? Are you on something ...? What exactly did you take this evening?'

I feel my cheeks burning with shame, and then suddenly I'm

so angry that I don't care if people can see that I've been taking pills. I couldn't give a damn what Viktor thinks of me.

'You knocked Teddi down,' I say in a low voice.

'No, Petra...' Viktor gives a hollow laugh but I can see through him. I'm sure I'm right.

'It was you, wasn't it?' I say. 'I bet if I asked your mother she'd say that you came home with a dent in the car that very same night. You did, didn't you, Viktor? And even if she can't remember, I'm sure it would be possible to find out from the insurance company. They keep information like that for their records.'

'No, look...'

'That's why you don't want me to tell. That's why you've never mentioned Teddi. Because you drove into him.'

'Will you keep your voice down,' Viktor hisses. Without warning he grabs my arm in a crushing grip.

'Let me go,' I say, jerking myself free. I lower my voice, trying to sound calm. 'Just tell me the truth, Viktor. Why lie? It was an accident, wasn't it?'

Viktor licks his lips but doesn't say anything.

'Wasn't it, Viktor?' I watch him scratching his neck, and it's then that it dawns on me that Teddi's death was no accident.

Lea Snæberg

There are some half-finished drinks on the table in reception and I drain one of them, although it stings my throat and I feel sick. Then I open the email but can't see any message. There's nothing there except the selfies I sent Birgir.

As I stare at myself, at the unfocused eyes and pouting lips, I feel my stomach churning with nausea. I can't believe I thought the photos looked good when I sent them. Now I can see myself properly: a silly, childish girl who thinks she's somebody. Inside me a voice keeps repeating: *Stupid, stupid, stupid...*

I wonder who would want to do this to me, who would hate me so much that they'd be prepared to spend weeks, months, talking to me. Surely a stranger wouldn't do that? It must be someone I know.

I make a mental list of all the people at school, the kids I hang out with, who are in my class. My girlfriends and ex-boyfriends. Would one of them go to all that trouble? Have I done something to them without intending to?

Or could it be the girls from my old school, who don't want me to get away, who think it was too easy for me just to move to a new school and escape them like that? I see their faces before my mind's eye and try to fix on one of them, work out who could have a reason to hate me this much, but I can't think of anyone.

Yet somebody out there has these photos of me and can do whatever they like with them. Send them to everyone I know or share them online. The purpose of this email must be to show me who's in charge.

Suddenly, I can't take any more. I hide my face in my hands and start howling like a baby. I don't care what I look like or what kind of noise I'm making. Right now, I don't care about anything at all.

Irma
Hotel Employee

Lea's obviously in real distress. She's huddled in a chair in reception, her phone on the table in front of her. Her hair has fallen over her face, veiling her expression, but I can hear her gut-wrenching sobs.

'Are you OK?' I ask.

Lea looks up, and I feel a stab of pity when I see the anguish on her face and the tears pouring down her cheeks.

She's strikingly like her mother, with the same dark, curly hair; that's to say, when she hasn't straightened it. I think it looks prettiest when she leaves it wavy. Just as it suits her best not to wear any make-up at all, especially not the heavy black eyeliner she sometimes uses.

'I ... I...' Lea stammers. 'I'm going to be sick.'

'All right,' I say. 'Come with me.'

I lead Lea into one of the empty bedrooms near reception and point her towards the bathroom. Through the door I hear her retching twice, followed by the sound of vomit gushing into the toilet bowl.

'Would you like something to drink?' I ask when she re-emerges, and open the minibar. 'Water? Coke? There's orange too.'

'Coke, please.'

I gesture to Lea to take a seat, open a bottle of Coke and hand it to her. She drinks half straight down, then wipes her mouth.

'Feeling any better?' I ask.

'Mm.' She stares at me with wide eyes, as though she's seeing me for the first time. 'Don't tell my mum and dad.'

'Of course not,' I reassure her. 'The first time I drank alcohol, I threw up in a floor vase in the middle of the night. Next day I'd totally forgotten about it and couldn't understand why Captain, my dog, kept sniffing around the vase. I didn't realise until Mum started asking about the revolting smell in the hall.'

'Seriously?' Lea wrinkles her nose. 'Ugh.'

'Mm.' I nod. 'It was disgusting. You can't imagine what it was like having to clean out the vase.'

'No.' Lea's eyes turn sad again. 'No, I can't.'

'Has something happened?' I ask warily.

'No ... well, yes,' she says. 'It's just ... I did something really stupid.'

'Stupider than puking up in a vase?'

Lea laughs dully. 'Yes. Much, much stupider.'

She tells me the whole story, though it's hard to understand everything she says. The story is incoherent and her tongue keeps tripping over itself, but I listen. After she's cried for a while longer, I notice that her eyelids are growing heavy, and I tell her she's welcome to lie down on the bed.

'Captain,' she says, as I help her into bed. 'Was your dog called Captain?'

'Shh,' I say, tucking the duvet round her. 'Just try to get some rest.'

'Thanks for helping me.'

'It was nothing,' I say.

'Pretty necklace.' Lea's words are slurring with drowsiness, and before I can answer, her eyes close. Her lips part and her ribcage starts rising and falling regularly. I watch her for a while, smiling to myself. Lea looks so young and innocent lying there that I'm filled with a powerful desire to protect her.

I rub the necklace between my fingers, wondering if it's possible to care for someone you don't really know.

Petra Snæberg

I can't move, though all I want is to run away from Viktor. But my legs won't obey me and my mouth is dry.

'Can we go somewhere and talk, Petra?' he says. 'My room's just round the corner.'

'What about?'

'About this,' he says. 'About us.'

'Us?'

Viktor scratches his neck again and moves a little closer. 'Come off it, Petra.'

'It wasn't an accident, was it?'

'Of course it was an accident,' Viktor shouts, then glances round nervously. We're still alone and the music is booming from the restaurant. I peer round him, hoping to see someone. Praying someone will come.

'All right, Viktor,' I say and force myself to smile. 'I believe you. And now I'm going to bed. Could you move?'

He doesn't budge. 'Where are you going?'

'Up to bed.' I try to keep my breathing steady.

Viktor is silent, and we stare at each other for what feels like an eternity. I'm backed up against the wall, I can't get any further away, and his face is looming so close I can feel his breath and see every gradation of colour in his eyes.

My thoughts are swirling round in my head, like pictures flashing up one after another: Viktor coming round to my house late in the evenings, saying he doesn't feel like sleeping at home, Viktor looking for me every time we go out clubbing and shoving away every single boy who comes over to talk to me. Always nearby, always so protective of me. At the time I thought Viktor was so caring.

I remember the look on his face after we kissed and him saying: 'You know we're not related, not really.'

But the idea is so absurd, so surreal. I would have known, wouldn't I?

Then I picture Maja, her smile and her hand stroking her belly. Did she leave the note to warn me about Viktor?

Suddenly, he reaches out and brushes a lock of hair back from my face, his fingertips gently tracing my cheek.

'Don't,' I say in a strangled voice.

Then, at last, someone calls our names. Viktor looks round, and I seize the chance to slip past him and walk quickly away.

Tryggvi

My hands are shaking so badly that it's hard to hold them still under the jet of water. While I'm washing them, I feel odd. The feeling's not unlike how I felt when I was told that Teddi was dead. The same numbness, somehow.

When I leave the gents, I meet Oddný coming towards me. 'There you are. Shall we go to bed? Things are winding down here.'

'No,' I say.

Oddný's eyes widen. 'Oh?'

'You go up,' I say. 'I'll come in a bit.'

Oddný stares at me for a few moments, then leaves me without another word. She's never been keen on talking about things and generally tries to wriggle out of difficult conversations. This time I'm glad because I don't want her company right now.

There's something I've got to do. Because there's one difference now from the despair I experienced when Teddi died: this time there's something I can do about it.

Irma
Hotel Employee

Viktor looks round when I call out, and Petra slips past him and starts walking hurriedly away towards the rooms.

'Petra,' I say again, and give chase.

'What?' she asks, swinging round. She seems preoccupied, her eyes fixed not on me but on Viktor, who's following us.

'It's Lea,' I say, watching Viktor take up position behind Petra. Is it my imagination or does she tense up?

'What about Lea?' Petra asks, hugging herself.

'She ran outside. I didn't know what to do but I thought I should at least let you know. She ... she seemed distressed.'

'What do you mean, ran outside? Why?'

'She...' I hesitate, then lower my voice. 'I think she was drunk. I found her in reception. She'd been sick.'

'Lea?' Petra says. 'Drunk?' Only now does she seem to be fully taking it in.

I nod, reluctantly. 'I tried to help her. I gave her a drink of Coke in one of the rooms, then just popped out to deal with something, and when I got back she'd gone.'

'Outside?'

I nod again.

'But...' Petra gives me a sharp look. 'How do you know she went outside?'

'I heard the front door slam, then caught sight of her through the window.'

Petra's staring at me as if she doesn't believe me. I take a deep breath, then add what I'd rather have left out.

'Lea told me she'd sent some selfies to a boy she was talking to online. She was in a bit of a state.'

'What kind of selfies?'

When I don't reply, I can see the realisation dawning on Petra. She opens her mouth, then closes it again.

'We should go after her,' I say. 'Before the storm gets any worse.'

Outside the wind is screaming and the noise of the weather mingles with the blaring music and loud voices of the revellers. Petra glances in the direction of the restaurant, where a burst of raucous laughter momentarily rises above the music.

'Is there someone you'd like me to fetch?' I ask.

'I think...' Petra breaks off, then seems to make up her mind. 'No, we'll be quick. She can't have gone far.'

'She's only just left,' I say. 'We'd better hurry.'

'All right,' Petra says again and sets off towards the front door, almost at a run.

'I'm coming too.' Viktor heads straight after her, but Petra doesn't acknowledge him.

I grab two coats from a peg in the corridor, without having a clue who they belong to, and hand one to Petra. I see her hesitate for a split second, then she pulls it on and zips it up to the neck. Viktor follows suit, seeming almost eager to charge out into the wild night.

I can hardly suppress a smile when I open the front door and we're met by an icy blast. The sky is heavy, black and starless, almost blotted out by curtains of driving snow.

'This way,' I say, beckoning them to follow my lead.

Petra Snæberg

It's blowing a blizzard outside and the visibility is very poor, but Irma leads us on confidently, as if she knows the area like the back of her hand.

Maybe it wasn't such a good idea to go out searching for Lea ourselves. It would have been more sensible to phone the search-and-rescue service and wait for the team, or at least to let the others know. I thought, briefly, of fetching Gestur but was put off by the memory of the accusation in his eyes after Lea waded into the sea. The last thing I need is to give Gestur yet another reason to blame me. I'm sure he'd find a way to make me responsible this time too.

But I'm not going to stand by uselessly, like I did earlier today, or that time she grabbed hold of a knife when she was three. This time I'm going to deal with the matter myself, catch up with Lea and bring her back to safety.

But the blacker the darkness becomes, the more grinding the cold, the more my conviction wavers. Maybe this wasn't the right moment to try to prove myself.

'Are you sure she went this way?' I call to Irma.

She looks back without stopping. 'Yes. At least, someone has come this way. Can't you see the footprints in the snow?'

I peer down but can't see any tracks that could be Lea's, only the prints left by Irma's big boots. Yet I follow doggedly in her footsteps, wondering what Lea's wearing, whether she's only got a jumper on in this cold. How long can an inadequately dressed person survive in these conditions? It's definitely below freezing

– minus two or three, maybe – a lot more if you take the wind-chill factor into account. Without shelter, I'm not sure an adult would survive an hour outside in this, let alone a slim teenage girl.

For God's sake, what can have got into Lea?

My worry briefly gives way to anger. How could she have rushed out into the lava field in the middle of a blizzard?

So what if she sent pictures of herself to some boy? It's hardly the end of the world.

But the more I think about Lea, the more it comes home to me that it must have seemed like the end of the world to her. She's like me in that she can be shy and lack confidence, though she's good at hiding it. And she's at the age when her self-esteem is based on what other people think of her. To her mind, the possibility that the pictures will be shared online must mean that her whole life will be destroyed. The kids in her class will look at her differently, jeer at her and humiliate her.

How bad can the photos have been? How much did she show?

I don't want to but I can't help picturing the greedy male eyes leering at the screen, poring over images of my child – who's still only a minor.

I have to find Lea, whatever it takes. Irma's some way ahead of me now, and I pick up my pace, stumbling and half running to catch up with her.

Behind me I can hear the crunch of Viktor's footsteps in the snow.

Tryggvi

For the first few years after Teddi died, I was consumed by a burning rage, like boiling magma inside me. I drank and went out and got into fights, but nothing could extinguish that rage. In recent years, though, I've found peace in my soul and finally managed to become reconciled to his fate, but now I can feel the magma erupting to the surface again. Feel it beginning to seethe and boil more fiercely with every drink I down.

I sit by the window, staring out, while the people around me chatter away. These people mean nothing to me anymore. All that matters is Teddi and what happened to him. I sit and wait for them to come back into the room, because I'm determined to tackle them. Look them in the eye and demand to hear the truth.

My whole body is itching; I have to do something to ease the torment. But it's not the kind of itch you can get rid of by scratching.

Then I spy a movement outside the window and make out three figures walking away from the hotel. As they pass the outside lights, the glow cast on their faces shows me exactly who they are.

Rising to my feet, I leave the small group who are still partying in the restaurant and make for the door.

Irma
Hotel Employee

The storm is worse than I'd bargained for, the gusts so violent, it's as if they're deliberately trying to knock us off our feet.

'We should turn back,' Viktor shouts. He's looking at Petra, but she appears to be avoiding his eye.

'No,' she contradicts him stubbornly. 'I'm going to find Lea.'

'But we should fetch a car. It's crazy to continue on foot in this weather. She could be anywhere.'

'Exactly,' Petra says. 'She could be anywhere. But probably not near any roads.'

'Are you positive you saw her go outside?' Viktor asks me.

'Yes,' I say. 'I saw her heading in this direction. There's a farm nearby. Maybe she'll take refuge there.'

We carry on walking. I've lost track of how long we've been out here. As unobtrusively as possible, I pull out my phone to find our location, but the little blue dot on the map is virtually no use at all.

I catch the sound of Petra sobbing. She's hopelessly inadequately dressed for the cold, the coat is too thin and she's trying to hold the hood over her head with numb fingers as she isn't wearing a hat.

'Would you like my hat?' I call out to her.

She looks at me as though she doesn't understand the question.

'Would you like a hat?' I ask again.

'No,' she calls back. 'No, it's all right.'

But Petra isn't all right; I can hear her teeth chattering. I try to put myself in her place and imagine what it would be like to have a child lost in these conditions. The feeling must be unendurable.

'For fuck's sake, we won't find Lea like this,' Viktor shouts, after we've struggled on for a while longer. 'We need to phone for help.'

'You go, then,' Petra shouts into the wind. 'Just go back to the hotel. But I'm going to find Lea.'

'Petra, you're not dressed properly,' Viktor says, more gently. 'We can go and fetch the car. Drive around the area and—'

'No,' Petra snaps, then adds, slowly: 'I'm not going anywhere with you.'

They stare at each other.

'It was an accident,' Viktor says.

'Really? Then why didn't you say anything? How could you have left him like that? Why didn't you call the police?'

'I...' Viktor takes a step closer to her, and Petra shrinks away. 'I couldn't.'

'Why didn't you say anything to me?' Petra says, her voice breaking on the last word.

Seeing that the situation is getting dangerously out of hand, I decide to interrupt them.

'I've found something,' I call, bending down. Picking the object up, I brush the snow off it.

Petra claps a hand over her mouth.

'Is that...?' Viktor asks.

'Lea's phone,' Petra says.

Now
Sunday, 5 November 2017

Sævar
Detective, West Iceland CID

Edda showed Sævar and Hörður into the room where they were planning to interview the guests. She was kind enough to make some tea, which they gratefully accepted. Sævar wasn't usually much of a tea drinker, but it was comforting to have a hot drink after spending a large part of the day freezing at the foot of the precipice. In spite of the sunshine and stillness, the cold was ever present, worming its way under your clothes before you realised what was happening.

The first guest they wanted to talk to, a tall, glamorous woman, entered the room a few minutes later. When she sat down, Sævar noticed her impeccable fake nails and two rings that, at a guess, must have cost a packet, not that he knew enough to judge.

'What's your full name?' Hörður asked.

'Stefanía Hjaltadóttir.'

'Thank you,' Hörður said. 'Could you take us through what happened yesterday evening?'

'Yes, of course. I, er ... Where do you want me to begin?'

'Wherever you like.'

'OK.' Stefanía lowered her eyes, and Sævar could almost see her brain cells working. There was no question that she was agitated.

'For example, you could begin at the point when you went into dinner yesterday evening,' Hörður suggested.

'I went down to the restaurant at seven. Before that I'd been with Petra and Viktor in his room. We were having a drink together.' Stefanía gasped and wiped away an invisible tear.

'Why did you meet up there?' Sævar asked.

'Petra invited me. The three of us wanted to talk.'

'And what did you talk about?'

'All sorts of things,' Stefanía said. 'We were reminiscing about old times and so on. We used to be inseparable when we were kids but ... since then we've all gone our separate ways.'

'I see.' Sævar smiled. 'Was there any tension between Viktor and Petra?'

Stefanía opened her mouth, then closed it again. 'No, not then.'

'What about later in the evening?'

'I couldn't really see,' she said.

'What couldn't you see?'

'Just...' Stefanía shifted in her chair. 'I think Petra was worried about that girl. About Viktor's girlfriend.'

'Maja?'

'Yes.'

Sævar glanced at Hörður.

'Did *you* think there was any reason to suspect that Viktor had been involved in Maja's disappearance?' Hörður asked.

Stefanía laughed as if the idea was ridiculous, but broke off when she saw the police officers' grave expressions. 'No, I ... Of course not. It didn't even cross my mind.'

'Did it cross Petra's mind?'

'She thought it was odd that Viktor didn't seem more concerned.'

'I see,' Hörður said. 'Did she seem angry with Viktor?'

'Angry?' Stefanía shook her head. 'No, I don't think so.'

'Was there any other source of friction between them? Anything you can think of?'

'No, nothing,' Stefanía answered firmly.

They asked a few more questions, but nothing Stefanía said gave them any clue as to what could have happened.

Once she had left the room, Sævar took two sheets of paper out of a file and skimmed the contents.

'Petra wasn't entirely wrong,' he told Hörður.

'Oh – about what?'

'Petra's concerns weren't entirely unjustified. In the last two months the Reykjavík police have twice been called out to Viktor and Maja's place,' Sævar said. 'The first time, the neighbours reported hearing a loud altercation in their flat. The second time, a passer-by alerted the police because he heard screaming.'

The Early Hours of the Morning
Sunday, 5 November 2017

Petra Snæberg

I've lost all sense of time now and have no idea how far we've come from the hotel. We stopped being able to see the lights ages ago. Hard pellets of snow are whirling out of the sky, stinging my eyes, disorientating me and making it hard to breathe. I don't know where we're heading, but we'll have to turn round any minute. We'll have to trust that Irma knows the way back to the hotel.

I keep calling Lea's name, but the wind snatches my voice away. I can feel the weight of her phone in my pocket and know that Lea would never have been parted from it unless something terrible had happened. She's as attached to her phone as to one of her limbs – to her it's as important as an arm or a leg. I try to push these thoughts away, picturing her back at the hotel, safely tucked up in bed, totally unaware that we're out here searching for her.

Lea was with Harpa all evening, and the two of them looked as though they were having a ball.

Though if I'm honest, I hardly remember seeing my daughter this evening. I've been too wrapped up in my own affairs and in everything that's been happening to spare a thought for her. Perhaps that's how it is generally. I get too preoccupied with work and my own worries to pay any attention to Lea's problems. I just write them off as typical teenage woes that will sort themselves out in time. Tell myself she's just going through a difficult patch like most kids her age.

But now I'm convinced I could have made more effort. I should have listened to her more and tried to talk to her. We should have gone on the mother-and-daughter trip I'd always planned. The two of us never do anything together. Nothing is the way I imagined it would be when Lea was small.

Lea was born prematurely, with one arm over her head like a miniature Superman. When they placed her in my arms and I saw her tiny hands and contorted mouth, I understood that all the clichés were true: nothing mattered except her; my heart doubled in size and was filled with more love for her than I'd ever felt for anyone else.

But in recent years it's as if I've forgotten that sensation. I've let us grow apart and haven't been there for her. I haven't been a good mother.

The tears are pouring unchecked down my cheeks now. But it's not as if anyone can see them in the darkness and blinding snow.

'This is crazy,' I hear Viktor grumbling behind me. 'Where the hell are we?'

Irma comes to a halt and peers back at us. She's the only one who's properly dressed and doesn't seem to be out of breath.

I turn a full circle in the hope of spotting Lea. In my mind's eye I can picture her lying somewhere, at risk of hypothermia. My little girl, I think, the tears flowing even faster.

'I'm going to make a call,' Viktor says, taking a few steps away. Not that he needs to, as the wind is roaring so loudly now we can hardly hear each other speak.

'Who are you calling?' Irma shouts.

'I don't know,' Viktor replies, waving his arm in an exaggerated gesture of uncertainty. 'The hotel or the emergency line. Lea might have gone back.'

'Viktor could be right,' I say to Irma, once he's turned away. 'Maybe Lea's back at the hotel.'

'It's possible,' Irma admits, appearing strangely calm. She probably doesn't have any children herself and can't understand how desperate I am to find Lea.

I yank at the hood, trying to pull it better over my head. My ears are freezing, and I feel as if my brain is slowly and surely freezing too.

'Should we turn back?' I ask, peering after Viktor, who is moving away, apparently unable to find a good signal. He's holding up the phone, his figure growing dim through the haze of snowflakes.

'Not quite yet.' Irma smiles, then adds, 'Don't you recognise me?'

'What?' Viktor has come back into view, still holding his phone, looking frustrated.

I'm suddenly filled with despair. As if we might not make it back to the hotel. As if we might even die out here.

'What did you say, Irma?' I ask.

'You're not seeing me,' she replies incongruously, her smile widening. 'Look at me, Petra. Haven't you worked out yet who I am?'

Sævar
Detective, West Iceland CID

The young girl sat there, straight-backed, waiting for their questions.

'What's your full name?' Hörður asked.

'Sigrún Lea Gestsdóttir.'

'Right, Sigrún—'

'Lea,' she interrupted. 'I'm always known as Lea.'

'I see,' Hörður said. 'Lea. Could you tell us about yesterday evening?'

'Yes, I…' Lea lowered her eyes and took a deep breath. 'I was with Harpa all evening. She came to my room before supper and … and we were drinking.'

She shot a look at them, expecting a reaction, but when neither of them said anything, she carried on with her story: 'Then we went down to the bar, and Harpa was a bit drunk by then. Me too. She kept bringing over more and more drinks, and I just…'

'OK,' Sævar said. 'We're not here to talk about that.' He smiled at Lea and waited for her to continue.

'Yes, anyway…' Lea closed her eyes as if she was finding it hard to go on. 'I wanted to go to bed but then I got a message. An email.'

Sævar knew that three people had gone out in search of Lea,

but what he still didn't know was what could have driven the girl to flee the hotel in that crazy manner.

'I, you see … I'd been talking to this boy, Birgir – or at least he called himself Birgir. He said he lived in Sweden and that he'd lived there since he was a kid. I was so stupid that it never occurred to me he was lying. I mean, he had an Instagram page and it all looked so normal. Loads of photos and friends and…'

'But you're saying he didn't exist, is that it?'

Lea's cheeks flushed. 'Yes.'

'So what did the email say?'

'Nothing,' Lea replied. 'It was just photos. Photos of me…'

Sævar and Hörður exchanged glances. Lea didn't need to explain. They had already dealt with several cases in which teenage girls had sent explicit images of themselves to boys who then circulated them. Often they weren't even boys, but men who paid for the pictures. In most cases the girls had been minors: the men had exploited their innocence and desire for easy money.

'What happened next?'

'I went and sat in reception because I was feeling so drunk I thought I was going to be sick. Then the woman who works here came in – I can't remember her name. She helped me and gave me some Coke to drink, and after that I just felt incredibly sleepy. The woman said I could lie down in one of the guest beds and I must have fallen asleep straight away.' Lea raised her eyes. 'The last part is a bit of a blur but she said … there was something she said.'

Lea frowned, and Sævar could see that she was racking her brains.

'What did she say?' he prompted.

'She said … said she had a dog called…' Lea gulped.

'A dog?'

Lea shook her head. 'Oh, it was nothing.'

'All right,' Sævar said. 'So you're saying you never actually went outside last night?'

'No, I didn't go out.' Lea shook her head again. 'I just woke up in the strange room in the morning, and that's when I realised my phone was missing.'

Sævar leant back in his chair. If Lea was telling the truth, it was evident that Irma, the maid, had known all along that the girl was perfectly safe, sound asleep in bed. This put quite a different light on things. He needed to know more about this Irma.

The Early Hours of the Morning
Sunday, 5 November 2017

Irma
Hotel Employee

Viktor is still trying to make a call. I could tell him that it's useless: there's no signal out here.

'Don't you recognise me?' I ask Petra, but I can tell from her expression that she doesn't.

But then why should she? We're not alike. I take after my mother, as I got to hear more and more often as I grew up. We both have round faces and pallid skin. Eyes that are too close together to be considered beautiful. The only thing I inherited from my father is my dark hair – as far as I know. Of course, I could have inherited all kinds of qualities from him – my temperament, quirks and expressions – without knowing anything about it. Because we don't know each other at all.

When he walked in the door of the hotel on Friday, I waited with bated breath to see if he'd recognise me, even though he hadn't seen me since I was a little girl. Whether I'd detect in his expression the tiniest sign that he knew me. But I saw no such thing, which told me that he hadn't taken the slightest interest in what happened to me after I grew up – if he ever had.

Not that I'd exactly been expecting him to. After watching my father for a while, I knew that all he was really interested in was himself and his money.

I felt no real desire to get to know him, but he wasn't the only person who mattered. Because when people have a child, the child doesn't just acquire a father and a mother, they also become connected to a whole branch of a family tree. A group of brothers and sisters, uncles and aunts, grandparents and cousins.

Ever since I was a little girl, I've dreamt of having a brother or sister, someone who would have moved house with me wherever I went. You see, when Mum and I moved I always had to leave behind the friends I'd made. But brothers and sisters would have come with me. As I got older, it became ever clearer to me how much I was missing out on. How much I'd been deprived of, because my father didn't want to acknowledge me.

One day, as I was sitting in my car outside my father's house, I saw Petra and Gestur pull into the drive, along with their children, Lea and Ari. They were all so good-looking, like a perfect family in one of those heart-warming adverts. I remember exactly what Petra was wearing that day: a light-blue shirt, her unruly hair held back by a large pair of sunglasses and the hems of her jeans rolled up to show off her slender ankles. She was barefoot in her sandals and had polish on her toenails.

I knew at once that I had to be part of their lives.

Although I was now living in a place of my own, my life was still affected by Mum's illness. I found it hard to hold down jobs and earn enough to pay the rent on my flat.

Petra and Gestur's life made such a contrast to mine. They were fixtures at all the important parties in Reykjavík, their smiling faces almost always turning up in the online reports of the events. Via social media I saw that they were forever on the move as well, travelling abroad, attending posh dinners, triumphing at work like they did everywhere else. All the glamour, the designer clothes, the swanky houses and cars and ... I wanted all that. I had a right to all that.

So I parked outside their house and sat in my car, watching them through the windows. I learnt about their daily routine, what they did at weekends and with whom. I tried to summon up the courage to knock on the door and introduce myself, but I didn't know what to say.

I've waited so long for the right opportunity and now, at last, it's here.

'Should I know you?' my sister asks, staring at me, bewildered. She seems suddenly nervous, as if I've said something unsettling. She folds her arms across her chest and draws away from me, throwing a glance in Viktor's direction as if to reassure herself that he's still there.

Petra's perceptive, that's something we have in common. I look forward to finding out what else we share.

Sævar
Detective, West Iceland CID

They were offered food at the hotel. Sævar accepted the invitation gratefully as he'd been trying to ignore his rumbling stomach for hours. Since being woken that morning by Hörður's phone call about the discovery of the body, all he'd eaten was one small pot of *skyr* on the drive up from Akranes.

Edda came into the room bearing two menus.

'Order whatever you'd like,' she said. 'On the house, naturally.'

'Thanks very much,' Sævar said.

After a quick look through the menu, he ordered a burger, while Hörður went for a chicken sandwich. They didn't have much time to eat, but Sævar was pretty sure he couldn't keep going without an injection of energy.

The series of events was still frustratingly vague. He couldn't understand what motive Irma could have had to lie about Lea going outside.

The food arrived quickly and neither of them said a word until all that was left on their plates was a few chips.

Sævar took a swig of a fizzy drink, then asked: 'Do you think she planned it?'

'Who?'

'Irma. The young woman who works here.'

'Hm, now you're asking.' Hörður put down his knife and fork.

'Why would she lie about Lea like that?'

Edda came back and took away their plates. 'Coffee?' she asked.

They both accepted the offer and watched her juggling the plates with professional ease as she left, closing the door behind her.

'She has dark hair like the hairs in the victim's fist,' Sævar observed. 'Could be hers.'

'But why?' Hörður asked.

Sævar didn't answer. The question puzzled him too. Why would the hotel maid lead two of the guests up to the top of the Knarrarklettir crags? And how the hell had one of them ended up falling over the edge?

All he could do was wonder whether the whole thing had been carefully planned.

The Early Hours of the Morning
Sunday, 5 November 2017

Petra Snæberg

'Sister,' I say so quietly that the word can hardly be heard over the wind. 'But that's not possible.'

'Isn't it?' Irma asks.

I'm about to insist that she must be mistaken, when Mum's words come back to me: *No one said marriage was easy.* I see her, wiping her mouth with a napkin and calmly telling me that Dad had cheated on her.

The snatches of memory fall into place like pieces of a jigsaw finally slotting together. Irma smiles when she sees my expression, but before I get a chance to respond, Viktor comes back.

He's given up on the phone and is looking from one of us to the other.

'What's up?' he asks.

Irma's smile vanishes as soon as Viktor reappears.

'I don't know, Viktor,' she says. 'Maybe you should tell us. Maybe you should tell Petra what's going on.'

Viktor stares at Irma for a moment, then shakes his head. 'What are you talking about? Who do you think you are?'

Irma takes a step towards me, saying in an undertone, so that only I can hear: 'He's not who you think he is, Petra.'

'What are you saying?' Viktor asks, coming closer.

'I've been watching you since you arrived,' Irma says. 'I know what you did to Maja. I found the broken vase under the bed and her blood-stained top.'

Viktor laughs. 'What the fuck...?'

I close my eyes and take a deep breath as Irma goes on:

'I saw you go into Petra's room last night. I saw you standing by her bed, watching her.'

'You're lying.' Viktor's nostrils flare as he stares at Irma, and I see a glimpse of something menacing, something so unlike the Viktor I know.

'If I'd known what you were capable of, I'd have acted far sooner.' Irma glances back at me. 'I'd never let him hurt you, Petra. We're sisters. I switched on the lights in your room to scare him off.'

'How did you get in?' I ask Viktor.

'The door was open,' he says. 'I just wanted to—'

'To what?' Irma interrupts. 'To stand there, watching her when you'd just murdered Maja?'

I feel sick. 'The note?' I ask.

Irma smiles. 'That was me. Perhaps I should have been clearer, but I didn't want to risk you mentioning it to Viktor or anyone else. I just wanted to put you on your guard.'

'But it was signed *M*,' I say.

'I thought the note would be more effective if you thought it came from Maja,' Irma explains.

Ever since leaving the hotel I've been so frantic with worry about Lea that I haven't given any thought to Viktor or Teddi. Or Maja. What did happen to her? Surely Viktor can't really have killed her?

My heart is crashing against my ribs, but it's no longer anxiety about Lea that paralyses my limbs but fear for myself. The sort of fear I imagine animals experience when faced with a predator.

Viktor starts moving towards me, but I stop him in his tracks.

'What happened to Maja?' I ask, though it's not really her I'm thinking about. My mind has flown back almost two decades, the image that has haunted me all these years blotting out everything else from my mind: Teddi on the road near Mount Akrafjall. Teddi waving. Blinding lights approaching.

Usually the vision ends there, but now it continues. I picture Viktor's hands gripping the steering wheel, his eyes meeting Teddi's. That expression I got a glimpse of just now, which I didn't recognise, although I've known Viktor ever since we were kids.

And I picture Viktor putting his foot down on the accelerator.

Sævar
Detective, West Iceland CID

After they'd finished eating, they resumed their enquiries.

Sævar was still puzzling over what reason Irma could have had to lead the two guests out to Knarrarklettir. He considered the possibility that she hadn't known who Lea was when she helped her that evening – that she had made a genuine mistake and thought they were looking for a different girl – but this seemed extremely implausible. Perhaps there had been some incident or falling-out between Irma and the family, and she had wanted to get revenge, but he found that unlikely too. He was inclined to think there was something else going on here.

Then it occurred to him to wonder why the family had booked the hotel where Irma happened to work – whether it was by chance, or there was something else behind it. Something that might help them find out more about Irma. He put these thoughts to Hörður, and they agreed that they should have another word with Edda.

It turned out that Irma had applied for a job on spec, though Edda said they hadn't been advertising for staff. Irma had been very determined, calling them up to introduce herself when she didn't immediately receive a response to her application. That was what had impressed Edda about her.

'And she's an outstanding member of staff, even if she is a little unusual,' Edda added. 'Always on time, and anticipates everything that needs doing without my having to ask.'

'When was this?' Sævar asked.

'That she applied for a job, you mean? Back in the spring. In April or May, I think.'

'Do you remember if the hotel had already been booked for the Snæberg reunion by then?'

'I have a feeling it was around the same time. Luckily, we only had one couple booked in for this weekend, and they cancelled when we explained that there would be a big family gathering here.'

'Who made the booking?'

'Haraldur's wife, Ester,' Edda said. 'She rang and booked the whole thing. Planned the trips and all the meals for the weekend.'

❄

'We started a Facebook group to organise the family reunion,' Ester explained shortly afterwards.

Edda had left, and Sævar and Hörður had called Ester in, telling her that they wanted to discuss the booking. Her eyes were red, and she was clutching a handkerchief.

'Was it open to everyone or was it private?' Sævar asked.

'I wouldn't know. My son, Smári, took care of that side. I didn't give any thought to whether it was open or not.' Ester paused to think. 'Wait a minute: no, you had to apply for permission to access the group.'

'Could you show us the Facebook group?' Hörður asked.

'If you've got a computer, I think I should be able to.'

Sævar got out a laptop, opened up Facebook and turned the screen towards her. It took Ester several attempts to get her password right before she could access her account and open the group settings.

'Here it is,' she said. 'The Snæberg Family Reunion.'

'May I?' Sævar asked, and when Ester nodded, he took over the computer.

Once he had called up the group members, he saw that there was quite a long list of Ingólfur's descendants, their partners and their children.

'Do you recognise all the names here?' he asked.

'Let's see.' Ester took a little time to go conscientiously down the whole list, reading every single name. 'Yes, they're all family members or partners.'

Sævar felt a stab of disappointment. 'Did you discuss the organisation of the reunion on any other platforms?'

'No, not as far as I know.'

'Could other people have learnt about the details of the reunion from the family members involved?' Hörður asked.

'Well, I don't know...' Ester hesitated. 'I suppose so.'

Sævar realised it was probably going to be impossible to establish exactly how Irma had got wind of the event – if she had. Perhaps the timing had been a coincidence after all.

'Can you remember any circumstances when it might have been discussed outside the Facebook group?' he asked.

'Well, of course the subject came up whenever we met. And Elín, Ingvar's wife, rang from time to time to check some of the details, because Ingvar isn't very active on Facebook and he was bad at keeping her up to date about what had been decided. She refuses to use any social media. Come to think of it...' Ester frowned and looked at the list of group members again. 'I could have sworn she didn't have a Facebook account. But her name's here – so I suppose she must have relented in the end.'

Sævar clicked on Elín's Facebook page and studied it for a moment. She'd only been a member for a few months. She had hardly any friends, and the only family member among them appeared to be Petra's daughter, Lea. Elín's profile picture was a photo of a woman wearing sunglasses and a hat, taken from too far away for her features to be clear. A woman who might have been Elín, or just someone who could be mistaken for her from a distance.

'Could you give Elín a quick ring and ask if this is definitely her Facebook page?' Sævar asked. It would save time if they could establish this without having to track Elín down and ask her to come in and join them.

'What's this about?' Ester asked suddenly, her eyes narrowing. 'Why are you asking about the Facebook group? What does this have to do with the accident? I don't like the idea of the family being interrogated as if we're criminals. Especially not after we've suffered such a devastating blow...'

'We should hopefully be able to explain later today,' Hörður said calmly. 'If you could just bear with us?'

Ester regarded them suspiciously for a few moments, and Sævar began to think she wasn't going to be fobbed off so easily. She struck him as a woman who was used to getting her own way. But in the end she sighed and took out her phone. Then, with their permission, she stepped out of the room to make the call.

'Elín doesn't know anything about a Facebook page in her name,' she announced when she came back. Her anger had subsided, and instead she seemed shaken. 'I insist on being told what's going on.'

Hörður assured her the family would be put in the picture once he and Sævar had finished interviewing all the staff and guests. Ester had to accept this, though she shot them both an extremely sharp look before leaving.

❁

Sævar and Hörður were sitting facing Irma, with a printout that they had placed on the table in front of her.

'Hello Irma,' Sævar said. 'We were wondering how long you'd been planning all this...'

'Planning what?' Irma asked, without looking at the printout.

'Was it when you started work at the hotel?' Sævar asked, putting still more papers on the table. 'Or did you apply for a job here precisely because the Snæberg family were planning to hold their reunion here?'

'I don't know what you're talking about,' Irma said.

'Or had you maybe started planning it earlier?' Sævar persevered. 'At the same time as you messaged Lea, Petra's sixteen-year-old daughter, claiming to be called...' Sævar bent forwards to read the name. 'Birgir?'

'I don't know what you mean,' Irma said, without turning a hair. 'I've never sent her any messages.'

Sævar's certainty wavered for a moment. Maybe they were wrong. At this stage they couldn't actually prove that Irma was Birgir. To trace the IP address, they would need the help of digital policing in Reykjavík, as well as a warrant and rather more time. But he was still feeling fairly confident as he pressed on with the questioning.

'Lea's been kind enough to show us the messages she received from Birgir,' he continued. 'They started chatting in the spring, at around the same time as the family started planning their reunion at the hotel.'

Irma didn't say anything, but Sævar caught a slight twitch at the corner of her mouth. Apart from that, there was no sign that his words had had any effect.

Nevertheless, he still thought there was a pretty good chance that Irma was guilty of posing as Birgir. But he was puzzled about why. He couldn't understand her motive or incentive for any of this, although all the evidence seemed to indicate that she had planned the whole thing, give or take the odd detail. What reason could she have had to lie, saying that Lea had run off into the night, and dragging Viktor and Petra out to search for her?

He decided not to push her further on this point just yet, but to try a different line of attack. 'You applied for a job at the hotel shortly afterwards, although they weren't advertising for staff. What made you do that?'

'I've always wanted to work at a hotel,' Irma replied. 'And this one is amazing. I mean, look around you. Who wouldn't want to work in a place like this?'

'So the timing was pure coincidence?'

Irma nodded, looking almost amused.

'We noticed that not long after the family Facebook group was set up, a profile was created in the name of Elín, Ingvar Snæberg's wife, though she wasn't aware of its existence. Do you know anything about that?'

'No,' Irma replied, appearing to suppress a yawn.

'Does the name Captain mean anything to you?' Sævar watched Irma's reaction closely, observing how she suddenly seemed more awake, as if something had been switched on inside her brain. He continued: 'Not a very common name in Iceland, though it's used for pets. Dogs, for instance...'

This was the source of Sævar's suspicions of Irma. Suspicions she'd just confirmed with her reaction to his question. When they'd interviewed Lea again, a little earlier, she had told them that Birgir had often talked about his dog, Captain. And that when Irma was looking after her the previous night, she'd mentioned a dog with the same name. It could be a coincidence but, as Sævar had learnt since working for CID, true coincidences were rare.

'You may remember telling Lea about your dog, Captain, when you were helping her into bed in one of the hotel rooms, just before you and two of the guests went out to look for her,' Sævar said. 'This is what we're having trouble understanding, Irma. Why this lie about Lea going outside? What was the plan?'

Irma finally dropped her gaze to the table and considered the printout of Lea and Birgir's chats. Sævar waited for an answer, but she remained obstinately silent.

'We can continue this chat for as long as it takes,' Sævar said in a conversational tone. 'But the truth will come out in the end.

At this moment, our forensics unit is busy tracing Birgir's digital footprint. You see, the thing about the internet is that it's almost impossible not to leave a trail, and I'm wondering what kind of trail you've left behind, Irma.'

This wasn't strictly accurate, but it was near enough. Sævar was confident that they had enough justification now to apply for a warrant to trace the IP address of the person claiming to be Birgir, and that this would lead them straight to Irma. 'So, what was the plan?' he asked again.

'The plan?' Irma turned to look out of the window. 'I just wanted to get to know them.'

'Who do you mean by "them"?'

'My family,' Irma said. 'The Snæbergs.'

Sævar was confused. 'But you're not—'

'Not related to them? Oh yes, I am. I may not look like it, but I am. About a year ago my mother finally told me who my father was.' Irma smiled and seemed to enjoy being able to add: 'Petra and I are sisters. Haraldur, her father, is my father too.'

Now it was Sævar's turn to fall silent. He was totally unprepared for this.

'I'd be happy to take a DNA test to prove it,' Irma said. 'He had a fling with my mother thirty years ago. Of course I knew who the Snæbergs were. I mean, who doesn't?'

'Not many people,' Sævar acknowledged.

Irma ignored this. 'For a long time I thought about going to see him, to find out what he'd say, but ... but in the end I couldn't do it. I was pretty sure he wouldn't exactly welcome me with open arms – he's not that kind of man. Not exactly the affectionate type.'

Sævar couldn't disagree with this assessment.

'But I wanted to get to know some of them, like Petra, for example,' Irma continued. 'My sister. I sat outside her house for ages, trying to pluck up the courage to go and knock on her door, but ... but I couldn't do that either. I didn't have the nerve.'

'So you decided to deceive her daughter instead?'

'It wasn't...' Irma began sharply, then stopped herself and continued in a softer voice: 'That was never the plan. I just thought if I knew more about them it would make things simpler. It would be easier to establish a connection with them when I finally introduced myself.'

'But you never did, did you?'

'No.' Irma tucked a lock of hair behind one ear. 'I thought it would be the perfect opportunity here at the hotel.'

'And was it?' Sævar asked.

'Yes.' A smile spread over Irma's face. 'Yes, I told Petra last night.'

'And how did she take it?'

'She was surprised, as you might expect,' Irma said.

'All right,' Sævar said, trying to picture the sequence of events. 'So, you find out where the family is planning to hold its reunion, you get a job at the hotel, and you create a fake profile for a teenage boy so you can chat to Lea. All this, just to get to know them?'

'You have to understand that they would never have let me in if I'd just knocked on the door. They'd almost certainly have turned me away. I couldn't take that risk.'

'OK, but what happened then, Irma? You still haven't answered my question. Why did you lie to them and say that Lea had gone outside?'

Irma leant back in her chair, saying nothing for a while.

Then: 'The family's different from what I'd been expecting; much more flawed. I've been watching them all weekend and seen how broken many of them are. I knew all about Lea, pretty much, but I was surprised to discover how many black sheep there are in the family. How unhappy they really are.

'And they're all so focused on themselves that they never noticed me, didn't see me, whereas I heard and saw everything that happened. I heard what went on in Maja and Viktor's room.

I found the vase and the blood-stained vest under his bed.' Irma suddenly made as if to stand up. 'I forgot the vest, I'll...'

'Irma.' Sævar gestured to her to stay where she was. 'We don't need the vest.'

'But Viktor was dangerous,' Irma protested. 'He killed Maja and threatened Petra. I was watching them last night and saw how frightened Petra was of him.'

'You thought Petra was in danger from Viktor?' Sævar was beginning to suspect that Irma was prepared to go pretty far for her newly acquired family.

'He was in love with her,' Irma said. 'You should have seen him around her. But of course she didn't notice anything. On Friday night he went into her room and just stood there, staring at her in bed. I had to switch on the lights to frighten him off.'

'So you decided to carry out your plan,' Sævar said. 'What for? To protect Petra, the sister you didn't even know?'

Sævar saw a twinge of pain pass across Irma's face. For a moment he thought he'd found a weak point. Then she smiled and said: 'I know them better than they realise.'

'Does that mean you admit to murdering Viktor?'

'Of course not,' Irma said scornfully. 'But I tricked them into going outside with me so I could show Petra Viktor's true face. I just wanted to teach him a lesson.'

'A lesson?'

'I wanted to force a situation where he'd admit what he'd done to Maja,' Irma said. 'I thought if we were there, with no way out, he'd tell us everything.'

Sævar didn't believe her. He was certain Irma had had a very different motive for leading them to the edge of the precipice at Knarrarklettir.

'You know what?' Sævar sat back in his chair. 'Maja turned up earlier, safe and well. She finally rang her parents to let them know where she was. She'd asked an ex-boyfriend to come and collect her on Friday night after having a row with Viktor. In all the fuss she forgot her phone in their room and didn't let anyone know where she was until a short time ago.'

Irma didn't say a word, but she raised a hand to her necklace and began rubbing the small gold heart that hung from it. She was clearly agitated by the news.

Hörður, who had been listening to the interview in silence, now leant forwards and asked: 'What happened last night, Irma?'

The Early Hours of the Morning
Sunday, 5 November 2017

Irma
Hotel Employee

I've imagined this moment a million times. Pictured countless versions, some ending well, others badly.

I realise this won't be welcome news to Petra. No one wants to hear about the sins of their parents, do they? We all long for the image we have of our parents when we're children to be true. It's always a shock to discover that they're only human and make mistakes.

I didn't know how Petra would react if I knocked on the door and introduced myself as her sister. But I didn't regard myself as a bystander anymore, as someone who would watch from a safe distance without intervening.

It was like an addiction. When I wasn't near them, I was thinking about them. When I was at home, I stared at my computer, waiting for notifications to pop up about new photos or profile updates. I couldn't get enough. Felt I could never know enough about them or get close enough to them. I longed to get inside their house and look at their things, but it was too difficult. Whenever they went out, they put on the burglar alarm. At night too. The only time the door wasn't locked was when they were all home, and then it was impossible to enter unnoticed. Though I did manage to slip inside once. Petra was alone at home and had stepped into the shower. The back door was open, and I crept in. I only meant to take a few pictures, then leave. But there was so much to see that I ventured further and further inside. I could hear the sound of the shower upstairs so I knew Petra wouldn't come out straight away.

All of a sudden I found myself standing in Petra and Gestur's bedroom. Opening the wardrobe, I ran my fingers over all the beautiful dresses and soft jumpers. I'd never seen such a full wardrobe. When I heard the water being switched off, I knew I would have to get out fast. Without pausing to think, I grabbed a necklace that was lying on the dressing table and fled.

But all this visit achieved was to increase my yearning to get to know them. And in the end I found a way to make it happen.

I never meant things to go so far that I would end up being sent nudes of Lea. I feel sick from having looked at them. In fact, as soon as I received them, I destroyed Birgir's fake profile.

I only created it as a way of getting closer to the family: I knew Lea would be the easiest member to approach. Seriously, kids trust anyone. They have no idea how easy it is to create a fake identity.

I rationalised it to myself as a necessity – a way to acquire the information I needed before becoming part of the family. At the end of the day, Lea's my niece; I've got a right to know her. Besides, I wanted to help her improve her self-confidence. I'd seen what she was like on social media, always trying to please everybody. She was so lacking in self-esteem, but Birgir helped her. He was her confidant, the person who cheered her up and praised her.

I never meant to hurt Lea.

But when I realised how dangerous Viktor was and saw that he was a threat to Petra, Lea became a tool. I'm not proud of the fact, but I needed Lea for everything to work. All I needed was a distressed teenager, a few sleeping pills and a good helping of luck to lure both Petra and Viktor away from the hotel. Actually, I'm astonished it worked out as well as it did.

'Nothing's happened to Maja,' Viktor is shouting. 'Nothing. We quarrelled – she got angry because I didn't react the way she wanted when she told me she was pregnant. I mean, what the fuck? Am I supposed to be happy when she tells me we're going to have a baby after we've only been together five minutes? Five minutes! Seriously, Maja's not as helpless as you seem to think. *She* went for me and was screaming – screaming like ... like a crazy bitch. All I did was back away, but then she fell and hit her head on the desk and the vase fell off and smashed. The floor's made of concrete, for fuck's sake. There was blood everywhere. Then she just left. Stormed out. I don't know where she went, but what was I supposed to do? Go after her?'

'Yes,' Petra yells, so loudly that I jump. 'Of course you were supposed to go after her. She was pregnant and didn't have a car, and we're miles from anywhere, Viktor. Didn't you care at all?'

'Of course I cared.' Viktor pulls off his hat and runs a hand through his hair.

'I don't believe you,' Petra says. Her voice is hoarse but she seems to have temporarily forgotten the cold. She makes no attempt to cover her head, though her hair is whipping around wildly and becoming encrusted with snowflakes. Then she adds: 'Everything you've said up to now is a lie, Viktor.'

'Petra.' Viktor shakes his head as though she's talking complete gibberish.

'You murdered Teddi,' Petra carries on in a low voice. Then she raises it suddenly, as if something inside her can no longer be controlled. 'You killed him,' she shrieks, her voice splitting on the words.

'OK,' Viktor shouts back. 'OK, I did it. I killed him. But only because he wasn't good enough for you. Steffý told me what happened. How he was all over you in the car and you were trying to push him off. He wouldn't stop when you told him to.'

'That wasn't his fault,' Petra said hoarsely. 'I ... I had a panic attack. Yes, I pushed him away, but he stopped at once when he realised I didn't want it. And it wasn't his fault.'

'Petra.' Viktor takes a step closer. 'You deserved better than him. I only wanted to protect you.'

'You killed him,' Petra repeats.

'Don't say that.' Viktor pleadingly reaches out a hand towards her, as if trying to calm her down.

And before Petra can slap it away, someone comes running towards them out of the driving snow.

Now
Sunday, 5 November 2017

Sævar
Detective, West Iceland CID

Petra's hand was trembling as she reached for the glass of water. She emptied it quickly, then put it down and wiped her mouth with the back of her hand.

'Sorry, I ... I...'

'Don't worry,' Hörður says with a smile. 'Just begin when you're ready.'

'Yes, right, er...' Petra's voice was husky, and she coughed to clear her throat. 'What was the question again?'

'Could you tell us what happened, starting from when you, Irma and Viktor left the hotel?'

'Yes, right.' Petra brushed a recalcitrant lock of hair back from her face, then blew out a long breath. 'Irma came up to me and Viktor, and said that Lea had gone outside. Lea's my daughter. She hasn't always been ... in a good way.'

Sævar nodded.

'Anyway, we went out to look for her, and the weather was terrible. It was snowing heavily and the wind was incredibly strong. I just followed Irma, as she seemed to know where she was going.'

'Didn't you find it odd that she seemed so sure about the direction Lea had taken?'

'Yes ... well, I was a bit sceptical, but then we came across Lea's phone.' Petra shrugged. 'I don't know. I was fairly drunk. We both were.'

Sævar knew that Irma had taken Lea's phone, presumably as a precaution, in case she needed to provide Viktor and Petra with further proof that they should follow her.

'You and Viktor?' he asked.

'Yes.' Petra licked her lips, and her gaze fell on the empty glass.

'More water?' Sævar asked.

Petra said yes, so he refilled the glass.

'Thanks,' Petra said, and drank, this time taking only a small sip. 'Before I knew it, we were up on some kind of moor. Or mountain. But I don't remember climbing up a steep slope; the gradient seemed quite gentle, so I couldn't work out where we were. I wanted to turn back and thought we'd be more likely to find Lea with the help of a search-and-rescue team. I was so frightened. People die of exposure in weather like that without the proper gear.'

'That's true,' Hörður agreed. 'But Lea never went outside, did she?'

'No. No, she didn't,' Petra said.

'What happened then?' Hörður asked. 'When did you find out who Irma was?'

'She told me we're sisters.' Petra seemed a lot less enthusiastic about this fact than Irma had been.

'You know it was her who sent your daughter all those messages, don't you?' Hörður said. 'Pretending to be a boy her age?'

Petra nodded.

'What happened next? What happened after Irma told you she was your sister?'

'We...' Petra started biting at her thumbnail. Then, apparently realising what she was doing, she jerked her hand away from her mouth and put it firmly in her lap. 'The weather was so bad. Viktor went in search of a phone signal, and we lost sight of him in the snow.'

'Is that true?'

'We searched for him but we couldn't find him. In the end, we found the path back – back to the hotel.'

'You and Irma?'

Petra nodded again. 'Then, when Viktor didn't turn up, we rang the police and the rescue team arrived and...'

'And they found his body early this morning,' Hörður finished.

Sævar studied Petra. Could she be telling the truth? He doubted it had been that simple, and wondered if Irma and Petra had used the time on their walk back to agree their stories, because they sounded identical. Would they go so far as to protect each other when they didn't even know each other? He couldn't see what incentive Petra would have for shielding Irma after everything the maid had done to her daughter, but Irma was a different matter. He had already seen how far she was prepared to go to protect Petra. Had Irma perhaps seen her chance to win her sister over and force her to accept their relationship?

'Why do you think Irma lied to you about Lea?' Sævar asked.

'Because...' Petra hesitated. 'Because she wanted to warn me.'

'Warn you about what?'

'About Viktor,' Petra said. 'She thought he was dangerous.'

'And you?'

'Sorry?'

'Did you believe Viktor was dangerous?' Sævar asked.

Petra lowered her eyes and ran a finger over a sore patch of skin by her thumbnail. 'I didn't know what to believe.'

'Couldn't Irma have found another way of warning you rather than hatching this elaborate plan?' Hörður said. 'Persuading you to go outside, taking you up a mountain ... It seems an awful lot of trouble just to deliver a warning.'

'I think...' Petra paused. 'I think she wanted Viktor to fall over the edge.'

'Over the precipice?'

'Yes,' Petra said. 'I think she led us up there because she genuinely believed he was dangerous. She was convinced he'd done something to Maja.'

'So Irma pushed him over the edge?' Sævar asked.

'No,' Petra replied. 'I didn't say that. I said she wanted Viktor to fall off, but when it came to the point, she didn't push him. Like I said. I don't think she's quite right in the head, to be honest. She hasn't had an easy life. Her mother's ill, she's lonely and...'

'And you don't find it rather a big coincidence that Viktor's life ended in exactly the way she wanted?' Hörður asked. 'Do you honestly expect us to believe that neither of you had anything to do with that?'

Petra bent forwards over the table. 'Irma felt she had to protect me. She thought Viktor was dangerous, but in the end it was an accident. We lost Viktor, and he fell off the cliff. Believe what you like, but that's the truth.'

Sævar placed a photograph on the table showing Viktor's fist clenched around a few strands of long, dark hair. 'Then how do you explain that?'

Petra stared at the photo for a while before turning away with a pained look. She closed her eyes, took a deep breath, then met Sævar's gaze with an uncompromising expression. 'Irma was right about Viktor in a way. He wasn't a good man. He...'

Sævar waited but Petra seemed unable to finish the sentence. 'What do you mean by that?' he asked eventually.

'It seems Viktor had harboured feelings for me for a long time. Feelings that I...' Petra inhaled sharply through her nose. 'That I hadn't a clue about. I've always regarded him as my cousin, but it seems he felt differently. That night he tried to ... to...'

Petra swallowed and dropped her gaze. Her eyes filled with tears.

'I see,' Sævar said.

Petra nodded. Then she looked up and the despair was plain

in her eyes. 'Does it have to go any further? Please, I don't want my family to find out.'

Sævar and Hörður exchanged glances. They couldn't promise anything.

'Whose hair is it, then?'

'Mine. Viktor tried to calm me down, saying everything would be all right. He always did that, tried to comfort me when I was upset.' Then, her voice suddenly thick with fury and bitterness, Petra added: 'But then it was Viktor's fault that everything went wrong in the first place.'

Petra Snæberg

My house is as chaotic as when we left on Friday, but now I couldn't care less. What's a bit of mess in the great scheme of things? I feel choked up when I'm greeted by the familiar smells, the complex aromas that are always there but which you don't notice until you've been away for a while. The lights come on inside, and I glance at the window. Outside it's pitch-dark, nothing visible except a glimpse of the bushes that grow right up to the glass.

I pull the curtains across the window. Gestur doesn't say anything.

'I'm hungry,' Lea says, opening the fridge. 'There's nothing in here.'

'I could go and get something,' Gestur offers.

'Sushi,' Lea suggests.

'I'd be up for sushi,' I say.

Ari shrugs to show that he doesn't mind either way.

'I can fetch the food,' I say. 'Lea, are you coming with me?'

Lea opens her mouth as if to object, then a smile lights up her face. 'Yes, I'll come. Can we buy some sweets on the way?'

❋

After supper, I go for a shower. I haven't showered since yesterday, but it might as well have been months ago. My skin is strangely tender and it's as if I can still feel that icy wind.

I stand under the scalding water for a long time, raising my face up to the jet until it's burning.

Every time I close my eyes I relive the moment when Viktor vanished. One minute he was standing there, the next he had disappeared, as if the earth had swallowed him up.

What remains is a sense of loss. I miss Viktor, miss who we used to be. Miss being part of our little threesome. I miss being a teenager and never thinking about the fact that one day it would all come to an end.

The bathroom is full of steam when I step out of the shower. It enfolds me in warmth. I don't want to open the window straight away so I wipe the condensation off the mirror so I can see myself. Newly emerged from the shower, with wet hair and no make-up, I'm exposed. I feel as if I'm seeing myself exactly as I am, with a few grey hairs showing in my parting and fine wrinkles at the corners of my eyes. I'm not seventeen any longer, and thank God for that.

In spite of everything, a heavy burden has been lifted from my shoulders. I'm still weighed down by secrets, more even than before, but somehow the burden feels more bearable. Perhaps because this time I have an inner conviction that some kind of justice has been done.

I realise this is an old-fashioned way to think. What's the proverb again? Oh yes: an eye for an eye makes the whole world blind. What does a life for a life do, then? Or, in this case, two murders?

Not that I think Tryggvi actually intended to kill Viktor. Tryggvi burst out of the darkness and falling snow, and grabbed him by the neck of his coat, dragging him away from me. Then he gave him a violent shove, making Viktor fall over backwards into the snow, and stood over him while he spoke.

I didn't immediately follow what Tryggvi was saying, but then it all began to make sense.

Tryggvi was Teddi's father. I remember that Teddi often used to talk about his dad. His parents had recently split up when we met, and he often went to see his dad at weekends and said he was sure his parents' separation was only temporary. At least, he hoped so.

Viktor struggled to his feet, but Tryggvi kept moving closer, forcing him to retreat. And then, quite suddenly, he was gone. I don't think Tryggvi had a clue about the cliff edge behind Viktor.

There was a split second, as Viktor started to lose his balance, when our eyes met and I sensed that he knew what was happening. His eyes were wide with fear and desperation – he didn't want to go.

Next moment Tryggvi had vanished too. He plunged into the dense haze of snowflakes, heading away from us. No one has asked about him today. Everyone seems to have forgotten about him in the confusion.

I wonder what happened to him. Whether he eventually found his way back to the hotel during the night or went somewhere else. I noticed that Oddný was sitting alone this morning. She didn't appear to be looking round for Tryggvi, so presumably she wasn't worried about where he was. I didn't like to ask.

✻

It's evening, and Gestur and I are sitting on the sofa together. Neither of us switches on the TV. The silence is companionable. From downstairs we can hear the noise of the film Lea and Ari are watching. If I know them, they'll be halfway through the sweets already, although the film has only just begun.

'How are you feeling?' Gestur asks, after a while. 'Is there anything I can do?'

'It's all right,' I say. 'I'm fine.'

It's true. I'm not feeling at all bad, in the circumstances. Gestur thinks I'm sad because Viktor's dead, but I can't tell him the truth. I can't tell him that Viktor's death has brought me release.

My family's not perfect, but then we've never pretended to be. It's not our fault if others see us differently. People think that having money and nice things is somehow desirable. For me, it's never been like that. From my point of view, our wealth is nothing but a burden.

I think about Irma, who's so eager for me to acknowledge her. I think about the lengths she's gone to just to get to know us, to get to know me. She's so desperate to be part of the family that I feel I can hardly refuse her.

The reality is that I have no choice. We came to an agreement about what to tell the police. I didn't want to reveal what Tryggvi had done and, in return for her silence, I promised Irma that we'd stay in touch. In fact, I promised to invite her round for a meal next weekend. I find the idea repugnant, after everything she did to Lea, and I certainly can't expect Lea to share a table with her. Lea's had so much to bear already. As if it wasn't bad enough that Birgir, the boy she was crazy about, turned out not to be the person she thought he was, it now transpires that there was an older man stalking her as well. He actually came to the hotel, looking for her. We still don't know who he was, but we gave the Snæfellsnes police a description of him and they seem to have a suspect.

I'm sure I'll manage to shake Irma off in the end. She must understand that we have nothing in common, in spite of being half-sisters. We couldn't be more different.

Gestur holds out a hand to me as if to make peace. He doesn't try to grab mine but waits patiently to see if I'll place my palm in his.

I take his hand and sense a relaxation of the tension between us.

He kisses the top of my head, and we sit like that for a while, our fingers clasped, listening to our children's laughter.

Sunday, 5 November 2017

Tryggvi

Theódór's grave is in Ísafjörður in the West Fjords. Nanna moved back there after he died. She wanted him to be buried in the place where he was born, and she wanted to stay near him. Besides, she still had lots of family living there.

Oddný didn't mind my taking the car. She got a lift home with her family. I told her I'd pick up my belongings when I got back to town, and she understood, though she was sad that our relationship had to end like that. But I don't think it came as a surprise to her. We don't belong together. All we really did was try to fill the emptiness in each other's lives; the emptiness that can never be properly filled, at least not in my case.

The journey takes almost half the day. Luckily, the weather's good, and, when the sun eventually rises after the long night, I enjoy the views of sea and mountains as I thread my way round the fjords. My shivering slowly ebbs away as the sun shines into the car, warming the interior. I tune the radio to a station playing oldies and feel for a while as if I've travelled back in time. As if I'm young again.

I stop at a service station for a coffee. The night came and went without my getting any sleep at all, but the caffeine helps, for a while at least. There's a peace inside me that I haven't felt for many years. When I think back to last night, I feel as if some other man was at work. In fact, I remember little after the moment when I overheard Petra and Viktor talking while I was in the bathroom. I only have a dim memory of following them out into the storm, but I can still hear the echo of Viktor's voice as he admitted he'd killed him. Killed my Teddi.

I don't know exactly what I meant to do when I charged out into the snowstorm after them, but I do know that I had no intention of hurting anyone. When I heard that note in Viktor's voice, though, that careless note that displayed no regret, I saw black. No, perhaps that's not right. I didn't see black, I saw Theódór. I felt Teddi's presence, heard his voice and pictured his smile and his laughing eyes. Like a punch in the gut, it came home to me what I'd lost.

❊

The cemetery in Ísafjörður is beautiful on this cold November Sunday. The faded grass is covered in frost, though the sun has thawed the ice enough for the odd drop of water to glitter in its rays.

I see her at once. She's standing by the grave, wearing a brown coat, leather gloves and walking boots.

'Nanna,' I say, when I'm close enough, as gently as I can.

Even so, she jumps. For a moment she stares at me, her mouth open, her eyes wide.

'Tryggvi,' she says. 'What … what…?'

'I thought I'd drop by,' I say. 'I hope that's all right with you.'

'Yes, of course,' Nanna says. 'I was just…'

'Visiting our Teddi?'

'Exactly.'

'The grave looks good,' I say, and it's no lie. The headstone we chose is made of black granite. We decided to have only his name and a short inscription engraved on it. In front of the stone is a lantern and a small vase of artificial roses.

'It's not easy to keep it looking good in winter,' Nanna says. 'The wind and the snow, you know.'

We stand there silently together, contemplating the grave. I think to myself that at last the three of us are together again, as we loved to be.

'Would you like a spot of coffee, maybe?' Nanna asks after a while.

'Yes, please,' I say. 'Coffee would be great.'

Sunday, 5 November 2017

Sævar
Detective, West Iceland CID

They drove home that evening. There wasn't a breath of wind, and the sky was bright with stars. The mountains didn't seem as menacing now as they had done that morning.

Sævar couldn't shake off the feeling that there had been more to Petra's final words, when she'd said that it was Viktor's fault everything had gone wrong. At first he'd thought she'd been referring to Viktor's feelings for her, but now he wasn't so sure.

Still, it was impossible to read anything into her words, as impossible as it was to prove whether someone and, if so, who, had pushed Viktor over the precipice. Perhaps it had been an accident, perhaps not. The police would do their best to uncover the truth.

'You can turn on the radio if you like, I don't mind,' Hörður said.

Sævar switched on Radio 1, which was playing the Bob Dylan song, 'Like a Rolling Stone'. Turning up the volume, he hummed along. He'd been a huge Dylan fan when he was younger; still was, in fact.

He was looking forward to getting home and taking a shower.

They had work to do tomorrow. Tasks which were far more tedious than today's groundwork, but just as important. Reports to write. Then more enquiries, though Sævar doubted now that anything new would come to light.

In a way he was relieved. All day he'd been afraid that Maja wouldn't turn up and that they'd have to launch a major search of the whole area. If the worst had happened and Maja had been found dead, the police would have had difficulty explaining to her family why they hadn't started the search much earlier. But, fortunately, Maja had phoned as soon as she realised her family were looking for her. She'd been sorry and apologised profusely. Sævar wondered if she had any inkling of the chain of events that had been set in motion by her disappearance.

They would take Maja's statement tomorrow, but a phone call had clarified most of the events relating to her. On Friday evening she had gone up to the hotel room with Viktor and broken it to him that she was pregnant. He had reacted badly, saying it was too soon to have a child and he wasn't sure their relationship would work out. Maja said they'd quarrelled. She said they'd certainly pushed each other a bit but denied that Viktor had been violent. She said she'd fallen over by accident, broken the vase on the desk and got a nosebleed. She'd changed her clothes, which was how her blood-stained top had ended up on the floor.

Sævar asked about the smears of blood inside the bathroom cabinet and Maja explained that she'd gone in there to clean up. While she was doing so, she'd rung her ex-boyfriend, who she was still on good terms with, and asked him to come and fetch her. When Viktor heard her talking through the door he got angry and their row had flared up again. In the end, Maja had stormed out, taking nothing but her coat. She didn't notice that she'd forgotten her phone until later but hadn't wanted to go back to the hotel to fetch it. Instead, she'd crouched, shivering, by the road until she saw her ex's car approaching.

Sævar gathered that they'd then spent the weekend together and been too busy reviving their relationship to think of letting anyone know where she was. Maja seemed in good spirits, in spite of Viktor's death. His parents, Ingvar and Elín, were understandably distraught, but Sævar found it rather strange how little his death seemed to have affected Maja. Perhaps things would look different when they spoke to her tomorrow.

He unlocked his phone and checked the online news sites. The accident was on all the front pages. The name of the victim hadn't been released yet on the two biggest news providers, but it had already been leaked on social media and those sites were on fire.

He selected the number of his partner, Telma, to ask her to pop out and buy some food before he got home, but she didn't answer. So he sent a message and a reply pinged straight back:

Just in Reykjavík, visiting Lóa. See you tomorrow after school.

Sævar stared at the message, feeling an overwhelming sense of emptiness. Telma wouldn't be there when he got back. Sometimes he felt as if he'd been coming home to an empty house all his life. But at least Birta would be there waiting for him, with her wagging tail and warm shaggy coat.

'Hey, my old mate, Jón, got in touch yesterday,' Hörður said suddenly, turning the radio down a bit. 'You know we've been having a bit of trouble filling Pétur's place now that he's leaving. Well, it turns out Jón's daughter is moving home to Akranes.'

'Is she a detective, then?'

'Yes, she's been working in Reykjavík for years. I had a chat with her colleagues there and they gave her a good report.'

'Great,' Sævar said. 'Excellent.' He wouldn't particularly miss Pétur, but he had mixed feelings about a new person joining CID. You could never be sure how an outsider would fit into their little team at the station.

'She's about your age,' Hörður remarked. 'You might remember her from school. Her name's Elma.'

'Elma.' Sævar thought back to his school years. After his family moved to Akranes, he had gone to the West Iceland Sixth Form College. His time there was a bit hazy. The fact that those were the last years when he'd had parents, been part of a family, made them seem almost dreamlike in retrospect.

At school he'd mainly hung out with a few well-chosen mates. They'd started a band. Rented a garage on Ægisbraut and spent the evenings there, trying to write songs that had sometimes seemed cool but, in hindsight, were mostly just noise. He'd played guitar and still did sometimes when he was alone at home. But now the songs were different; gentle ballads, shot through with melancholy. The lyrics he wrote weren't intended for any ears apart from Birta's. Not even Telma had a clue about the existence of the little notebook containing his song lyrics.

'Do you remember her?' Hörður asked, breaking into Sævar's thoughts.

'What? No. No, I don't remember anyone called Elma,' he said.

Acknowledgements

Growing up I used to go to my family cabin in Arnarstapi, Snæfellsnes a few times a year. Every time I went there with my grandparents I was told the names of the landmarks on the way and surrounding the cabin. Every cliff, every mountain, waterfall and stone had its name and its story. There was Bjarnafoss, the waterfall where you could see a woman comb her hair in the stream. There was the story of Oddný-píla, the teenage girl who haunted a valley between Arnarstapi and Hellnar. And there was the story of Axlar-Björn, the first and only serial killer in Iceland, who was buried in three parts only a short distance from our cabin. I was fascinated by these stories and remember sitting in the cabin during the dark winter months, oil lamps casting a dim light inside and the northern lights dancing outside, as I begged my grandparents to tell me the story just one more time…

Arnarstapi is where I fell in love with storytelling. There were so many stories about the landscape around the cabin, most of them very dark and often supernatural, and they were my main inspiration when I started writing myself. This book is set in Snæfellsnes, my favourite place in the world, and I hope that it will allow readers to travel there with me.

As always, I had an army of people around me that made this book possible. First, thank you to my Icelandic publishers at Bjartur & Veröld, Bjarni and Pétur, who encourage and cheer me on whenever I need it.

To the awesome team at Orenda – thanks a million, Karen, West and all the people that work so hard on every book. I am forever grateful for your work. Thank you to my translator, Vicky Cribb, who has such an amazing eye for detail. It is truly a privilege to have such a talented group of people working on my novels.

Thank you to my amazing literary agent, David Headley, for his friendship, support and encouragement.

My husband, Gunnar, who is my first reader and my greatest supporter – thank you for making me laugh whenever I don't feel like it.

Finally, I want to say how blessed I feel to have experienced the childhood I had. I'm lucky to have a big and close-knit family, and for that I am so grateful. Thank you to my grandparents especially, for sharing their knowledge and their stories. I will forever be grateful to them for taking the time to teach their grandchild what they know, and it is truly a privilege to tell those stories again. I will do my best to pass them on to my children, so hopefully they will live on through future generations. I believe that is how true value is created.